Emma Eleanor Elizabeth Minto, Gilbert Elliot Minton

Life and Letters of Sir Gilbert Elliot

Vol. II

Emma Eleanor Elizabeth Minto, Gilbert Elliot Minton

Life and Letters of Sir Gilbert Elliot
Vol. II

ISBN/EAN: 9783744675413

Printed in Europe, USA, Canada, Australia, Japan

Cover: Foto ©Raphael Reischuk / pixelio.de

More available books at **www.hansebooks.com**

LIFE AND LETTERS

OF

SIR GILBERT ELLIOT

FIRST EARL OF MINTO

FROM

1751 TO 1806,

WHEN HIS PUBLIC LIFE IN EUROPE WAS CLOSED BY HIS
APPOINTMENT TO THE VICE-ROYALTY OF INDIA.

EDITED BY HIS GREAT-NIECE

THE COUNTESS OF MINTO.

IN THREE VOLUMES.

VOL. II.

LONDON:

LONGMANS, GREEN, AND CO.

1874.

LIFE AND LETTERS

OF

SIR GILBERT ELLIOT

FIRST EARL OF MINTO.

———◦◦◦———

CHAPTER I.

LADY MALMESBURY'S letters having carried us on to the summer of 1792, we must now retrace our steps to the spring of that year, when Sir Gilbert went up to London to attend to his parliamentary duties, and resumed his place as his wife's correspondent at head-quarters.

A slight delay was caused in his journey to town by a collision with a runaway couple to Gretna, who had carried off all the horses. 'The lady is a fortune, and pays all the post-boys largely herself, so she is not carried off by force, though she looks a miserable little creature.'

'London: March 24, 1792.

'. . . I dined yesterday at the "Star and Garter," at a sort of party club for members of the House of

Commons to dine every Friday during the session. There are seldom above a dozen, but they are generally the leading people. Fox was accordingly there yesterday, and Grey. Sheridan came in late in the evening, just as we were parting. Fox is always pleasant in these sort of small and cosy companies; and he has exactly the merit which he said he liked yesterday in Lord Sandwich, which was being very much engaged and eager in whatever he was about; with this difference, that Fox is generally eager about better things than Lord Sandwich whose objects were mostly trifling and childish to the greatest degree. Lord Sandwich is supposed to be dying. Gerard Hamilton has had a severe paralytic stroke, which is not his first, and he is not expected to recover. . . .

'I am glad to find, I think, an appearance of greater moderation about the French affairs and our own constitution, etc., than there seemed to be last year. The conduct of France is not commended in *everything* as it was, by *anybody* that I have met with, and Fox spoke as ill of Payne's book yesterday as other people, which he did not do last Parliament of Payne's first book. There are certainly a certain number of people in the kingdom who are desirous of confusion; but there always are, and always must be, some such men in every country. They do not appear to produce any effect, and that matter is now in the hands of Horne Tooke and such persons, who will probably never be able to raise even a mob of the populace, but will certainly make no revolution. Francis, however, I am sorry to say, is very furious, and, I think, wrong-headed on these points, and seems to have no objection to a convulsion. Sheridan is also one of those who think: they might gain by confusion, and I am persuaded that he wishes to stir the lower ranks of the people even by the hope of plundering their betters. But I class him in a form very little above Horne Tooke in character and estimation, and therefore in *effect*, in this country. . . .

'There is one of the finest pictures of Sylvester Douglas at Lawrence's I ever saw. Lawrence seems to me much improved this year. There is a picture of Grey just begun, wonderfully like.'

'London: Monday, March 26, 1792.

'I dined on Saturday at Burlington House, where there was but a small party. The Duke was kind as possible in his manner, and desired me to come, whenever I was disengaged, in a family way, which I propose to do now and then. If I can break through the Duchess's cold and particular ways, I should find it a pleasant resource. Lady Charlotte is a good-looking girl, but not up to beauty. I dined yesterday at Lord Sheffield's; we had Lord North, the Douglases, and *Lally Tolendal*, a French emigrant; I was entertained with his company. He was a principal leader of the moderate party in France, whose plan for their constitution was formed very much on the British model, and which is equally distant from the extremes of the two other parties. He is, of course, detested by both,

and has been in exile a good while; he is now returning to Paris, not without some expectation of being
hanged.'

' Yesterday was a busy day.   I attended Mr. Grey's
committee on the laws concerning debtor and creditor
at eleven in the forenoon, and had no opportunity to
write a line to you before I went to the House for the
motion on the slave-trade.   The question for a *gradual*
abolition of the slave-trade was carried by a great
majority.   Wilberforce moved for the immediate abolition.   Dundas proposed the amendment of *gradual*,
and was supported by the Speaker, who, by the way,
did not make a figure, but a much better one than
mine on the Test Act, so I have no right to criticise.
Fox licked both Dundas and the Speaker soundly, and
stuck to Wilberforce.   Young Jenkinson [1] then spoke
and proposed a scheme of his own.   It was a set speech,
composed and delivered in mimicry rather than imitation of Pitt, but so inferior, and I think so puerile in
manner in spite of all the confidence, arrogance, and
conceit that could belong to a veteran, that he put me
in mind of a monkey brought in to dance on the rope
after a principal performer.   He will do, however, in
the world; for those qualities which make a man odious
and unamiable in private life are very successful in
public, especially when added to great application, and
probably both to ambition and every other branch of
the selfish and interested passions.   I was, on the

---

[1] Afterwards second Earl of Liverpool and Prime Minister.

whole, disappointed with him, but he is nevertheless an
extraordinary boy.   He makes more faces than his
father, and is so ludicrous in action and grimace that
his language has hardly fair play.   Pitt delivered one
of the greatest and most eloquent speeches I ever
heard in my life, and *being right,* it went so far that
one could hardly help almost *liking* him.   But enough
of *speeches,* which you don't like long accounts of.

' N.B.—I voted with Pitt and Fox for the immediate
abolition.'

' London : Thursday, April 5, 1792.

' . . . I have seen more of Fox and his set this year
than usual, having made a point to dine at a weekly
club with him pretty regularly, and having been now
and then at Brookes's.   I should wish to get over the
little reserve, both on his side and mine, which has
kept us at a distance so long ; but I imagine, that
without living something of the same life, which I am
not equal to, this is not very easy to accomplish.   I
have seen a good deal of Douglas and Lady Katherine,
and I am really happy to tell you that you have a very
good chance, almost a certainty, of seeing them at
Minto.   I dined yesterday at Mrs. John Pitt's with
the Cholmondeleys and Bellinghams.   Cholmondeley
is more absurdly uxorious than ever. . . . He had hold
of her hand under the table from the time the dessert
was set down, not only squeezing but perpetually
shaking it ; and if he quitted hold an instant to
make some gesture or action, he snatched it again
as if they had met after a long separation.   The whole

was a great display, and would almost make one sick
of being in love with one's *own* wife. His mother is
now living at Hartingfordbury, enjoying conjugal feli-
city with her husband at his parsonage. I am sorry,
however, to find she is entirely broken in her health
and mind, to the extent of not knowing people nor
remembering anything. Miss Palmer, Sir Joshua's
niece, has about 30,000*l.* by his death, and everybody
is marrying her. Who should you guess to have the
best chance in most people's opinion, but Lord *Inchi-
quin,* a fool of at least sixty or seventy years old?
Young *Dick Burke* is the most talked of, then Dr.
Blackden, Mr. Malone, Dr. Lawrence, and Walker
King. She has as many suitors as Penelope, but all
of them taken together would not make one Ulysses.
Lord Ossory, who had the first choice of a picture, has
taken the Reclining Venus, with a boy piping at her
feet. You probably remember it as a beautiful picture.
Lord Palmerston, who has the next choice, has taken
the Infant Academy. . . . I am going to-day at
length to Beconsfield. Burke has been there ever since
I came, except a day or two that he came to town on
business, when I called in Duke Street but missed him.
I wrote in the beginning of this week to say that Elliot
and I proposed to go to Beconsfield to-day if he was to
be at home, and I received the answer which I inclose
to you. You will observe a little stiffness in it. I
believe there was something of the same sort in mine.
The truth is, that I have had a horror at this meeting,
and that he does not know how to feel on the subject

either.   I believe his disposition towards me to be
affectionate and kind as usual, but I know his sanguine character so well that I cannot doubt of his
being at heart deeply hurt and affected at my withdrawing myself from the proceeding of last year.   My
own wish, and a very anxious one it is, is to return to
the most unlimited cordiality and affection with him in
point of private and personal friendship; but, besides
that I am unable to go all lengths with him on the
subject which most engrosses his mind—*the French
question*, I have felt so sensibly the evil of admitting
any sway over my mind so powerful and sovereign as
his was, and have found myself so often led to a fluctuation of opinion on important points by yielding first
to the influence of his authority, and then having to
combat the same point with my own reason, and I
think the particular subject of his present attention is
so likely to lead to questions of immense moment on
which every man should form an opinion of *his own*,
and regulate his conduct by an unbiassed and *temperate*
judgment, that I cannot again surrender myself so unconditionally even to Burke; and this is a resolution
which I *must* acquaint him with.   I doubt whether, on
these terms, we *can* be as *cordial* as I wish, although
our habits and intercourse may be undoubtedly kept up
with the same *external* intimacy—if these two words
can go together.   I had a long conversation yesterday
with the Duke of Portland on this subject, and there
seems the less chance of a perfect recovery with me, as
I find even the Duke is far from being on the same

footing as he was with him.   The Duke is strongly and
fondly attached to him; and I never saw anybody
more deeply wounded than he seems by this interruption in their former habits.   Burke, I believe, feels
the same on his side, and they have met, and still
meet, as often as opportunities offer, in the way of
private friendship and society, both in town and country,
but they have never *once yet* touched on the subject of
last year's catastrophe, or of Burke's last pamphlet.
I own I go in a great funk, and wish I was back again
already, although I have a strong desire to express to
Burke the continuance of my attachment for him.
Elliot is a sort of mediator between us; and I think is
the only one out of Burke's family who is *now* as entirely his as we all were before.'[1]

                    'London; Monday, April 9, 1792.

   '. . .   I am very much relieved in my mind by
the renewal of my intercourse with Burke, as that
subject has weighed pretty heavily on me ever since I
left town last May.   His reception of me was full of

---

[1] The following passage, which occurs in a letter of a later date,
written by Mr. Elliot of Wells to Sir Gilbert, gives an instance of the
influence exercised by Mr. Burke over his friends:

'Young Burke had applied to Lord Fitzwilliam for the seat of
Higham Ferrars, and was refused, Lord Fitzwilliam conceiving that
young Burke would follow his father's footsteps. and in conversing with
young Burke he used some unguarded expressions, and called old Burke
the standard-bearer of Pitt.   This produced a severe remonstrance from
old Burke, which affected Lord Fitzwilliam so much that he kept his
bed, and was actually ill for several days.   When Burke heard this he
was so much hurt in his turn, that he went to Lord Fitzwilliam and the
whole thing was made up.'

kindness, and I have reason to be satisfied that there is much less difference in his affection for me than in the case of any other of his friends, with perhaps the exception of Elliot and the Duke of Portland. But with all this, I own I did not feel perfectly comfortable. He talked his own language about the French Revolution, and his difference with his former friends on that subject, as freely as if I had no share in their dissent from him ; and this, Elliot tells me, is a distinction in my case, for with all his other friends he avoids the subject entirely. But the conversation on these points was necessarily all, or next to all, on his side ; and he never led to the only topic really interesting between us, or which seemed naturally to call for explanation—I mean my withholding all concurrence or countenance last year on that memorable and unhappy day, and the total suspension of all intercourse between us ever since. I saw that it was a *measure* with him to avoid this explanation, and I was not earnest to bring it on. But in the course of our conversation I did take occasion to say that I had found my mind fluctuate on this subject, and that I was so made as to be incapable of forming a judgment on which I could depend myself in any other way than by preserving the most temperate and cool tone of mind, and rather weighing and balancing all that was offered on all sides in a judicial way than trusting myself with anything like enthusiasm even for those sentiments which I am most inclined to approve and to partake in. I told him also that I was fully sensible of the great importance of the questions which seemed not unlikely to arise in this country, and to require a decision from every one of us, and that my thoughts were really not a little occupied with them; and that the possibility of our being called upon to treat these questions as more *practical* than they had hitherto been in England added to my anxiety to be in possession of my own judgment on these points, and to put myself, by coolness, in a capacity to satisfy at least myself with the part I might think it right to take. The Duke of Portland called there yesterday, induced to do so I believe on account of my being there, and being pleased, both for my sake and Burke's, that we should meet in unity again. Dick is fortunately in Ireland, and the brother at Bristol. Mrs. Burke has been ill, and is a little altered in looks. . . . The weather has been charming—the primroses and violets in full blow, many of the shrubs in leaf, the blackthorn and all the cherry-trees in blossom. You do not know what pretty walks and woods there are beyond this place. Elliot and I strolled among them all yesterday forenoon while Burke was at church, and I often wished I had you for my companion instead of one who, with every excellence of heart and character, is dead to every sensation and enjoyment, and is therefore like a wet blanket to a fire, or a blight to the blossoms I was admiring. . . .

'The Duke of Clarence applied in form to Burke, *at court*, as one of Sir Joshua's executors, for a cast which Sir Joshua had of *Mrs. Jordan's leg;* and Burke sent it to him accordingly, for which the Duke sent a note with his own and *Mrs. Jordan's thanks.* The cast was made by Mrs. Damer some time ago, before Mrs. Jordan was a princess, so that this testimony of her beauty was given to merit and not to rank. Burke showed us the King of Poland's present to him on account of the honourable mention made by Burke of the late Polish revolution. It is a gold medal of the King, extremely well executed and extremely like him. It is accompanied by a very pretty note in the King's hand, and written in English. Besides this there was a festival given in Poland expressly in honour of Burke, at which there was a great display of magnificence, and a general illumination with devices expressing his name—such as his cypher *E. B.* combined with the arms of Poland, etc. This may be set against Fox's bust in Petersburg.

'. . . The King of Sweden had received an anonymous letter the day on which he was assassinated, informing him of his danger and advising him not to go to the masquerade. The letter said that its writer was not his friend, but on the contrary one of his most determined enemies, but that he scorned to take his life in that way.' (*This letter is not completed.*)

'April 14, 1792.

'. . . Grey and Dr. Moore, brother of Sir John, dined with us yesterday. Lord Lauderdale, Grey, Francis, Courtenay, and a few others, among whom is Mackintosh,[1] the author of a book on the French Revolution

---

[1] Afterwards Sir James Mackintosh, author of *Vindiciæ Gallicæ.*

on the democratic side, which is much commended by those who are of that way of thinking, have formed an *association* for procuring Parliamentary reform in England; that is to say, some new mode or other of electing the House of Commons. This association is in its infancy at present, but is likely enough to grow and to succeed in their first object, which is to excite a clamour and to raise a flame on this subject. They are to invite and promote associations all over England, and after giving notice in Parliament this year of a motion for Parliamentary reform next session, they are to employ the recess in forwarding the agitation of the question all over the island. A thousand schemes will therefore be formed; the most violent will have the greatest number of supporters and the greatest clamour, and the business will soon be taken out of the hands which moved it and placed in worse. If any effect at all is produced by this association for Parliamentary reform, the business will not be confined to that object, but will of course run wild through the whole field of innovation. I was surprised at Grey's taking this part, as he seemed to me more temperate and considerate than most of my friends last year. He is fairly in for it now, and I see they are already dubbing themselves the only patriots in the country, and are making one another drunk with expectations of distinction and glory in this new course. I am very sorry for this, as I think it always possible in such a country as this, and perhaps in any country if people of weight and authority set about it, to create confusion, and always impossible

to know what the issue of confusion will be ; but on
the whole, I think a great majority of the nation will
be for quiet, and that the example of France may rather
secure than endanger us.   At the same time, it is certainly possible that, like other examples, it may operate
just the other way. . . . Dr. Moore seems to me a dull
and rather foolish man, with the pretensions of a
traveller and author, and a good deal of that unmeaning
sort of Scotch philosophy which is so universal with that
class of my countrymen. . . .

'There had been a report the day before yesterday
that the Duke of York had shot himself at Newmarket,
and it got into the *World*, I mean the newspaper of that
name ; but there was not the slightest foundation for
it.   It was occasioned by a post-boy coming into
Whitechapel, who, being asked by somebody, What
news from Newmarket? gave this account by way of
wit.   The fact is, however, that the Duke of York, and,
I believe, the Prince, lost everything they played for at
Newmarket, which was to a great amount.   If anything
can make a democracy in England it will be the Royal
Family.   People seem to think the Prince cannot live
above a year or two, and that he has been threatened
with apoplectic symptoms, but I do not know much of
the foundation of this story.   Others say he is going to
marry a Princess of Brunswick, a beautiful woman.   I
went the day before yesterday to Sheen, and found a
large company come like myself on chance.   Sir Ralph
and Lady Payne, Mr. Payne, Lady Stawall and your
friend Mr. Somerville, who seemed a pair; Lord Pem-

broke, Miss Whitworth,. Tommy Tinker, etc. Lord
Pembroke is the ruin of a man of gallantry, which is so
far a melancholy spectacle, that when the gallantry decays
there is nothing else left, and it forms a perfect companion, or, as the French call it, a *pendant*, for a de-
cayed fine lady and beauty. Though these companions
are no longer good company to each other, they are
like two game-cocks exhausted by a long battle and
lying by each other—still natural enemies, but both
unable to fight. Lord Pembroke is perfectly grey, and
otherwise old-looking. However, he has certainly
something of a natural manner, and of a man of fashion
about him, that may yet procure a tolerable place for
him in society. Lady Payne is still more ruinous than
he. But, like Lord Pembroke, her manners and polite-
ness will make her just as good company as ever for all
except the fighting cocks. Mr. Somerville I think a
ton-ish young man of bad ton—a little of the coxcomb
in the groom line.

' Lady Palmerston told me, by way of secret, that they
are going abroad this summer with all their children
for a year or two. Italy is their object. I wonder when
you and I shall make a *grander* still ; but I own it is
hope without much reason to feed on. By the time we
are ready, I fancy we shall have no occasion to go abroad
to see antiques and ruins though I flatter myself we
shall never be able to perceive antiquity and ruin at
home *ourselves*, whatever travellers who visit us may
do. . . .

' I am going directly to Beckenham, and shall

stay till Monday, when I shall come to town as usual
for the post. The post is the first blessing of absent
lovers, but it is hard work waiting for it. God bless
you!'

'April 20, 1792.

'. . . . This new association for Parliamentary reform and the rising spirit for promoting innovations, is
beginning to attract notice, and is likely to form an
interesting future in our politics, if it does not come
even nearer home than politics. Fox, I believe, does
not join it or approve of it; at least I hope not.

'I was yesterday at the new play written by Mr.
Richardson, whom I think you must have seen at Mrs.
Carew's. He is a good-natured, pleasant-tempered, and
poor man, and had a strong support of friends, particularly of *our* cloth. But in fact it is a flat play, and the
moral but indifferent. The hero is a copy of Charles in
the 'School for Scandal,' and it is meant to prove that
a young man is the *better* for vices—which is a fashionable doctrine, and came clearly out of Sheridan's school.
Modern moralists may be allowed at most to preach indulgence for vices, at least of some sort, but not to
preach the vices themselves. Mrs. Jordan's character is
serious, but seems to suit her full as well as the broad
comedy in which she usually shines. This was my first
play this year. The house is amazingly fine from its
size and form, but it is far too large for a playhouse.
One cannot distinguish a feature of the actors from a
great part of the house, and one hears very imperfectly.
New Drury Lane is to be less, but much larger than it

was. Covent Garden is also to be rebuilt on the same plan as Drury Lane. I saw Mrs. Crewe yesterday for the first time this year. She is as fat as me, and looks very old, but she refined and puzzled me as well as ever.'

'London: April 28, 1792.

'. . . I dined the day before yesterday at the Pechels', who purpose to be at Wilton Lodge this summer. Lord Charles Spencer, and his son Mr. Spencer with his wife Lady Elizabeth Spencer, second daughter of the Duke of Marlborough, were there. She seems a gentle, good sort of girl, tolerably well-looking but not to be called handsome. They seem unusually well and comfortable together for that sort of young couple of fashion. His passion is playing on the organ, and they have accordingly set up an organ in their parish church in the country, where *he* plays, and she has taught the children and girls to sing. They sing psalms together in company in London as other people sing Italian duets. But what I mentioned them for was to describe Lord Charles' delight with them in his quiet way. He is as much in love with his son as *you* are with any of yours.'

' Tuesday, May 1, 1792.

' This new association for Parliamentary reform begins to make a noise, and the subject has excited here the greatest possible anxiety, with considerable alarm for the possible consequences. You will see their paper, or manifesto, in Monday's " Morning Chronicle." Yesterday Mr. Grey gave notice in the House of his intention to move something on this subject next session; and he accompanied his notice with a short speech. This gave occasion to a long debate, or rather conversation, on the matter both of Parliamentary reform and of this association for bringing it about, which you will see in this day's paper. You will see that many of Fox's friends have declared themselves strongly against this measure. Amongst those who think extremely ill of it I am one, and *ought* to have said so yesterday, but did not find resolution to rise. I was, indeed, exceedingly fatigued and worn out, having sat the whole day in and about the House from ten in the morning, and ate nothing till past ten at night, and eating at that time had not the effect of brightening me. If anything can prevent the mischief of agitating such questions for half-a-year together, without even hinting at any particular point that they purpose to confine themselves to, and at such a time as the present, it is the very general and forcible disavowal which they received yesterday from every side of the House, and which I hope they will receive in every part of the country from all those who have anything to lose by confusion. I am very sorry to see that Fox has taken a part in their support, although he has not signed the Association; but he might just as well have signed it as made the speech he did yesterday. One effect will be, if not certainly to divide and break up our party, at least to expose it to very great danger of being separated, and drive Fox still further than ever from any hope of reconciling to him the moderate and prudent part of the country. The Duke of Portland is extremely displeased with the whole proceeding, and so, indeed, is much the greater part of his friends of every description. Fox, I believe, was sincerely angry and dissatisfied with the Association, because it put him in the disagreeable dilemma of either changing his former conduct on the same question, or differing with a great part of those who act with him, and, indeed, with the most weighty and respectable part of his support. We all profess to desire not to break on this ground, but whether it can be avoided time will show.

'I must just tell you what it is which engages so much of the leisure I had for writing. The Stryning Committee disposes of one completely till it is time for the House, or for some engagement of business or other, and I have this day or two been in company in the evenings. I took Elliot to Beckenham[1] on Sunday. The Abbé Gautier was there on purpose to meet me, and teach me his method of teaching everything by games, and I made some progress. I shall bring down all his books and games, and shall both *teach* and *amuse* my pupils a little, but I am not for carrying his system so far as he does himself. I returned from Beckenham yesterday in time to dress and breakfast before the Committee met at ten o'clock. Then came the slave-trade. I ate a chop upstairs with the Duke of Buccleuch, in perfect good humour and charity and civility on both sides. I am sorry to see him look very

---

[1] Lord Auckland's country seat, Eden Farm, was at Beckenham.

indifferently. I went last night to a ball given by
Mrs. Gally, in honour of the birthdays of Miss Judith.
Beresford and me; we were both assured that we
looked extremely well for our age. I have got Elliot
into Brookes's. I put him up without telling him of it,.
and he was chosen unanimously in the fullest room
there has been this year. I consider this as very
flattering both to him and me. I am very glad he is
chosen, as it will brush him up a little, and be a resource to one of his political turn, who has no society of
his own, male or female, and there is no danger of his.
playing.

' London: Saturday, May 5, 1792.

'. . . The news from Lisle[1] is true, but is told'
different ways. Some accounts say that almost all the
French corps were destroyed, but I believe the truth to
be that about 150 of them were killed by a regiment or
two of dragoons, who pursued them from Tournay.
They cut Dillon, their own general, *into pieces*, and
mangled and massacred him in the most brutal and
savage way. Some say they also beheaded his wife,
but for that I have no good authority. They certainly
hanged, or otherwise murdered, several of their own
officers. . . . It is universally allowed that this business is very prejudicial, and may perhaps be fatal to
the interests of the ruling party in France, but I have

---

[1] On April 20 the National Assembly by the voice of the King
declared war against the Emperor of Austria. On the 28th, the garrison of Lisle sallied out to attack Tournay, were repulsed, and fled into
the city, where they murdered two of their officers.

no confidence in predictions on any side. It certainly proves that *anarchy* is a *severe* government, and that the most civilised people becomes a wild beast when every man in a country is left to decide for himself what is lawful and what is not. I was at Beckenham on Thursday to dinner, and stayed all night to take leave of them before their departure. They[1] are on their way to Harwich this day, and expect to be at the Hague on Monday.

' I dine with Francis to-day. Francis is at present very wild indeed for one who is *at large*. He is a ringleader in the reforming confederacy.'

' London : Monday, May 7, 1792.

'. . . . I dined yesterday at Lord Carlisle's with a party of lords and great people. We talked a great deal of the new Association, and were all of a mind in condemning it. I do not know what impression they may make with time, but at present it is difficult to be more *alone* than they are in the class of people with whom the principal associators have been used to be connected, and with whom they certainly wish to stand well. The fact is that they feel themselves already to be in a scrape and in a disagreeable situation. On one hand they are disavowed by the better sort, and they disavow the other sort themselves. There is nothing they are so sore upon as the imputation of any connection with, or resemblance to, Paine or Horne Tooke's followers;

---

[1] The Edens.

and Paine [1] and Horne Tooke [2] are quite ready to reject
them in their turn.   I was very sorry, as well as surprised, that your friend Dudley North was in this
nonsense, and he seems to repent it heartily himself,
although none of them dare say so in plain words.   I
am sorry to tell you too that Dudley North looks extremely ill, and I fear is so.   He got into the Association merely by his connection with Lord Lauderdale,
who is very light-headed on all subjects, and I believe
very little in earnest on any.   Colonel Fullarton is one
of them, and is heartily ashamed of it.   He confessed
this to Douglas, and says that he only wishes for a fair
opportunity to quit them.   He is like many of the
rest, in having been engaged merely from a sort of
table companionship, and from a heedless kind of
assent that people sometimes give to a proposal that
seems to promise a kind of hearty and lively intercourse
among friends. . . . On the whole, this affair seems
less formidable than it might have been, and is likely
enough, by want of heartiness in many of the members,
and by divisions among themselves, to dwindle and
expire pretty quietly.   Yet there is no answering for
anything at present.   I am sorry to tell you that Lord
Guildford is thought to be in a very indifferent state
of health.'

---

[1] Thomas Paine, author of the *Rights of Man*. For this publication
he was prosecuted by the Government in December 1792, and was found
guilty, in spite of a brilliant defence by his counsel, Thomas Erskine,
then attorney-general to the Prince of Wales.   Erskine was removed
from his office for the part he took on this occasion.

[2] Horne Tooke, author of the *Diversions of Purley*. He was tried for
high treason in 1794, was defended by Erskine, and acquitted.

'*Tuesday.*   I have done a great deal of business to-day.   I began by sitting for my picture.   It is only chalked out this sitting, but Lawrence does a great deal more in chalk than is usual, and makes out the likeness completely before he begins to paint.   What he has done appears to me very like.'

'May 12.

'France is in a state of perfect confusion.   The late disasters[1] seem to have shaken the popularity of the Jacobin party, and will probably give some advantage to those who have rather more moderate views of Government; but I think it very doubtful whether much progress will be made towards a real settlement of the country, as anarchy seems so thoroughly established in the constitution and character of the people themselves, that *no form* of government can make much difference without such a *force* to assist it as cannot be expected at present.   The Kings of Hungary and Prussia will probably endeavour to take something from them which they wish for, and will leave them to settle their own troubles as they like ; but no political speculation or re diction is worth a farthing, and I not only do not attempt to look forward, but do not listen to the wisest of those who do.'

[1] The French army, which, under General Lafayette, had invaded Flanders at the end of April, had been repulsed in various engagements with the Austrians.

'London : Monday, May 14, 1792.

'. . . . There seems reason to apprehend that I may
not get away quite so soon as I was convinced I should
only yesterday. I had a long conversation with the
Duke of Portland this morning on the subject of these
associations, which have come to be thought much
more seriously of than one could so soon have imagined.
In consequence of the part many Opposition members
had taken against these novelties, Pitt desired to communicate with the Duke of Portland, telling him that
he had the King's permission to do so. . The Duke and
he met alone. Pitt expressed his satisfaction at the
disposition that had been shown by the Duke and his
friends to co-operate in preserving tranquillity, and
desired that an unreserved communication might take
place on that one point. He then informed him of
the only measure which Government had thought of
maturely ; which is, a *proclamation* against seditious
writings and publications, and calling on the magistrates to be vigilant in suppressing any appearance of
tumult if it should be necessary. This is intended to
bring the matter immediately before Parliament, as the
proclamation will be communicated to the Houses and
become the subject of addresses in which Parliament
may express its sense on these proceedings, and show
the disapprobation which *all parties* entertain of them.
I believe this to be a good measure, as the reformers
will at any rate be active on their side, and would draw
many to their measures if nothing is done to counteract them ; and the notice bestowed by King and

Parliament, with a general concurrence of respectable people of all descriptions, will at least induce the public to consider the subject as serious, and to deliberate well before they pledge themselves thoughtlessly to all this mischief. Pitt proposed that the principal members of Opposition should attend the Privy Council when the proclamation was ordered, and he offered to make those Privy Councillors whom the Duke should recommend for that purpose. This was very properly declined, as it was thought that our concurrence would have more weight and do more good if any appearance of union or junction with ministry should be avoided, as it might be subject to misinterpretation. If it had not been for this delicacy, you might have directed your next letter to a Right Honourable. The rest of the measure was approved of, and will be executed this week, probably on Thursday. Pitt told the Duke that he had undoubted information of many foreigners who are employed to raise sedition in England, and that money is sent from France to assist in this attempt. Several other measures were talked of as in contemplation, but not yet reduced into form, or indeed maturely considered. The Duke acquainted Fox with this communication; but he said he saw no danger to warrant any unusual measure, and declined taking any part in support of what is proposed either in Parliament or elsewhere. This is the state of things, and the moment seems so critical that the Duke expressed the strongest objection to my leaving town while this matter is depending. You will perceive that

there is a thorough schism in the party. I flatter
myself I am in the much most numerous, as well as.
respectable, side ; but as it appears that much good
may be done by the members of Opposition discoun-
tenancing these mischievous proceedings, there certainly never was an occasion where every individual
voice was of more consequence.   It seems just possible
that the proclamation and addresses, which will certainly
take place this week, may include all that will be
expected of us, in which case I shall still keep my
time; but I confess I think it more probable that
things should continue a week or two longer in such a
state as to render my departure extremely improper. . . .'

'London : Thursday, May 17, 1792.

' The proclamation is not yet out, and I imagine
there is some hitch in it. I am sorry for it on two
accounts—first, because I think it a right measure and
likely to do good, but that the effect is a good deal
weakened by delay, especially after it is publicly expected ; secondly, because it delays my departure.
There seems no chance now of any measure coming into
the House of Commons this week on this subject ; and
it is the general opinion that some regular discussion or
other should take place there on this matter before the
end of the session.   In my opinion every day that is
lost does mischief, for while nothing is done on one
side, the greatest possible activity is used on the other ;
and many persons who might be startled if they saw
that the thing was thought serious by almost the

whole of the House of Commons, are daily dropping in to the reforming societies without learning that they are taking any important step; and when once they get afloat at all, they are sure of going down the stream wherever it may lead them. Our neighbour, David Earl of Buchan, is one of their number; and I am sorry to see a more considerable person has lately added his name—I mean Professor Miller of Glasgow. Lord Lauderdale was his pupil, and lived, I believe, in his house while at college, and it is through that connection, I suppose, that he has been drawn into the Association, probably on a very fallacious account of its tendency and a very imperfect notion of its consequences. . . . Some of *us*, who disapprove of the Association and of Parliamentary reform, and think much as we do about the times, object, however, to the proclamation as too personally hostile to our old friends. Lord North, I believe, suggested the difficulty, and Adam is of that opinion, and probably several others. This has been mentioned to Government, and it is possible it may have made them hesitate about taking the measure without a more general promise of support. The fact is, however, that since the proclamation was returned by the Duke of Portland with a few amendments and with the approbation of those whom he had consulted, we have heard nothing further from ministry, and do not positively know what they mean to do. The forged news from India appears to have been a stock-jobbing fraud, and has succeeded, as it is said, in occasioning the loss and the gain of a

great deal of money.   It has exposed Dundas to some
ridicule on account of the violent exultation with which ·
he received the account.   When he read the letter he
called out—" Damn them (meaning the Opposition),
here is a bone for them to gnaw at."   He set off immediately in a chaise and four for *Kew*, to carry the news to
the King in person.   He was met on the road tearing
full gallop by the Speaker, and Dundas put his body out
of the chaise, and waved his hands over his head by way
of huzzaing, hallooing out that Seringapatam was taken.
All this is more natural than dignified, and somehow or
other it diminishes one's confidence in statesmen to see
them so like common men, or rather common boys.
But this is a reproach which fits statesmen of *all sides*
in this *natural,* and therefore *boyish* country.   However, I think it not only a defect in dignity, but a real
defect in more important requisites of a statesman, that
he should be much and violently affected, and thrown
off his bias, by events either good or bad.   He should
preserve equanimity, and discover neither great exultation nor great depression in any circumstances, if he
would be thought very superior to those whom he
governs, and worthy of trust in difficult times.   At the
India House the news was told to the proprietors, who
happened to be assembled for a ballot, with *three
cheers.*

'I went with Sir George (Cornewall) to Eton on
Tuesday, and gratified my curiosity concerning the
future haunts of the boys.   Nothing can be more
charming to the eye than the whole scenery of Eton,

and if *place* can make a difference in the happiness of
that age, I shall feel great comfort in the local merits
of Eton.   I was happy indeed to see that there is every
appearance in the boys themselves of the *highest health*,
and of the greatest satisfaction and enjoyment of their
situation. . . .   We invited a large party to dinner—
viz. James Harris, Sandy Douglas, four Mundys, and
Lord Maitland. . . .   Lord Maitland is but eight years
old, and although he has been at school these six
months, there was not one of the *company* who had even
heard his name or known him before.   It seems a most
strange and monstrous plan, or rather total want of plan,
to throw such a child as that alone upon that world,
to shift for himself in learning, in principles, in habits,
in everything.   It seems to me very like the conduct
of those birds who lay their eggs upon the sand, and
leave the sun to hatch them, and chance to rear the
young.   Lord Lauderdale persuades himself that it is a
right thing to make a boy fight his own way, and take
his chance in the world ; but I cannot help thinking
that there is less system and principle in this method,
than want of instinct and natural affection.'

'London : May 19, 1792.

'. . . There is some expectation of the proclamation
this evening, but it is not certain, but there have been
strange events and surmises within these two days.
The Chancellor actually gave in his resignation yesterday, but was prevailed on by the King to remain ; but
whether only for a time or for good is not known.

There is a very strong and general idea that some change or other is approaching. The King is supposed to want to get rid of Pitt, but dares not in these times. Pitt and the Chancellor are so ill together, that it seems impossible for them to hold together long. The division in our party is not so inveterate, but is equally certain on this new subject of reform, and I do not see how any strong government can be made of such materials as compose *all* the parties now existing. You see the impossibility of my coming just at this moment. Do not quote me for more than the resignation of the Chancellor, and the breach between him and Pitt.'

‘London : May 22, 1792.

‘ The proclamation appeared yesterday, and was laid before the House. The address is to be moved upon it on Friday. . . . The Chancellor is decidedly turned out—that's to say, he has received an intimation from Dundas, as Secretary of State, that he may retire. He may, perhaps, continue to sit in Chancery in order to wind up the business of the Court, but he is certainly dismissed, and it was even understood that he was to give up the seals last night. There has long been, indeed I believe from the beginning, a decided hostility between Pitt and him ; some recent provocations from the Chancellor in opposing some of Pitt's Money Bills, seem to have made the cup that was full before at last run over. It is thought the seals will be put in commission. . . . It is supposed that a few (I suppose very few) of the Chancellor's friends will follow him

and go out of office. The public, of course, speculate
on further coalitions ; but I am convinced that nothing
of that sort is possible, and that although our party is
almost as much broken up as the cabinet was, no part
of it will think of going into office without the other.
I have, at the same time, no doubt that the Duke of
Portland and his friends would by no means be unac-
ceptable to the King, and perhaps not to Pitt.'

'London : Thursday, May 24, 1792.

' I cannot afford you five minutes to-day, but I hope
our correspondence is at length drawing to a conclusion. . . .

' I sent you the proclamation last post ; an address is
to be moved on it to-morrow, and both the proclamation
and address have been communicated to, and suited to
the taste of, the Duke of Portland and some of his
friends. All the alterations made in it were suggested
by me, and approved by all those who attended the
meeting. That part of our party, however, who are reformers, are violent in abusing this measure, which
might be expected; but they have, I fear, drawn in
several of those who disapprove of reform, associations,
etc., to object to the proclamation, which will very much
weaken the effect intended by it. It was thought
advisable that some pretty solemn warning should be
given to the country that mischief is afloat, and that
the union of *all parties* in opposing sedition and confusion should induce the people to consider well at least
what they are about before they took a part in promo-

ting the various schemes that are offered to them. A proclamation from the King, backed by addresses from the two Houses, and supported by men of all descriptions in Parliament, was thought likely to do good; and I think it as good a measure for the purpose as could have been adopted, it being always difficult to know how to counteract that sort of mischief which does not amount exactly to a legal crime. We are to have a curious meeting this evening at Fox's, of reformers and anti-reformers; that is, of Grey and his party, and the Duke of Portland and us who are against these irregular measures. The intention of Fox is to prevent things going to extremities to-morrow in the debate, and to soften, at least, all personal asperity that a difference on this subject might lead to. Fox is in a difficult and uncomfortable situation, and has reason to apprehend the loss of half his present support, on one side or the other, whatever he does. He endeavours to trim, which is not natural to him, and he does not do it well. He does not sign the Association on one hand, but on the other he defends it, and all the measures they have taken, and he handles pretty roughly the opposition we are making to it. If this matter continues long to be a principal object of our politics, a total separation of the party will be impossible to avoid; but as few subjects hold very long, it is no doubt desirable to preserve good blood amongst us, that we may not be entirely disabled from reuniting on other points after this foolish business is at rest. However, it will, I think, be difficult to bring about much conciliation in the business we are to meet on to-night, or to avoid a considerable risk of greater sharpness and alienation than has yet taken place. Notwithstanding this, I have an engagement with Grey to go with him to the north, if we can agree about the day. The only business here of my own which is not finished is my picture.'

'London: Saturday, May 26, 1792.

' Yesterday is over, and I have not said a syllable, which on the whole is, I think, the worst of my delinquencies in that way. I passed my time pleasantly at home all the morning in expectation, and, as I conceived, in the certainty of speaking; and I passed from five o'clock in the evening till four in the morning equally pleasantly in momentary *hope* of getting up the whole of that time. I ought to be in perfect despair about speaking, from the experience of late years, and of none more than the present ; for I cannot complain either of want of leisure or opportunities, or any other impediment. I certainly have some *impediment in my speech*, however, or other ; yet I go on with something like a hope that I may do better next year, and make one trial of one session in speaking on all occasions well or ill, but above all *ill*, for that is the only true and *good* speaking ; and if I fail entirely either by not speaking at all or by continuing to speak ill the whole of a session, then to go out and make room for Elliot or some other impudent and loquacious fellow.

' What has passed on the subject of the Association and the proclamation has obtained the greatest possible

credit with the country and the House for the Portland part of our party, and will go further than anything that could have happened to reconcile both King
and people to that branch of us, and it is by very much
the most numerous. We have given the strongest
proof that the country is safe in our hands from those
dangers of schemes and popular projects and irregular
practices, the fear of which has so much alienated the
sober part of the nation from our whole party. But I
trust it will not *divide us*, and I am really sincerely
glad that it will not ; both because I like Fox and think
his abilities necessary to the country if kept in a good
direction, and because I have always thought that a
connection such as the Whig party is a very desirable
thing for the country whether they be in or out. Strong
professions of this sort were made on both sides of our
divided party yesterday. The associations have taken
as moderate a tone as they can. I think what has
passed has done good in this respect, and they must
see so plainly that this business threatens dissolution
to Fox's party that I am persuaded they will slip out
of it pretty quietly next year, after losing the first
motion they make for reform. I feel all notion of Parliament and of business off my mind for this year, and
my thoughts are all bent on home.'

'London : May 29, 1792.

'Mr. Grey, who is to be my fellow-traveller, has
obliged me once more to defer my setting out till

Sunday, as he has a meeting of the *Friends of the People* to attend on Saturday.'

' Monday, May 31, 1792.

' . . . I was up at six this morning, in order to sit to Lawrence at seven. My picture is perfectly like at present; and if it turns out a capital picture I have thought of playing Coutts a trick, and having a copy done for him, and presenting you with this.

'The times are full of speculation on politics; but I see no more reason to expect that things will come to a point now than six months hence; and it would be quite endless to stay here on that account. I suspect strongly that the breach in our party is incurable, although much has been said to keep us together, and there is a real unwillingness on all sides to come to a rupture—some thinking it disadvantageous to their own interests to lose the benefit of our numbers and weight, and others thinking it disadvantageous to the country to dissolve the *only* connection that has ever professed anything like a public principle, and most of us having a real feeling of attachment even to those from whom we differ at present. However, we differ so *widely* and so fundamentally, and I fear there is also in *some* such a design of setting up a new *head* and a separate interest in the party, instead of the Duke of Portland, that I think it very unlikely that a total and open rupture should be avoided. I think it equally unlikely, not to say impossible, that either *half* shall, with any advantage to the public, or credit and comfort to themselves, form any new connection, or have a share in any administration.   There is, however, reason to believe, or rather to know, that such an event has been thought of as desirable by the present ministers, or at least some of them.   Dundas has certainly thrown out such an idea; but I do firmly believe it to be impossible, at least in the present circumstances.   What is to happen in this eventful world a twelvemonth hence, my eyes are too shortsighted to conjecture.'

CHAPTER II.

SIR GILBERT left London for Minto on the 2nd of June. During the recess he received accounts of the political situation from various friends who remained in or near London; selections from whose letters are now given very nearly in the order in which they were received, and among these will be found some characteristic notes from Lady Malmesbury to her sister.

The political letters give us the deliberate opinions of a certain school of politicians on the exigencies of the time. In Lady Malmesbury's letters we are reminded of the circumstances which were daily moulding those opinions; she wrote as they reached her the reports of the hour—reports often false and exaggerated, yet accepted as authentic in the political society of London; and in these we see the fuel which made the fire burn—in other words, we learn the facts, real or so-called, which were exciting the passions of a whole people, not excepting the class which pretended to think for the people.

Mr. Elliot of Wells was perhaps more than any one in the confidence of Burke at this time. 'Burke's admiration of Elliot is extreme, and nothing can be

more perfect than his character,' wrote Sir Gilbert in
one of his letters to his wife ; 'and his judgment is
strengthening considerably, though he will probably
never venture far out of truisms.'   It may be thought
that the letters of his now given verify in some degree
Sir Gilbert's prediction ; but, as even truisms have
their day, they may be worth reading when they have
grown unfamiliar to our ears ; and such questions as
those discussed in the following correspondence—questions concerning the rights and relative duties of
governments and subjects—which resolved themselves
into the one question, as to whether political institutions are made for man, or man for the institutions,
will never again be viewed from the point whence
Burke and his friends considered them.

Fox said of Windham that he owed his fame to his
'having been much frightened;' but in the letters
before us, fear is not the predominating sentiment,
rather a firm resolution to defend, at all risks and costs,
the constitution which the writers believed to embody
the spirit of English liberty—a spirit not the less free
because self-reverent and self-controlled.

To this end they were prepared to suspend the action
of the institutions themselves; and the alarm with
which they beheld the events that necessitated such
measures never shook their faith in the worthiness of
the object to be defended, or led them to shrink from
the duty which they thought it behoved them to do.
It is remarkable that while in all discussions of the
politics of this period Burke and Fox are accepted as

the representatives of the opinions of their respective parties, neither of them was in perfect unison with his own so-called followers. Burke far exceeded his friends in his vehement hatred of the principles of the Revolution, and in the ardour with which he advocated 'strong measures' abroad and at home. Fox, on the other hand, never shared the extreme views of those whose influence over him had perhaps a greater part in his rupture with his old connections than difference in fundamental principles. Who was right? who was wrong? will be debated as long as the antagonistic opinions exist which were attacked and supported by Burke and Fox; but amid the long array of statements and arguments brought forward in support of either view, two propositions seem incontrovertible—1. That the French Revolution did not give liberty to the continent. 2. That strongly-repressive measures did not stifle liberty in England.

If these points be admitted, it ensues that Burke had the clearest insight into the ultimate consequences of the French Revolution; for on that wide-spread destruction he saw that no healthy organism would grow. Philosopher as he was, his antagonism to the revolutionary doctrines was much less philosophical than practical; he dismissed their metaphysics with scorn, and attacked the inevitable mischief of their results.

Fox had the truest appreciation of the causes which led to the French Revolution, and the most generous sympathies with its origin and tendencies. To him

'the light that led astray was light from heaven.' To
Burke all lights were *ignes fatui*, except the She-
chinah which shone from the ark of the Constitution.
Fox abhorred a war against a people struggling for
liberty.   Burke would have waged ten thousand wars
rather than risk the loss of English liberty in license.

To save England from the infection of revolutionary
doctrines the war began ; and before it ended, the
despotism which Burke had foretold had enslaved the
continent, and was persistently opposed by England
alone ;[1] the Tories, who then directed her councils,
being described by Madame de Staël as ' *les Whigs de
l'Europe.*' Before the storm had ceased to rage the
chief part of the statesmen on whose heads it had burst
had passed away—Pitt, Fox, Burke, Windham, Elliot,
were no more ; and when condemning the arbitrary
policy inaugurated by the administration of Mr. Pitt
in 1793, it is only fair to remember that that policy
was felt to be exceptional, and to be directed against
temporary dangers.   Its effect on the national character was therefore widely different from what it would
have been had the same restrictions been imposed by a
despotic government for its own ends.   Those who

---

[1]   ' And we are left, or shall be left, *alone ;*
        The last that dare to struggle with the foe.
        'Tis well ! from this day forward we shall know
        That in ourselves our safety must be sought ;
        That by our own right hands it must be wrought ;
        That we must stand unpropped, or be laid low.
          O dastard, whom such foretaste doth not cheer ! '
                WORDSWORTH—Extract from *Sonnet dedicated to
                              Liberty.* November 1806.

framed and those who suffered under the new laws were equally engaged in a life-and-death struggle with a gigantic enemy. The measures which cramped and confined the free action of Englishmen were designed as walls and ramparts against a foreign foe. When he fell they were doomed. Within a year after the peace of 1815, the writings of Cobbett, pointing out Parliamentary Reform as the only certain cure for misgovernment, were being read throughout the land ; and the popular party, ever increasing till it included the bulk of the people, prepared to take up the work, and ultimately to decide the questions which at the close of the last century had been the subject of political discussion and parliamentary warfare.

William Elliot of Wells to Sir Gilbert Elliot.

'Reigate : June 11, 1792.

'My dear Sir Gilbert,—I came here on Thursday. Lord Malmesbury arrived within three hours after your departure, and was much disappointed at missing you. I had only an opportunity of seeing him for a few minutes, but I thought he looked remarkably well, and is, like yourself, grown fat. Before I left London I called at Burlington House. The Duke, I perceive, continues to wish anxiously for an arrangement with the ministry, *including Fox*. Nevertheless, Fox's sentiments respecting the French Revolution seem to raise an unsurmountable bar against his admission to office. An administration founded on dis-

cordant principles could not fail at the present juncture of producing the most calamitous consequences to
the country; and it is too evident that, if Fox were
now to come into power, he must necessarily be in perpetual conflict with the rest of the cabinet upon the
topic of France, which is of late become so important
an object as to involve in it almost the whole system of
our politics, both foreign and domestic. It is con-
sequently believed that the great seal will be put into
commission for some months. Lord Loughborough
cannot accept it without the direct requisition of his
friends ; and the Duke of Portland is not much
disposed to promote such a measure.

  · · · · · ·

' The most interesting intelligence I have to send you
is that of the secession of five members from the
Association of the Friends of the People. The five
were Baker, Christian, Dudley North, Courtenay, and
Lord John Russell.

  · · · · · ·

' We are to have a meeting at Epsom on this day
se'n-night for the purpose of voting an address of
thanks to the King for the proclamation which I believe will be carried without opposition.'

'London: June 19, 1792.

' My dear Sir Gilbert,—I came to town yesterday
evening after the meeting at Epsom, where an address
to the King was voted, with only six dissenting voices.

Its principal opposers were *Sir Joseph Mawbey* and
Mr. Horne Tooke; the former of whom was not heard
at all, and the latter was soon interrupted, in consequence of his presenting a letter to Lord Onslow from
Mr. Paine; after which he was hooted down, and the
letter, without being permitted by the meeting to be
read, was delivered into the custody of the sheriff.
Lord William Russell expressed a *strong* disapprobation
of the proclamation, but said that since the measure
had been adopted he should vote for the address. This
seems odd logic, but it is nevertheless the logic of
Bedford House, which is at present very fluctuating
and unsettled in its politics. Francis was at the meeting, but did not vote. I afterwards dined with him at
Mr. Johnson's on Putney Common, where I left him
bewailing the degenerate and base servility of the times.
After I got to town I called at Burlington House, but
as the Duke was not alone I had no particular conversation with him. However, I breakfasted with Lord
Malmesbury this morning, and he read to me from his
memorandum-book all that has passed since I last
wrote to you. There has been a direct proposition
from Pitt for a coalition. The last conference upon
the subject was between Lord Loughborough and Pitt,
who supped together on Thursday night at Dundas's.
Lord Loughborough asked Pitt whether the intimation
which had been made to the Duke of Portland was
known to the King. Pitt's answer was that the
proposal did certainly not proceed from the express
command of his Majesty, but that he had reason to

believe that the coalition would be very acceptable both to the King and to the Queen. Lord Loughborough then mentioned the necessity there seemed for including Fox in any arrangement that might take place. Pitt, I understand, acknowledged that he had thought the breach which existed in the party was greater than it really proved to be; but at the same time he declared that nothing had ever passed between Fox and himself in the House which could induce him to wish, upon any *personal ground*, to exclude Fox from a share in the government. The difficulty would be *where* to place him, and that also the King might have some hesitation upon the subject, in consequence of some of Fox's late declarations upon French and some other topics. He said likewise, that if such an arrangement had been proposed in November last, all impediments on this head (I mean on Fox's admission into power) would have been easily obviated, as the King would not *then* have felt indisposed to Fox—his conduct in the year '83 and during the time of the discussion about the Regency being entirely obliterated from the *Royal memory*. The present difficulty would probably arise from the opinions which Fox has delivered in the last session of Parliament. I do not find, however, that Pitt by any means deemed this an insurmountable obstacle. Lord Loughborough, towards the close of the conversation, suggested to Pitt the principal topics upon which an explanation with ministers would be necessary before any arrangement could be effected; amongst which, I believe, he men-

tioned French politics, the reform of Parliament, and
the slave-trade. Pitt said that the slave-trade was a
point on which both parties must make concessions.
There has as yet been no explanation between the Duke
and Fox. That, however, will be an essential step, and
the points upon which I understand an explanation is
likely to be demanded on the side of the Duke, will be
the affairs of France, the reform of Parliament, the
repeal of the Test Act, the slave-trade, and the repeal
of the Act against the Unitarians. Fox does not seem
averse to coming into office, but Lord Malmesbury told
me that the first time he conversed with him upon the
subject he was very impracticable on many points.
He had some short discourse with him a second time,
and then he was rather more tractable. To-morrow is
a court-day, and as the King will be in town, it is
possible the negotiation may be resumed. Lord
Malmesbury says he will write to you on Thursday. I
shall stay in town for a day or two, and you may
depend upon hearing from me if I should have any
news to send you. Farewell; I wish you may be able
to read what I have written. The truth is, I did not
come in till a quarter past five, and I have still to dress
for dinner. I am to dine at Burlington House.—Your
ever affectionate   ' W. E.'

                                    ' Reigate: June 29, 1792.

' My dear Sir Gilbert,—I have still to thank you for
your letter of the 15th, which I found here upon my
return from town on Saturday, and which I intended

to have answered by Monday's post, but was prevented. I had, however, little news to communicate, since I left things precisely in the same state as when I wrote to you on Thursday, no further intelligence having been received at Burlington House from ministry at eleven o'clock on *Friday* night.   The King is not unacquainted with the negotiation, as he has mentioned it to one or two of his friends in terms which betrayed *no aversion* to the measure.   The Duke and Fox had a long conference in the middle of the last week; and the Duke told me, that in the course of it, after talking of the many difficulties attending a coalition, Fox said, " *It is so d—d right, to be sure, that I cannot help thinking it must be,*" or words to that purpose.   But I did not learn that they came to an explanation on any controverted topics.   In truth, the more the obstacles which oppose a junction with ministers, *including* Fox, are considered, the more insuperable they appear.   If a treaty should be fairly set on foot, it is likely to be deemed an *essential* condition that Pitt should quit the Treasury, and that *at least* a *neutral* person should be placed there.   This is a concession which Pitt, in the plenitude of his power, can scarcely be expected to make without reluctance; and even if he himself were inclined to it, it is not probable that his friends will readily. be brought to grant their concurrence to so great a sacrifice.   Indeed, I cannot help believing that, if Pitt should consent to relinquish his situation, he would feel less objection to resigning it to the Duke of Portland than to anybody else; and such an event is certainly devoutly to be wished. But admitting this part of the negotiations to have the most favourable issue, there must arise another difficulty, which the Duke sees in the strongest colours; I mean the arrangement of Pitt and Fox, *not only* in the Cabinet, but in the House of Commons. For, supposing Pitt to be Chancellor of the Exchequer, and Fox to be Secretary of State; or supposing them both to be Secretaries of State—one for the Home, and the other for the Foreign Department; Pitt has been so long established as the leader in the House of Commons that it seems impossible that, whilst he holds any high and conspicuous office in it, he should not retain that pre-eminence which is at present in a manner attached to his character. And this kind of distinction and precedence on the part of Pitt cannot fail of being unpleasant and mortifying to Fox. It is also doubted whether Fox may not insist upon bringing in Sheridan, and perhaps some other of his friends, though I do not know that he has yet directly intimated such a proposition. Sheridan might be provided for by some lucrative employment (for he cannot have a cabinet office), but you will recollect he belongs to the Association; and, if that is to be a rule of exclusion, it will not be easy to decide upon what principle of justice an exception can be made in his favour. These of themselves appear to be impediments of sufficient magnitude to preclude all chance of an arrangement on the present plan; but the most serious and lamentable difficulty still remains untouched—namely Fox's sentiments and declarations relative to the French Revolution in the two last sessions of Parliament. Without a complete recantation from him on this subject, both in public and in private, the whole benefit to be derived from a coalition must inevitably be defeated. The principal objects of such a measure are to furnish the Government of this country with the means of preserving tranquillity at home, and of interposing with effect in the affairs of the continent. Until order shall be re-established in France, it is too plain that neither this nation, nor indeed scarcely any other in Europe, can be reckoned in a condition of even tolerable safety ; and if England should not permit the period of her influence to pass by unexerted, she may, perhaps, by mediation alone, without resorting to force, be able to restore something in the shape of government to France, and may at the same time be instrumental in preserving Poland from the oppressive and tyrannical ambition of the Empress. I remember that last year many of our Gallican enthusiasts were strenuous in representing it to be the right policy of this country to treat the French Revolution as an event purely of a domestic nature, and unlikely to produce, at least for many years, any very important *external* consequences. I confess I never could prevail on myself to think this doctrine, which teaches us to regard England as completely separated from and wholly unbiassed by the interior politics of France, sound in point of theory; and it is, beyond dispute, historically false.[1] We know that even in the

---

[1] Burke, writing to Lord Grenville almost at the same time, says, ' I perceive that much pains are taken by the Jacobins of England to pro-

proudest days of her despotism, France operated as
much by her example as by her arms. She presented
to the world a splendid and a stately fabric, which
attracted the admiration and imitation of surrounding
courts. The liberty of England was in peculiar danger
from her influence; and it seems somewhat pre-
sumptuous to imagine that we shall be less sensible to
the contagion of a system certainly more flattering to
the natural dispositions of mankind, and formed upon
principles seducing and corrupting to the taste and
morals of society. It is surely not a rational speculation to believe that a great and striking change, or
rather *inversion*, both of government and opinion, can
be accomplished in a vast and flourishing country like
France, the Greece of modern Europe, without exciting
some sympathy of spirit among nations which have for
centuries acknowledged her as their mistress in manners, arts, literature, and science. But in truth we do
actually at this moment feel the weight and power
of her example; and therefore to assume and to act
upon the contrary hypothesis, would be to reject the

pagate a notion that one State has not a right to interfere, according to
its discretion, in the interior affairs of another.   This *strange notion*
can only be supported by a confusion of ideas,' etc. etc.—*Edmund Burke
to Lord Grenville*, August 1792.

Windham's opinion of the doctrine of non-intervention may be seen
in a letter to Burke, published also in Burke's correspondence :—' Why
is all right of interference in the affairs of another country, even without the plea of aggression on the part of that country, to be universally
given up?   The more I have thought on that opinion, the more satisfied
I have been that it is a mere arbitrary assumption, wholly unsupported
by anything in reason and nature,' etc. etc.—*W. Windham to Edmund
Burke*, November 7, 1793.

testimony of past and present experience. Sheridan, in one of his speeches towards the close of the session, observed that one of the distinguishing excellences of the English constitution is that it contains the principles of its own internal correction and amendment, and that it is, by its very frame and texture, capable of almost indefinite improvement. The remark must be allowed to be both beautiful and just. But whilst we have a French Revolution at our door we are overawed; the faculties of our constitution are, as it were, suspended, and it is bereaved of all its nerve and energy. This state of *privation* is in itself alarming, because it leads to decay. We must then exert our influence, whilst it remains, to annihilate the source of the danger which is the object of our apprehensions. If this reasoning is admissible, you will grant that the advantage to be expected from a coalition *comprehending Fox* must be frustrated unless he should undergo a complete *conversion* on the topic of continental affairs. Indeed, without such an alteration in his sentiments, I do not see how he can be included in the intended arrangement with *safety* to his character; for, if he adheres to his admiration of the French Revolution, and continues to deny the existence of any peculiar *peril* in the temper and disposition of the times, there really is, *as far as relates to himself,* no sort of foundation for the measure; and the whole transaction can appear to the public in no other light than as an act of egregious political profligacy. Should this embarrassment be found to be unsurmountable, and should it prove fatal

to the *present* negotiation, another and most momentous
question must of course claim the attention of the
Duke of Portland and his friends—whether an arrangement should be made with ministry, exclusive of Fox?
It is evident that, whilst the party is permitted to
remain on its present footing, its Gallican friends
constitute the most efficient branch of it, and therefore have a decided advantage. Fox is usually considered as the mouth of the party, and it is said that
foreign courts regard him as the *entire director* of it.
This is very credible, because the same opinion prevails
in some degree in England, and it is not unnatural
that it should. The great aristocratical leaders of the
Whig interest are not much in the habit of debate;
and those members of the Whig party in the House of
Commons who differ from Fox in their sentiments on
French politics, speak but seldom, and when they do
they are looked upon by the public rather as expressing
their own *individual* opinions, than the *sense* of a
large description of the body to which they belong.
Thus the French Revolution goes forth to the world
carrying with it in a manner the weight and sanction
of the Whig interest of this country. Under these
circumstances, I cannot resist thinking that it would
be highly beneficial to the nation that the Duke and
his friends should support the Government as an *independent* party, unconnected with ministers on the
one hand, and *distinct* from Fox on the other. But
their conduct in this respect must, to be sure, be regu-
lated by the number of their forces, which, I fear, has

not of late received any great accession. At least there
are persons who are now clamorous and forward in condemning the proclamation that were supposed likely to
have voted for it, if there had been a division upon the
subject in the House. If the Duke should be able to
make a coalition on such terms as would decidedly add
to the future strength of his own party, and at the
same time give vigour to the present councils of the
nation, it would indeed be in every point of view a
most fortunate event. But it must always be remembered that the people are the avowed enemies of *coalitions* ; and if the aristocratical party were to come into
power immediately upon their division from Fox, they
might incur the risk of losing the public confidence,
and of increasing the popularity of the democratic
faction. I fear you will not entirely approve of *all*
these sentiments, since I must confess they tend to a
separation from Fox, which certainly affords a most
melancholy prospect, both to his friends and to the
country. But I much dread England is at present in
a state in which she has only a choice of evils. I do
not, however, believe that a division from Fox is ever
likely to take place. The personal attachment of the
leaders of the party to him is too strong to admit of it.
Many people seem to think that even the Devonshire
family would be divided upon the subject. The Duke
of Portland desired me to tell you that things were in
so very uncertain a state that he did not see the least
occasion to trouble you to come up at present, but that
he could nevertheless wish you to keep yourself in

readiness. Burke is at Beconsfield. Before he went he had a long discourse with Lord Malmesbury. The principal tendency of it was to show that, in case the negotiations with Ministry should fail, it would be advisable for the party to request Lord Loughborough to accept the great seal, in order to open the door to some future arrangement. They likewise talked a good deal upon the subject of foreign politics, and the general state of Europe; and I thought Lord Malmesbury seemed to be considerably impressed with the conversation. The Revolution Society have lately published some of their correspondence with a variety of the Jacobin Club in France. The publication amounts to an octavo volume, otherwise I would have sent it you by the post, as it is a complete illustration of the means employed for the propagation of French principles. Lord Malmesbury says that there was scarcely a state through which he passed, from Naples to Ostend, in which there were not emissaries employed by the French for the purpose of disseminating their new doctrines. . . . Pray make my kindest love to Lady Elliot and the children, and believe me ever, my dear Sir Gilbert, your most affectionate

'WILLIAM ELLIOT.'

'Reigate: July 11, 1792.'

'My dear Sir Gilbert,—I shall begin by correcting the passage you allude to in my letter of June 19, which, from your representation as well as my own recollection of it, I am sure bears a meaning very different from that I intended to convey. The points which I stated, or rather ought to have stated, as probable topics for explanation between the Duke and Fox, I believe, *merely* occurred to the Duke and Lord Malmesbury in the *course of private conversation*, as subjects upon which it might be necessary to come to some understanding with Fox, before a Cabinet could be formed. I certainly did not enter *minutely* into particulars on this head, but I had not the least ground for conjecturing that more would be expected from Fox than that he should refrain from *proposing* those questions, on which there existed a difference of opinion amongst the leaders of the party. The slave-trade, you will observe, was mentioned by Lord Loughborough in his discourse with *Pitt*, who said it was a measure on which he thought both sides must make concessions.

'As I had some business which carried me to Croydon on Saturday, I went from thence to town, and returned on Sunday. I saw the Duke on Saturday night, from whom I learnt that Lord Loughborough has had another interview with Pitt, and that the negotiation is at an end. The substance of Pitt's answer was, " That on consulting his friends, he found them very averse to an arrangement including Fox; that he believed their objection was principally grounded on Fox's declarations and conduct on the proclamation; and that upon the whole he did not feel the emergency of the times to be so urgent as to justify him in adopting such a measure, *contrary* to the *advice* and *senti-*

ments of his friends. He expressed himself in the handsomest terms towards Fox, and particularly requested that nothing that passed might be imputed to any reluctance on his part to act with him, for that if in the course of events they should ever happen to be together in administration, there was no man to whom he should be more disposed to give his implicit and entire confidence than Mr. Fox. He also desired it to be understood that, as the measure had not the sanction of his friends, he had deemed it unnecessary to trouble the King with it, and that therefore no difficulty was to be considered as proceeding from that quarter."

' From this circumstance I conclude that when the King mentioned the subject to some of his friends he could have had only some *general* notions of a coalition, and probably did not know what were likely to be insisted on as the essential conditions of it. The Duke seems to imagine that ministry have not been quite in earnest in the negotiation, and that Dundas set it on foot under an idea that the breach in Opposition was wider than it has proved to be. However, he still does not think it impossible that the treaty may be renewed before the meeting of Parliament, as the affairs on the continent before that time call so pressingly for the interference of this country as to render the union of political parties very desirable even to Pitt. Both the Duke and Fox concur in esteeming Pitt's resignation of the Treasury as a primary and fundamental article in any arrangement, and I understand Fox rather blamed

Lord Loughborough for not having sufficiently enforced that point in his conferences with Pitt. Lord Loughborough, I suppose, conceives it to be too great a sacrifice to expect from Pitt. Though Lord Loughborough has conducted himself throughout the whole mediation with the utmost staunchness and integrity, yet the Duke, I perceive, considers him as somewhat biassed towards a coalition by his desire for the great seal. This, however, the Duke is very delicate of saying, and particularly desired that any hint he dropped on this head might be understood to be in the strictest confidence. I remember Lord Malmesbury in the beginning of the negotiation appeared to think that Pitt's *abdication* of the Treasury was rather *too strong* a concession to extract from him. But I do nevertheless believe that an arrangement including Fox would be perfectly impracticable without it. Perhaps if the Duke and his friends were to join ministry, exclusive of Fox, Pitt's resignation might not be so immediately requisite, though even in that case it would certainly be very desirable. Fox is of opinion that a coalition would be barely feasible with a neutral person at the head of the Treasury. I breakfasted with Lord Malmesbury on Sunday morning, but as Pelham was with him we had no conversation upon any but general topics. He promised to write to you before he goes into the country. The Duke also requested me to tell you that it was his intention to have written to you, but that as he had a good deal of business to do before he left town, and had related to

me all the particulars of Lord Loughborough's last
interview with Pitt, he trusted you would not think
his writing necessary. Pelham is a great enemy to
the reform. He is, however, no friend to the proclamation, and spoke against the address in Sussex; but
I believe he was induced to speak by a fair opening
given him by the Duke of Richmond, which he could
not resist taking advantage of. The Duke of Portland
seems to consider the members of the Association as
persons entirely separated from the party, and says
though he may not positively mean to shut the door
against their return, yet that, even in that case, he
should not receive them with the same cordiality that
some other persons might be disposed to do. I find
there has been a great meeting in Edinburgh relative
to Parliamentary Reform. The Duke read me a part of
a letter from Sir Thomas Dundas, by which I understand that the anti-reformers, of whom Sir Thomas is
one, wished to adjourn the meeting without coming to
any resolution ; but as they were fearful of not having
sufficient numbers to accomplish so strong a measure,
they determined to endeavour to turn the attention of
the delegates merely to the correction of the acts relative to the Scotch elections. Harry Erskine has
written to the Duke in terms which give him great
satisfaction. He expresses himself as a general friend to
reform, but is a decided enemy to urging such important
topics at the present critical juncture. I did not see
his letter, as the Duke had lent it to Lord Stormont.

'Pray remember me most kindly to Sir George

Cornewall. I am very sorry he has such bad weather for his excursion. It rains very frequently with us, and I therefore suppose that with you it pours eternally. I do not, however, insist upon your communicating this supposition to my lady, as I know she does not much approve of insinuations against the climate of Scotland. Douglas is, I imagine, by this time at Aberdeen.

'I am, with love to my lady and all your family, my dear Sir Gilbert, your ever affectionate

'WILLIAM ELLIOT.'

Henry Erskine to Sir Gilbert Elliot.

'Edinburgh: June 14, 1792.

'My dear Sir Gilbert,—As there is no person with whom I stand connected by blood, friendship, or political party, for whom I have a more sincere respect or to whom I feel a more sincere attachment than yourself, you will easily believe that I could not chance to differ from you on any point of great importance without particular concern, and that, on the other hand, I must receive a very great degree of satisfaction in finding that, on any point of consequence, my sentiments coincide with yours. I therefore embrace with eagerness the opportunity your friendship has afforded me of giving you my opinion and determination on the very important question that at present so unfortunately divides our political friends.

'For myself, I have ever been of opinion that,

however excellent the principles of our constitution
may be, it certainly admits (particularly in respect to
Parliamentary representation) of many very salutary
amendments; and whenever at a *proper time*, and in
a *proper mode*, there shall be brought forward a plan
of reformation in that respect, it shall meet with my
cordial support. But I am decidedly of opinion that
this is of all others the most improper *time* that such
a plan could have been suggested; and that the mode
adopted is, at the present conjuncture, the most unfortunate that could have been devised. Though I
rejoice in the downfall of despotism in a neighbouring
kingdom, and am by no means certain that, wildly
democratic as the system which has been substituted
in its place may appear to be, it was in the situation of
that country avoidable, yet I am perfectly certain that
it has excited in the minds of many men in this island
ideas on the subject of government highly hostile to
our happy constitution, and which, if not repressed by
the firmness or moderated by the address of its real
friends, may lead to consequences of the most dangerous nature. At such a time, therefore, that *general*
complaints of the defects of the British Constitution
should have been brought forward from so respectable
a quarter I most sincerely regret; and I still more
seriously lament that the remedy proposed has been
left so vague and undefined; and, however in other
circumstances I might have been inclined to join the
respectable Association, who from the purest motives
have stirred this business, I have been under the neces-

sity of *not* adding my name to the list, though my
attention was called to the business by my brother
Thomas,[1] with whom it must naturally be my desire to
act so far as my own feelings of duty or prudence will
permit.

'I am satisfied that the vague and indefinite nature
of the resolutions of that Association will lead all those
whose wild and extravagant notions on the subject of
government are taken from, or at least inflamed by,
several late publications, to join in a general cry of
reform.   They will grapple themselves close to the Association, till they find (which I trust they will do) that
the objects they have in view fall short, very far short,
of the high democratic notions to which I have already
alluded ; and thus two very serious evils will arise :—
First, A flame will be excited in the country which the
exertions of the Association will in vain attempt to ex-
tinguish ; and, *secondly,* Those very individuals who,
independent of their being so committed, would most
probably have been able to quiet the minds and
moderate the exertions of the wilder reformers, will
find that they have lost the confidence of the lower
ranks of the people, by means of which they might
have been able, at some future period of a different
complexion, to have obtained by means of the
moderate sound of the public voice—that rational
degree of reform of which I have already said I really
think that our constitution would admit.

'Under these impressions I have resolved (though

---

[1] Lord Erskine.

without any change in my abstract sentiments on the subject of reform) to join in no public exertion towards it in the present delicate situation. But, on the contrary, so far as I may have any influence, to exert it for the purpose of moderating the violent spirit of innovation I perceive, with regret, to be rising in this part of the United Kingdom; and so far as lies in my power to prevent all my friends who, like myself, are attached to a moderate and constitutional reform, from exerting themselves to obtain it at a period when their endeavours would not only lead to a very imminent political danger, but might tend to preclude the hope of obtaining, in safer times, those meliorations of which I think the constitution of this country stands in need and would admit of, to the effect of renovating, instead of impairing, the admirable foundation on which it rests.

' I thus, my dear Sir Gilbert, though very sorely pressed as I am with the hurry of business, throw out my ideas on this important subject. I know not precisely how your ideas on the general subject of reform may stand, but I have the satisfaction to think that our line of conduct will be the same. I shall be happy with your leisure, and with mine, which is now fast approaching, to communicate more particularly on the subject; and, in the meantime, with respectful compliments to Lady Elliot, and kind love to the young folks, I remain, my dear Sir Gilbert, your very affectionate and faithful servant, ' HENRY ERSKINE.'

Sylvester Douglas to Sir Gilbert Elliot.

LAST ILLNESS OF LORD NORTH.

'London : Friday, July 27.

'Dear Sir Gilbert,—You will be surprised to see this letter dated from London; but on my arrival at Gloucester on Wednesday, I found a letter from Lady K. informing me that Warren had pronounced Lord Guildford to be in great danger, and desiring me to come to town immediately. I set out accordingly without stopping, and found him on my arrival so weak and so altered that I have not the smallest hopes of his recovery, though the physicians think he may continue to languish for some time. Thank God, he suffers little pain or none, and his mind is in such a state of mildness and benignity, that to see and hear him would disarm the rancour of his greatest enemies, if he, whose character is a total stranger to the passions of hatred and resentment, can have any enemies among those who have had an opportunity of knowing him, except such as have no indulgence for human frailties, because they are equally devoid of the weaknesses and the virtues of humanity. In the present circumstances, I do not foresee that it will be possible for me to return to the circuit. You will guess the scene of distress in this family, and the least I can do is to share the sufferings which I cannot alleviate. I find the Duke of Portland is in town, and I hear that the wish on the part of the ministers still continues to obtain some accession from Opposition. I found my little boy quite well. Give my love to your little boys and girls, and remember me affectionately to Lady Elliot.

' Ever yours,   SYLVESTER DOUGLAS.'

In August came the terrible news of the massacre of the Swiss Guard and the removal of the King and Queen of France from the Tuileries to the Temple. It is curious to see in the following letter from Lady Palmerston how few outward signs of the coming catastrophe were to be discovered by strangers in the aspect of Paris only two days before.

Lord and Lady Palmerston, with their children, having passed through Paris on their way to Italy, on the 13th of August Lady Palmerston wrote to Sir Gilbert from Lyons :—

' We got to Paris on the 2nd of August, and meant to have stayed a fortnight, but we found things in so critical a state that we were advised to leave it as soon as possible, and the events we have received an account of to-day justify the prudence of that advice. We saw and visited all day, and night, and I really think this the only town for a gentleman to live in. I propose taking a fine hotel, and passing my winters there instead of living in London. Mr. Stanley and Mr. Crosby were almost the only English there. I went one day to the Assembly, which to have seen and heard will be a pleasure all my life. I left it with great regret on the 7th, and we arrived here on the 12th, having

had a particularly pleasant journey ; the weather prov-
ing to me what sort of season summer can be. We have
travelled all the way from Calais here without meeting
with difficulty, danger, or inconvenience, except in
leaving Paris, when owing to the postillions carrying us
through the Faubourg St. Antoine, the people surrounded and stopped the children's coach, but it was
only to prevent their leaving Paris. When they had
obtained their point of carrying them back to the
section, the mob were appeased, and by the good conduct
of the greffier and Monsieur Emmanuel, after an hour
and a half the crowd dispersed, and they set off attended
by eight of the National Guard on horseback, who accompanied them almost to the first post.   Our anxiety
till they arrived, and we heard they were in safety, you
may easily imagine, for we were particularly advised
not to return.   Except that distress, which we brought
entirely on ourselves by not leaving the town a
more quiet way, we have travelled just as we might
have done in England, and the civility we have met
with from all the people in office with whom we have
anything to do is very uncommon.'

In the following month the news of the horrible
' September massacres' filled Europe with dismay.
Lady Malmesbury having seen a letter from Paris,
which came ' by a private boat,' and confirmed the
account of those dreadful events, wrote to her sister as
follows :—

Lady Malmesbury to Lady Elliot.

' They opened the prisons last Monday, and murdered everybody in them, to the amount as it is said by a *democrat* who writes, of 20,000 people. Amongst them, it is supposed, all the Queen's ladies, Madame de Lamballe, etc. etc., and certainly the two Montmorins; M. d'Affrey, who deserved it, as he betrayed the Swiss on the 10th. Seventeen people, either French or foreigners, who had taken advantage of the gates being opened for a few hours to go out, were driven back and murdered. It was not over; and these infernal monsters had declared, that when they marched to oppose a foreign enemy they would leave no domestic ones behind, so probably Paris will be a heap of ashes before the Duke of Brunswick gets there. . . .

' They do not allow any women to go near the Queen, who is obliged to empty her own slops. She begged only that a woman might be admitted once a day to clean her room, and they told her a free people was not made to serve tyrants.'

' Brookwood : September 12, 1792.

' . . . I saw Lindsay,[1] who arrived on Saturday from Paris. He said it was impossible to describe the state he left it in the Wednesday before. Madame de Lamballe's death was too horrid to describe. She would

---

[1] Described in an earlier letter by Lady Malmesbury as ' Ellis's half-brother, the finest of the fine gentlemen, but pleasant.'

have escaped (for they said they would spare all the women), but she fell into convulsions, and the people decided to kill her.   They brought her to herself by all kinds of torments, that she might be sensible before she died.   They then cut out her heart, and afterwards cut off her head, and deputed six of their ringleaders to carry these horrid trophies to the Queen; but the guards at the Temple persuaded them to desist from this intention.   They then carried the head on a pike to the Palais Royal, where Lindsay was dining with the Duke of Orleans, and of course started back with horror, seeing it under the windows.   The Duke said only, " Je sais ce que c'est ; " and then walked into the next room and sat down to dinner with complete coolness.[1]   You are to observe she was his sister-in-law.   Lindsay passed by the church when they were murdering the 160 priests, and heard their groans.   In all about 7,000 had perished when he came away.   La Fayette and Lamartine are at Luxembourg, waiting the Emperor's orders on their fate.   All their companions are released and gone to Holland.

' Don't you feel ashamed of having a little French blood in your veins?   I do : et je me tâte to find out whether I have not a natural inclination for murder.'

---

[1] In another letter Lady Malmesbury says—' I knew Madame de Lamballe very well, She was a silly, good-humoured, inoffensive woman. I am intimately acquainted with her sister-in-law, Madame de Carignan, and saw a good deal of her family at Rome ; her two sisters are married to the two first people of rank there—the Prince Doria and the Connétable Colonna. I am really grieved for them.'

Lord Auckland to Sir Gilbert Elliot.

'Hague : September 29, 1792.

' My dear Sir Gilbert,—Eleanor and I, and your nine nieces and nephews, are all well, and as happy as cheerful minds and the right employment of time can make us. But all my ideas of happiness are shaken by the calamitous history of France, every circumstance of which passes, from day to day, through my hands, and disturbs my mind both sleeping and waking. It is not an exaggeration to say that above 20,000 cold-blooded murders have been committed in that devoted country within the last eight months, and that above a million of orphan families have been reduced to beggary. . . . To this are to be added the proscriptions, emigrations, and banishments; the desolations still going forward under foreign invasion and civil fury: and the near prospect of a famine. When we see all this (not to mention the destruction of all the statues and palaces) it is impossible not to acknowledge that we are at best a wretched race of beings, without any security for the enjoyments, such as they are, that we possess. But it strikes more particularly those who know France and its interior; and I venture to say that old recollections made you sigh over the downfall and destruction " de notre bon Henri " on the Pont Neuf. Eleanor and I were so familiarised to all the scenes which have gone forwards, by having travelled so much through the provinces, by having lived so much with

the unfortunate prisoners of the Temple, by knowing
personally many of the victims to the late atrocities,
and by having lived in friendship and correspondence
with some of them to the last hour, that our life is
embittered by the details which we receive, and we can
talk of nothing else.   I wish I could tell you that
the Duke of Brunswick is advancing rapidly to Paris ; [1]
but that is not the case.   He is, however, advancing.
On the 22nd (our latest accounts from the army) the
column under General Clairfait was near to Rheims ;
and the main army, after driving Kellerman on the
20th from a strong post between St. Menehould and
Dampierre, was moving to Chalons.   The delay had
been occasioned, in some degree, by the extreme wet
weather and badness of the roads, but chiefly by precautions necessary on the subject of provisions.   It is
probable that the next accounts will be of a bloody
kind ; but there is every reason to believe that the
French will be defeated.   Duke Albert, with 16,000
men, is now before Lille, and has taken one of the
suburbs ; but the place is strong.   A dentist (l'Evesque)
has lately been arrested at Frankfort, and has confessed that he had received 50,000 livres to poison the
King of Prussia.   He had passed a part of this summer
at Berlin, and had been recommended to the Princesses,
and employed by them, and was nearly employed by the
King of Prussia.   The Jacobin Committee are known

[1] On July 25 the Duke of Brunswick broke up from Coblentz and
entered France at the head of 70,000 Prussians and 68,000 Austrians
and Hessians.   He published at the same time his famous Proclamation.

to have offered large rewards to anybody who will assassinate either him or the Duke of Brunswick in their camp; the consequence is that every Frenchman, who approaches on any pretence, is strictly searched. It is a wonderful circumstance to see a nation in the eighteenth century so totally lost to every idea of character, order, honesty, religion, morality, and humanity.

'I hoped to have been re-established about this time at Beckenham; but what La Fayette calls "an imperious concourse of circumstances" detains me here, and I cannot with propriety leave the Hague at present. I console myself with the hope of passing the next spring and summer at Beckenham.

'Your nieces are growing very tall: they complain of your want of punctuality as a correspondent.

'Our love to Lady Elliot, who will have totally forgotten us all.—Yours very affectionately,

'AUCKLAND.'

Lady Malmesbury to Lady Elliot.

'October 16, 1792.

'Well, what do you say to the Duke of Brunswick?[1] —this Alexander foiled by a Sans-culotte? he and his army are running away as fast as they can, and will certainly winter in Germany, instead of Paris. The sick

---

[1] The Allies commenced their retreat on September 29, having entered France on July 25. From the time of the retreat of the armies under the Duke of Brunswick, France was the aggressive power in the war which desolated the Continent, and until 1814 was not again called upon to defend her soil against invasion.

amounting to ten thousand; and no wonder they had
the dysentery, for they found nothing to eat but sour
grapes in Champagne. The emigrants desert by hun-
dreds, and call it *re-emigrating*—pretty creatures! On
the other hand, the Austrians do nothing, and the
French have taken Nice and Worms, and, I daresay, by
this time half the Palatinate. All I grieve at is the
loss of so many innocent victims, for I persist the best
scheme, instead of assisting, would be to draw a cordon
round all France, and block up their ports with fleets,
just as if it was the plague, and so leave them to destroy
each other, and prevent them doing mischief elsewhere.

'Lady Palmerston got to Turin a few days before
the Sans-culottes entered Savoy.[1] She says the whole
of it must fall, as there is no means of defence; but I
can't conceive but what a handful of men might stop
an army in those defiles in the Alps.'

The Same to the Same.

'Bath: Wednesday, October 17.

' As you are so much interested about news, I must
just write you a few lines to tell you I received a letter
from Madame de Balbi, from Luxembourg, yesterday.
The Duke of Brunswick having advanced as far as
Chalons, and enclosed Dumouriez in such a manner it

---

[1] The French declared war against the King of Sardinia in September
1792, having been previously called on to do so by a Republican Convention in Savoy.

was impossible he could escape, let him remain peaceably thus during six days, and the seventh sent orders to the Princes to retreat, and followed their example the next day. As this conduct is incomprehensible, many people suppose the Duke of Brunswick, in his conference with Dumouriez, obtained from him a promise that he would with his army go and fetch the King and bring him to him. The Duke was not certain of his subsistences. He feared to leave so large an army behind him, that the massacres would recommence at Paris, and this made him consent to this arrangement. But this appears to me like ringing the bell for a servant to give you the cup that is in your hand. The campaign is decidedly over, and the Princes are ordered into their winter-quarters *out of France*. There is to be a congress at Luxembourg, to be called *Le Congrès d'Union*. All the powers will send ambassadors except France, Poland, and Turkey. In this congress will be decided *Les Indemnités à donner*. She adds, " *à qui?* " which is very true. Monsieur has been very ill. In short, everything is as bad as possible ; and Burke, whom I saw this morning, is almost mad. I feel very sorry for my friends, and it is very likely that I shall soon be sorry for myself, for the success of these wretches is our destruction. . . . I hope we shall be *the last*—as this place is complete retirement !

' Poor Madame de Balbi is in such distress ! She has been obliged to sell everything. She says they cannot conceive the cause of the Duke's retreat.

'The King's house at Winchester is fitting up to
receive the priests, and the country begins to dislike
it; I am convinced the very presence of the French is
poison and corruption.'

The Same to the Same.

'London : Wednesday.

'All the world is black, and the alarm is very great
and very general. To give you an idea how serious
the evil is, I will say that even Lord Malmesbury fore-
sees the storm, and you may guess how men's minds
are when I add that Louisa read to-day, written upon
Privy Garden-wall, "No coach-tax ; d—n Pitt ! d—n
the Duke of Richmond ! *no King!*" In short, there
is no doubt there will be a struggle. I assure you I
speak the opinion of evreyone I see ; and, so far from
being black, I am sure we shall conquer at last, but the
struggle will be a hard one. The people at Brussels
rose and turned out the governors, and set open the
gate for the French. These mean to attack Holland,
which they will certainly carry with as much ease as
they have done the Low Countries ; and what then
remains to be done? As for Fox and Grey, I wish
they would utter treason at once, and be beheaded or
hanged.

'I heard from two emigrants to-day nothing but
misery and distress. All the Frenchwomen who were
here are gone back to get divorced from their husbands,

and by that means keep their estates. So the knowing ones will be taken in by their own laws.

'There was an outburst of loyalty at the play the other night—loud calls for " God save the King " before it was given. It is shameful that, at the Haymarket, the orchestra is always a quarter of an hour after it is called before they will play " God save the King "— this is a *Sheridanism*. Did I tell you that he is so in love with Madame de Genlis's Pamela[1] that he means to marry her if she will have him ?

'I expect Madame de Coigny here; she is literally starving, and this is the only way of feeding a gentle-woman. Mentz is taken by the French. It does not appear that either want or disease was the cause of the Duke of Brunswick's flight, and he has not alleged either; it must either be treachery, bribery, or dissension between the German armies, in which case, in ten years, France will be the greatest country in Europe—*so there's an end of that.*'

In these few sentences Lady Malmesbury hit the very heart of the matter with a precision which Sir Gilbert's masculine correspondents failed to attain after reams of argument, and she disposed of the vexed question of party politics in an equally just and summary manner when she wrote, 'The Duke of Portland is our *Duke of Brunswick*—no party will be led to victory by either.'

---

[1] Pamela, supposed to be the daughter of Madame de Genlis and the Duke of Orleans ; married Lord Edward Fitzgerald.

William Elliot of Wells to Sir Gilbert Elliot.

'Reigate: November 19, 1792.

'My dear Sir Gilbert,—I thank you for your letter which I received yesterday. . . . I do most perfectly accord with you in your sentiments concerning the imprudence of concessions at the present juncture. Reform, as you observe, implies innovation ; and innovation, which is in itself dangerous, cannot fail of leading to destruction when the people are under the dominion of frenzy. If the discontent proceeded from any specific grievance, the remedy would be easy ;—you would redress the grievance, and the ill-humour of the people would subside. But the object of the modern fanatics is of entirely a different nature. It is much more capacious and comprehensive in its tendency. Their scheme amounts to the total and complete subversion of all existing institutions and establishments. They say civil society, as it now subsists, is ill constituted, that it must be pulled down, and reconstructed upon new principles. In such circumstances all subordinate reforms are worse than useless ; they betray weakness and timidity on the part of the Government without conciliating the mind of a single insurgent. To concede, therefore, at this moment is to surrender. If you concede with a view to prevent *contest,* the concession must include nothing short of the *whole.* . . . The spirit of sedition has now been evidently advancing in this country for two years past, and yet no means have

been employed to oppose it except the proclamation,
the permanent efficacy of which much depended upon
subsequent events.   It clearly showed the sense of the
higher orders of the people; and, if the great leading
political interests in the State could have afterwards
been *immediately* united, I do believe the virtue,
wisdom, and property of the nation so embodied, and
ready to be exerted on any pressing emergency, would
have exceedingly awed and checked the proceedings of
the unsound part of the community.   As it is, however,
the proclamation has lost its influence on the minds of
the lower classes, and perhaps it for some months served
to lull the upper ranks into a dangerous sense of security.
Europe seems menaced with universal convulsion and
change; England, I much dread, must expect her share
of the calamity.   Recent examples prove that no government can now resist the insurrection of its own
subjects without at the some time encountering France.
The French are a part of the seditious in every country;
this is their mode of conquest.   It is so that they have
conquered Avignon,[1] Savoy, Brabant; and Montesquieu
stands at this moment impeached by the Convention
for not pursuing the same method of victory at Geneva.[2]
When once political seduction is systematically prac-
tised, armies and navies will be but brittle weapons.   I
will, however, dwell no longer upon this gloomy pros-

[1] The French had annexed Avignon and the Venaisin, which state
belonged to the Pope, in 1791.   This was their first act of aggression
on independent territories.

[2] The revolutionary party in Geneva delivered over that city to the
French troops on December 28, 1792.

pect, but I do assure you if you were as much within the focus of sedition as I am, you would participate in my apprehensions. I saw a letter the other day from Windham to Baron Maseres. It was chiefly written upon mathematical subjects, but at the end of it he touched upon politics. He seems much alarmed, and as far as I could judge from the little he dropped on that point, he appears to be against concession.

'Farewell! This letter has swelled to a much greater length than I had any notion of when I sat down to write. But I really cannot think, speak, or write upon the topic of the French Revolution without being so voluminous as to be a burden to my friends.—Believe me ever, my dear Sir Gilbert, your truly affectionate

'WILLIAM ELLIOT.'

On the very day on which the preceding letter was written, the Assembly passed unanimously a decree to the effect that 'the National Convention declares, in the name of the nation, that it will grant fraternity and assistance to all people who wish to recover their liberty; and it charges the executive power to send the necessary orders to the generals to give succour to such people,' &c.

When it was proposed in the National Convention, on the motion of M. Baraillan, to declare expressly that the decree of November 19th was confined to the nations with whom they were at war, the motion was negatived by a large majority.

On December 15 a still more violent decree was

passed, and transmitted to the generals on the frontier. After various clauses enjoining the confiscation of all the property possessed by any privileged class or body in the territories occupied by French troops, it concludes thus :—' The French nation declares that it will treat as enemies the people who, refusing or renouncing liberty and equality, are desirous of preserving their princes and privileged castes, or of entering into an accommodation with them. The nation promises and engages not to lay down its arms until the sovereignty of the people on whose territory the French army shall have entered shall be established, and not to consent to any arrangement or treaty with the princes and privileged persons so dispossessed, with whom the Republic is at war.'—*Ann. Reg.* xxxiv. 155.

Of this ' decree Fox expressed great horror,' writes Lord Malmesbury in his journal.

These arrogant and insulting measures naturally excited great indignation in England, and on December 19 Lady Malmesbury wrote to her sister that she is ' prodigiously cheered by the great efforts of courage shown on all sides. The Duke of Portland says Charles Fox's speech was not like that which was printed in the " Star," but as he has not contradicted any part of it I am inclined to think the Duke is mistaken ; he is, as Mr. Burke says, " a very wretched man." You cannot think how odd this sounded in my ears when I heard him utter it of Fox ; but I vow I begin to believe he is right.'

'Brookwood Park : December 18, 1792.

'Mr. Ellis has written a sermon applicable to the times, and Mr. Lowth preached it last Sunday at our parish church of Hinton. I never heard altogether so fine a thing. The thing itself was a charming piece of writing, and Mr. Lowth delivered it as well as Garrick could have done. At one part he was so affected that his voice faltered and he could not restrain his tears. You may suppose the effect this produced on the audience, and several of the common people wept bitterly ; one woman was obliged to go out. It was quite a tragedy, and unfitted me for doing anything the rest of the day. I have sent it to Lord Malmesbury, and I daresay it will be printed, as it certainly ought. I am very sorry for Charles Fox's behaviour and the general dissensions prevailing in the party, and Windham's speech was incomparable. I desired Lord Malmesbury to send you a parcel of "A Pennyworth of Truths," one of the cleverest things I ever read. Lord Loughborough I saw yesterday, and he thinks matters very serious. People call "No King!" in the streets ; the London tradesmen are supposed to be ill-affected.'

CHAPTER III.

'THE career of conquest,' says Alison, in his 'History of the French Revolution,' 'having brought the French armies to Antwerp, a decree of the Convention was passed on November 16, ordering the French commander-in-chief to open the Scheldt;[1] and by another decree, passed on the same day, the French troops were ordered to pursue the fugitive Austrians into the Dutch territory. These directions were immediately carried into effect by a French squadron, in defiance of the Dutch authorities, sailing up the Scheldt to assist in the siege of the citadel of Antwerp. The French did not attempt to justify these violations of subsisting treaties on any grounds recognised by the law of nations, but contended that treaties extorted by cupidity, and yielded by despotism, could not bind the free and enfranchised Belgians.'

Alison goes on to say, that only eight years before the French had successfully interfered to prevent a similar opening of the Scheldt by Austria, on the ground of a violation of the rights of the United Provinces, as established by the treaty of Vienna in 1731.

---

[1] It had been provided by the treaty of Munster, 1648, that the Scheldt should remain for ever closed.

Under these circumstances it was thought desirable to assemble Parliament, and in the speech from the throne the King said that 'he had observed a strict neutrality in the internal affairs of the Continent, and had strictly abstained from any interference in the internal affairs of France; but it is impossible to see without uneasiness the strong and increasing indications of an intention to excite disturbances in other countries, to disregard the rights of neutral nations, and to pursue views of conquest and aggrandisement.'

Parliament met on December 13, and on the same day Sir Gilbert wrote from London to his wife as follows :—

'Spring Gardens: Thursday, December 13,' 1792.

'I arrived here yesterday at 4 o'clock in fifty-six hours from Minto, which, considering long nights, bad roads, and tired horses, was reasonably quick. I was not at all tired. The back of the chaise being let down and the seat folded down, made a good bed, and, with the help of a pillow, diminished the fatigue of travelling to a degree that you, with all these "appliances to boot," will hardly understand. Lord Malmesbury is here as a bachelor without a footman, and he gives me such entertainment as I should find at the Hummums—that is to say, a bed and a fire. . . . I dined with him yesterday at Burlington House. There was a meeting of Peers after dinner, at which, of course, I did not assist. But Windham came in, and Elliot and I passed

---

¹ Parliament met that day.

the evening with them. I find everything much more unsettled than it ought to be. There has been no meeting whatever of our party in the House of Commons, and we are going to-day to open this remarkable session without three people having conversed together on the part that should be taken. Fox is warmer, more determined, and further than ever in his separation from the Duke of Portland and his friends. He is to have an amendment and division on the address, so that it is now unavoidable that we should publicly go to the right and left. For my part, I am determined to support Government in its measures for suppressing sedition and putting the country in a state of defence against the many dangers it is exposed to both at home and from abroad. At the same time, the mismanagement of the ministry has thrown great difficulties in our way in supporting their very first measure. They thought it necessary that Parliament should meet *immediately*, and the only way which they had left themselves of calling it was calling out the militia, for it could not in any other case meet at so short a notice.[1] The militia cannot be called out during a recess of Parliament, *legally*, except in the case of actual insurrection or *imminent* danger of invasion. They are therefore obliged to justify it on the ground of *insurrection*; and as no insurrection has taken place in England, which seems, I think, rather

---

[1] Parliament could not legally meet within fourteen days of the summons being issued, except in the case of its being required to call out the militia.

more quiet than usual, they lay it on all the *insurrec-tions* which have taken place in Scotland, and, I believe, Ireland. The Scotch insurrections consist of the plant-ing of the Tree of Liberty at Perth, and the Dundee mob, and some others of less note. This is certainly ridiculous to those who live in Scotland and know the truth. This conduct of ministry imposes on those who wish to stand by Government the heavy task of defend-ing, or at least approving, an *unconstitutional* act re-lating to the military, a subject on which it is easier to raise jealousy than any other. All this might have been avoided if they had made short prorogations of Parliament, or rather if they had seriously turned their thoughts to their business earlier. Yet, with all these objections, I think it the peculiar duty of the present hour to support the Government in measures right in themselves, though irregular in their form, and I shall vote against the amendment. I understand there is some uneasiness concerning the part of the numerous French now here; some of the *Marseillois*, or actual murderers of August 10 and September 3, are confi-dently said to be in London, and that French emissaries are active in promoting mischief. Of this it is im-possible to doubt, the French Government having avowed that system.[1] Associations and declarations in favour of Government are very general and numerous in England—especially in London. I hope they will be equally so in Scotland. It is thought that the

[1] See decrees of November 19 and December 15—*Ann. Reg.* xxxiv. 155.

alarming aspect of affairs has cooled the wishes of many reformers in England, and that it would not be pressed or supported strongly in this country. How that may be in Scotland, I do not personally know. . . . I daresay the Scotch borough reform will be granted; as to the Scotch county reform, I do not yet know. If English reform is postponed, I imagine the Scotch counties will have to wait, and I am sure it is much their interest to do so; for one year of confusion will entail more misery on the whole nation, and every individual in it, high and low, than any reform can compensate in half a century, or during the present generation. . . . I am going to the House; if I can send you a line from there I will. No coalition, which I heartily rejoice at.'

'Spring Gardens: Saturday, December 15, 1792.

' . . . We have had hard service in the House, having had two late days running, and we are to have another to-day although it is Saturday. I cannot enter on politics to-day, because I can say but a few words more, and it is impossible to be understood on the affairs of this period without a pretty full explanation.

'Fox is losing the good opinion and confidence, almost irrecoverably, not only of the country, but of many who were most attached to him. The Duke of Portland's indecision and feebleness of character is doing much mischief, and laying his friends under great difficulties, as well as exposing his character to much suspicion and question in the country, which his intentions do not merit. I have been labouring, and I think successfully, to diminish this evil, and it will not last many days longer. All that is wanted is, that he should declare himself distinctly in public to entertain the opinions which he daily professes, and enable his friends by that means to act in a body and with the weight of connection, instead of separately, and as individuals *quitting* their connection, as we now appear to do. A war, or considerable preparation for it seems unavoidable, and great as that evil is, I have no doubt of its absolute necessity. There is reason to believe that the King of France has been executed this very day. That scene is probably enacting at this very instant of time. A general massacre of those suspected of any attachment to the King, and hostile to the present anarchy, is also much expected to follow the King's death, or rather to accompany it. They have met with a serious check at Frankfort, and have lost that town. They seem indeed to apprehend at Paris some greater blow to Custine's army. I understand they have given up the invasion of Holland, in consequence of the steps taken in England lately.[1]

---

[1] An angry correspondence, which arose out of the King's speech, had been carried on between Lord Grenville and M. Chauvelin, the French envoy. 'England,' said Lord Grenville, in a note to M. Chauvelin, 'never will consent that France should arrogate to herself the power of annulling at pleasure, and under cover of a pretended natural right, of which she makes herself the sole judge, the political system of Europe, established by solemn treaties and guaranteed by the consent of all Powers. This Government will also never see with indifference that France shall make herself, either directly or indirectly,

'Spring Gardens: Tuesday, December 18, 1792.

' There seems little doubt of my coming down at
Christmas. . . . The Duke of Portland's conduct is
giving us all great uneasiness, and is not only hurting
our cause but is destroying his own character. He is
perfectly agreed with us in supporting Government in
the measures necessary in this crisis, and in condemning the conduct and principles of Fox; but he allows
the world to think otherwise, and has not yet taken
any step to counteract the misrepresentations of Fox's
newspapers &c., by which he appears to be acting with
Fox, and we appear acting in opposition to *all* our
friends. We are on the point of sending a strong representation to the Duke of Portland, signed by his
most attached friends, and requiring him to declare
himself openly. I have had several long and strong
conferences with him on the subject, sometimes alone,
sometimes with Lord Malmesbury and Elliot, by which
no effect was produced but giving him extreme pain ;
and his manner on these occasions is exactly the same
as *George's*.[1] He does not utter one word, admitting,
however, all you say, and sobbing grievously. The
King of France seems to have rather a better chance
than he had ; but the improvement in his prospects is

sovereign of the Low Countries or general arbitress of the rights and
liberties of Europe. If France is really desirous of maintaining friendship and peace with England, let her renounce her views of aggression
and aggrandisement and confine herself within her own territory, without insulting other governments, disturbing their tranquillity, or vio-
lating their rights.'—Alison's *History of the French Revolution*.

[1] Sir Gilbert's second son, a child of eight years old.

very slender. . . . You can hardly conceive the degree
of reprobation in which Fox and his party are held.
They are sensible of it, and testify some wish to avoid
the loss of such a body of support as they have driven
from them ; but I know that Fox's passions and *connections* are too powerful to let him approach towards
the opinions which we entertain, and that any pretence
of union would only produce destruction amongst ourselves and mischief to the public. It is said that
about seventy have already gone over ; many of those
who acted with him have disclaimed him in the most
violent language — particularly country gentlemen ;
and the country itself appears to be of the same mind.
You see there has been a mob at Manchester against
Republicans. Manchester was thought to be one of
the most disaffected places. Our wish is not to join
Ministry, but to support *Government* in a separate
body. The Duke of Portland is, however, making this
difficult, and if he continues many days more, most of
his party will go over individually to Ministry. Not
I, however.'

'Spring Gardens: Thursday, December 20, 1792.

'Your Friday and Monday's letters came together
to-day, and were a great relief as well as great joy. If
one could ever forget one's love, the pining for letters
would put one in mind of it. When the post misses it
always seems impossible to get over the interval till
the next day, and as the time approaches again the
minutes become as troublesome as the hours were
before.

'Affairs here are much as they were. The Duke of
Portland was brought to a determination, and promised faithfully to go to the House of Lords yesterday
to *declare* himself openly. He contrived, however, to
be too late, and the thing is yet undone. He has
determined, however, to do it to-morrow. It is become
extremely necessary, for I never knew so much character lost in so short a time. It is, I think, certain
that Lord Loughborough will be Chancellor. He is
extremely desirous of it himself; and it is not only
right, but no good reason can now be brought against it.
I have had a long conversation with him on the subject
to-day, and have indeed seen a good deal of him every
day. I am at present grand mediator. I imagine
that we shall have a formal deliberation in a day or
two concerning the footing on which *we* are now to
act. Whether as a separate party, *all* out of office,
except Lord Loughborough, or with a *few* leading
people in office, the rest engaging to support and to wait
—or with a more general coalition. The latter I think
out of the question, because I do not think the ministry are hard enough pushed to want it, and it must be
thoroughly against the grain. The second would perhaps be the best practicable plan both for the public
and for maintaining any degree of connection amongst
us—I mean amongst those of our present party who
think as we do. The first would be the most comfortable to our own feelings, and seems most likely to be
adopted. But, then, farewell the Duke of Portland's
party; for, while a few of us are standing out, the mul-

titude will melt into the ministry, and will never be
seen again in their old form.   However, it has been
a great fault in the Duke of Portland not to have settled all these important points deliberately long ago,
and informed the public of the footing we stand on.
The last week of indecision, or rather *worse*, in the
Duke of Portland, together with the offensive part
taken by Fox, has sent crowds over to Government,
and I see no reason to expect that they will now consider
the Duke of Portland in their future conduct.   Windham stands higher at present, both in the House and
in the country, than any man I remember.   I think he
might have a cabinet office if he liked.   All this is
very confidential.   I am going to bring these points to
some decision immediately, if it is possible.'

'Spring Gardens: Saturday, December 22, 1792.

'. . . Our political situation is no better than it
was, and the Duke of Portland will find it difficult to
regain even *my* good opinion.   Weakness is the cause
of his misconduct; but that quality prevails so much
that his insufficiency for leading a party, and more especially in arduous times, is become manifest.   His
conduct has gone beyond indecision, it has amounted
to duplicity; and two parties professing sentiments
exactly opposite to each other, are *each* entitled to
claim his concurrence, and accordingly do so.   While
the public knows not what to think between us; or
rather, while the public has grounds for ascribing to
him those opinions which in private he disavows, and

to which he has always encouraged the opposition of his
private and particular friends. We had determined to
present a strong remonstrance to him. I actually
drew one, which was approved of; but understanding
from him that he was to declare himself in the House
of Lords on Wednesday, it was dropped. He told me
even what he would say. The substance was to be a
declaration of an unequivocal, fair, and honourable
support of Government, in the measures which related
to the present situation of the country. Yesterday he
spoke, but has contrived entirely to disappoint the
purpose of his speaking. He supported the particular
bill,[1] but without any expression of general support.
Lord Lauderdale and *Lord Lansdowne* supported the
bill immediately after, and there was no opposition to
it. The Duke, therefore, still stands exactly on the
same footing with Lord Lansdowne—that is to say,
with Fox and all his party. I am convinced that this
was even concerted; for very lately Fox had determined and declared that he would *oppose* the bill; but
probably thought it better, in order to preserve the appearance of agreement with the Duke of Portland, that
if the Duke should not declare a general support, he
should agree with him in supporting this particular
measure. Something will probably be done this very
day, either to fix the Duke of Portland to one line of
conduct or to dissolve our connection with him—in
which case we shall disband, and stand each man on

---

[1] Alien Bill.

his own ground. My mind in that case is made up to
declare that I am entirely unconnected; that I will
concur where it is possible, on the present crisis, with
those who are charged with the safety of the State,
but that I will form no connection with them or any
others; and of course that I will accept of no office or
situation that could render the motive of my conduct
suspicious. I told you in my last letter that Lord
Loughborough was likely to be Chancellor. It is
settled, however, in the negative. The Duke of Portland has given a second and positive dissent, and Lord
Loughborough acquiesces, and is determined not to
accept without the Duke's approbation. It is also
determined that the Duke and his party shall form no
connection, great or small, with ministry, but shall
support Government out of office. This is what the
Duke says to us; but as to supporting Government,
either one way or the other, he will not say a word on
the subject anywhere but at his own fireside; and
whatever is done by us has the appearance of being
merely the act of individuals—what is worse, of individuals falling off from their party. I hope we shall
get into a more settled way before I leave town.

'I went last night, after the House of Lords, with
Elliot and Sylvester Douglas, to the play, and saw Mrs.
Siddons in the last act of "Jane Shore." This is my
first *pleasuring* since I came to town.'

'London: Tuesday, December 25, 1792.

'I wish you all a merry Christmas. Our affairs here are in a better state than they were, for we have brought the Duke of Portland to a decision. I must take a great share in the merit of this achievement, for I have been daily employed, sometimes in my individual capacity as a friend, sometimes deputed by others in this work. There was a meeting at Lord Malmesbury's on Sunday, at which it was determined that a representation should be made to the Duke, and that he should be desired explicitly to take his line, and either to continue at our head on the principles which he and we profess, or disband us at once. Lord Malmesbury, Windham, and I were deputed to execute this commission. We went yesterday morning, and I had the honour to be *l'orateur de la députation*, which I assure you was not a pleasant office. My colleagues, however, flatter me with my execution of it, and the fact is that we had a most unexpected success. He is to make an explicit declaration of his sentiments to-morrow in the House of Lords. Lord Titchfield is to do so in the House of Commons on Thursday, and he authorises everybody to quote his opinions as coinciding with ours and as differing from Fox. With all the loyalty of England, and all the zeal shown all over the kingdom for tranquillity and for the present Government, it seems as if it would require all the weight that can be collected to resist the very active and persevering spirit of the various

descriptions of our adversaries. I apprehend, however, that there is no real risk, if it is not in Scotland,
and I do not know that there is any there. I cannot
think that any quantity of arms can be disposed of at
Jedburgh, or in our part of the country. I should be
glad, however, to have the truth of this report.

'The number of French here is very great, and it is
believed that some of them are here with bad intentions, but to what number I do not know. I imagine
they are disappointed by the spirit which has been
shown in favour of Government. Some of the very
worst of the French murderers on the 10th August
and beginning of September have been here, particularly one *Rotundo*, who was a principal performer in
the massacres of the prisoners on the 2nd and 3rd of
September. He was one of the executioners of
Madame de Lamballe, of which I understand he
boasted when in England, for I hear he is gone back.
Madame de Lamballe underwent all sorts of insults
besides cruelty.

'Windham took me the other day to Madame de
Flahault's, a French lady who escaped from the Louvre
on August 10, and seems a very agreeable woman. I
found Lord Wycombe there, and several other French
and English, crammed into a little miserable lodging,
where she sees company every evening, as if she were
at the Louvre. Their spirits under their misfortunes
are surprising.

'I expect to set off on Monday. The Duke's indecision and insufficiency require the constant stimulus

of his friends. . . . Although I have not yet spoken, yet the number of our party who can speak at all is so reduced, that I cannot but take my share.

'I hope to profess myself before I come away.'

The conference referred to in the previous letter as having been held between the Duke of Portland on the one side, and Lord Malmesbury, Sir Gilbert Elliot, and Mr. Windham on the other, was reduced to writing immediately after it took place, and was then shown to the Duke of Portland, who admitted its perfect accuracy. The original minute of the conversation, preserved in a volume of political memoranda, is as follows :—

'Monday, December 24, 1792.

'In consequence of the meeting held yesterday (describe it), and by their desire, Lord Malmesbury, Mr. Windham, and Sir Gilbert Elliot went to Burlington House this morning.

'They stated the sense of the meeting, and the specific points to which the Duke's assent was desired—viz., That Mr. Fox and some gentlemen formerly acting with our party, having taken a line and expressed sentiments in Parliament contrary to those of the majority of our party, and on subjects which we think too important to the interests and safety of the country to make it possible that we acquiesce in, a division has thereby taken place in the party. That Mr. Fox having been reputed the leader of our party in the House of Commons, we cannot otherwise avoid being involved ourselves in his opinions, or prevent their being ascribed generally to the party, than by declaring explicitly that we no longer consider Mr. Fox as speaking our sentiments. That although by these means Mr. Fox and his present friends stand divided from the party, yet the party itself remains connected on its ancient principles, and under its natural head and leader the Duke of Portland. That, knowing the Duke of Portland to agree with us in our own sentiments, and in our dissent from those of Mr. Fox, it is important that some declaration to that effect should be made as an act of the party, sanctioned by the Duke of Portland as its leader. That the Duke of Portland should take the proper steps for assembling those members of our party who agree with him and us ; and for placing our Parliamentary proceedings on the footing of connection and concert, and for preventing the dispersion of his party, which is become probable if some steps of that nature should not be taken.

'The result of the conference was that the Duke admitted the truth of these propositions, and the necessity of acquiescing in the points recommended to him. He stated very strongly, and indeed manifested still more strongly, the great violence that this determination did to his private affections and attachment to Mr. Fox, and ascribed the backwardness which he had hitherto shown to take these explicit and decisive steps, to that cause, rather than to any doubt on the reason and the necessity of the thing, or on the nature of his public duty. But that his mind was in some degree reconciled to these strong measures from an opinion that, however disagreeable they might appear to Mr. Fox in the meanwhile, yet they might ultimately tend even to his benefit and comfort ; because it seemed more desirable, even for the interests of Mr. Fox, that the party should be held together under its old connection, and in a form, therefore, that rendered a reunion of all its parts possible, if change of circumstances should seem to render his public principles and ours compatible with that reunion, than that a total dissolution of the party should happen, which in a short time would render its reassembling entirely impossible.

'That he was much flattered and affected by the continuance of our confidence, and that he accepted the offer we made him of acting in party under him with great pride and satisfaction.

'With regard to assembling us at present, he stated some objections which related only to the present moment, such as the uncertainty he was in concerning the sentiments of several of his friends ; the absence of others &c. But he would take the earliest opportunity and the best means that occurred to him of complying with this part of our request.

'With regard to a manifestation of his own sentiments, and those of his party, he would immediately complete the declaration of his opinion on the present state of public affairs, and the necessity of giving a fair and honourable support to Government in the measures which the interest of the country required.

'That Lord Titchfield would declare the same

opinions in the House of Commons on the earliest opportunity.

'That any friend of his, in declaring those sentiments which we profess, and which have been expressed in our present communication with him, may state himself to speak the sentiments of his Grace and his party, and to be authorised to say so. . . .'

'London: Thursday, December 27, 1792.

' The Duke of Portland has once more failed us, and prolonged his own dishonour and our difficulties. He went to the House of Lords yesterday, under express promise to declare himself and determined to do so. The House waited for his arrival; a long debate took place affording many opportunities, and increasing most extremely the necessity for his speaking. He sat through it as fixed as the lady in Comus, enchanted, I do believe, like her, without uttering a syllable. If one did not know the man with certainty, it would be impossible to defend him against the imputation of treachery, but the fact is quite otherwise. He was kept down by mere nerves and the horror of public speaking, and he was as unhappy and miserable afterwards as we are angry. What is to be done I know not. Lord Titchfield has engaged to speak for him either to-day or to-morrow in the House of Commons, and if that is performed it may do some good. The Alien Bill is to be fought hard by Opposition, and the House will hardly adjourn so soon as Monday. . . .'

'London: Saturday, December 29, 1792.

' I have at last delivered my mind of some part of its burden, and spoke yesterday in the House of Commons. It was meant only as a declaration of my general sentiments on the affairs of the present period, and of the line I mean to take. I expressed very distinctly the *entire* difference between my opinions and those of Fox and his present party, and the improbability there appears of anything like a general agreement between us while the present circumstances continued. I then stated my opinion that it was my duty to give a fair and honourable support to Government in defending the constitution and saving the country; that if I had stood alone in this resolution, I should have had courage to do my duty even in that situation, but I was fortunate enough to believe that I agreed with a majority of those with whom I had long acted; that those who differed with me, though weighty and respectable, acted only as individuals, and did not express the sense of any party, but that I, and those who agreed with me, stood precisely on the same footing that we had ever done—perfectly unconnected with ministry, but connected amongst ourselves, as formerly, on our ancient principles, and under our ancient chief (the Duke of Portland), who I knew agreed with me, or whose sentiments I knew I had expressed on this occasion. I then said a few words in support of the Alien Bill. ·

' You will see Fox's answer. He was extremely agitated, and expressed his surprise at my quoting the Duke of Portland, from whom he thought he had understood the very contrary. I own I felt most extremely uneasy, for if the Duke of Portland should disavow me, an imputation of falsehood was left on me. I not only had his authority for what I said, but it was given in presence of Lord Malmesbury and Windham, in consequence of the deputation I mentioned to you; the result of which was reduced into writing by me the same day, approved by Lord Malmesbury and Windham, *shown to the Duke of Portland and assented* to by him as a just report of what had passed.[1] However, his extreme indecision and wavering on this subject was alarming. I went last night to Burlington House with Windham. Fox came soon after, and we had a most unpleasant conference, each of us claiming the Duke of Portland, who is involved in such a labyrinth of inconsistencies as he can never extricate himself from. I was, however, extremely relieved indeed by his avowing explicitly that I had his authority for all I had said in his name, or intended to pledge him for— that is to say, as to the resolution to support Government in those measures which the present crisis required. The fact is, that as to the remainder of my speech—viz. my difference with Fox—I did not quote anybody, but spoke for myself. I was so understood by Windham and several other persons; and indeed I told Windham the morning before I rose, that I should

[1] See Minute of Conference with the Duke of Portland.

quote the Duke of Portland only on the *support to Government*. This, however, being understood differently by some, and Fox resting much upon it, I have resolved to make the matter clear on Monday. I am to expect a furious attack from Fox, who is violent to the greatest degree; but danger creates courage, and I do not feel at all afraid of making a good battle, and I shall be well supported by Windham and others. I understand from everybody that I spoke well and with great effect; and I have gained an advantage of late—I mean courage. I did not feel the terror of speaking, either before or at the time, nearly so much as usual.'

Sylvester Douglas to Sir Gilbert Elliot.

'Bushy Park: Saturday.

' My dear Elliot,—We have just received the account of your speech, which, even in the very imperfect report of the "Times," we all agree to think excellent. But that you have at last done yourself, your talents, and your principles justice, is a much greater pleasure to me than the particular merit of the speech.

' It has never been problematical that you must speak well, but it was growing every session and every day more doubtful whether you would ever speak. The ice is now fairly broken, as you have, for the first time, come forward without a lash.

' Many things in your speech and in Fox's answer have added greatly to the desire I expressed in my last note of knowing from you what has passed of late.

' I conclude that you spoke of the Duke with his explicit authority, and that he would so explain himself to
Fox.   I intend to ride to town to-morrow in order to
see you, and will arrive at Lord Malmesbury's by eleven
or a little after, and shall be obliged to you for a little
breakfast.   I want to consult you about signing some
resolutions relative to the Scarborough reform.

' I have seen with deep concern that the good dispositions you mentioned have prevailed over the good
principles.   The younger brother, who thinks and acts
as you and Windham, is delighted with your speech.
I was happy to learn from him that in manner his
brother's speech was extremely good.   Perhaps you
will have time to-morrow to read part of the " Impiad."

' Frederick North will be in town on Monday if his
attendance in the House of Commons should be wanted.
Pray, if this find you at home, send a few words of
answer.

' S. DOUGLAS.'

Sir Gilbert to Lady Elliot.

'London : Tuesday, January 1, 1793.

' I wish you all a happy New Year.   You will see
me again in the papers ; and I don't know when I shall
be out of them, as I seem in for speaking every day,
besides paragraphs.   I don't know how my speech of
yesterday will be in the " Star," but it is put in so
wrong in the " Morning Chronicle " that it must be
intentional.   I explained distinctly what I had quoted
the Duke of Portland for the day before—viz. for

support to Government; and I took care to assert, strongly and intelligibly, that what I had said on that subject was *correctly* and precisely authorised by him before, and correctly and precisely avowed and approved of afterwards; but I explained also what I had spoken only in my own name—viz. the great difference between my opinions and those of Fox. The Duke of Portland heard me read, the night before last, in the presence of Windham and Lord Fitzwilliam, the report of my first speech in the " Morning Chronicle," and he said, clearly and distinctly, that those were the sentiments he had all along professed, and which he had authorised me to deliver in his name. He told us also that he wished Windham to come the next day (yesterday), to settle what Lord Titchfield should say. Windham went accordingly, and made a speech for Lord Titchfield, which he delivered immediately after I spoke, and which was an avowal and support of mine; but after what Windham had settled, he added a sentence or two, evidently dictated by Fox, and which he did not say a word of to Windham. In short, the Duke is *two men*, and has contrived completely to destroy his own honour, as well as to endanger that of his friends. I expected a strong attack from Fox, but he refrained, either from want of ground or from policy. He manifested, however, in his manner, a decided hostility towards me, and I hear the tone at Brookes's is violent against me. All this is nothing. I have not only done my duty, but have done myself credit. But the Duke of Portland's conduct defeats the good effect of ours, both as to the interests of the party and those of the public.

'Lord Edward Fitzgerald has married Pamela, Madame de Genlis' daughter.   Sheridan is said to have been refused by her.'

Sir Gilbert left London for Minto on January 6, and while there he described in detail to Sir David Carnegie the nature of the political crisis, and the causes which had led to it.   The letter, though incomplete, is here given, for the same reason which has led to the preservation of the preceding series of letters from Mr. Elliot of Wells—i.e. that it gives a full and candid account of the causes which operated on the minds of the leading men of the Duke of Portland's party, and which finally led to the disruption of the party.

Sir Gilbert Elliot to Sir David Carnegie.

'Minto: January 1793.

' My dear Sir David,—If anyone had told me the day I received your letter that it would be unanswered at this time, I should have thought it very strange, and very unjust to suspect me of anything so impossible. I am now to confess, however, that if you forgive me this extraordinary delay, I shall owe it entirely to your indulgence, and not to any excuse I can offer, for I am conscious that none can be sufficient.   Whenever my friends mean to flatter me very much, or, I presume, to abuse Lady Carnegie, they say to me, this or that is

exactly like her. It will be happy for me if I can find
favour in your sight, as well as that of her other
admirers, for some of my faults, under this merit; in
which case, however awkward my imitations may be, I
shall certainly pass them off for graces.

' A very short question sometimes requires a very
long answer; and possibly this consideration, added to a
good' many pretty interesting avocations during a short
stay in the country, may have discouraged me from
attempting to give you the satisfaction you desire on
the politics of this session. I learn with real pleasure
the general approbation you appear to have given to
the part which I and most of our common friends have
taken. It will be impossible for me to enter fully into
the history of the late proceedings, because it would
make a book, and would lead me back to the last session,
if not further, as well as require an account of last summer during the prorogation. I will endeavour, however, to touch quite generally on the points which I
suppose most likely to interest you. Our party has
been in danger of *schism* ever since the French Revolution began, as, however remote from our interests that
subject might at first appear, it did in fact attract our
serious notice from the beginning, and it appeared very
early that our opinions differed *widely* and *warmly* on
the topic. The first explosion of this difference was, as
you know, between Burke and Fox. I remember that
both were blamed on the occasion for bringing forward
a subject which could not be treated without endangering our union, and which was not thought sufficiently

connected with the affairs of this nation as to *require*
discussion in Parliament, or to lay us under an obliga-
tion to take our side.   Our respective opinions were
not the less formed, nor the less known and understood ;
and in the division of the party on that point, I think
we stood pretty much as we do at this moment on
matters which have since arisen out of it, but concerning us more nearly.   You must have observed how this
question of the French Revolution has been gradually
approaching more and more near to us, and how it has
at length grown into the Aaron's rod, and swallowed up
all the other business and concerns of the world.   It
has at least generated all those questions on which we
are now at variance, and which have grown into so
much importance that they are become truly the just
criterion of public conduct and connection.

'The first general alarm manifested by the party or
the nation was towards the close of last session, when,
in addition to seditious exertions of inferior clubs and
individuals, the spirit of change, and the promotion of
popular discontent, received the countenance of considerable names by the association called the Friends of
the People.   You know what passed at that time.   The
most weighty and respectable members of the Opposition took a decided part in support of Government
against the danger that seemed approaching, and invited the ministry to act with vigour.   The proclamation
and address were concerted, altered, and almost made
at Burlington House last year ; and they were supported
by that description of the party in Parliament.   Fox

did not sign Grey's Association, and took a line in
debate which it was affected to consider as neutral in
the dissension of his friends ; but his neutrality was
like the Irish reciprocity, all on one side, and it was
plain where his heart was, and his tongue indeed was not
far off.   The recess was passed in the same contest in
the country, till the evil getting head we were all called
up suddenly by the late proclamation for the militia,
and found ourselves compelled, by the very nature of
the only business we had before us, to bring our several
principles into action, and to manifest unequivocally
and unavoidably the wide and radical difference in our
opinions.

'From the beginning to this time the Duke of
Portland and a great majority of our party have
thought as I, and I believe you, do on these subjects,
and we have throughout acted with constant communication and concert with him.   His public principles,
and indeed the fundamental principles of his party,
have at all times been such as to make the country
expect this conduct at his hands.   The points to which
that conduct may be reduced I think are—an opposition
to all seditious practices ; to the dangerous innovations
projected under the title of Parliamentary Reform ; to
all levelling doctrines, and to such as aim at the sup-
pression of the intermediate orders and gradations of
rank ; to the extension of French principles and of
French power, either by arms or by any other mode of
proselytism ; and lastly, a support to Government in
the measures which the danger of the times requires.

So far all is clear and well. But I say it in confidence (and indeed I wish you to consider it really in that light), we have had some reason to apprehend, or rather to feel, that the Duke's *firmness* is not equal to his principles, nor perhaps equal to the trying nature of the times and of the vigour and sturdiness which every crisis demands in a chief and leader of a party. His private virtues and good dispositions counteract his public principles and perplex his conduct. There has not only been some appearance of unsteadiness, and something problematical and equivocal in his own acts, at a time when everything should be clear as day, but his friends have found themselves strangely embarrassed, entangled, and obstructed in the services they have endeavoured to render the country in concert and in connection with him, by a want of steadiness and uniformity very unlike every notion which had been formed of his character and mind before. The fact is that his principles and those of Fox are black and white. Every act of their public lives must in the present state of the world be in direct opposition with each other.

' A declared and distinct separation from Fox can alone reconcile the Duke with himself; and this exertion he has not nerve to make. Fox has a sovereign command over his mind and his heart; and he does not neglect his advantage. Such is the present state of things—a fluctuation between private affection and public duty, between an amiable disposition and good principles. The consequence is that his friends are . . . .' (*This letter is incomplete*).

Lord Malmesbury to Sir Gilbert Elliot.

'Monday, January 21, 1793.

'My dear Elliot,—Parliament certainly will meet
for the despatch of business on Monday the 28th. War
is a measure decided on, but don't *proclaim* it in the
North before it is known in the South. I wish you
would seriously turn in your mind whether you would
or would not accept office if it were to be offered you, for
the *sole* purpose of deriving more benefit to the country
from your abilities than would be drawn from them
through your simple support out of office, and if such
an offer came to you, not as *a follower of any arrangement*, but in consequence of what is supposed to be
your own sentiments and feelings on the present
times, independent of any other consideration.

'I mention this, perhaps prematurely, rather because
I *suspect* than know such an idea to be in contemplation. It is, however, sufficiently probable for me to
submit it to your attention, in order to give you time
to revolve it deliberately in your mind, and it is very
essential for me to know your opinion, as it will go a
great way in deciding mine.

'After what we have declared so explicitly, it is
difficult to suppose we can again return to Fox, and it
is very clearly proved (whatever we may have till of
late believed), that it was his party, and not that of the
Duke of Portland, we have been following.

'The first consideration is to do what is strictly
right; the second, what is desirable and convenient.

' If they can be made compatible, so much the
better ; if not, we must not hesitate. Yours most
affectionately,   ' MALMESBURY.

'*Mem.*—The King of France was sentenced to death
on Thursday.[1]

' The mob forced the Convention to unanimity on
this measure, and are disposed to murders of all sorts.'

To this letter Sir Gilbert replied:—

' Minto: Sunday, January 27, 1793.[2]

'. . . You will feel the difficulty, or rather the impossibility, of my forming a decisive judgment on the
question you put to me, until I have an opportunity of
knowing all circumstances down to the latest date, and
of communicating and comparing my own thoughts in
a full and satisfactory way with you and other friends.
If I were called on for a decision *now*, and where I am
now writing, I should say *No*; and I confess my inclination runs so strongly against the coupling a separation from former friends (and perhaps from party altogether) with the acceptance of office, that I can hardly
give the question a fair consideration, nor describe the
circumstances in which I should think it necessary or
advisable to do so. Such circumstances, however, may
exist; and I should for that reason wish for the means

---

[1] He was executed on the 21st, and M. Chauvelin received notice to
leave the British dominions within eight days.

[2] This letter has been already published in the ' Correspondence of
the first Earl of Malmesbury.'

of knowing the state of things, as well as of full consultation with friends, before I should decide.

'A return to Fox, or of Fox to us, appears, as you say, highly improbable ; and every step he and those with whom he has exclusively connected himself seem to take, renders our separation wider, and anything like co-operation more irreconcilable with our principles.   By a newspaper report of the last Whig Club, I observe that Fox is made to conclude the day by drinking very emphatically the *Majesty of the People.* I have often heard the expression ; but the equivocation of the term *Majesty* appears to me to be a strong and unequivocal declaration, in the present times, of Fox's intentions, and to require more than ever the disavowal of those who are friends to the interests and liberties of the people, but decided enemies to its majesty. The last proceedings of the friends to the liberty of the press, who are Fox's immediate adherents, place him and us in direct opposition ; and so far from seeing any prospect of our approaching to each other, I cannot doubt that he has chosen his side in the troubles which threaten the world, and that it must be our post to oppose and combat him in Parliament and elsewhere. The Duke of Portland—I fear this part of the subject will afford but little comfort or remedy for the other evil.   The existence of our party depends on his *firmness, decision, vigour, activity, consistency, uniformity of conduct,* and *honourable support* of his friends, as head of that party ; and unfortunately the party is like *Snip,* and would look much better without

its head.   It is like the sign of the Good Woman.   I
fear the Duke has proved himself *entirely* unfit for his
station, both in character and talents, and that we are
hopeless there.   What remains?   To quit party; to do
what the public good requires out of party, since we
cannot do it otherwise; and to do this, as many others
have done, on independent ground.   The necessity for
so much as this, I fear, cannot be denied; but I own
that a connection with Ministry, the acceptance of
office, with all the suspicions belonging to such a step,
does not appear to me to be equally enjoined by public
duty; and in our circumstances it is certainly strongly
opposed by private feeling.   When I parted with the
Duke of Portland he had no reason to think that I then
thought such a step advisable, nor that any important
change would take place in my relation with him, unless
it should be grounded on some future proceedings; and
I cannot be reconciled to the idea of giving him the
first notice of our rupture by a step so strongly connected with private and personal interests.   With
regard to Lord Loughborough, I think the question
stands on different ground.   His acceptance of the
seals I believe sincerely to be eminently necessary
for the public service.   His conduct has been highly
honourable, and everything like personal claim, or
even party claim, on him, by the Duke of Portland,
is certainly at least cancelled, if not converted into a
direct *provocation*, by what has passed since the com-
mencement of this session.   But the public good, in
my opinion, *requires* his services; and from that they

are *due* from him. I shall certainly not only approve, but applaud, his acceptance of the seals. It is for every man to consider whether the public has the same claim on him. I cannot feel that my services *in office* are of the smallest moment to the country; but the circumstances of the country may become such as to require all our aid in every way in which it is called for. A war, in the present temper of the world concerning the cause of that war, and, in addition to this danger, any serious efforts of faction to obstruct our success by internal division and discontent, may possibly impose on us all the duty of lending a hand, and setting our shoulders to the work, and of firing any gun we are placed at. . . . Ever your affectionate ' G. ELLIOT.'

Lady Malmesbury to Lady Elliot.

'Spring Gardens: Monday, January 28.

' All ranks of people have put on mourning for the unfortunate King. There surely never existed such fiends on the earth. His will is the finest thing I ever read, and forms a most angelic character. . . . I heard yesterday that the little Dauphin had been found almost at the bottom of the stairs the day of the murder, and that he said, "Je vais prier le peuple de ne pas tuer mon papa." Who knows, if he had got among them, whether this might not have produced an emotion in his favour? Everybody, of all ranks, is in mourning, and nothing but the humanity of John Bull makes it safe to be a Frenchman in London. You know the story of the play, and that, upon Kemble's announcing it would be shut up the next night, the people refused to hear the farce, and all retired with half their diversion.

'This does more honour to a nation than all the triumphs and conquests can do.   Lord George Gordon comes out of prison to-day, which I am sorry for.   I own, notwithstanding the loyalty, I don't like the times.   I think there are civil and political revolutions as well as physical ones; and this I take to be a great crisis.   I am very black on the subject; and the Dominie says, "You know you will never live to see the end of it, for you will be murdered one of the very first."   This is, I think, a comfort.'

CHAPTER IV.

On the 5th of February Sir Gilbert was again in London.

'Winkle Place, Pall Mall:
'Half after four, Tuesday, February 5, 1793.

'I am this moment arrived. I called at Spring Gardens, but Lord Malmesbury is in Wiltshire with Mrs. Robinson,[1] and does not return till Thursday. I saw Harriet for a moment. Elliot, who is here, tells me that, through Lord Loughborough, Mr. Pitt had expressed a regard for Windham, Lord Malmesbury, and myself, with a clear intention of offering office, if we are disposed to take it. Windham may be Secretary of State for the Home Department if he chooses, but no specific office has been mentioned for Lord Malmesbury and me. . . .

'My mind is still extremely disinclined to office. I understand that Windham's is much in the same state. I do not intend to do anything except in conjunction with him.'

'Saturday, February 9, 1793.

'The declaration of war by France against us and Holland arrived in town to-day;[2] the accounts of

---

[1] Mr. Robinson died on December 28, 1792.

[2] It was declared in Paris on the 3rd. When England went to war

it came yesterday. · Pitt sent the letter immediately to Burke, and desired that he would communicate it to Windham and me ; and he generally joins us in anything like confidential communication. The House has not sat since I came.'

Sir Gilbert Elliot to Lady Elliot.

'Tuesday, February 12, 1793.

'. . . We have had a meeting at Windham's last Sunday of the former members of Opposition who agree with us. As the Duke of Portland will not call us together, nor act as our chief, we have taken this method of manifesting that we are not individual deserters, but a strong body. There were only twenty-one present. It was only members of the House of Commons. Windham was so dilatory and undecided about it that the cards went out only that day, and many more would have attended if they had had notice. We are to have another meeting immediately, at which, I suppose, we may muster about fifty. The company resolved unanimously on Sunday to support Govern-

with France in the spring of 1793, the position of the latter power was as follows :—Having expelled the invading armies from her own soil, she had driven the Austrians out of Flanders and occupied Brussels, Liége, Namur, Aix-la-Chapelle, etc.; had seized the Palatinate and Mayence, the most important fortress on the Rhine; was in possession of the citadel of Antwerp and the line of the Scheldt; had sent (Oct. 1792) a French fleet to anchor in the bay of Genoa, in which town a Jacobin tribunal had been established ; had annexed Savoy to the Republic (Nov. 1792) under the name of the Département du Mont Blanc, and Nice and Monaco under that of the Département des Alpes Maritimes ; and on December 27 the revolutionary party in Geneva had delivered over that city to the French troops.

ment. Windham, in opening the business, mentioned distinctly the difference with Fox, and the impossibility of holding any communion of counsels with him, which was unanimously assented to. He mentioned the hope, or rather the wish, that our meeting might lead to a restoration of the Duke of Portland to his natural place as our leader, which was also the general wish of the company. Windham was our leader on this occasion; I was also considered as standing forward in the business, and in general his name and mine are apt to go together. This meeting has a good effect. It silences the imputation of desertion. It must show the Duke of Portland that we are determined to take our own line even without him; and it has pledged Windham more distinctly than he was before to a separation from Fox. The Duke of Portland was informed of it by Windham before it took place, and expressed no disapprobation. This measure appears to me to give a weight and consistency to our present conduct, but does not amount to such a party connection as can embarrass or perplex us hereafter. Indeed a party without the Duke of Portland, or some such name, and without a distinct and considerable object to unite it, is out of the question. The Duke is still entirely of our mind, but he sees hardly anybody but Fox and his friends, and *cannot* act with us as a party, because he must next day associate with, and treat himself as connected in party with those whose conduct we are directly opposing.'

' . . . Nothing has happened in politics, nor seems likely to happen.   One reason of this *calm*, I think, is Lord Loughborough's having attained his own point. Lord Malmesbury is now equally still on the subject; we neither meet, nor converse, nor bustle with him as we did a few months ago.   The fact is that he has also settled his point, and will accept of the first foreign mission that is offered to him.   One strong and indeed just and reasonable inducement for his taking this line is, that it will restore him to a claim to his pension— 2,000*l.* a year.   He was, in fact, entitled to it before in point of professional claims.   All this, however, being settled in his own mind, a comfortable apathy and quietness has taken the place of his former animation.'

'Westminster Hall: Tuesday, February 19, 1793.

' I did not speak yesterday, which I am more sorry for than surprised at. . . . Our division was sufficiently decisive, and there is no reason to doubt of the hearty approbation and support of the country in the war, although nobody can like war in itself.   But its necessity is felt, and I cannot doubt that we have no other way to avoid much greater evils.

' You will be glad to hear that Charles Tweedie is appointed clerk in the Navy Pay-office.   Finding that Dundas only wished me to say that I˙ desired it, I thought that not to do so, after all the civility he had volunteered on the occasion, would be to sacrifice

Tweedie to a false feeling of delicacy; so I went on
Sunday, and obtained it instantly. He said it should
be done next day—that he had intended to give me
the first vacancy, though he is pressed by other persons,
and *"particularly by the Prince of Wales!!!"'*

'Thursday, February 20, 1793.

'I saw a letter yesterday from the sister of
Edgeworth, the King of France's confessor, giving a
short account of his attendance on the King at his
execution and the day before. Edgeworth made his
will and delivered it to his sister the day on which he
was sent for to the Temple, desiring his sister not to
inform his mother of his having undertaken that
service until it should be over, expecting at that time
that his own death would immediately follow that of
the King. He went to the Temple the evening before
the execution. The King asked him what he should
do. He answered that he must retract his signature or
assent to any acts which had been extorted from him
in prejudice of the Catholic religion. The King
answered that he had foreseen that this would be
required of him, and had already provided for it by
his will, which he then produced to Edgeworth and asked
him if that would be sufficient to entitle him to the
sacrament, to which Edgeworth assented. He then
proposed to administer the sacraments at five o'clock
next morning, and applied to the Commissioners on
the subject. They at first objected that he might
administer a poisoned wafer; but Edgeworth suggested

that they might themselves provide the wafer and other necessaries, if they suspected that he or the King could be guilty of so great a crime, and this was agreed to. Edgeworth passed the night in the Temple, and administered the sacrament at five in the morning. From that time the King's behaviour was firm and composed to the last. Edgeworth was on the scaffold with him, contrary to the report which has commonly prevailed, that none but the executioners and officers were there. It is thought that this false account was circulated in order to facilitate any misrepresentation of his behaviour that his enemies might wish to make. It had accordingly been put about that the King expected an attempt to rescue him, and that when he was prevented from haranguing the people, he had shown great emotion and had called out "Ah! je suis perdu!" This story seems to detract in some manner from the courage which his behaviour indicated. It appears, however, from the letter I am mentioning, that no such thing happened. It is true (the letter says) that he shrank when the executioner began to bind his arms, but Edgeworth said to him, "Il faut suivre votre modèle jusqu'à la fin,"—meaning our Saviour. The King answered, "Cela est vrai ; c'est le dernier sacrifice." He was immediately extended and placed for execution. Edgeworth continued still to speak to him and pray ; and he was so near him and so earnest, that the first notice Edgeworth had of the stroke, was receiving the King's blood on his clothes. Edgeworth then descended the scaffold, expecting to be massacred ;

but the people made a wide passage for him, and he walked slowly through the crowd, the people looking at him with a sort of awful respect. He is now in. retreat in the neighbourhood of Paris. The King's shrinking from the touch of the executioner was owing to a notion of dishonour attached to that circumstance.

'This is a melancholy subject, but I thought you would like to hear particulars so authentic.'

'Westminster Hall : Tuesday, February 26, 1793.

'. . . I got up at half after five yesterday morning to see the three battalions of Guards march off to Greenwich, where they embarked for Holland. It answered perfectly, and I felt much pleasure and interest in the scene. They are about 2,000 men, all young, and almost all fine men ; some uncommonly so. They were all animated by a spirit natural on the occasion, not to mention spirits of a different sort, of which they had had more than one could wish. Many of them were too drunk to walk straight. On the whole, however, their zeal and eagerness to go on service, which does not promise to be child's play, was very striking. The regret and dejection of those who were left was no less so. I saw myself a recruit belonging to one of those squads that we used to see fagging under our windows in Park Street, beg very hard to go, saying that he could do the exercise as well as any of those that were in the line, as he was in the first squad. Two men stole down to Greenwich, and were detected in smuggling themselves into one of the transports; and I believe by mere dint of entreaty, and even by *crying*, when they were found out, they obtained the Duke of York's leave to go.

' None of them, neither officers nor men, had more than three or four days' notice. Bosville, one of the officers, was married the day before he received the order. The poor women who are left behind are to be pitied, only seven being allowed per company.

' The King was on the parade, with the Prince of Wales, the Dukes of York, Clarence, Gloucester, and Prince William of Gloucester. The King, I think, in the character of an equestrian statue on a fierce white charger, a sufficient gigg, but looking so pleased that one liked to see him. The Grenadiers, when they began their march, sang "God save the King!" of their own accord as they passed by him, which overcame him a good deal. I did not see this myself, but was told so. I did not follow them to Greenwich, supposing that the crowd there would be beforehand with us, and that I should see little of the embarkation. I was sorry afterwards, finding I might have seen it very well, and that it was very fine. The Prince of Wales was in his new Light Horse uniform, which is very handsome and theatrical, and I daresay delighted him, but it displayed an amount of bulk which entertained Mundy and me, and probably all beholders. The Duke of York is gone with them to Holland. I hear the Duchess is much affected, as she really likes him. It is impossible to be more hearty in a war, or more satisfied of its necessity, than the people here seem to be. There is no news I know of. I saw a new play last night, in which Mrs. Jordan appeared for the first time for a considerable while. The play was dull, and did but just escape damn——n, but Mrs. Jordan was as excellent as ever, and your friend young Bannister as entertaining.'

'Saturday, March 2, 1793.

'We have had the trial every day this week, not excepting to-day. But we have had another employ-ment for some days which has helped to consume the time I should otherwise have employed in writing to you. You will see in the papers to-day an advertise-ment concerning the Whig Club, with my name and some others. Preparing this meeting, calling on people, and settling the business, have cost us, who are not yet handy in these operations, a great deal of trouble and time. The letter to the secretary will be printed as soon as it is delivered. It was written by me. Elliot has been very active in writing and running on the occasion. I hope our example will be followed by many, but we are not sure of it. . . . The ladies' subscription for the war goes on prosperously; it is now for the relief of the widows and orphans of soldiers and sailors who are killed in battle or in service. The Duchess of Buccleuch and Lady Pembroke subscribe each 100 guineas, Lady Malmesbury fifty; I have put you down for ten. This plan sounds very well, and may tend to give a sort of spirit to the country con-cerning the war. But it will, in fact, do little or no good; these exertions of individuals never amount to more than expression of their own zeal.'

After mentioning the capture of Breda [1] as a disagreeable circumstance, because said to be by treachery, Sir Gilbert goes on :— .

'March 7, 1793.

'There is an immense power confederating against France, and allowing for the uncertainty of war and of all human calculations, there seems reason to expect a successful issue to this most important struggle between all the order and all the anarchy of the world. There has been a good deal of uneasiness in the public concerning the apparent slowness of our preparations and slackness of our exertions, especially in the naval line. Burke, Windham, and I desired a conference with Pitt on the subject yesterday, and we had a long one with him and Dundas in the Speaker's chamber. Pitt was of course all civility, and desired that we would never make the smallest scruple of applying for any information we wished, or suggesting anything we thought useful, promising to attend to it with great care, and assuring us of a perfectly confidential communication of all information. He gave us a good deal of satisfaction concerning naval preparations, and on all other points gave us encouraging information. Burke gave him a little political instruction, in a very respectful and cordial way, but with the authority of

---

[1] Breda, with a garrison of twenty-five hundred men, capitulated after a siege of three days, and when the French were on the point of retiring.

an old and most informed statesman ; and although
nobody ever takes the whole of Burke's advice, yet he
often, or rather always, furnishes very important and
useful matter, *some part* of which sticks and does
good.   Pitt took it all very patiently and cordially.
This was more like a cabinet than any council I have
yet attended.   The Duke of Portland has behaved as
usual about the Whig Club business.   He went there
with Lord Titchfield, and countenanced the proceeding
of the club on the subject of one letter, which was as
adverse to us, and as decidedly a support and adoption
of Fox, as possible.   In their speeches and toasts we
were treated as *deserters* from friends and principles,
in all of which the Duke, by his presence, evidently
held himself out to the world as taking part against us.
You will see the letter in the papers, and judge how
the Duke of Portland could concur in any proceeding
adverse to it or those who signed it.   I give him up
completely now, as this is direct duplicity and open
hostility with us.   .   .   .

' The defeat of General Miranda,[1] with 2,000 French
killed and 9 pieces of cannon, is true, and is important
news.   The arrival of the Guards is said to have produced the best consequences already by giving spirits
and confidence to the Dutch.   More troops are going
there.'

---

[1] General Miranda was, on the 2nd and 3rd of March, forced to raise
the siege of Maestricht, and to retire beyond the Meuse, by an Austrian
army under the Prince of Coburg.

'London : Thursday, March 14, 1793.

'. . . Lady Charlotte Bentinck's marriage with Charles Greville occasions a great deal of conversation. . . . It is certainly a bad match for Lady Charlotte, and I should think it must be very contrary to the Duke's wishes ; but he is not famous for firmness in any point just at present. I think Charles Greville a very disagreeable coxcomb, with very little merit to recommend him excepting his face. This might have been a natural title to favour and influence upstairs, but I understand he has long governed despotically the whole family, not excepting the Duke or even Lord Titchfield. Charles Ellis [1] is coming into Parliament immediately, in the room of Lord Barrymore. He gives 3,500*l.* for the remainder of the Parliament, about 1,000*l.* a year.

' He thinks, I believe, on the present state of affairs exactly as we do.'

Many of the letters of this period are omitted ; for as they relate entirely to the rumours in circulation in town concerning the progress of the war in Holland and the state of the continent, they have no interest at the present date. One day Sir Gilbert wrote that ' it is believed the Duke of Orleans, Egalité, is about to be made Protector or King of France.' The next day's

---

[1] 'Charles Ellis, upon receiving his fortune on his coming of age, wrote a most charming letter to George Ellis, inclosing ten bank-notes of a thousand pounds each ; this is a sort of Belcour trait which Sir Gilbert will admire.'—*Letter of Lady Malmesbury.*

letter contradicted the report. On March 15, stocks rose 3 per cent. in consequence of news from Holland, which on the 16th was proved to be unfounded. ' *March* 16.—It is astonishing how little any report is to be depended on. This news was sent in a letter from Colonel Grenfield of the Guards from Holland. Lord Grenville believed it so much that he sent Colonel Grenfield's letter to the Prince of Wales. This was the authority on which I said the news was certain.'

On the same day[1] he wrote, on more authentic information, that ' Sir James Murray, who is considered as one of the most intelligent and scientific officers in our army, is just returned from the Prussian army through Holland. I understand that he has brought accounts which create uneasiness about *Dort*, where the *Guards* are with the Duke of York. An attack was expected from Dumouriez to take place the day before yesterday. It was supposed that he would attempt it with 10,000 men, for whom he had procured boats to cross the Mardyke. They had 10,000 men to oppose him, besides some force on the water ; but as the Guards are sure of being put, or rather of putting themselves, forward, and as the Duke of York's spirit may not be restrained by sufficient prudence, there is naturally a just anxiety concerning him and our handful of English troops.

' The Prince of Wales is become impatient of his present inglorious life, while his brother and all the

---

[1] March 16.

Princes of Europe are acting personally in their common cause. He wishes to serve abroad, and to have his share of the glory that is going. He says it is by no means jealousy of his brother's fame, and that on the contrary he is willing to serve *under* the Duke of York's command, but that he does not like to remain at home merely a parade officer, or an idle spectator of the great events in Europe, while everybody else is acting a part in them. I do not know what will come of this, but the feeling he has on the subject is creditable to him, and it would be a way to recover character and favour with the country.'

'London: March 19, 1793.

'. . . . I have subscribed ten guineas to the emigrants, laity and clergy, who were on the eve of starving in the streets. A thousand pounds have been sent within these two days in one sum, but without any name. It is supposed to be the King, but that he is afraid to appear in it, for fear of giving offence or jealousy to the English common people. I was invited on Sunday evening to Madame de Flahault's, a French *bel esprit*, and friend of Windham's, to meet Madame de Staël—Necker's daughter—a celebrated woman, on account of her influence in France at a certain period, on account of her father's situation, and on account of her own qualities. She is one of those women who are greedy of admiration, and lay themselves out for it in all ways, purchasing any quantity of anybody at any price, and among other prices by a traffic of mutual flattery. She is also to have the whole conversation to herself, and to be the centre of every company she is in. I was not sorry to see this sort of sight, and was not ill amused, though we sat in a miserable lodging over a grocer's till two o'clock.'

Sir Gilbert and Mr. Windham had had some thoughts of a journey to Holland during the Easter recess; and the Duke of York, on hearing of their intention, had promised them a '*warm*' reception in every sense of the word. The project, however, seems to have been abandoned; and Sir Gilbert wrote to his wife, ' that there was just a probability of the packet's being molested by French privateers and frigates, and it would be no joke to be a prisoner to these cannibals. Windham would be sure of swinging, and they might think me just worthy of being a pendant to him. Eight of our Levant traders have been taken by the French fleet in the Mediterranean, which is a natural consequence of our having no fleet there. The French fleet which sailed from Brest proved less formidable than was at first apprehended. It consists of ten ships, but only three are of the line; the rest frigates. It is supposed we shall very soon have a small fleet at sea.'

'March 25, 1793.

' I am writing this at two in the morning, and have hardly recovered from a severe headache which I earned, together with immortal glory, as toastmaster

at the Scottish Hospital on Saturday. I left the company in as great admiration of me as was possible for
those who could not speak plain, and saw double. I
succeeded the Duke of Montrose and Lord Moreton,
who had the chair before me ; but I certainly eclipsed
both my predecessors. I should be very happy that
this were sure of being the last time I should ever
have a headache in that vile way, but there was no
avoiding it.

‘I am extremely sorry to tell you of poor Lord
Herbert's shocking affliction—Lady Herbert died to-
day. It was in consequence of her lying-in, but I
believe was unexpected, in a fainting-fit. Both he
and Lady Pembroke are much to be pitied.’

‘ Tuesday.

‘ Dumouriez's defeat on the 18th¹ is a very important
event; and I went yesterday, at Pitt's desire, with
Burke (and Windham was also expected but did not
come), to Downing Street, to assist at the settling some
of the clauses of the bill now depending against traitorous
correspondence with France. Some clauses have been
objected to by some of *our* friends, meaning Windham's, etc. ; and, indeed, Windham and I had both expressed difficulties on one clause in private conferences
with them. I found myself yesterday in company that
seemed   very   strange : — Pitt,   Lord   Hawkesbury,

---

¹ Battle of Nerwinde : a division of the Austrian army was commanded by the Archduke Charles ; a division of the French by the
Duke of Chartres, afterwards Louis Philippe, King of the French.

Dundas, the Chancellor, Master of the Rolls, Attorney, and Solicitor-General, Ryder, and Lord Mornington. Pitt conducted the business civilly and pleasantly; and gave way in all that we, or rather I, wished; for Burke, as usual, was for the strongest measures. The Malmesburys go to Brookwood on Thursday, Elliot goes with them, and the two Ellises. I shall go there on Tuesday. Dundas is to be married in a few days to Lady Jane Hope.'

'House of Commons: March 26, 1793.

'Since my letter great news is come. A most complete and decisive victory was obtained on the 22nd near Louvain over Dumouriez. In all the late actions there have been 7,000 French killed, besides prisoners—an immense slaughter and loss. Dumouriez had two horses killed under him, and is wounded. He was *taken* by a Hungarian soldier, but the Hungarian was shot before he had secured him.[1] The Austrians are in possession of Brussels, and it seems probable now that the French will evacuate Austrian Flanders entirely. Government here has determined to embody four battalions, or about 2,000 French emigrants, who are, it is thought, to be employed in Holland. The news from Louvain comes from Ostend by letters to different people, but has not come officially to Government. It is, however, universally believed.'

Lady Malmesbury, giving the same account, adds, 'Dumouriez, they say, has fled to a strong position *in a wood*, and I shan't *holloa* till he's *out of it.*'

' By letters from Lord Auckland yesterday and to-day Dumouriez was beat on the 22nd, and has retreated to Hal, leaving great magazines at Louvain. The Austrians entered Brussels on the 24th. In short, the French have now given up Brabant; Ostend is evacuated by them. . . .

' Nothing can be more promising than the operations of the combined armies hitherto, and the spirit of insurrection in France against the present system is not less so. There are some considerable districts and some large bodies of men in arms, headed by good officers, in actual resistance.'

Sir Gilbert spent the Easter holidays at Brookwood, a place in Hampshire which Lord Malmesbury had hired on his return from the Continent in 1792, and where he and Lady Malmesbury seem to have resumed the agreeable life and pleasant intercourse which had been interrupted at Grove Place by their journey to Italy.

' The party,' wrote Sir Gilbert, ' is Elliot and the two Ellises, and Mr. Lowth, parson of the parish and son of the Bishop Lowth. . . . Lord Malmesbury and I have made a large circuit on horseback to-day, describing a complete circle of about twenty miles around Brookwood. It has been a warm sunny spring day, and I have seen the country to the greatest advantage. It is extremely pretty and pleasant, highly dressed in point of fences and cultivation, with a great number of little woods and copses. The cottages picturesque; the inhabitants thriving, but preserving a *sylvan* sort of character. There is a good deal of wild common ground on the skirts of the woods, and the distant views are of downs. Everything is in the highest possible order, and this country affords a specimen of general prosperity and comfort which should make even a *Sansculotte* think twice before tearing off the breeches of the world, and making us sit bare under the Tree of Liberty, instead of on a good, broad, well clothed, aristocratic basis, as they do in Hampshire.'

'London: April 16.

'. . . I went on Saturday to Lady Hardwicke's, to hear Madame de Flahault's novel.[1] I think few Englishwomen could sport that sort of exhibition. She read two hours, which gave us a specimen of her work. I thought it pleasing and well written, but without any extraordinary merit. I never felt an inclination either to laugh or to weep, though the author seems to propose both effects; but I felt no inclination to sleep, which, in the absence of the other two affections, is a proof of merit in the book, at midnight. Douglas, who had heard or read it before, was placed next the authoress to *support* her; and he fell into a profound sleep after the two first pages, to the great

---

[1] Madame de Flahault is better known as an authoress under the name of Madame de Souza, which she acquired by a second marriage. Her writings are marked by considerable power of pathos, and a very graceful style. *Eugène de Rothelin* is perhaps the best of her novels.

horror of Lady Katherine, who kept saying to Lady
Ann North and me, "I am sure he will snore aloud
soon." We had a very late supper, at which I could
have snored very willingly an hour or two before we
parted. I went on Sunday with Douglas to Bushy
Park, to see their new acquisition called the Pheasantry.

'From thence we went to Richmond, and Douglas
and I paid a visit to a Madame de Cambis, an old lady
of high rank, and a remarkably sensible and agreeable
woman, whom I saw every morning for six months at
Madame du Deffand's, when Douglas and I were together at Paris. She has been in exile these two years,
and I never had the grace to visit her before. . . . It
was fine weather, though cold, and I passed a very
pleasant day. Douglas and I talked *Greek* and ex-
changed *Homer* all the way.'

'House of Commons: Thursday, April 18, 1793.

'I am sorry to say that I *cannot* send you half a
page. I was unluckily broken in on from breakfast
till I came to the trial, and there was not one other
manager except Burke, so that I could not stir from
the box a single moment. I am now waiting for
Sheridan's impeachment of Lord Auckland, which will
come on this moment. It is nonsense, and will be
serviceable to Lord Auckland, as it gives an opportunity, or rather makes it quite necessary, to vote an
approbation of his conduct.'

'1793.

'. . . I have got into the midst of French society lately. I dined with a party at Douglas's a few days ago, and had a good specimen of a debate in the Constituting Assembly, of which they had all been members. Two of them were very distinguished— M. Malhouet and Lally Tolendal; the third the Prince de Poix. The curiosity was to see the total impossibility of any of them proceeding two sentences without interruption from both the others, and much the greatest part of the time they all three spoke at the top of their voices, all equally confident of his own triumph and the absurdity of his adversaries. We had several emigrant ladies at the same time, and in the evening all the Parlezvous in London. There was really a considerable part of our old circle at Madame du Deffand's, assembled strangely in London, after a dispersion of above twenty years. Fish Crawfurd—with whom Madame du Deffand, being blind, was in love—was of the party the other day. Douglas, myself, Mrs. Cholmondeley, Madame de Cambis, &c. &c. Poor Mrs. Cholmondeley is shockingly altered. She is like ninety years old, tottering as if with palsy. There are many fine pictures now in London, and indeed fine things of all sorts for sale from France. Part of the Orleans collection, from the Palais Royal, is now exhibited, and selling at exorbitant prices. It is only the Flemish school, but the Italian pictures are also in town, and will be sold in their turn.'

'I was, last night, at a *ball*. It was at Lady Anstru-
ther's. I should not have gone, but Lady Ann North
and Lady Charlotte took me there from Lady K.
Douglas's; and I stayed just long enough to see some
of the dancing generation. There were one or two
instances of the modern fashion of dress for young ladies,
by which they are made to appear five or six months
gone with child. Perhaps you do not believe this
fashion, but it is quite literally true. The original idea
seems to have been an imitation of the drapery of
statues and pictures, which fastens the dress immediately below the bosom, and leaves no waist. The
consequence of which is a slight swell of the figure, as
you may see in pictures; but this being attempted by
artificial means of pads placed on the stomach is an
exact representation of a state of pregnancy. This dress
is accompanied by a complete display of the bosom—
which is uncovered, and supported and stuck out by the
sash immediately below it.

'I am giving you a faithful description of Lady
C—— C—— as she was at the ball last night. She is
the most exaggerated in this fashion, but it is followed
in considerable degree by many others.[1]

'There is no news of consequence, except the marriage of one of the princes in Italy to Lady Augusta

---

[1] 'As to gowns, they are very pretty, something between a *chemise*
and a *pierrot*. Nobody ever wears caps, but twist handkerchiefs etc.
round their heads; and nothing can be so picturesque and pretty as
dress is now, excepting, indeed, that some ladies have made themselves
into the most extravagant shapes possible. Lady A —— and Lady

Murray. The marriage is not legal, but it is still a scrape both for her and him.'

'April 27.

'The duel between the Duke of York and the Hereditary Prince of Orange is false, but they are not on pleasant terms with each other. The Prince of Orange is a cold, formal, ceremonious character; the Duke of York just the reverse, and they are supposed to dislike each other.

'Things do not look so well as they did. The French seem determined to fight it out. Dumouriez's defection has not produced great effects. They have three strong towns to employ the combined army, and the French are assembling a numerous army in the field. Coburg's whole army has not one piece of artillery with it except field-pieces, and he cannot have any heavy artillery these three weeks; of course they can undertake no siege during that time, nor make any important attack, and it is well if they keep their ground against the French artillery, without any to defend themselves. The Prince of Coburg commands only the Austrians, and has no authority over Prussians, Dutch, Hanoverians, or British troops, who have each their own commander. There is therefore no commander-in-chief, and no certainty that the combined forces will cooperate. The army extends forty miles, which scatters

C—— C—— actually wear false stomachs; and the former literally goes so naked, that at a ball the other day all the men swear she had nothing on but a thin calico dress over her shift, and the whole clung like wet drapery. Gold chains marked the shape of the neck.'—*Lady Malmesbury to Lady Elliot.*

it extremely, and exposes it to accidents on weak
points.   On the whole, I fear the generals themselves
are not sanguine of success.   I heard all this from
Captain Bentinck, who is just come from the army
through the Hague.   There is a transport of ours
taken with troops and officers going from Ireland to
Plymouth.   Dumouriez has certainly quitted the
Austrian army, and is supposed to be gone to Switzer-
land to seek for shelter.   The troops that came over
with him are still with the Austrians, and puzzle them
very much what to make of them.   I dined yesterday
at Burke's,[1] with the Chancellor, Lord Hawkesbury,
young Jenkinson, whom I like very much, Windham,
etc.   Harriet had a grand supper last night; I stayed
till one this morning, when supper not being yet ready,
I came home to bed.'

'Thursday, May 2, 1793.

'. . . If William Alderman' (a servant) 'is so bad
as you seem to think, would it not be best to part with
him while I am in town, and have an opportunity of
finding another?   If it is quite ascertained that he
pilfers and supplies his wife from the house, I should
certainly part with him. . . . At the same time, I
confess I am always unwilling to take extreme measures
on the supposition of such offences, and am slow to
believe in them entirely, or to act on that belief,
because I see every day the difficulty of knowing the

---

[1] In another letter of nearly the same date, Sir Gilbert says—' Burke
is now in closer communication with ministers than anyone out of
office.'

truth, and the ease with which false reports gain credit on all sorts of subjects, *abroad* and at *home*, in *war* and *peace*.   I fear there is no choice but to remove Paul. I am very happy to find him acquitted in point of character, and I really believe him to be an honest well-meaning creature ; but good intentions will not sow the land·nor get in the harvest, and I remain satisfied that he is incapable to do what his place requires.   I therefore leave it to your discretion to part with him, wishing only that he may be let down as gently as the nature of the case admits of.

'I dined on Tuesday at Lord Fitzwilliam's with the Duke of Devonshire, Lord Spencer, Frederick Montagu, four Burkes, Dr. Lawrence, and some others.   The Duke of Portland was to have dined there, but was detained at the House of Lords.   It was settled after dinner that the same party should dine at Burlington House next Thursday.   Burke has now got such a train after him as would sink anybody but himself:— his son, who is quite *nauseated* by all mankind ; his brother, who is liked better than his son, but is rather oppressive with animal spirits and brogue ; and his cousin, Will Burke, who is just returned unexpectedly from India, as much ruined as when he went many years ago, and who is a fresh charge on any prospects of power Burke may ever have.   Mrs. Burke has in her train Miss French, the most perfect *she Paddy* that ever was caught.[1]   Notwithstanding these disad-

---

[1] Madame d'Arblay describes a party at Mrs. Crewe's when all ' the train ' were present.   The hostess received them in a blaze of beauty

vantages, Burke is in himself a sort of *power* in the
State.　It is even not too much to say that he is a sort
of *power* in *Europe*, though totally without any of those
means, or the smallest share in them, which give or
maintain power in other men.　Mirabeau said, like a
true Frenchman, but with some truth at one time—

which not even a black veil half-dropped over her face could obscure.
First among the guests came Richard, 'the comic, humorous, bold,
queer brother of Mr. Burke.' Mrs. Burke, 'soft, reasonable, and
obliging,' brought with her Miss F., 'a wild Irish girl, just imported,
speaking with a prodigious brogue, and sputtering in one's face from
excessive eagerness.'　Burke himself followed, 'easy, cordial, wonderful;' but if politics were mentioned, showing so 'extreme an irritability'
that his countenance assumed the 'expression of a man going to defend
himself against murderers.'　Mr. Elliot of Wells completed the party.
He is described as 'a tall, thin young man, plain in person, dress, and
manners, but sensible, and possibly much more, as he was very reserved.
The conversation at dinner is admirably described, for Madame d'Arblay
had a peculiar power of either rendering conversation with entire accuracy, or else of making her personages speak so perfectly in character
as to persuade the reader that he assists at their actual discourse.　The
picture of Burke is complete, when, on the party being unexpectedly
joined after dinner by Lord Loughborough and Erskine, he (Burke) retired from the conversation, took up a book, which happened to be the
Satires of Boileau, and read *aloud* to himself.　Madame d'Arblay does
not tell us what passages he selected, but one hopes that among them
may have been the following lines:—

> 'A-t'on vu quelquefois dans les plaines d'Afrique
> Déchirant à l'envi leur propre République
> Lions contre lions, parens contre parens
> Combattre follement pour le choix des Tyrans?
>
> .　　.　　.　　.　　.　　.　　.
>
> L'Homme seul, l'Homme seul en sa fureur extrême
> Met un brutal horreur à s'égorger soi-même.
>
> .　　.　　.　　.　　.　　.　　.
>
> Et pour comble de maux, apporta dans la France
> Des *harangueurs* du Tems *l'ennuyeuse Eloquence.*'
> *Satire* viii.

'Ma tête aussi est une *Puissance.*' The same sort of
thing is almost true with regard to Burke, who does
not, however, say it of himself. The Duke of Portland's
character used to be a puissance, but his hand has
dropped the crown which his heart alone had placed
there. He is more entirely sunk into nothing than one
could have thought possible. I cannot feel in charity
with him yet for having betrayed me so deliberately as
he did, besides ruining and betraying his own friends,
in compliance with those who were betraying him.
But I have returned to private habits with him, and
see him now and then with an affectionate sort of compassion. So there end the honours of the house of
Bentinck. I was yesterday in the evening at Mrs.
Herbert's, Lord Porchester's sister, to keep May-day.
She is as fat as I am, and I shall be content to be as
good-humoured as she is. I rather like Lady Porchester, for she seems to unite a good deal of sharpness
with good nature. I went from there with Lord
Malmesbury to Lady K. Douglas's, where the most
remarkable thing I saw was Lady A——, the founder
of the *pads.* I never saw such a figure. Lady C——
C—— carries the thing off to a certain degree by her
beauty—her figure being naturally very pretty; and
which, being not only pretty but naked, gives at least
something undisguised and undistorted by this strange
fashion. Lady A—— has not the plea of beauty to
excuse her.

'Harriet says you desire to hear something of what
the world is doing, for you see or know nothing of love

except what the crows are making. I can give you
little information of this sort ; I believe it is so general
one don't see it now. I have been constantly in the
Managers' box the whole of this day, there being nobody else to sit by Burke till this moment that Sheridan
is come. God bless you ! This is the last month of
our separation.'

'Friday, May 3, 1793.

' Your letter did not come this morning as it ought,
and I must take patience till to-morrow. I have been
at work all day to-day at Parliamentary Reform, and
I begin to have some hopes of mustering stuff and
courage enough to speak on Monday. I dined to-day
at the beginning of a political dining-club of Wind-
hamites. The beginning was but slender, but it was
owing to Windham's total neglect of the invitations.
We were only six, instead of twelve who were expected
—Lord Malmesbury, Lord Beauchamp, Lord Porchester,
Burke, Windham, and myself. We have agreed to go
on with it, and to bring gradually as many of those
agreeing with us as like to come. I then walked with
Burke twice up and down the Mall in the dark, and
am come home in hopes of securing a page or two for
you, and keeping as much of to-morrow forenoon for
Reform as I can. I had an unexpected visit this forenoon from an old French schoolfellow, whom I had
neither seen, heard of, nor thought of since I was at
school with him at Paris. His name is le Comte de la
Porte. He is a man of family, military, and an
emigrant. He has been two years driven from France,

and served last campaign with the Princes. He was the oldest boy at school, and indeed, left it to go into the army soon after we went there. I was really happy to see him again. I found, on inquiry, that there is another of our comrades in London—a Monsieur de Sebville, whom I have desired La Porte to bring to me. They are both very unlike the other two specimens you have seen of our school—I mean Mirabeau and Verneti. La Porte is a tall, handsome, and gentlemanlike man, though not a boy now, being some years older than *forty-two*. I have often asked the French here after Verneti, but have met with nobody who knows any-thing of Avignon; but it was the scene of so much horror that I should be much afraid he will never again explain the propagation of silkworms. One of our French friends here is in a bad way—Madame de Flahault; she seems far gone in a consumption. I was admitted the other day to her bed-room. You need not be alarmed for my virtue, however, for Farquhar was of the party. She had company the whole evening in the next room, and people went in, two or three at a time, to see her in bed. Necker's daughter, Madame de Staël, was one of the party. Her husband, M. de Flahault, was arrested long ago at Boulogne, and his prosecution has been going on ever since. She has just heard that he is ordered for *trial*, and removed to Arras in Flanders, which is a very bad —that's to say, bloody—town; so that there seems little doubt of his being hanged or beheaded in a very short time. She speaks of this *nouvelle affligeante* to

everybody, and begs that her friends will come to her
on the occasion; they are odd people.   Having a
husband, or a father, or a son, beheaded, however, or
in danger of it, is really now so habitual to them, and
so much neighbours' fare, that one ought not to judge
them by our notions.'

' Tuesday, May 7, 1793.

' The debate on Parliamentary reform was adjourned
at two o'clock this morning, and goes on to-day.
Windham made the most famous speech he ever made
before.

' I did not speak yesterday, but must to-day; and my
tooth not being out, as Windham's is, you will understand that I cannot and must not write a line more to-
day.'

' Westminster Hall: Thursday, May 10, 1793.

' After all the expectation I excited in you last post,
and after all my own labour and anxiety, I did not
speak at last.   I feel, as I always do, sorry and even
dejected that it is so; but there is so little profit in
describing those, or any other uncomfortable feelings,
that I shall spare you and myself on that subject.   No
evil, perhaps, is entirely without its comfort, and
though I regret in a higher degree than usual that I
was not prepared to my mind on this occasion, yet I
confess I consider it in some degree as an escape; for
it was not a subject or an occasion to do ill, or even
moderately on, when every other person who appeared
at all was displaying so much excellence. . . . Another
consolation is that the number of persons who wanted

to speak, and who were not permitted on account of the great length of the principal speeches, was so great that no man could be missed, and in fact I was not so by anybody but the few who knew that I intended to speak.'

'Tuesday, May 11, 1793.

' Lady Abercorn had a ball the other night at which there were twelve ladies in the garb of statues—that is to say, with the girdle close up to their breast and the drapery falling, or intended to fall, statue-fashion below. They were not uncovered, but by all accounts it produced almost all the effect of nakedness. George Ellis asked Mrs. Poole, who was one of them, whether she was really as naked as she appeared to be, and she said she really was very near. People say that women observed that men would not come to their assemblies or society unless they had gaming, or some other stronger inducement, and that they try this cheaper and safer method of attracting them. The style now certainly makes private society much more like a masquerade or public place where you see a mixture of pures and impures, and the latter pursuing their own business in their own way. I am glad that A. and H. have excellent skins, for by their time I see that it is possible they may dress *after Eve* in the Ranelagh season and warm weather. The twelve statues at Lady Abercorn's had all girdles with these letters on them, L L T P. There were various readings of this. Some said it was Long live Tom Payne ! others, Long live the *Pads !* But the real meaning

was Long live the Prior! It seems Lord Abercorn
has a house called the Priory.'

'London: Sunday, May 12, 1793.

'. . . Harriet talks now of the Ellises coming to
Minto with us. . . . There seems a better prospect
now of our keeping our time—that's to say, of not
sitting later than June 15, possibly sooner, for the
India Bill does not meet with the tedious sort of opposition that might have been expected. . . . Pitt says
Parliament may be up by the 5th or 6th of June;
Hatsell, who is better authority, says the 14th. I am
heartily impatient on all accounts, but chiefly from a
desire to be again among you all, with the children on
my knees and shoulders. I am thinking how many
forenoons I am losing of reading on the grass; and I
am losing too all the young green, and the green
beauty of Minto that must be in perfection just now.
All I know of the country is Kensington Gardens, where
I walked on Sunday with La Porte, one of my French
schoolfellows. It was really extremely pretty; but its
rusticity was in some degree diminished by the resemblance of the entrance and the battle to get in to the
pit-door when Garrick acted. It is literally hardly
safe for a woman. I went out to the furthest end of
Tottenham Court Road to find Sebville, the other
French friend. He was just gone to mass in Soho
Square. I followed, and heard high mass, in hopes of
seeing him, but did not find him till the *scaling*.[1] I

---

[1] Scotch for the dispersion of a congregation.

then proposed Kensington Gardens to him, but he
could not go. I went, however, to La Porte, whom I
found lodging in a garret in Great Pulteney Street,
and he went with me. It is the only thing I could
think of to show them any attention, for they cannot
afford to dress themselves so as to dine anywhere.
These two men are supported by their wives, who
remain in France, and whose fortune or income is not
yet confiscated. They send them by stealth all the
money they can get. La Porte says the wives have in
general behaved incomparably. That some few have
taken advantage of the new law of divorce and have
married Democrats, but that such conduct has been
very rare, and that these women are held in great
contempt ; but that the wives of the emigrants have
in general shown the greatest fidelity and fortitude,
and have been the means of saving their husbands from
absolute want. La Porte heard from his wife lately,   .
but the letter was a month old. Sebville has had no
account whatever of a wife and nine children since
March. The situation and misfortunes of these people
—I mean the gentry of France in general, the greatest
part of whom are outcasts all over Europe—are really
interesting and affecting. I never knew such dirty
beasts, however, men and women, gentle and simple.
Sebville lodges in a perfectly new nice-looking house,
almost in the fields, and has the first floor for himself
and a friend. It might be as sweet and comfortable
as he likes himself, without any expense but a pail of
water and a broom. I was obliged to hold my hand-

kerchief to my nose while I was in his drawing-room, and his bed-room was too filthy to go into ; but I saw that, for economy, he and his friend (a man) sleep together. This man, however, has a large house with a decent fortune in Normandy, and is of a very good family. They certainly feel less inconvenience from poverty than we should, on account of their total ignorance of comfort even when they are rich.[1] I dined on Saturday with Charles Ellis ; his first dinner since he has got into his new house and before the world.'

'London : May 21, 1793.

'. . . I went to the Culverdens' (at Sheen), and stayed all night. I found a large party as usual. They played at casino till 12, and set off for Guildford races at 10 this morning. Mrs. Culverden received a letter from Lady Palmerston while I was there last night. They talk of coming to England this autumn. The letter gave a long and particular account of an accident which happened to Lady Palmerston and Miss Carter, in a walk to Virgil's tomb, near Naples. A peasant took some dislike to them or their servants, and after frightening them in various ways, he fired at them from a vineyard, shot Miss Carter in the legs and elbow and filled the servant's back full of shot. Miss Carter's petticoats and pockets were also full of shot-holes ; and two men, whom they had got to join them, were shot in the head. They got home without further mischief, but it was truly a trial of courage.

[1] Lady Malmesbury, writing to her sister on the same day as Sir Gilbert, mentions an interesting fact in connexion with the war related

Lady Palmerston happened to be a few paces before the rest, and escaped unhurt. The man was in prison and the trial going on when they left.'

At the end of May, Sir Gilbert went down to Minto. While there he was offered the government of Madras, which he refused; but, apparently in consequence of the overtures made him by ministers, he returned to London in June.

In the early days of the schism Sir Gilbert had repeatedly written to his wife, even more frequently than appears from his printed letters, that he deprecated a coalition with Ministry on the part of the party, and of course was opposed to the dissolution of the party by the drifting over to Government of individuals. He considered the connection which looked to the Duke of Portland as its head, as sufficiently powerful to exercise a salutary control over the policy of the ministers, there being no such radical difference of principles between them on the immediate questions at issue as between certain sections of the Opposition; and he recognised only two conditions as absolutely essential to the action of an independent party, with credit to themselves and usefulness to the public— namely, union and forbearance. Time, however, con-

---

to her by an eyewitness:—'Copley, who was present at the engagement of the 8th, tells me that they found the bodies of fourteen women dressed as National Guards amongst the dead at the batteries; and Dumouriez says the best cannoneers he had were women. And after that they gravely tell you that the spirit of the nation is against the Revolution and its "enormities!" The Prussians retired at the second shot quite out of the wood.'

vinced him that such conditions could never be fulfilled.

A party including amongst its chiefs the Duke of
Portland, Fox, Windham, and Burke, had become as
little formidable as a herd of deer when all the stags
are fighting. The Duke, though an excellent amiable
man, was not made to lead ; he was in the most literal
sense *un homme drapeau*; for when the storm raged
round him, he could only flutter in the breeze. Fox,
who attracted the affection of all who approached him,
seems, by the very easiness of disposition which made
him so lovable, to have failed in the power of control-
ling those whom he could not persuade. It was in
open disregard of his wishes and interests that Grey
and Sheridan joined the Society of the Friends of the
People. Windham, possessed of a scholar's refinement
of mind and tastes, was by nature indolent and uncertain ; and even at a critical moment it was doubtful
whether he could be brought up from his favourite
Fellbrigg to attend a debate.[1] Burke, the last and perhaps the greatest of the Whig leaders, was in truth no

---

[1] For instance, when the third reading of the Traitorous Correspondence Bill (in the earlier stages of which he and Sir Gilbert had taken
an active part, having been instrumental in procuring alterations of
certain clauses) stood for April 5, he wrote to Sir Gilbert on the 4th,
that his love of ease, or the idea of going up for nothing, prevailed,
though his chaise was at the door, his things packed up, and he remained some days longer where he was. 'There was always, too, the
chance that I should have failed myself, and after coming 140 miles, as
at the election for Speaker, for the purpose of speaking, have let the
occasion pass without saying a word. One hope I have, that my
absence and the absolute want of some one to utter a word, may put
you upon performing the task.'

longer one of them. Maddened by the crimes committed in the name of liberty, he was ready to exclaim

'Twere perjury to love thee now!

When repressive measures were under discussion, he was for the strongest, and having begun by quoting to his friends the saying of Montesquieu, 'Qu'il y a des cas où il faut mettre pour un moment un voile sur la liberté comme l'on cache les statues de Dieu,' he was rapidly preparing to convert the veil into a strait jacket.

From such men no union, no clear and definite line of action, could be hoped ; and as to the second condition which Sir Gilbert had conceived to be essential to the usefulness of an independent party—forbearance towards those in power, by which it is to be supposed he meant an avoidance of a system of constant carping criticism calculated to disgust the people with the measures determined on by the general sense of the House—if Sir Gilbert had persisted in the belief that such forbearance was possible to any political party, he would have been a very sanguine man.

When he arrived at the conclusion that nothing could be hoped from his party but discord and antagonism, it seemed to him that the only course remaining, in face of a great common danger, was to strengthen the Government, which, as he had written years before, ' is, after all, whether we like it or not, responsible for the honour of the country '—trusting that the accession accruing to it from the Liberal ranks would enlarge the spirit of the policy to be pursued while strengthening the executive.

Up to this point Sir Gilbert's most intimate friends shared in his views; the only question which remained to be considered related to the expediency of an imme-diate adhesion to Government on the part of the recal-citrant followers of the Duke of Portland, or of further delay until a more considerable section of those who had been accustomed to act together should be prepared to enter into a new arrangement.

It was obvious that their weight in the coalition to be formed with Ministry must depend on the numbers and individual importance of the seceders; on the other hand, it was no less obvious that under the strong solvents of inaction, uncertainty, and want of leader-ship, the party was in a condition of rapid dissolution. Some thought that by waiting until the increasing gravity of the crisis should have forced the Duke of Portland to separate himself finally from Fox, the old connection might still be saved; others, and Sir Gilbert among them, were convinced that before the Duke of Portland arrived at a decision the connection would have ceased to exist.

While such was the diversity of opinion among Oppo-sition, the Ministry plied them with offers of office.

Sir Gilbert to Lady Elliot.

'Spring Gardens: Tuesday, June 25, 1793.

' I arrived here about two o'clock to-day. The Chancellor[1] called a few minutes after, and I told him my decision concerning Madras; he then talked of other arrangements, as if they were in actual agitation, and said that Pitt had had a conference with Windham after the motion made by Fox on Monday, and that Pitt had only told him (the Chancellor) that the conversation with Windham had been perfectly satisfactory. . . . I then went to Dundas and communicated my decision. He appeared much disappointed, etc. He then mentioned other arrangements, and particularly Pitt's conversation with Windham. The result of which is, that with mutual professions of entire agreement, and of a disposition to unite, all arrangement is, however, suspended for the present. He understood from Windham that his mind was made up to think it must come to his accepting office, but that it might be better some time hence. That Pitt acquiesced in this idea (and I fancy the more readily) as Dundas went on to say that indeed, with regard to the particular office to which it might be supposed that Windham might look (Secretary of State), there were great difficulties in changing, in the present circumstances, in the midst of a war, the correspondence of which was conducted through that office. . . . Lord Spencer has refused

---

[1] Lord Loughborough.

Ireland on private grounds of family convenience, but
has explained it carefully to be on no other grounds,
and Dundas is equally satisfied with his professions,
considering him also as prepared to accept of office. . . .
Windham dines here to-day.'

A few days later he wrote :—' Windham and I have
had a great deal of talk.'

The offer of Madras was followed up by other overtures ; Mr. Dundas proposed the Irish secretaryship to
Sir Gilbert—an office for which he had himself said, in
former days, that ' nerves and bad taste were specially
required.'   ' He told me that they proposed to make a
great reform in the Irish Government, and to convince
that country that it was the wish of Great Britain to
govern Ireland on a less corrupt system than formerly,
and said they wished to appoint such a new government
there as might give credit to their professions.   He
lamented extremely Lord Spencer's refusal, considering
him peculiarly well fitted for the situation.'   Pitt, in
his conversation with Mr. Windham, had held out a
still more tempting bait, in the shape of the Secretaryship at War, with a possible seat in the cabinet ; and
Lord Loughborough, with the zeal of a recent convert,
drew on his imagination for posts suitable to his friends,
and pressed on Sir Gilbert's acceptance the post of
Vice-President of the Board of Trade—an office which,
he said, Pitt thought of creating.   Sir Gilbert, however,
saw no necessity for any such creation, and, looking on
it in the light of a job, desired it should not be per-

petrated in his favour. 'I mentioned to Dundas my objection to the Chancellor's proposal. He held up his hands in surprise, and said he could not imagine where the Chancellor had got such an idea; that Pitt "had never thought of any such board, and *would not think of any new job*." The Chancellor is certainly very little in their confidence, and the most random talker I ever knew.' 'I dined at Wimbledon on Saturday; the party was Lady Jane Dundas, Miss Dundas her daughter, Lady Louisa Hervey, Mrs. Digby (Miss Gunning that was), Miss Stuart, daughter of General Stuart, a General Dundas, the Duke of Buccleuch, Mr. Ferguson of Pitfour. We passed the evening in guessing riddles and discovering thoughts by twenty questions. The Lord Chancellor and Lady Loughborough arrived next day. She seems a good sort of woman, and has so much sensibility that her eyes are perpetually filling with tears. I am serious in thinking that, notwithstanding the extreme misery of her face, person, and manners, she may be much more agreeable to those with whom she is at her ease than I ever thought her before. My passion, however, must be hopeless, as she went so far as to tell me she was attached to another person—Elliot, who is so much the fashion that all the ladies are sighing for him. To be sure they think they may confess their admiration of him without facing the censure of the world, and consider him somehow as an amiable circumstance, as Miss White said of Rauzzini.'

The negotiations between the ministers and the leading Whigs were dropped for a time, in consequence

of the determination of the latter not to take office
except under conditions which could not then be fulfilled ; and in July Sir Gilbert returned to Minto, but
before doing so he took a degree of Doctor of Laws at
Oxford, and wrote thence to Lady Elliot the following
letter :—

'Christ Church, Oxford : Wednesday, July 3, 1793.

' I came here yesterday in the evening. Everybody
was at the theatre when I arrived, and I found Oxford
a solitude, like in long vacation, but without a scout, a
bed-maker, or any other living face that I knew. I
posted alone round Christ Church meadow, and many
other haunts, recovering the traces of past things, which
had become fainter than I should have thought. At
night I got into the world. I found a grand confusion
about Burke. When his book on the French Revolution came out, it was of course extremely approved of
and admired by this loyal and pious body ; and there
was a proposal made to give him the degree of Doctor
of Laws by diploma, which is the greatest compliment
the university can pay. The proposal, however, was
not adopted, as *they* say, because it is not usual to give
degrees for writings of a political nature ; but in truth,
I believe, because it was not yet clear how far he was
favoured at court. Burke and his friends took the refusal ill, of course. He is now here to wait on the
Duke of Portland ; and it being moved to grant
honorary doctor's degrees on this occasion to persons
of note, the Duke of Portland gave Burke's name
among many others, for a doctor's degree, which was

immediately complied with by the heads of houses. On this, Burke, with the approbation, or rather at the desire, of the persons who had formerly proposed a degree by *diploma*, wrote a letter to the Vice-Chancellor, declining the intended honour on the ground of his having been thought unworthy of it before. This has vexed the Duke of Portland extremely, who appears to have drawn this affront on the university by proposing Burke's name without knowing whether he would accept. All this has made a grand rout. I supped at the Dean of Christ Church, with Lord and Lady Darnley, Lord Malmesbury, Lords Stormont and Mansfield, Lord Dalkeith, and others.

' I am going this moment to the Chancellor's.'

'Spring Gardens : July 6, 1793.

' I took my degree at Oxford on Thursday. George Cornewall spoke some English verses, and really did extremely well. . . .

' I set off for Minto on Monday. The heat of this town is equal to that of the tropics.'

Soon after their parting in London Mr. Windham carried out the project he had been obliged to abandon at an earlier period of the year, and went over to Holland to see the military operations there. A letter addressed by him to Sir Gilbert from thence, and dated ' Camp before Valenciennes: July 26, 1793,' though too long to be given in extenso, contains passages of sufficient interest to warrant their insertion here.

After describing a visit to the trenches, ' one of the things that people do here by way of a lounge,' he says, ' I feel myself to owe to you such a free communication of the state of my mind in all cases where you may be interested in any way to know it, that I would tell you frankly if I had felt very much frightened. But the fact was very much otherwise, and the result of my experience of myself in this and some subsequent instances, and of my observations of all about me is, that courage such as is wanted for common military purposes is not only a quality very generally possessed, but acquired with very little effort. The danger to be sure in the cases of which I can speak, was on the whole very inconsiderable, but there were moments at which it was otherwise, and the effect of danger on the mind is perhaps rather in proportion to the appearance than the reality. You cannot conceive how much the habit of a camp lessens the value which any man sets on his own life.

.   .   .   .   .   .

' The grandeur of the scene, such as it comes to the eye, and still more as it is presented to the mind, exceeds all that one could ever have hoped to see in one's own time. No one in fact for these forty years has seen so regular a siege, and in a much longer period no one has seen an army composed of troops of so many different nations, of characters so various, and brought from places so remote. There is a regiment of Keyser

(Kaiser) Hussars, arrived within these few days, and which I saw just after their arrival, that have been five months on their march. They reckon up among the different corps of the army some twelve or thirteen languages. In the midst of all this the great action of the piece is continually going on, and you are sipping your tea and eating your mutton with a siege roaring below you, and with the air at night illuminated as by the finest fireworks. You cannot conceive anything more calculated to strike the eye and fill the mind with great and awful images.'

Here follows an account of the progress of the siege, and of ' a great coolness' which had sprung up towards us on the part of the Austrian engineers, in consequence of 'a foolish vapouring speech' of a British officer who had offered to take the place in sixty hours ; thereby giving so much offence that the English artillery were either excluded from the operations altogether, or were placed in situations where the credit to be acquired was in no proportion to the danger to be incurred. And the letter closes with a P.S. written on the 26th (three days later) describing a successful attack on the outworks of the town, and confessing the writer's self-reproaches that it had not occurred to him that he might with propriety have formed one of those who stormed 'the covered way; ' the only consolation he can receive for this oversight being the reflection that the satisfaction he would have derived from the thought of having taken part in the storm[1] of

---

[1] The storm of the outworks is intended, for Mr. Windham opens his

Valenciennes could bear no proportion to the misery he must have occasioned to one or two others had he fallen. 'The English troops behaved exactly as one could wish, equal to any in point of courage, and far exceeding them in humanity and generosity. Our friends the Austrians, who are perfect patterns of soldiers in all other respects, so as to be looked up to rather by our troops as elder brothers in the art of war, do not shine on the side of humanity. They are, to be sure, a set of unfeeling savages as need be brought to thin the human species.'

Early in August Sir Gilbert was invited by the Government to undertake a service which on various grounds was peculiarly acceptable to him.

The siege of Dunkirk was at this time going on, and the ministers had it in contemplation, should the town, as was expected, surrender to our forces, to send a commission there of the same character and with much the same objects as that which they did subsequently send to Toulon. The fall of Dunkirk was expected from day to day, and it had become necessary to find a man suited by abilities, character, and position, to take the chief place in this commission. Sir Gilbert Elliot was, according to Mr. Dundas, *unanimously* agreed upon by the Cabinet as the most fit person for the post could he be induced to take it. His early education in

letter to add a few lines ' at half-past ten at night,' to say that the town would surrender, and that a storm would hence be spared, ' than which nothing could be so dreadful.'

France had given him a familiar acquaintance, not only with the French language, but with the personal history, habits of thought, and prevailing sentiments of the French royalists, and the relations he had kept up in England with the principal emigrants had prevented such early knowledge from becoming rusty. Above all, his natural moderation, candour, and liberality of mind, joined to a temper of unfailing sweetness, combined to fit him in a special degree for a service which required all the conciliatory qualities, as well as prudence and discretion.

The feeling with which he undertook it is expressed in a letter to Lady Elliot :—

‘Spring Gardens: September 17, 1793

‘ . . . Now, thinking as I do that our internal safety depends entirely on a successful issue to this war, I see nothing to be done but to support and assist ministers in carrying it on, to obtain additional confidence to their administration by our accession to their counsels, and to make ourselves responsible, as well as them, for this measure, which is fully as much our own as theirs. We are completely responsible for the conduct of the war now, since we are so for its issue. If the war which we advised fails, we shall not be let off by blaming the conduct of it; and it is clear that we, as well as the ministers, whether we are in or out, must stand or fall with this war. It would even be shabby to do otherwise. But is it not childish to be finding fault with the mode of carrying on the war

at the very time when we refuse to assist in doing it
better? Besides, Windham's view of renewing the
connection with and dependence on the Duke of Portland is to me quite inadmissible. It will be fatal to
everything like useful exertion, and fatal probably to
our private honours. The only way in which the
Duke of Portland could be of any use would be by
coming directly into office. He would then be fixed to
one system, and nothing would depend on his indecision
and his conflict between duty and inclination.'

To Lady Elliot.

'Spring Gardens: September 10, 1793.

'It is intended to be a *special* and *temporary*
mission[1] for the purpose of settling and ordering the
government of the town and its district, and not a permanent station as governor. My office at Dunkirk is
to be entirely independent of the military com-
mandant; the title of the office is not settled, but I
am to represent the King. No further conquests are
to be made in that quarter in the name of Great
Britain, nor is it intended to retain Dunkirk after the
peace. . . . Dundas is extremely disappointed indeed
at Lord Spencer's refusal to go to Ireland. He says it
is impossible to express the importance of his taking
that employment, and that there is not another man in
the kingdom whom it is advisable to send there. He
named as candidates Lord Abercorn, Lord Moira, the

---

[1] Mission to Dunkirk

Duke of Leeds, Lord Carlisle; but it seems determined that if Lord Spencer will not go, the present governor of Ireland shall continue another session.

'They have not filled up Madras.'

'Spring Gardens: September 11, 1793.

'The siege of Dunkirk is raised, and all thoughts of it are given up, and I wish with all my heart the consequences may not be still worse; but as it is, it will make a glorious clamour, and will in all probability require the sacrifice of one or two ministers to save the rest. The Duke of York, I am told, is violent against the Duke of Richmond and Lord Chatham. On the other hand, I suspect the Duke of Richmond will be found less to blame than is thought. The opinion of Lord Chatham's insufficiency in his office is quite universal; although I know how totally inconclusive even the most general rumours are, yet I can hardly disbelieve all I hear on that point. Some, I think, will blame the Duke of York for precipitation in commencing the siege not only before the necessary succours were had from England, but what is more material, before the Prince of Saxe-Coburg could co-operate with him, as the Austrian army was engaged in the siege of Fresnoy. . . . I have seen Dundas and Pitt since the bad news. Dundas seems much dismayed; Pitt tried to carry it off better. . . . I believe you will be relieved rather than disappointed by this issue; to me the pleasure of returning to you, and the hope we shall not part, is a complete and perfect compensation for all disappointments.'

'Spring Gardens: Saturday, September 14, 1793.

' I send you excellent news. It is a full compensation for the miscarriages at Dunkirk. The *Gazette* will inform you that Lord Hood is in possession of Toulon, in alliance with the Royalists ; fifteen sail of the line of the French are in his custody, and, although held for the King of France, they are in the meanwhile *hors de combat*, or, possibly, even ready to be employed on our side. The same thing would have taken place at Marseilles, if the Republicans had not got possession of the town by surprise the very day before the treaty was concluded. There is, however, a reasonable expectation that the south of France will in general declare for the King. Nothing can be more important than this event. It is more likely than any other to hasten a peace, and while the war continues it deprives France of half her naval resources. It sets a great part of Lord Hood's fleet at liberty to act elsewhere. The Corsicans have declared against France, and are not only able to defend themselves, but offer 2,000 men to co-operate with us. Naples will furnish 6,000 men. The King of Sardinia has a fair prospect of advancing against the French in the county of Nice, and may thus afford assistance in the south of France. It is supposed the Swiss will join the allies against France. So much for the south. Coburg has taken Fresnoy. . . .

' Somebody was saying something in the King's presence, since the retreat from Dunkirk, disadvantageous to Colonel Moncrieff; the King said, very handsomely and honourably, " For God's sake, wherever the blame may be, do not let us lay it on the dead man." Prince Adolphus is come home while his wounds are healing. He is to return immediately after. He is some inches taller than the Prince of Wales, and large in proportion. The Prince of Wales told the Chancellor that Prince Adolphus told him he had resolved *not to be taken*. If he had not effected his escape, he would have resisted and got himself killed. This is very noble, if true. He felt the disadvantage it would be to the war that he should be a hostage in the enemy's hands. Lord Mulgrave is with our old friend the Comte de St. André among the mountains between Nice and Turin with the Piedmontese army.

' Lord Malmesbury is to be employed directly, and seems to like his destination [1] extremely. We are living with cabinet ministers. We passed the evening of the day before yesterday at Somerset House, with Pitt, Dundas, and the Chancellor. . . .

' I go to Beconsfield to-morrow ; to Windham on Thursday.'

' Spring Gardens: Tuesday, September 17, 1793.

'Fortune is at her tricks again with us, and I am under the necessity of giving you more agitation. I am to ·be employed immediately at Toulon, in a ministerial character, for transacting all affairs of a civil and political nature that must arise at that most important post. By Toulon is meant, in effect, the south of France ; although Toulon will be my place of residence. This commission I consider as the most

[1] Vienna.

honourable that it is possible to entrust any man with
at this crisis, and in this respect it will be gratifying
both to you and to me.   It must also prove sufficiently
advantageous in other respects; the duration must
depend on events.   A very considerable military force
will be there as soon as possible.   General O'Hara
will, I believe, be sent from Gibraltar to command the
troops.   I am told I shall be expected to go in a week
or ten days.   I hardly know what to say about your
coming to town.'

'Spring Gardens: Thursday, September 19, 1793.

' I am in great haste to-day. . . . I dined yesterday
at Pitt's with a full· Cabinet, and some others, among
whom was Lord Hugh Conway, who brought Lord
Hood's despatches from Toulon.   I was at the levée
yesterday.   The King spoke a great while to me, which
I suppose he meant as a civility.   After the levée
Dundas had an audience, and the King said to him, " I
see Sir Gilbert Elliot is at court to-day; when does he
go to Toulon ? "   Dundas said he was just going to
mention the subject to his Majesty.   The King said,
" Oh, I took it for granted you would send him there."
Nobody had spoken to him on the subject before.   I
had a very long conversation with Pitt after dinner.
He ended by saying he was extremely glad I had agreed
to go.   I told him that the commission appeared to me,
from its importance and from the nature of the duty,
the most gratifying that could be offered to any man in
this country; but that my pleasure was a little mixed

with anxiety on account of its delicacy and difficulty. After a little pause he said, " It certainly is attended with very great difficulty, but if it had not we should not have desired you to undertake it." '

' . . . Good news from Toulon. A small body of English, Spanish, and French have dispossessed Carthaux, the general of the *Sansculottes*, from a strong post which he had taken before Marseilles and Toulon, with great slaughter, and the loss of all his cannon. Lord Hood says he is not now afraid of twenty Carthaux. This seems to make our footing at Toulon more secure.'

Lady Elliot joined her husband in London on hearing of his appointment on foreign service; hence no further letters passed between them while he remained in England. He embarked at Dover for Ostend on the 18th of October 1793, and was accompanied as far as Brussels by Mr. Elliot of Wells, who returned to England in time to see Lord Malmesbury off on his mission to Vienna. ' My Dominie,' wrote Lady Malmesbury on this occasion, ' goes with Lord Malmesbury as far as the coast ; for I believe he always attends, like a confessor, in the last moments. Lord Malmesbury's passage to Ostend took *fifty-six hours*, the longest ever known. This is "pour encourager les autres." '

The last sentence was aimed at Lady Elliot, who was

meditating a journey with her children to Italy, in order to lessen the distance between herself and Sir Gilbert.

What was thought of Sir Gilbert's acceptance of office at this juncture by his most intimate friends and counsellors, Mr. Burke and Mr. Windham, may be seen in the following letters, which will fitly close this portion of the correspondence :—

Edmund Burke to Sir Gilbert Elliot.

‘ September 1793.

‘ My dear Sir,—The event of the taking of Toulon, or rather of its surrender into our hands, is such that when I consider the dead stupidity with which it is received, I take the worst possible augury of the sense and public spirit of England from their feeling, or rather want of feeling, about ˙it.   I am afraid that sufficient pains have not been taken to animate the people to take an interest in the war.   As to the ministry, their nomination of you is a pledge that they mean to improve this event, so glorious to the national character.   It is in itself worth twenty victories, and you go to let the people see that their confidence in this nation is not misplaced.   The thing is arduous indeed in the extreme, but it is a task worthy of you, and you owe yourself entire to your country at this instant.   You are happy to have a friend and companion who has as good a heart as ever I knew even in a young man: and I have never observed a more

sound and mature judgment in the oldest.[1]   Well, God
give you both success! I trust it is his cause, though
his ways are in the great deep.   I hope to see you
before you depart.   I have many things floating in my
mind with regard to your destination, whether worth
talking of or not I cannot tell.   The state of unforti-
fied Flanders, in which we must be constantly victorious not to be wholly ruined, fills me with anxiety
and apprehension.   The conduct of the King of
Prussia with regard to Wurmser is equally alarming.
But we must bear up with magnanimity, for our all,
body and soul, is at stake.   We must be the victims of
Jacobins, or what is worse, we must be Jacobins if
this whole is not levelled with the ground.   I suppose
we are   preparing everything for a vigorous winter
campaign, for rest and repose we shall have none.   As
to their (the Austrians) talking of Maubeuge, surely it
is quite idle.   If Fouchard is not put out of the question, they will have to think how they shall keep their
own Netherlands, without troubling themselves with
anything further.   I shall say nothing to Cazalès about
you till you desire me, but his mind is all on fire with
this business.

'I have not been quite well since you left me with
an indigestion.   A French gentleman, the Chevalier de
Cambon, who was at Toulon with his regiment for a
considerable time, has come to see him (me?).   I have

---

[1] Elliot of Wells had been intended to accompany Sir Gilbert, as
secretary to the mission; he did not do so, but for what reason is not
given.

talked to him a good deal about it. But there is nothing much worth troubling you with.—I am ever, my dear Sir Gilbert, most faithfully and affectionately yours &c.,   'EDM. BURKE.'

William Windham to Sir Gilbert Elliot.

'September 19, 1793.

' My dear Elliot,—Our opinions are not so different but that I can rejoice most heartily in the news you send me, and at the prospect of your appointment to a situation where not only great credit may result to yourself, but where your abilities and judgment are likely to prove of the utmost importance to the public. There are many situations in which the advantage to be derived from one man's talents, more than from those of another, is, after all, perhaps very problematical. But this is not one of that sort ; and as I really think that everything depends on the man employed, so my genuine opinion is, that probably in the whole compass of the three kingdoms there is no one to be found so qualified for the service in all respects as yourself. I don't know that this declaration is calculated to quiet the anxiety which you describe yourself to feel, and which one cannot blame you for, but neither ought you to be alarmed at it.

' My judgment of you and of your qualifications will be so much more firmly fixed than any that I shall be able to form of the circumstances of the situation that, should events not answer to your wishes, I shall only conclude that it was not in the power of skill and prudence to have made them better.

'While I think in this way of the importance of the service, and of your qualifications for it, it will be easy for me to be satisfied with what you have done, and at the same time to keep my former opinions about myself. . . . . The present case stands on grounds of its own; and though there are other situations, likewise of great importance, and for which you would be eminently fitted—in which I know not whether at this moment I should have heartily wished to see you; yet here all other prospects and considerations are lost in the urgent and critical nature of the service, in which, if good can be done, it is of such prodigious amount as to allow of no choice or hesitation. You will of course go fully charged with Burke's ideas upon the subject, whose correct and powerful judgment comes out every day more and more. Had his opinion of the plan of operations prevailed, this fatal check would have been avoided that we have experienced at Dunkirk. The success at the other end of France will, I hope, compensate it. One principle I hope we shall adopt—to act with the most high and clear honour and good faith. There is nothing in the transactions with nations that one contemplates with such warm feelings of satisfaction, and nothing in my opinion that will be so calculated to give us that authority in the affairs of Europe that the nature of the times calls for. I shall follow you with all the solicitude of private friendship, and with the most awful impressions of the important nature of the service. It will be an infinite satisfaction to you, and no small one to me, that you will have Elliot with you. I think of him in all respects, both as to judgment and character, as I am sure you do. So far as anxiety will allow, I think the service a most pleasant one ; and in that light, and with a view to the company that I should be in, can regret that I am not going with you. You are to let me hear from you again before your departure. You need not be told how glad I shall be whenever you or Elliot can afford me a line during your absence. As little need you be told that you will carry with you, there and everywhere else, my most earnest wishes for your success, honour, and welfare.—Yours ever most truly,

' W. W.

'Thursday Night, 19th.'

Mr. Windham joined Pitt's government in July 1794, at the same time with the Duke of Portland, Lord Fitzwilliam, and Lord Spencer.

Edmund Burke to Sir Gilbert Elliot.

'September 22, 1793.'

'My dear Sir,—When I wrote to you I did not imagine that your letter had expressed so strong a wish as on reading it over again I find it did, that I should go to town. I should, however, be happy to go, not only to town, but to the remotest part of Europe or of Asia, if I thought I could be of the smallest use in this momentous crisis of human affairs ; but a letter which Mr. Cazalès received from Monsieur Lesardieres, a

---

[1] This letter has been already printed in the ' Correspondence of the Right Hon. Edmund Burke.'

gentleman of Poitou and connected with the principal
people there, made me almost despair that anything
will be done in a way correspondent to any ideas of
mine, or in which, of course, I can be of the least
service.

'I cannot help thinking that we are got again on the
wrong tack; and that we are resolved either to consider
ourselves as in war with the whole nation of France,
merely on common political points, or that we have
taken up some of the Republican factions, in order to
establish their power and to crush the remainder of
the Royalists in that unhappy country. If I understand at all the true spirit of the present contest, we
are engaged *in a civil war;* but on a far larger scale,
and on far more important objects, than civil wars
have generally extended themselves to or compre-
hended. I consider the Royalists of France, or as
they are (perhaps as properly) called, the Aristocrats,
as of the party which we have taken in this civil war.
I regard, therefore, the abandoning them *exactly* in
the same light of morality and policy as I should, had
I lived in the time of Charles the First and served in
the King's army in Yorkshire, the voluntary sacrifice
of the army of Sir Bevil Granville, or any other
Royalists serving in the west. Strongly impressed with
the soundness and justness of this idea, I have always
looked on the proceedings in Poitou with greater
interest, and in truth as of more importance, than the
proceedings of the combined powers on the side of
Flanders. These brave and principled men, with very

inadequate means, have struggled, and hitherto vic-
toriously, for upwards of six months, and have, in fact,
by the mere dint of courage and constancy, done more
against the common enemy, and deprived him of a far
larger extent of territory, than all the regular armies
of Europe put together, though they have in the field
perhaps not less than 400,000 men, and all the resources of so many mighty kingdoms.   They amount
to about 40,000, though ill armed and ill provided in
every respect.   To this moment I understood that our
Government had from the beginning an earnest desire
of communicating with the Royalists in that quarter,
and only lamented that they had no possible means of
doing so, having all sorts of supplies in readiness to
send to them.   The communication is now obtained.
The royal and Christian army has sent us word that
they desire to be owned by some great power ; that
they want to be furnished with arms, etc., and some
French leaders of their own principles ; that if they
can obtain this recognition and this succour, they shall
be able to resist the common enemy ; but if they continue to be discountenanced and unsupported, they are
apprehensive they shall be overpowered.   That the
city of Nantes will, with such a countenance, declare
in their favour, otherwise not.   Certain it is that
hitherto the only effect they have seen of the interference of those great powers is the enabling the Jacobins
to send one great army against them from Mentz, and
another from Valenciennes.

    ‘ The capture of neither of these places has been of

so much advantage to the common cause as the sending of the troops employed there to extirpate our friends in Poitou has been of prejudice to it.   By actively assisting the enemy, and by refusing the least countenance to the Royal (our own) party, I fear we shall not be free from the guilt or the mischief which will accompany the barbarous cruelties and massacres with which the most savage of all enemies will utterly destroy our friends, together with the country they inhabit.   They have begun the incendiary part already. Here is an opening, which, if neglected by our Government, whether as statesmen or as lovers of mankind, they will one day sorely repent.   I understand that the answer given to Monsieur Lesardieres was through a young gentleman who had distinguished himself by some writings in favour of the French Revolution.   He is now a clerk in office, and has the department of the gentlemen who are the victims of that Revolution delivered over to him.   That answer, I understand, was truly discouraging.   No politician can make a situation.   His skill consists in well playing the game dealt to him by fortune, and following the indications given by nature, times, and circumstances.   Where can we hope to plant 40,000 men in the heart of the enemy's country at less than a hundred times what the support of that would come to ?   I know that we were hurried on by the torrent of circumstances to send the body of our forces to Flanders.   I don't blame the measure, but indeed I lament it, and am quite sure

that the fourth part of these forces sent to Poitou
would have by this turned the scale in our favour.

' I truly and unreservedly rejoiced at the affair of
Toulon, not only on account of the immense and un-
paralleled advantage of it as a military stroke, but
because the war was at length put upon a proper footing—the only rational, manly, and honourable footing
it can be put upon. Instead of refusing to acknowledge the ancient, lawful, prescriptive government of
that country in the monarchy, the acknowledgment of
it by the French Republican magistrates of Toulon was
made the very condition of our receiving their city and
all it contained. The Royalists of Poitou are now at
that point to which we ourselves have brought the
Republicans of the south. Having acted on the principle of supporting the Royal cause as our own cause
on the Mediterranean, how comes it that we act on the
very reverse principle on the ocean ?

' It cannot be that we have taken up the wicked and
frantic project of what is called the Constitution, and
that we mean to consider all those as enemies who
were not concerned in that mother rebellion and all its
evil principles. When we were offered such a town
and port as Toulon, with a fiduciary deposit of twenty
sail of the line, we should have been the most contemptible of pedants and sophists, when the fundamental point was gained (indeed, whether it was gained
or no does not turn the question), if we were to chicane
with them about their fopperies of a Constitution.
Lord Hood consulted, I suppose, the humour of the

time and place, as a man of sense would. He did not himself talk the *feuillant* language, but he wisely let them talk what language they pleased; which *feuillant* language, however, to do them justice, they spoke only very faintly and very generally. It was a point gained, to get a town where the fiercest Jacobinism had so long prevailed, to go so far. By the way, they hoisted the white flag, not the colours of the first Revolution:

' But if, in such practical affairs, we were to rest upon abstract principles of any kind, we must give the preference to those of Poitou. Very wisely and very temperately, they have held out nothing but the general principles of religion, loyalty, and civil order, leaving everything else to be discussed when Jacobinism, the enemy of all those principles, is driven out of the field. But for us, against the sense of nine in ten, at least, of all the land proprietors now despoiled and banished, to set up the idol of the Constitution, would be a madness equal to that of the makers of that mock Constitution. The present, with which we are now at war, is substantially the same, but a little more coherent, uniform, and rational. That pretended Constitution was, in truth, the very cause of all the evils which at this moment afflict Europe ; and if even it could be set up again (God, of his infinite mercy, avert so great a calamity!) by our arms and politics, be assured, my dear Sir Gilbert, that things would move on again in the very same circle, without the same means of checking them in any part of the course of their revolution. All I can do is to clear my conscience, by leaving nothing said or undone on my part, publicly or privately, to prevent the system of considering the body of the emigrants, and those who hold the same cause in France, as not the real body of that nation. The rest are either to be got under by force, or by tenderly and wisely managing their distemper according to the circumstances of the case ; but never ought we to take *practically* any steps, by way of curing some symptoms of a distemper, to fix its radical cause for ever.

'I take it for granted that I shall embrace you before you go. I assure you I am as heartily concerned as the Ministry themselves can be, that they may get out of this arduous war with honour and advantage. The paper I gave you to read at going shows you how decided I am. Pray send it to me, that I may transmit it to the quarter where it was intended to go. Adieu, my dear friend, with every, the most cordial wish for your success.—Yours ever faithfully and affectionately,   'EDM. BURKE.

'September 22, 1793.

'I suppose you have got my letter. It was directed, as this is, to Lord Malmesbury's.'

The principle which Burke desired the ministers to adopt was one of unflinching and indiscriminate antagonism to the Revolution : the standard of the old monarchy was to be raised; the 'government to be restored that was there before '89;'[1] and the émigrés

---

[1] The quotation is from a letter of Burke's son to Mr. Elliot.

were, we suppose, to re-enter Paris as a holy army of martyrs. The English ministers—and Sir Gilbert Elliot agreed with them—were of opinion that in adopting these views wholesale, they, with their historical antecedents, would have been inconsistent and unjust : whereas the aggressions of France in Europe, and her repeated declarations of the principles on which she professed to act, made it a matter of necessity to England to arm in self-defence.

A well-known foreign writer, Henri Heine, tells us that it is in the nature of Englishmen to transmute intellectual ideas into substantive facts—to resist the encroachments of mind with matter, and to be themselves brutal as facts (brutaux comme des faits); but at the time of which these letters treat, the ideas of the French concerning the benefits of liberty and equality had taken the concrete form of annexation of their neighbours' territories, *before* England replied, not altogether illogically, ' on the holy text of pike and gun.'

A letter from Burke to Sylvester Douglas, after Sir Gilbert's departure, contains a passage which shows the keenness of Burke's feelings on the personal and political questions involved in Sir Gilbert's mission, and also his entire misapprehension of the position in which his friend was placed at Toulon :—

' We both of us love Sir Gilbert Elliot very sincerely,' wrote he from Beconsfield, November 14, 1795, ' but we are not without many rivals in our esteem and affection for him. There is hardly a quality wanting in

him to engage every person to wish him success, and to
ensure the success of their wishes. If there be one which
he possesses in a less eminent degree, it is that kind of
exertion which is necessary to tax the resources of which
his mind is full, to the complete extent of their productive power. You observe that he is in a situation
of great responsibility; that he feels it, and that he is
not overpowered by it. All this is exactly how it ought
to be. To be sure his responsibility is great, but he is
not alone responsible.

'We are all responsible for him; I mean such of us
as by the unhappy circumstances of the time, by the
extravagant conduct of some persons, and the undecided
conduct of others, have been separated from the party
we once belonged to. He and we, who, on account of
our principles, have suffered ourselves to be torn from
our affections, must take double care that the principles to which he sacrificed so much should be maintained by us with all that firmness and consistency
the want of which we blamed, and blamed so justly in
those for whom, in every other particular, we had a
true respect and a most sincere regard.

'Sir Gilbert Elliot is not found in a common shop of
the diplomatic exchange. When a man is found in
that line, as in a profession, if he obeys his instructions
with judgment and dexterity, he has performed all
that is required of him. But our friend does not take
his politics from his commission; he takes his commission on account of his politics. His mission is not fit
for his acceptance, if it includes a probability of being

obliged to compromise with his principles. I do not say (God forbid!) that in some incidental particulars which do not affect the body and substance of our cause people should not yield to circumstances. Indeed he will have as far as regards France very little occasion for dexterity or management. He will be in a condition to give the law with an authority which no statesman before him ever possessed, or he will be nothing at all. The sword must open his passage.

.   .   .   .

' Sir Gilbert Elliot, if he cannot protect those whom he calls his party, ought to come away from a situation which by its nature subjects him to act a part compounded of fraud and imposture. Persons much his inferiors are able to act that part.

' It is not permitted to Sir Gilbert Elliot to be an ordinary man, neither his nature nor the times will suffer it.

' Si paulum a summo decessit vergit ad imum.'

CHAPTER V.

Sir Gilbert set out for Toulon on December 19, 1793, Lady Elliot returning to Minto on the same day, and Lady Malmesbury remaining in solitary occupation of her house in Spring Gardens: 'dark, dismal, dreary, and *all the d's* besides.'

The letters written by Sir Gilbert on his journey are devoid of important matter, while they teem with characteristic touches, terribly seductive to an Editor with a natural propensity to hold the writer in affection. Modest by nature and exceedingly simple in his habits, few things tried his patience more severely than to find himself an object of constant observation. Hence his first experience of an official position was not wholly agreeable. The attentions of a member of his suite, whose own vanity found gratification in ministering to the importance of his chief, drove him to desperation. 'I have more than once fairly jumped out of my chaise and distanced him by running up a steep hill;' a method of getting rid of a bore which is surely no less amiable than arduous. 'Of all plagues dignity is the greatest. I am constrained to own that between the position of a great man with an assiduous attendant, and that of a lunatic with a keeper, the difference is but trifling; but I do hope to teach him a more natural indifference to such trifles without hurting his feelings.'

In graver mood he poured forth his horror and detestation of the Jacobins, who had just guillotined the Queen of France, that vindictive and purposeless murder being less wicked than 'the horrible, horrible, horrible subornation of her own child against her, a deed I should have thought not to be conceived on this side of hell.'

No words were strong enough to paint his execration of the crimes committed by 'men among whom the devil had broken loose.' But before the letter closed he came across a detachment of French prisoners on their way to Hungary, and straightway his political aversions were stifled in compassionate sympathy for their misery. 'Poor miserable wretches in greatest misery, dying in numbers of want, hardship, and disease. Walking up a hill I fell into conversation with their officers, the Colonel of the battalion being in appearance and accomplishments equal to a journeyman blacksmith, and the rest great blackguards; but they were very wretched, so I left ten louis d'or to be divided among the three who appeared most miserable.' [1]

---

[1] So great were the straits of the French army at a much later period, that, after the victory of Albenga, an order of the day conferred a gratuity of three louis d'or on every general of division.—*Scott's Life of Napoleon.*

Though the journey to Toulon was unmarked by events
calculated to give interest to his correspondence, it
was productive of experiences which must have considerably modified his expectations of great results to
Europe from the operations of the Allies on the
Continent. At Brussels his interviews with 'Ministers and considerable people' convinced him that the
opinions of continental statesmen, and of all descriptions of people at Brussels, were unfavourable to the
capacity of the Prince of Coburg,[1] the commander
of the Austrian army in Belgium, who had just raised
the siege of Maubeuge.

At Genoa Sir Gilbert had hoped to meet Lord
Mulgrave returning to England from Toulon, where he
had held the chief command, and had conducted some
successful operations. In this, however, he was disappointed, and they missed each other on the road. The
tenor of Lord Mulgrave's communications to his
Government had led them to anticipate with confidence the results of the defence; but it now appeared
that during his recent passage through Genoa, his
personal communications to various persons there were
of a less cheerful tinge, and Sir Gilbert learnt with
dismay that Lord Mulgrave's opinions of the English

---

[1] To a letter recording this fact, Mr. Windham replied: 'Much of
what your letter told me in way of fact, was altogether new to me, and
not of the most satisfactory kind. I lament exceedingly this opinion
entertained of the Prince of Coburg, which, whether well or ill-founded,
is equally unfortunate, and sets one's whole hopes and confidence so
many per cent. lower than they were.' A few months later Colonel,
afterwards General, Mack was placed in virtual command of the army,
though it continued ostensibly to be under the Prince of Coburg.

commanders at Toulon, and of the troops they led, were on a par with those entertained at Brussels of the military talents of the Prince of Coburg. It is impossible not to suppose that if the English Government had been better informed of the condition of affairs at Toulon in the month of November 1793, they would have thought it scarcely worth while to open a political Commission under the circumstances then existing. The town, closely besieged by the Republican armies, was cut off from all communications with the interior, and could therefore be of no use as a *point de départ* for diplomatic negotiations with the Royalists in the south—for the organisation of a system of defence among whom this Commission had been chiefly designed. Moreover the town and port were so entirely commanded by the heights around them, that a successful attack on certain outworks could not fail at any moment to place both at the mercy of the enemy, and to oblige the fleet to seek its safety in immediate departure; as was actually the case within a month of Sir Gilbert's arrival. The chance of a successful resistance by the garrison was felt by those who had any opportunities of observing its composition and character to be very remote.[1]

[1] From Genoa Sir Gilbert wrote:—'This place has professed neutrality; but it has been in fact more adverse to us, and more useful to the French, than open hostility, and it has been thought necessary to bring it to an explicit declaration either of war or of alliance. I found all this decided and on the point of execution at my arrival, and I can hardly form an opinion one way or the other—nor shall I take this measure at all on myself. It turns on facts which passed before my arrival, on provocations which I did not witness, and on a knowledge

It is not easy to appreciate the extent of the difficulties against which the statesmen of eighty years ago contended, in obtaining information concerning events passing in distant countries. Foremost amongst these were the excessive slowness and uncertainty of communications, and the limitation of their sources of intelligence to their own official agents.

It is often said at the present day that by means of the correspondence of the Daily Press, the public is as well informed of foreign affairs as the Government; but it is no less true that the Government has been an equal gainer with the public in the increased amount and variety of the information laid before it, often on the authority of observers as impartial as intelligent. When Ministers were confined to the information derived from the reports of their own agents, it was no fault of theirs that the view presented to them was necessarily a limited one, while in some cases it was designedly so, and it is possible that the self-same circumstances which acted prejudicially on the practical side of their policy, may have been beneficial to its general scope and determination. In their ignorance of many disturbing causes, they worked with sanguine energy towards the attainment of their mark, the creation and direction of the great forces needed to set Europe in movement. But if, as seems admitted, English statesmen detected at an earlier period and

of the disposition and character of the people here, with whom I am unacquainted. I confess I should rather wish to concentrate our whole force and use our exertions where they are most wanted.'

with far greater clearness of vision than their Continental allies, the nature and the magnitude of the danger threatening Europe from the armed propagandism of revolutionary opinions, it is certain that they were not so clearsighted with regard to the secondary causes on which the success of great enterprises must ultimately depend. They knew little of the resources of the Powers whose co-operation they sought, and of their consequent ability to fulfil their engagements; less still of the secret aims, far more faithfully pursued by them than were the avowed objects of their policy; and least of all were they acquainted with the personal qualities of the Continental leaders. In the following correspondence it will be seen that the knowledge possessed by the English Ministers of their own instruments was not much more accurate, that their warlike preparations were fitful and feeble, and that the multiplicity of their military expeditions was a main cause of their defeat.

When, in the month of November 1793, Sir Gilbert joined the naval and military forces assembled at Toulon, an English contingent of less than 20,000 men, commanded by the Duke of York, was co-operating with the Emperor's army in Flanders.[1]   An

---

[1] Some of the causes which led to the failure of the expedition to Holland may be seen in the following extract from a letter from Mr. Elliot of Wells. Having accompanied Sir Gilbert on his journey as far as Brussels, he proceeded from thence to visit the head-quarters of the Duke of York, who, placed and maintained in the position of Commander-in-chief by the King's desire, was destitute of the talents

expedition under Lord Moira was preparing to leave
England for the coast of Brittany, and another to the
West Indies was in contemplation.   The Continental
Powers meanwhile were busy with their own objects.
Russia was bent on the acquisition of Poland and
Turkey, Austria of Bavaria, and Prussia was exercising
her usual political good husbandry at other men's
costs.[1]

requisite in a military leader, and was becoming a source of serious
difficulty to the Government. 'Almost all the persons immediately
about the Duke,' wrote Mr. E. from Tournay, November 2, 1793, 'are
very young men, and as they live at head-quarters, they fill his table,
and prevent him from inviting the general officers and colonels of
regiments as frequently as it is usual for a commander-in-chief to do.
This is one source of disgust. The youth of the circle which surrounds
him occasions also a levity of manners at head-quarters, hence arises a
lamentable deficiency of discipline among the officers. The Duke feels
this, and sometimes *expresses* himself harshly, when he ought to *act*
with severity. His own deportment is perfectly steady and unexcep-
tionable, and the stories which are spread of his drinking are absolutely
false ; but he has not had the training and military education required
for a commander. The Commissariat's department is very ill-arranged.
To-day, which has been extremely wet, the men had not sticks to boil
their kettles with, though the camp is on a plain surrounded by *large
woods*, and Lord Herbert told me that on some former occasion the men
had been six-and-twenty hours without provisions, a piece of negligence
which is never known to happen in the Austrian army. The French
troops are well appointed and well clothed. The whole of the army
under the command of the Duke of York does not amount to 20,000
men.'

[1] '*Nov.* 20.—Lord Malmesbury has shown me a most curious paper
that has just been transmitted to Lord Grenville by M. Jacobi, the
Prussian Minister : it states that the King of Prussia will require between
three and four millions sterling annually in order to maintain his army
on its present establishment, and that of this sum he expects this
country to pay a million and a half, the Empire to pay about half a
million, and the rest to be made up by the states of the Empire. But
as the complexity of the constitution of the states of the Empire renders
it difficult for them to raise a large sum of money in a short space of

Sir Gilbert to Lady Elliot.

'Toulon : November 16, 1793.

'The scene from the harbour answers my expectations fully in point of beauty. It is extremely fine. What I call the harbour is in fact a pretty extensive bay, and we are at a considerable distance from the town. I breakfasted on Friday with Lord Hood on board the "Victory," and we agreed to delay going on shore till we could open the Commission in form in the presence of the principal people of the town. Lord Hood dined on board the "Victory" as I did also, and it was settled that we should open the Commission to-day; but it blows so hard that boats cannot be conveniently got ashore, and to-morrow being Sunday, Lord Hood has appointed the ceremony for Monday. In the meanwhile we are entertained with the view of little battles, and the music of cannonades and musketry all round us. The important posts are all in our possession, but the enemy is close to them, and there is a pretty constant skirmishing and cannonading between them, enlivened with a few bombs to and from the harbour. I saw the first bomb in my life yesterday evening; they are so cheap a sight here that I am already too lazy to turn round to look at them. As these battles are hitherto pretty bloodless, one may really look at them as at fire-works.

time, the King proposes that *our* Government should *advance* their share of the subsidy; he also demands that the payments should be made every quarter.'

'As this ship has been absent for about five-weeks, and nobody has been on shore, nor anyone from the shore here, I am as much in the basket as if I was on Minto Pond.'

'*November* 18.—It blows so hard and rains so much that it is impossible to get on shore. At least Lord Hood cannot go, the " Victory " being to leeward of the harbour. I am determined to go to-morrow, if I go alone. I find Lord Hood very pleasant and comfortable in our business. He does not feel the smallest jealousy on account of this Commission, which takes in fact a great share of the business which he has been transacting out of his hands. He has, however, so much more to do than a man can accomplish, and there is a great deal of it so much of a sort that he is not accustomed to, that I believe he really feels my arrival a relief.'

'*November* 19.—Lord Hood still stays on board on account of the weather. I am therefore come with O'Hara, and am at length on terra firma. If the day had been better, and Lord Hood could have come, we were to have had a ceremonious entry, with salutes &c., but I was very glad to escape these honours.'

'*November* 21.—I am now completely in office and shall not have a sinecure. This has been a day both of ceremony and business. I was visited in the morning by all sorts of corps both civil and military. There were at times nearly 100 in the room at once. Of

course little passed beyond bows and a few compliments.
What everybody expects of me is money and bread for
this populous town, which has hardly any of those
commodities left.   There seems a great degree of confusion in their method; but there are clever distinct
men among them, and I do not despair of getting
things into order.'

'Distinctness' was not the characteristic of the
policy adopted at Toulon by any of the parties concerned.   The Continental Powers were impatient of
operations which England would not allow them to
abandon, but which weakened their action in other,
and to them, more important, directions.   The French
looked to the English Commissioners for their daily
bread, but wondered all the time for what object of her
own she dispensed it.   'Our Spanish allies,' wrote
Sir Gilbert, 'hint that we want to make a second
Gibraltar of Toulon;' and as selfish objects are always
readily credited, this view no doubt obtained many
adherents.   What England did want was undoubtedly
less clear than it might have been.   She was not committed to a dynastic restoration, nor did she profess any
peculiar preference for the Constitution of 1789.   She
was at war with the Convention, and therefore sided with
the enemies of the Convention, but she failed to enlist the
passions or selfishness of any one of the French factions,
for nothing is so difficult as to inscribe a negation on a
standard, unless it be to get men to follow it when
raised.

Sir Gilbert was clearly of this opinion when he wrote, in a despatch to the Right Hon. H. Dundas :

'It has been hinted to me that the sections have deliberated lately on the propriety of inviting Monsieur to Toulon, and that they are inclined to that measure. All persons and parties are dissatisfied with the present state of things. They are, in fact, so terrified that they care not what refuge they come to, provided it be strong, and the more powerful the protection is, the more likely it is to attract them.

'The interests of the Monarchy, which (although H.M. is not ultimately pledged to that principle) we have in the meanwhile avowedly espoused . . . would surely be much promoted by the presence of an ostensible and legitimate representation of the royal authority. I am persuaded it would detach from us no support on which we can depend, and it would add a great accession of numbers and zeal in the service. The white cockade is universal, and " Mon Roi " in every mouth. There seems some affectation of pure royalism. I perceive much less solicitude about the Constitution of 1789 than I expected.'

The exigencies of the military situation became speedily so pressing as to throw the political question into the background, and the result of Sir Gilbert's observation of the Toulonese during the few weeks he spent among them may be thus summed up: A mortal dread of the Republicans,[1] a display of loyalty verging

[1] Fugitives from Lyons brought into the town accounts of the horrors committed by Fouché and Collot d'Herbois in Lyons—increas-

on affectation and a genuine indifference to all constitutional reforms.

Sir Gilbert to Lady Elliot.

'24*th*.—O'Hara thinks as ill as possible of the business as it now stands; but reinforcements may be expected before the worst may happen; besides, I never saw a man half so nervous, or half so blind to every side but the black one, as O'Hara. His strange rattling, and to all appearance absurd and wrong-headed manner of talking, and indeed acting on some points, is more alarming in my eyes than any other circumstance. He is not without sense in his profession, and he has considerable military experience and knowledge, with personal courage in the highest degree, but he sees all the difficulties and can think and talk of nothing else. The means of surmounting them he cannot bring his mind to dwell on, and hardly to admit. Although there is much reason for O'Hara's despondency, I do not, however, for the reasons I have given, pin my faith on him.

ing the terrors already in everybody's mind. When Frenchmen accuse Frenchmen of want of patriotism for having sided with the Allies, it should be remembered that the cruelties committed by one part of the nation on the other, and not any political bias, were the cause and justification of their conduct. And though on the whole the proportion of the nation that took arms against the Republicans was insignificant, not so was the number of those alienated from liberal principles by the horrors of 1793. Even in 1873, the temper of mind produced by the events of that fatal year is an element of difficulty in the establishment of constitutional government in France.

'Lord Hood, again, is perhaps over confident, and will never admit the slightest doubt of our keeping the place. . . .

'This, like all other human affairs, depends so much on the manner of playing the game on both sides, and on so many accidents that can neither be foreseen nor provided against, that I confess I do not see sufficient ground either for confidence or despondency. We have had extraordinary disappointments, which were not known when I left England ; our situation would other-wise have been much better.

'Five thousand Austrian troops were promised by the Emperor from the Milanese, and might have been here before us. The Emperor has countermanded them, and there is not the slightest chance of their being here in time to do any good ; and they are not expected to come at all. This is a severe loss, for they would have been the only troops, except the British, who are much to be depended on. In the next place, 2,000 Neapolitans out of 6,000 who were supposed to be here, are not yet come. Thirdly, 1,200 or 1,300 British troops from Gibraltar, which ought to have been here long ago, and had positive orders to come from Government, have been detained by Sir Robert Boyd, who is about ninety years old, and has lost any sense he may ever have had. Fourthly, the whole body of Spanish troops, full 6,000, are worse than useless. It is impossible to de-scribe them. There never were beheld such wretches to the eye ; and as for soldiers, they carry their musket on the right or left shoulder, as it happens, and *always*

run away, officers and men together. The Spaniards,
however, claiming an equality with us at Toulon, and
one of their admirals having been appointed by the
King of Spain Commander-in-chief of *all* the combined
forces, English and all, they will not listen to any
orders or any advice given by O'Hara. These people
are necessarily entrusted with very important posts,
and the first time a serious attempt is made upon them
I fear the worst is certain. All these crosses were un-
known when I came away. Neither Lord Hood nor
Lord Mulgrave seem to have given correct accounts.
Lord Mulgrave, as everybody here says, was very glad
to get off. He had done some brilliant and successful
things, and left the place quiet ; but saw the difficulties
approaching. The Neapolitan troops are well-looking
men, tolerably clothed and appointed, and not without
spirit, but perfectly raw, having never seen fire before.
The Piedmontese troops, about 1,400, under our friend
Revel, are extremely good, and may be depended upon
to follow the English.[1]   The superiority of the English
is something beyond one's imagination. In looks and
dress and discipline and courage they are a higher

---

[1] Sir Gilbert mentions more than once in his despatches the admirable
quality of the Sardinian troops, commanded by the Chev. de Revel. 'It
is a great satisfaction to me, who am a *Nissard* in my heart, to see the
good understanding and great cordiality that appears on all occasions
between the British and the Sardinian troops.   This is as strong
between the common soldiers as between the officers. They have a
confidence in and esteem for each other, and always want to be together
when business is to be done. The Chev. de Revel is as remarkable for
judgment and conduct as for personal bravery, and the affection which
exists between him and his soldiery is quite affecting. He is a

order of beings. You will not be sorry to hear that I have eight of them as a guard—two at my door and the rest in the hall, night and day.'

' *November* 25.—Messenger not yet gone. Graham,[1] of Balgowrie, who came here with Keith Elphinstone to dissipate his grief for the loss of his wife, has left the highest character possible, both for understanding and courage. Although he was not in the army and had nothing to do with the business, he always went out when there was anything to do, and was foremost in all dangerous and difficult enterprises. He was gone to England before my arrival.'

'Toulon : December 1, 1793.

' Yesterday was a bad day for us. A sortie was made in order to destroy a new battery of the enemy's, which is nearer both to an important outpost and to the town than is convenient. It ended unfortunately, and we have suffered great loss without effecting the object. O'Hara is taken prisoner, and is wounded in the arm ; several other officers are wounded. Our loss in British exceeds 200, of whom about 40 are killed. You will see the account in the Gazette. The provoking thing is, that if the troops had been less spirited or better disciplined, all would have been well and everything would have succeeded. They attacked the battery and

passionate admirer of the excellent qualities of his countrymen, and they return his regard with a degree of affectionate respect which I never witnessed before.'

[1] Afterwards Lord Lynedoch.

got possession of it with very little loss. Their orders were to form there and remain for further orders ; and if they had done so, the guns would have been brought away or made useless and the battery destroyed ; but as soon as they got to the summit where the battery was they dashed down to the other side of the hill in pursuit of the enemy, and spread in great disorder all over the country to the right and left, and above a mile forward. The enemy rallied in consequence of this confusion, and poured down with great superiority of numbers, pushed them back and recovered the battery before any material business could be done. The British again found their way into the battery, but, not being supported by the other troops, were obliged to retreat. It was in the retreat that so many were killed and wounded. Revel commanded the Piedmontese troops, who are exceedingly good, and he has returned safe to my great joy.

'I was not able[1] even to go out to the ramparts to look on ; but Mr. Hardman brought me the news all the time of the action. First he rode in to say we had succeeded and were in possession of the battery. Soon after, that the event was doubtful, and one officer brought in dead and several wounded. At last, that we had lost the day and were retreating. It was as shocking as new to me to see dead and wounded men carried by my window. O'Hara's wound is slight, and he is well treated.

---

[1] Sir Gilbert had had a short attack of illness, brought on by bad diet.

'The night before the action he was as nervous as it is possible to conceive, and was wretched about the whole business and its possible issue. . . . He is perfectly brave in action, but there never was a man so unfit for a situation as he was for this one. General Dundas, I am sorry to say, thinks of our affairs as ill as O'Hara did. He is old and has bad health, and is quite overcome with the sudden load that has unexpectedly fallen upon his shoulders. He has desired earnestly to be relieved by some officer from home. He is a sensible man, however, and knows his profession. I have no doubt of his doing all that is possible, and, to say the truth, I feel more confidence in him than in his harum scarum predecessor.'

'*December* 6.—I live very pleasantly as to good understanding and harmony with everybody here, and particularly with Lord Hood, but I have nothing that can be called society.'

'*December* 9.—I consider our possession of this place very precarious, which is not surprising considering that I have heard that opinion from every military man of rank since I came here. It would require 5,000 or 6,000 good troops more than we have to make us tolerably secure, and where they are to come from I don't see. Dundas and Pitt promised that 5,000 hussars should be sent from Flanders a fortnight after me, besides troops from Ireland. But by sending additional troops to Flanders, and by the uneasiness which seems every now and then to be entertained in that quarter, I am doubtful of the fulfilment of their promises.   5,000 Austrian troops from the Milanese, promised by the Emperor, seem finally withdrawn from me. . . . In short, I fear the great hope we had been encouraging of making an impression on France from this quarter will be disappointed for want of despatch and vigour.[1]   The great misfortune is that nobody seems to have the real object of the war at heart.   We are all running after this conquest and that advantage, instead of making war on the French Convention. . . . We have still room enough for a good walk, and even ride, and nothing can be prettier than the country.   I walked to-day with two young men to their father's country house, about a mile and a half out of town, and pretty high up the hill ; nothing can be prettier ; the house is a very nice one,

---

[1] This was so much the opinion of Mr. Windham, that almost at the same date he was writing to Mr. Elliot of Wells as follows: 'I think if you see Dundas it may not be amiss to urge the danger of running after distant objects, while the great question lies still—of hunting the sheep till you have killed the dog. The most fatal error will be, I apprehend, the seeking to preserve the popularity of the war, by feeding the avarice of the nation with conquests. Not to mention that such popularity is of the most slippery sort, the nation, to do it justice, seems, as far as I can observe, to judge very rationally in that respect, and to understand (that) impression in France is a great means of terminating the war speedily and effectually. Among other places for which force may be wanting, I cannot help thinking of Toulon. They have been importuning, I find, the Pope to send to Toulon 2,000 of his troops. My fears would be lest this request should be complied with; for unless the Pope's troops are of a better quality than they have ever been supposed to be hitherto, such an accession to the garrison would be an accession of weakness and danger. The strength of a chain is the strength only of its weakest link, and we have seen by the specimen of the Spanish guard at the redoubt at Faron, to what the behaviour of a single corps may lead.'

but plundered almost of everything, and in it live all
their old animal companions—dogs and cats, a horse,
a mare and its foals, an ass and a goat, who all come
round about them when they go there, as Robinson
Crusoe's parrot did.

'They seem so used to ruin here that their spirits
are not much affected by it. The name of my friends
is Amyot. One of them was in the king's apartment
during the whole of the 10th of August. He escaped
afterwards into the country, and was kindly received by
some poor peasant in a retired part of the country, and
there paid his share of the housekeeping by day labour,
to which he became sufficiently inured not to feel it
very severe, and now he says he is secure and independent.

'This walk was secure because it is within our out-
posts, and is backed by a great hill called *Faron*,
now in our possession ; but our batteries and theirs
are firing away at each other about a mile on one side
of us, and we have never two minutes together
without the whizzing of a cannon. It would not do
for you ; and much as I always long to have you with
me in any pretty country scene, I confess I do not
desire your company here.'

'Toulon : December 12.

'Thank God ! I have at last heard you are all well
up to November 1. I cannot tell you what pleasure
the sight of your handwriting gave me. . . .

'We have received 700 Piedmontese troops, which
are next to the English in quality. . . .

' General Dundas is in very low spirits, and seems to despond more than ever. The misfortune is that a great proportion of our troops cannot be depended on. We have 7,000 Neapolitans, who are well-looking and well-appointed, but they do not like danger. Yesterday four of them were killed by bombs at an outpost, and the rest of the party sent to the commanding officer of the post to beg to be relieved as they were all *sick*. If a serious attack is made, such troops as these will beg to be excused ; the post will be lost, and then the place cannot hold out.

' Sir Joseph Erskine brings us as bad news as possible—that there is no intention in England to send us a single man except Sir Joseph's regiment of Dragoons of about 300, which will be of no use and will plague us for forage ! They cannot be much blamed, for by all former letters and accounts from hence, and by the number of men we actually have, and still more by those we are supposed to have, we must have appeared very strong. It was not yet known in England that the 5,000 Austrian troops from the Milanese were stopped. The consequence is that they have stopped the troops which were to come from Ireland and also the Hessians.'

' On Board the " Victory," Bay of Hyères : December 20, 1793.

' You will not be surprised, after what I have been writing to you ever since I got to Genoa, to learn that Toulon is no longer in our possession ; and you will not be sorry to see that we are all well, that my head is on my shoulders, and that I have escaped, as Mac-

heath says, both rope and gun. . . . There has seldom
been crammed more misery and more terror in a short
space than we have witnessed these last four days, and are
likely to witness still longer. On the 16th we received
accounts from Gibraltar that two regiments would be
sent immediately from thence ; that the West India
expedition was given up, and that we should probably
have a great part of the force destined for that
service to reinforce the army at Toulon. We were all
cock-a-hoop, and the prospect of great events opened
again before us. If we could only wait long enough to
receive all this aid, our affairs were sure to prosper ;
but that was the doubt, and every hour seemed critical.
For the enemy had already received their reinforcements.
They had come close to all our posts, and their deserters as well as our own spies promised us a general
attack immediately. This triumphant news was received from Gibraltar on the 16th in the forenoon, and
I never saw any man more delighted than Lord Hood.
He came skipping into my room, out of breath with
hurry and joy. On the 17th, at five o'clock in the
morning, somebody came tumbling in the dark into my
room over chairs and tables, and woke me in a start.
This was an officer from Lord Hood, to tell me that our
principal post, called Fort Mulgrave, was just taken by
the enemy. I knew immediately that the thing would
do no longer. I got up and went to Lord Hood's, where
I found General Dundas, and from that time till the
evening we remained, without stirring, at Council and
preparing measures. Soon after I got to Lord Hood's

we heard that another important post, the heights of Faron, was also carried by the enemy. This settled the matter. A council of war was held; the evacuation of Toulon was determined on, and measures concerted for carrying it into execution. It was determined to take place on the night of the next day. Lord Hood packed up his goods, and went on board that evening, the 17th. I sent off all my papers with him, but slept in town that night.

' The effect of these events on the inhabitants of the town being extremely doubtful, I for the first time took precautions. I got a pair of pistols on my table, went to bed in my clothes that I might be ready, and had all my things packed up. Next morning, about five, General Dundas stalked into my room with a long and careful face. The day he had to pass, and the doubtful issue of all he had to do, justified it. To be short, he wished me to go to Lord Hood to hasten the execution of all that had been determined on, which I accordingly did a few hours earlier than I intended. I took this opportunity to carry off and save the lives of two worthy French families who would have been among the first victims. The day was employed in embarking, first, the sick and wounded, about 4,000; during the whole day the miserable and terrified inhabitants were crowding into boats with children of all ages to escape the death that waited them on shore. Thank God! at least 4,000 lives have been saved in this way. We have between 2,000 and 3,000 on board the English

ships alone.[1] The French ships were burnt in the
evening and during the night. The troops were embarked in the night, and the whole was happily performed without loss or accident. The weather was
providentially favourable, and the fleet got safe out of
Toulon roads early in the morning of the 19th, and
anchored in this bay. Had the weather been such as
it has been ever since, that is to say blowing strong
from the eastward, we must have all—fleet, army, and
refugees—inevitably perished.

‘ The scene has been shocking, and when one considers
that some thousands of ruined families are now our
messmates, the prospect is not much less affecting than
the past. I find myself the guardian of many widows,
and of many orphans, who have hardly a friend left
but myself. I shall first secure a temporary asylum for
them somewhere or other in Italy, and provide for their
present support till Government determines what to do
further ; but so much we owe them, and I shall take it
on myself to make our Government do at least so much
good.

---

[1] ‘Les jours suivants’ (the entry of the army of the Convention),
says Lanfrey in his account of the siege of Toulon (vol. i. p.
42), ‘plusieurs centaines d’habitants qui n’avaient pas cru devoir
s’enfuir, choisis en pleine place publique, sur la simple désignation de
leurs concitoyens, furent mitraillés sans autre forme de procès.’ He
goes on: ‘Fouché, le futur grand dignitaire de l’empire, accouru de
Lyon pour prendre part à sa manière au triomphe de nos armées,
écrivait le 23 décembre à Collot d’Herbois:—“Nous n’avons qu’une
manière de célébrer la victoire. Nous envoyons ce soir 213 rebelles
sous le feu de la foudre. . . . . Adieu, mon ami, les larmes de la joie
coulent de mes yeux; elles inondent mon âme!”’

' I stay in this part of the world till I receive orders to return, which I have desired to have immediately, unless they think my commission may still be useful hereabouts, as Lord Hood thinks it may.

' My favour with the people of Toulon has always been everything that could gratify me, and *now* it is more like worship than any other sentiment. You would not be sorry to see me with my populous family, all grateful for past kindness and looking up to me for future salvation. The little children particularly come as naturally to my knee as my own. God bless you, and preserve you and yours from such widowhood and orphanship as theirs whom I have now married and adopted.'

Writing to Mr. Dundas, he dwells at greater length on the deficiencies of the military force which had rendered a recovery of these losses impossible; and closes his letter with an appeal to the justice of England on behalf of the Toulonese fugitives—the first note of a strain repeated through every phase of his career from Toulon to India, the responsibilities incurred by England towards those she admits to her protection.

Despatch to the Rt. Hon. Henry Dundas.

' "Victory," Bay of Hyères: December 20, 1793.

' . . . . . The state of the garrison, both as to numbers and quality, rendered it utterly impossible to recover the posts. The troops at each, if they had all been steady, would perhaps have been sufficient to

defend them against superior numbers, but regular
reliefs could not be afforded, and the same men were
left long enough exposed to shot and shells with very
little shelter, to fatigue the hardiest of troops, and to
disgust them with the service; but with troops of an
inferior quality, it appeared evident that the enemy
would obtain most of the material posts by mere
cannonade and bombardment, without an assault. If
the state of the garrison did not secure the defence of
the posts, it was still less capable of furnishing such a
considerable force as must have been necessary for going
out to drive the enemy from their conquests; and if
that had been practicable in one place, it was quite
impossible in two. Possibly all those difficulties might
have been struggled with, or it might have been at
least advisable to make the attempt with troops of a
different description: with those who acted with us at
Toulon, everything was difficult, and every difficulty
was insurmountable. This was the true cause of our
failure, and, in justice to the officers who commanded,
as well as to part of the troops composing the garrison,
it is a point that cannot be too well understood or too
much attended to. Whatever the nominal number of
the garrison was, there were not more than twelve
thousand effective men capable of duty and of bearing
arms. Of these there were something less than 2,000
British, and about 1,600 or 1,700 Piedmontese troops;
there were also a few hundred French, of the Royal
Louis, in all, making about 4,000 good soldiers. This
was the whole amount of troops that could be relied on;

for although there were some of the Spanish corps who were not so destitute of every good quality as the rest, yet none could be depended on for obeying orders or pursuing any plan that was resolved on. But the bulk of the troops of that nation really beggars all description; their total want both of courage and discipline rendered them perfectly safe to the enemy, and extremely dangerous to their friends, and make it superfluous to insist on their other qualities, which, however, are not less remarkable or characteristic.[1] The Neapolitans are good-looking men, extremely well appointed, and aiming in their dress at a distant resemblance to Germans. They have, however, one small fault as soldiers, which is an insurmountable dislike to danger, and a determination not to incur it. It is remarkable that this peculiarity is quite as prevalent and as universal among the officers as the men. The instances of this quality that have occurred during their service, but especially on the last days, are hardly credible where they have not been witnessed, but have rendered a Neapolitan quite proverbial at Toulon. The effect of these circumstances was to make it absolutely certain that, whenever a serious attack should be made by the enemy, it would succeed, and be absolutely impossible to recover any advantage that was lost. The

---

[1] At the same time, the pretension of the Spanish commanders to the chief direction of military affairs was a constant source of embarrassment to their allies. In all their conduct they showed much of the spirit of the Spanish historian who began one of his chapters thus: ' The victorious Spaniards ran away.'

Spanish troops not only admitted the enemy at Fort Mulgrave, but when our troops placed themselves between them, the Spaniards, by awkwardness and fright, killed and wounded as many of the English as the French did. The Neapolitans declared their intention of not defending a post at Cape Brun, if they should be attacked; they quitted the Sablette Mississi, the ramparts and gates of the town, and the grosse Tour, contrary to repeated orders; but the best evidence of their unsoldierlike character, both officers and men, was what happened under the orders of their officers on the night of the 17th and the next morning. A regular plan had been resolved on at a General Council of War, and the particular detail of the retreat had been concerted with the general officers of the different nations. The practicability of the retreat, without opposition or loss, seemed in a great measure to depend on the adherence to this plan. Certain posts were to be withdrawn, others to be maintained to the end; and the retreat and embarkation of the troops was to commence at eleven o'clock on the night of the 18th.

'These arrangements were made on the 17th before dinner. Without notice to General Dundas or Gravina, or any other person concerned, the Neapolitan officers packed up their baggage, and crowded the streets and quays with their preparations for departing on the evening of the 17th. Their baggage was actually sent on board, their general, Prince Pignatelli, actually embarked that evening, and the troops, quitting every post where they were stationed, continued their em-

barkation, publicly from the quays of the town, from
the evening of the 17th to the middle of the next day.
Their eagerness, impatience, and panic were so great
on the 18th, in the forenoon, that the embarkation of
the inhabitants was made not only difficult but dangerous, the Neapolitan soldiers firing on those boats which
they could not get admission to.   Many of themselves
were drowned in attempting to crowd into the boats,
and there was a temporary appearance of confusion and
insurrection in the town.   The Neapolitan Admiral
Forteguerri seems to have been in as great haste as the
military.   He sailed long before either the British
or Spanish squadrons, and, without waiting to make
any arrangement either about troops or refugees,
pushed off for Naples, leaving a good number of
Neapolitan troops on board our fleet to find their way
home as well as they can.   The scene of private misery,
beginning with terror and ending with the certainty of
ruin and want, which we have witnessed, and are still
witnessing, cannot be described.   Most of the fugitives
thought themselves too happy to get afloat with the
clothes they had on their backs, and have not saved the
least wreck of their fortunes.   They have not even
changes of linen, and there are whole families that
have not five guineas in the world to-day who were
masters of competent and considerable fortunes a few
days ago.   What is to be done?   My opinion is—and I
trust it is yours—that we have been too closely connected with them in the events which have preceded

this calamity, as well as in the last scene itself, to shake them off at this moment, and leave them to their miserable and certain fate, while we pursue our own better fortunes with indifference.

' I shall promise nothing, however, beyond present support and asylum, until I have your authority to go farther. The returns are not yet completed, but the number will be between 1,500 and 2,000. Some of these have saved a little. Others are young, and can struggle for themselves. Others have friends. The number for whom considerable aid would be wanted will, I hope, not be very great. I have got lists of them expressing their conditions of life, and I have the means of knowing the circumstances of most of them, which I shall make it my business to do, and shall transmit any material information to you. I shall also mention those who are entitled to particular notice, by the employments they have held and the services they have rendered during our government at Toulon. In the meanwhile, I consider it as the most important, if not the last office now belonging to my commission, to attend to this object, for which Lord Hood's and General Dundas's occupation cannot leave them any leisure. The first object will be to get them on shore somewhere, and for that purpose, I fear it may be necessary to negotiate, for there is a general backwardness to admit and shelter the French fugitives everywhere but in England. No plan is yet settled. We think of beginning with Corsica, and trying the ports of the Grand Duke of Tuscany, the Pope, and perhaps Naples.   In the meanwhile they will be placed in one of the Isles of Hyères.'

To Lady Elliot.

' The fleet has remained at anchor in this road ever since the evacuation of Toulon, that is to say since December 19.   There were several reasons for this: one of which is that it is in sight of the harbour of Toulon, and is the most convenient situation for preventing the entrance of ships there who may not have learnt the late change of circumstances.

' Many of our refugees have already been shipped for Leghorn and other ports, but the bulk still remains, and we wait for an answer from Leghorn, to tell us whether they will be received before we send them from thence.   In the meanwhile it is a strange and melancholy scene notwithstanding the light heart and animal spirits of this climate.   There is indeed a great deal of noise and laughing, and playing and all the out-side of mirth, but it is so checkered with tears and melancholy that the gay parts only enhance the sadness of the whole.   It is some sort of gratification to me to be considered the saviour and friend of all these forlorn families and individuals young and old.   I had the pleasure of saving several lives, and of being the sole instrument of any succour or comfort which they have any of them obtained.   There is one little boy, whose father is unfortunately missing, who has taken as kindly to me as if he were my own ; if he misses me longer than usual he says *vienne pas*, provençal for " he don't come." The men apply to me for serious wants ; the women for an additional mattress, a shirt by way of shift, or anything else they may require.

'About twenty of them, men, women, and children, sleep all together on the floor of our cabin. You may conceive the sort of scene with French ease on such subjects, and the English officers wondering and laughing.

' I shall see them safe on shore somehow or other, probably at Leghorn, and find bread for them for the first six weeks : I must then wait for the orders of Government, which I trust will enable me to launch them with something short of absolute despair into the wide world on which they are cast, many of them out of comfortable and pleasant homes of their own.'

' Bay of Hyères.

' Your letter, my dearest Maria, gives me the greatest joy of which I am capable. I am extremely happy that Gilbert continues so excellent ; George to promise so tolerably ; that A. M. missed Papa on November 15 ; that H. talks such good French ; that W. is so like Gilbert. Very full letters are the best substitute for yourself, and best comfort for your absence ; a poor resource when compared with your presence, but inestimable if your absence is necessary.'

' *January* 10.—I go to-day on board the " Lowestoft "

frigate to Corsica, to settle with Paoli the cession of Corsica to England.

'Lord Hood and the fleet will follow in a few days.

'The Grand Duke of Tuscany has agreed to receive the refugees into Port Ferraio in the Island of Elba; and so, having a place to rest the soles of their feet, they may now descend from this ark.

'On the 3rd I went on shore to the Island of Torquerolli, which is very beautiful. On my return I took your picture out of one of my red boxes, and holding it fast in the palm of my hand during the rest of the day, commemorated very devoutly the holy 3rd of January.[1] The weather was not quite so fine seventeen years ago.'

[1] His wedding day.

CHAPTER VI.

THE circumstances under which Corsica became annexed to Great Britain were as follows: The condition
of anarchy prevailing in France under the Convention
having encouraged a large majority of the Corsican
population to rebel against a yoke to which for thirty
years they had been constrained to submit,[1] they, in
the course of 1793, succeeded in shutting up the French
troops in three fortresses, S. Fiorenzo, Bastia, and
Calvi; but not being able to take these strong places
without assistance, they sought it of Lord Hood, at
that time commanding the British fleet off Toulon. In
return for the aid and protection demanded of Great
Britain, General Paoli[2] was authorised by his country-

---

[1] The acquisition of Corsica by France in 1768 had been considered
at the time as a brilliant achievement of the Choiseul Ministry, and
Burke, with characteristic exaggeration, described it in the course of
debate as pregnant with danger to England.

[2] It is well known that when, in 1753, the death of Gaffori had left
the Corsicans without a leader in the resistance they had so long (since
1729) maintained to the Genoese, they gave the command of affairs to
Pasquale Paoli, whose father had taken a prominent part in the war of
independence. The success of Paoli's administration was such that the
Genoese, despairing of being able to retain their hold on Corsica, sold
their right of sovereignty to the French, who immediately took possession of the island. Paoli forced to leave his country, sought an asylum

men to propose the annexation of Corsica to the British Crown, 'in any form and under any conditions His Majesty may think proper to dictate,' due regard being had to the laws and liberties of the Corsicans.

During the siege of Toulon no further enterprises of the nature suggested could possibly have been undertaken by the English commanders, but after the evacuation, it was determined by Lord Hood and Sir Gilbert Elliot, acting as Commissaries Plenipotentiary of the King of Great Britain, that a confidential mission should be sent to Paoli to ascertain from him what would be the probabilities of success before engaging the British forces in an attempt to wrest Corsica from France, and also to ascertain the genuine desires of the Corsicans on the point of annexation to Great Britain.

'In order to obtain from the people of Corsica a confirmation of those engagements which General Paoli had already contracted with His Majesty in their name as well as in his own,' it was suggested by the Com-

in England, and remained there until in 1789 a decree enjoining the recall of the fugitive patriots of Corsica was proclaimed at the instigation of Mirabeau in the French Constituent Assembly. Paoli then went over to France, where Louis XVI. bestowed upon him the rank of Lieut.-General and the military command of Corsica.

On his return to Corsica he was received with enthusiasm by his countrymen, who placed him at the head of the National Guard. From that time, though he continued in constant and confidential communication with the leading members of the Constituent Assembly, he secretly used his influence against the French rule, and after the death of Louis XVI. he took no pains to conceal his sentiments towards the Revolution. In the course of 1793, a price was placed on his head by the Convention, while Corsica declared him generalissimo of her troops and president of her councils. In this capacity he sought the protection of Great Britain.

missioners, in a letter from Lord Hood addressed to Paoli
and delivered by Sir Gilbert Elliot, that a General Consulta [1] should be summoned ; ' this being the only mode
by which the sanction of the people can be regularly obtained.' The mission consisted of Sir Gilbert, of Lieut.-
Colonel Moore, and Major-General Köchler. It was
the business of the officers to inform themselves of the
aspect of the military situation ; the attention of Sir
Gilbert was given to the political question.   The
English mission found Paoli in an old ruinous monastery
at Murato del Nebbio, where he had come with the intention of passing a few days, and where he had been
detained some months by the necessity of his affairs.
He had neither 'books nor papers, nor, indeed, any
conveniences of life near him,' and was apparently no
less ill supplied with its necessaries.

His stock of arms, powder, and lead were all but
exhausted, and his funds and provisions were in an
equally low state.   A sum of 4,000l. was stated by him
to be absolutely required to meet the immediate
exigencies of a body of 2,000 men, and ammunition
and stores of biscuits and cheese were urgently asked
and forthwith supplied.

Sir Gilbert's first conference with Paoli convinced
him that the calling together of the General Assembly

[1] ' This is the name given to their Legislative Assembly, which meets
once every year, and is composed of representatives chosen by the provinces and towns.   It is also assembled on extraordinary emergencies,
on which occasions the number of deputies is greater than in the Annual
Consulta, and it may then be considered as a Convention with full
powers to pledge the national faith and bind the people by its act.'

was, in the existing situation of affairs, utterly impracticable. Every Corsican, not excepting the priests, was in arms. The General was himself within six or seven miles of the enemy, of whom it was necessary that he should not lose sight. To assemble a General Consulta at Cortè under these circumstances was out of the question; and Paoli succeeded in satisfying Sir Gilbert that it was unnecessary for the object for which it had been desired. By the minutes of the General Consulta in May 1793 it was clear that Paoli was invested with sufficient authority to speak for his countrymen. He had already distinctly pledged them and himself by his letter to Lord Hood, and he did not hesitate to assure Sir Gilbert that he would call a General Consulta as soon as it was possible to do so, which would ratify the terms previously agreed on by himself and the English Commissioners. Sir Gilbert adds that his faith in Paoli's sincerity towards his new allies, and in his power over his fellow-citizens was strengthened by evidence obtained during a week's residence in the island of the temper of the people. 'They are, indeed, passionately attached to Paoli, and the violence that was threatened to his person by the French Convention was the signal for the most general and instantaneous rising among the people ever known in that country of general insurrection; but they and he knew too well the impossibility of maintaining the absolute independence of this little state by her own separate resources, and they prefer the powerful protection of Great Britain to that of any other nation in Europe.

' These dispositions have undoubtedly been cultivated by Paoli and those who act under him ; but their
existence cannot be doubted by anyone who has had
an opportunity of witnessing it on the spot.   I do not
believe there was a man, woman, or even a young child,
amongst many thousands whom we saw, that came
within hail of us without calling, " Viva Paoli, e la
natione Inglese ! "   The number and description of persons who had this sentence in their mouths rendered it
impossible that they should have been tutored, or that
it should have been an artificial cry, prepared for the
purpose of deception.   Whenever we talked of making
them independent, they rejected that idea, and said
they would be English.   Leonetti, and indeed Paoli
himself, constantly and unequivocally held the same
language ; not privately to us, but on all occasions in
public and in the hearing of the people.   I am
satisfied that Paoli's sincerity in the design is as little
to be doubted as that of his countrymen.   He is old,
extremely infirm, harassed and fatigued beyond his
strength, and impatient to return from this scene of
labour, perplexity, and danger as soon as he has
brought his country safe into a British haven.

' It has always occurred to me, that Paoli's personal
situation might create a difficulty, and that he might
be unwilling to surrender into foreign hands a
dominion of which he is in possession under circumstances so flattering even to a laudable ambition ; but
he has assured me that he is determined to retire out
of the island, as soon as the public tranquillity and

safety are firmly established under the protection of
the British Government.   The state of his health,
which is visibly impaired, added to his age, convinces
me that he is sincere in these professions.   He has
no family for whom he entertains ambitious views.
Leonetti, who is his nearest relation, is a sister's son.
It is evident Paoli intentionally, and almost affectedly,
avoids every appearance of bringing him forward, and
that he keeps him in the background, even more than
his near connexion with him seems to justify.   On the
other hand, Leonetti, though a worthy man, and much
respected, is by no means qualified, either by attainments
or by natural endowments, to sustain the arduous part
of a successor to Paoli, especially in any attempt that
Corsica might make singly to maintain its independence against the powerful pretenders to the dominion
of that country.

' I had much conversation with Paoli concerning the
form of Government that might best suit the common
interest and views of both countries, and I had the
advantage of consulting several persons of ability and
knowledge, who are conversant with the Corsican laws
and constitutions.   The result appeared to be that the
Government should be placed in the hands of a person
deputed from England, and representing His Majesty,
under the title of Viceroy, Lord-Lieutenant, Governor,
or any other that might be thought proper.   The
military to be entirely under his control, and what is
generally styled the Executive Power to be administered by him in His Majesty's name, with a

negative in all Legislative Acts.   The Constitution of
Corsica to remain in all other respects very much on
its present footing.   I shall not dwell on the particulars of that Constitution, which is described in
several publications.

' The general plan of this Constitution, modified in
such a manner as to adapt it to the necessary super-
intending authority of a British Government, together
with some stipulations for the preservation of their
national laws and religion, and for the security of
property, would satisfy, to its full extent, the desire
entertained by the people for a reasonable and
moderate share of internal liberty, and would, at the
same time, answer every just and rational object of
British Government in that country.'[1]

A lively account of the impressions made on Sir
Gilbert by his first introduction to the people of
Corsica is given in a letter to Lady Elliot.

' I sailed on board the " Lowestoft," with Colonel
Moore and Major Köchler.   We got in two days off the
Isle Roussa, half way between St. Fiorenzo and Calvi.
These two latter places were in the possession of the
French.   L' Isle Roussa belonged to Paoli's party.
We—Colonel Moore, Major Köchler, and I—went ashore
from the frigate, which lay better than a league off, in
a boat with four lads to row us, but without arms.
When we came close to the little harbour we looked out
for the people to see what they were, and when we had

---

[1] Despatch to the Right Hon. H. Dundas.

got nearly in, so as not to be able to get out again, we came in sight of the landing-place, which was close to us, crowded with people, all of them armed, many evidently wearing the French national uniform. At that moment I observed that we all three looked at one another, but we said immediately all together that whatever they were we were in for it now, and ordered the lads to pull in. This uncertainty, however, did not last two minutes, and we quickly found ourselves in the midst of friends. Corsica having been so lately French, the people wore the national uniform there as they do in other parts of France, many of them wearing it out from economy; but it is not the best economy in the world, as by this means many of them have been killed in skirmishes by their own friends. We were conducted on landing to the Commissary's house, where we found Paoli's nephew, Signor Leonetti, who, having served at Gibraltar with a party of Corsican troops, knew Major Köchler, and they fell a-kissing one another as if one of them had been a pretty girl. They set refreshments before us, consisting of almonds, chestnuts, oranges, new cheese, and wine, and the rooms filled with all ranks to see us. This is the universal custom throughout Corsica. Everybody walks in that likes and *cracks* [1] with you, and such celebrities as ourselves are constantly in a crowd and gaped at. This was in the forenoon, and we agreed to spend the day at Leonetti's house, two miles off, and he engaged to accompany us next morning on our journey to Paoli.

---

[1] Gossip: Scotticè, crack.

We set off for Leonetti's house on foot accompanied by
what are called soldiers—that is to say, peasants with
guns. I was very much struck with this first specimen
I had ever seen of a real national militia; the inhabitants of a country carrying arms of their own, for their
own defence and for their own purposes, and every man
entirely after his own fashion. There is no such thing
as uniforms, or regiments, or company, or officers, but
they come from their houses when they choose or when
they are wanted, with a gun slung behind them by a
belt on their shoulder, a cartouche bag buckled before,
and a bag of chestnut flour behind, a pistol hanging
from their girdle on one side, and a dagger stuck into
the pistol belt. They march before and behind and all
round you without any order, just as their fancy directs.
They are a handsome people, about middle size, perfectly well made, active in their bodies, and full of
spirits and vivacity in their characters. Many of them
with dark lively eyes, and some with the finest classical
antique features I ever saw. I speak now of the men,
for although I saw one or two handsome girls, female
beauty appeared to me more rare than that of the other
sex. They wear in general a short jacket like our
shooting jackets, of coarse stuff made of thick wool un-
dyed; waistcoat, breeches, and buff leather gaiters.
This is so general that it may be considered as the
Corsican uniform. Their guns are most slight fowling-
pieces, which they carry from their childhood, and they
are almost without exception excellent shots, hitting a
pigeon on the wing, or a hat in the air with single ball.

Leonetti's house is perched upon a high hill, and is
very significantly called Monticielo. The buildings I
have seen in Corsica are not sumptuous—indeed, just
the contrary. Leonetti's house is the best I have seen,
and it is considerably inferior to the worst of the smallest gentleman's house in Teviotdale. He had a neat
and well-furnished room or two, however, and a most
beautiful view over two miles of country to the sea.

‘ To show the state of life and society in the island,
his drawing-room windows were built about half-way
up in brick, with loop-holes to fire through. We employed the remainder of the day in walking about the
hills.

‘ This country has one of the merits of Minto, that
one can never walk many paces on a level; and my
education at home puts me on a par with the best
Corsican walkers, and gives me a clear superiority over
many of them.

‘ Leonetti is a son of Paoli's sister, and his nearest
heir and relation; his family consist of his wife, a young
son, his wife's mother, and grand-father. The wife
was neither handsome nor clever; her mother is for
my money; she is a clean, clever, brisk, talking old
lady, and presently told me everything in the world
about herself, and asked me everything about me and
mine; and in talking she lays hold of one, sometimes
by the arm, sometimes by the leg. In short, she is
charming! I indulged my growing passion for her by
considering that at her great age there could surely be
no harm in the friendship. I was, therefore, quite

shocked when I heard from Leonetti that this ancient
dame was (will you forgive me for saying it?) four
years younger than my own wife! This seems pretty
general in Corsica. I thought that they all seemed
remarkably old of their age. To comfort you for this
lady's youth, I should tell you that I saw an old man,
with a grey beard and wrinkled face, leaning like an
old stooping man on his firelock, and when Paoli asked
him his age he said it was thirty-eight; no one guesses
within seven or eight years of my age. The next day
we all set out before daylight, very small horses, asses,
and mules being provided for the servants and baggage,
and we on foot. Our journey was really charming.
The country pretty, picturesque, and romantic; the
people not less interesting and pleasing. Our road
was hilly, steep, and rocky, but varied by change of
ground scenery; some valleys were tolerably rich and
very pretty.. Every soul that met us greeted us with
" Viva Paoli, e la natione Inglese!" Our guides and
guards told everyone within reach of their voices who
we were and why we had come. The news ran before
us, and met us again at every village in the shape of
volleys of musketry—fired in our faces as a welcome.
Every soul turned out to see us, and great numbers
always escorted us from one village to the other. We
breakfasted at Palasca and slept at Pietralba. The
houses where we halted belong to persons of good
family, being indeed Paoli's relations; but the houses
were in no respect superior to a tolerable hedge ale-
house, and the way of living and dressing something

on the same scale. They gave us a great profusion of
victuals, ill cooked, with abundance of garlick; the
wine was extremely small, but perfectly pure with an
agreeable flavour. They make very good things with
milk in the way of cheeses, syllabubs, &c., and though
it is all *ewe-milk*, without any of the peculiar flavour;
a light new cheese called *Bruccio* is specially good.
We arrived on the second day at Murato del Nebbio,
where Paoli now resides, passing a very high and very
steep hill called Tenda, and then near Murato getting
down on a little rumbling highland river which is quite
beautiful. This day I fairly out-walked our soldiers,
who, though they could walk longer, could with difficulty keep pace with me, not being used to *put on* as
you do when you are whistled forward.'

The letter ends abruptly here. Sir Gilbert apparently never found time to conclude his narrative, but
in a letter to another correspondent he mentions the
week passed in Corsica as 'the most interesting and
entertaining time he had ever spent; which perhaps
you will not easily suppose, recollecting Paoli only at
the *Tabby* assemblies in London. But in Corsica,
and at this time too, both he and his people were
truly interesting. He is much altered and broken
both in health and looks, and very impatient for the
repose which these events are likely soon to give him.
The people of Corsica are unanimous, I may say, for a
connexion with England.'

The result of the mission was so satisfactory, that

early in January 1794, Lord Hood concluded a convention with Paoli, by which it was agreed that the
British forces should assist the Corsicans in the expulsion of the French from the island, and that its
annexation to Great Britain should be the immediate
consequence.

Pending the success of the military operations no
further diplomatic action could be taken with reference
to the relations of England and Corsica. Sir Gilbert
Elliot, therefore, left the fleet for a while, and proceeded to Florence to treat with the Grand Duke of
Tuscany on behalf of the French refugees from
Toulon, who, having been landed from the fleet at Leghorn, remained there on sufferance until some place
of refuge for them could be agreed upon.   Sir Gilbert's
passage to Leghorn was not unmarked by adventure.
' It is clear to me,' he wrote to Lady Elliot, Leghorn,
January 31, 1794, ' that having, like Macheath, escaped
both rope and gun at Toulon, I am not born to be
hanged; I have now reason to believe I am not intended for drowning, and I flatter myself I may be
reserved for the fate chosen by Harlequin, when
ordered to choose the manner of his departure—death
by old age! The fact is, I was yesterday ship-
wrecked—but nevertheless I arrived at Leghorn without even having wet my feet ! We sailed the day before
yesterday in the "Amphitrite" frigate, with two transports under our convoy, from Porto Ferraio.   Yesterday between 9 and 10 o'clock, just after breakfast,
when we were all very jolly and comfortable in the

cabin, the morning being fine and the breeze fair, we felt the ship strike, without the least previous notice, on a rock. There can be few situations in which the change is either greater or more sudden than between the moment before and after striking on a rock. We were about seven miles from shore, and the rocks were about two fathoms below the surface. In this misfortune there were several fortunate and providential circumstances. The day was before us. The weather extremely moderate. There was little sea. We had been lamenting the delay caused by waiting for the two transports, but, to show how little we knew what was good for us, we should have been very forlorn without them. They were far astern when the accident happened, but in less than half an hour they lay to, at a moderate distance from us, and every expedient having been tried in vain to get the frigate off the rock, we were put on board one of the transports and sent off to Leghorn to procure further assistance as soon as possible. I remained on board two hours after she struck, and she was all that time thumping her bottom against the rock, and when our boat was pushing off, her mainmast did everything but come by the board.'

On the passage to Leghorn the wind became un-favourable, and the transport, a ' mere tub,' could not weather the point next to Leghorn. The master had no knowledge of the coast, both rocky and dangerous, and was at last obliged to drop his anchor within a

cable's length of the sunk rocks. 'If the wind fresh-
ened, we were pretty sure of going on shore with little
hopes of escaping for our lives. A boat from Leghorn
ventured sufficiently near us to tell us we were in a
very dangerous place, and that if it blew harder we
should all be lost, but they would not take any of us
on shore. In this critical situation the day passed.
Towards sunset we were relieved from it by a small
row-boat belonging to the Health Office, in which we [1]
embarked, and after two hours' tossing on a high sea
in pitch darkness were safely landed at Leghorn.
Shortly afterwards we found ourselves in a box at the
opera surrounded by painted ladies, men in dominos,
and all sorts of luxury and magnificence. It is the
fashion to receive visits and transact business at the
opera.[2] The Consul was in Lady Harvey's box. We
literally walked out of our wreck into this scene of
splendour and gaiety. It was more like enchantment
than is generally found *before* the curtain.

'I could not but reflect on the vicissitudes of human
affairs! The day before yesterday I was on board the
"Victory," and might almost have commanded that
three decker. The same day I had a frigate to attend
me. Next morning I am fortunate in having a trans-

---

[1] Sir Gilbert, with two English and two French officers.

[2] From Florence, a few days later, Sir Gilbert wrote: 'I was at the
opera with a bit of London—the Websters, Lord Granville Leveson, the
Herveys. At the opera, ladies of fashion quit their boxes and stroll
masked into the pit, and talk to every man that pleases them, stranger
or not. One of the most agreeable of the Italian ladies is Madame
d'Albany, the Pretender's widow—very sensible but plain.'

port to take shelter in. That evening I was reduced to a row-boat, and from thence jumped up again into My Excellency with a squadron to attend me !'

In a subsequent letter Sir Gilbert says : 'I am very happy that Captain Hood of the " Amphitrite," and all his officers, have been acquitted by their court-martial for the loss of the frigate. It appeared that the rocks on which we struck were not laid down in any chart. Lord Hood says to me in his letter, " that it was providential the weather was good, for otherwise we must all have perished." '

The disposal of his flock of fugitives was a task of no small difficulty. The protection extended to them by the British Government at a time when, in Sir Gilbert's own words, 'a most savage spirit had gone forth against the unhappy French,' was creditable to the national character—as it was creditable to Sir Gilbert that no amount of ill will on the part of those to whom his representations were made, and no amount of unreasonableness on the part of those in whose interest he worked, caused the slightest relaxation in his efforts to find a settlement for these unhappy people.

'I am sorry to observe,' he wrote in a despatch to the Rt. Hon. Henry Dundas, Leghorn, February 21, 1794, 'that the expense already incurred in the relief of the Toulonese is very considerable;[1] it has hitherto been unavoidable, and, indeed, I cannot yet see any means of preventing the continuance of a very heavy

---

[1] The expense of the refugees at that time is stated by Sir G. as 150*l.* per day.

charge for some time to come, without abandoning these helpless people to a fate which they have no possible means of averting by any exertions of their own. They are hunted from place to place, without the possibility of settling anywhere, and turning their talents or their industry to account ; and indeed wherever I have been, I have found the prejudice of the people, with too much countenance from the better sort, set so strongly against everything that bears the French name, that they are excluded from the usual resources of industry, and are in effect forbid to earn their bread.'

About 4,000 had taken refuge on board the English fleet, on December 19. Of these, 2,000 had been crowded into the town of Porto Ferraio in Elba, granted to them as an asylum by the Grand Duke of Tuscany ; a few hundred more had been admitted into Leghorn ; but the remainder were not permitted to land, and it was considered as an indulgence that the vessels themselves were allowed to remain in the mole, instead of being sent to Porto Ferraio, 'where there was not room for a man more.' On the very day of Sir Gilbert's arrival at Florence an order was published for the departure from Tuscany, within a month, of all French who had not come there before the month of May, 1793.

The Courts of Rome and Sardinia, and the Republic of Lucca, evinced no less unfavourable dispositions ; but Sir Gilbert's representations gradually produced a better state of feeling, and the business was finally arranged by the consent of the Grand Duke of Tuscany and of the King of Sardinia to designate certain places within their territories for the reception of the refugees.[1] At a somewhat later period the Court of Rome also consented to receive a limited number in the Roman territory, but not until the negotiation had well-nigh come to an untimely end, in consequence of certain pretensions on the part of the Pope which Sir Gilbert was not able to admit.

As no official intercourse existed between the Courts of St. James's and of Rome, Sir Gilbert had addressed himself to Mr. Hippesley,[2] a personal friend of his own, who resided at Rome and was believed to have some influence there, entreating him to obtain from the compassion of the Papal Court an asylum for a small number of the Toulonese. The answer, 'not otherwise unfavourable,' came 'clogged with the condition' that Sir Gilbert's demand should be officially made, subject to the subsequent approval of his Government. With such a condition it was impossible for him to comply ; and he therefore withdrew his application, with an expression of regret that no other course was open to him, 'since this little business of charity had become

---

[1] 'The Republic of Lucca refuses to have anything to do with the French. The King of Sardinia consents to receive 800 to 1000 in the province of Oneglia, on the condition of our importing grain and some other articles of provision for them. The island of Sardinia is refused on account of the animosity which has prevailed there against the French of all descriptions since the expedition undertaken last year by France against that island. Tuscany names four small towns in her dominions for the reception of the refugees, on condition that they are finally removed from Tuscany after a few weeks.'

[2] Afterwards Sir John Hippesley.

entangled with considerations of a nature so distinct,
and at the same time so delicate and important,' that
he had neither 'skill to untie the knot nor power to
cut it.' 'You will be glad to hear,' he says in closing
his letter, 'that by the opportunities I have lately had
of distributing considerable numbers in Piedmont, and
dispersing others in different ways, I shall avoid any
immediate distress by this disappointment. If, however, it were possible to separate this one Christian and
charitable work from other temporal and spiritual
objects, and to permit only 400 or 500 families to
breathe inoffensively in the territory of the Roman
State, my present views and wishes will be answered to
their fullest extent.' 'The hard-heartedness shown in
all quarters to these poor people is little to the credit
of Adam's posterity.'

Not long afterwards, the desired asylum was conceded.
Next to the difficulty of finding a settlement on terra
firma for the refugees, came that of persuading them to
submit to their miserable destinies.

To Lady Elliot.

'Leghorn: February 21, 1794.

'You have no conception of the life I lead here. I
never was so worked or worried, or so fairly tired out,
in my life. The French come before I am up, and
from that time till dinner I have on most days
not one instant's release from the most vexatious and
harassing of all business, the importunities of the
unreasonable, and, what is much worse, the reasonable

prayers and tears of the unhappy, to whom I can give nothing like reasonable comfort.

'The same unhappy story, repeated almost in the same words by them all; everyone convinced that his own case was the only one that deserved attention, and not one in twenty in which it was possible for me to give any relief or comfort. I have stood with my back against a table between the windows *eight hours* in this employment. And it was by absolute violence that the door was ever defended long enough to let me write my despatches or even a letter to you. . . .'

'*March* 4.—It has been as much, or rather perhaps more, than I have been able to do to keep my humour as sweet as it ought in such a case; and when I have got to the end of a day without a hasty answer or anything like harshness to any of them, I always congratulate myself, as I have several times been very sorry for the contrary; but by this difficulty you may judge of the quantity as well as of the kind of work I have had to do.[1]

---

[1]
'Tunbridge Wells: March 31.

'I received your letter of the 4th yesterday. I am heartily glad you are removed from so much plague and tiresome business. I can conceive nothing more wearing than the continued demands of those whom you cannot relieve, and the number of unreasonable characters which must exist everywhere in such a crowd, much more so among a nation who never take the trouble of reflecting; even here, amongst my small acquaintance, I find one and all of a mind that they have a *right*, whenever the war ceases, to a restoration of all their property and effects. They will not listen to the *impossibility* of its taking place, or the regaining that which is destroyed or subdivided, but go on saying it is but just and fair. I fear that great troubles are in store for that devoted nation, even after the foreign wars cease, and the continuation of civil discord will be as long as the lives of the present generation.'—*Lady Elliot to Sir Gilbert.*

'We have got off near a thousand of the lowest people to Oneglia and Leghorn.'

Six weeks passed in harassing occupation before the business was concluded, and it was with a feeling of intense relief that Sir Gilbert found himself restored to tranquillity and leisure on board of the 'Britannia,' the flag ship of Admiral Hotham, appointed to carry him to the fleet off Corsica. 'Nothing can be more agreeable than our *manière d'être* on board this ship. We are afloat and sailing, which I am still enough of a big boy to be tickled with; there is breeze enough, with a smooth sea, to give us all the appearance of life and motion without the possibility of a qualm ; we have sunshine by day, and a clear starlight sky with a young moon at night. If I go on I shall make a convert of you, and you will say, " Almost persuadest thou me to be a sailor." I have certainly seen the sea in its holiday wear by coming to the Mediterranean ; but I have observed so much good in a sailor's life, and I think the general character and dispositions of the Navy so pleasant, as well as their way of living together, that my former repugnance to the profession (for one of our boys) is much diminished.'

'The best of men have ever loved repose ;
They hate to mingle in the filthy fray,
Where the soul sours, and gradual rancour grows
Imbitter'd more from peevish day to day.'

So felt Sir Gilbert—but at this period of his life it

was more often his fate to fish in troubled waters than to float on smooth ones.

On his return to the fleet, he found that a considerable change for the worse had taken place in the relations of the naval and military commanders. San Fiorenzo having been taken on February 17, the French were reduced to their last stronghold, the town and fortress of Bastia; this, the most important of their positions, Lord Hood now desired to attack with the combined naval and military forces. General Dundas, however, considered the plan proposed to him by Lord Hood to be impracticable, and refused his co-operation unless he should be previously reinforced to the amount of 2,000 men from Gibraltar.

To Lady Elliot.

'St. Fiorenzo: March 13, 1794.

' A considerable change has taken place here. Lord Hood and General Dundas never were on a cordial footing. Their differences have come to a head since their arrival in Corsica, and the result is that General Dundas has retired. He sailed yesterday.'

' *March* 14.—Lord Hood's difference with General Dundas was founded on an original disinclination to each other, or dissimilarity of character; and neither of them has ever appeared to me disposed to avoid the consequences of this situation by laying any restraint on his own humour, or by endeavouring to make the best of the other. The breach has therefore gradually widened. One annoyance has been the want of communication and of consultation, and the service has undoubtedly suffered . . . The true cause of the final rupture is that Lord Hood is extremely sanguine and enterprising, and General Dundas has the opposite qualities of caution and backwardness.   He seems always ready to throw the game up instead of playing it, and has not vigour and animation enough for an active command.   Lord Hood may possibly err on the other side ; may either not see difficulties, or may underrate them ; but it seems to me that this is a fault on the right side in war, where activity and enterprise are generally so well seconded by the fears of the enemy, as to succeed beyond a reasonable calculation. Nay, an attempt will often succeed because it is not reasonable.   I have learnt that fear is a more general and governing principle than I knew before.   One constant effect of it is to diminish your own advantages and to magnify those of the enemy ; it is like a fog, which makes one shrink into oneself and makes things at a distance loom larger than the truth.   If military operations were more frequently calculated on the fears of the enemy instead of being directed by our own, I am convinced they would oftener succeed.

' It was next thing to violence which made General Dundas attempt anything here, as it was the extraordinary exertion of the Navy which enabled him to succeed.   Having taken San Fiorenzo, he now refuses to attempt Bastia, which he says is a wild and visionary scheme, with our present force.   Lord Hood offers to take the place in three weeks.   It was, in fact,

on this point that the difference between them has
proceeded to extremities.'

The senior officer who, on the retirement of General
Dundas, became by accident Commander-in-chief, was
totally unequal to the position; until he could be
superseded from home, it was vain to attempt any
military operations, and thus five or six weeks of the
best season were lost, while the French had just so
much more time to strengthen their works. The
second in command, Colonel Moore,[1] a ' young enterprising man,' might, it was thought, if left to himself,
have done his work well.

' I am extremely hurt,' wrote Sir Gilbert, ' at the
idea of stopping short and giving up the point in
Corsica, after undertaking it. Coming immediately
after the evacuation of Toulon, and exposing our
Corsican friends to a similar fate with the Toulonese,
our characters will suffer deeply in a military and
every other way.'

' St. Fiorenzo: March 28, 1794.[2]

' I am extremely impatient of this long inaction,
and am less able on that account to enjoy the pleasant-
ness of the country and climate. I divide my time
between the fleet and the army, the " Victory," with
which I have most to do, being in Mortella Bay,
between three or four miles from the town. Mortella
Bay means Myrtle Bay, and is no doubt so called from
the quantity of myrtle which grows round it; as in

---

[1] Afterwards Sir John Moore.
[2] To Lady Elliot.

Teviotdale we should speak of Broom House or Ferny
Lee; and in this country the weeds are myrtle and
arbutus, and the fields are covered with a hyacinth of
which the stalk is often three feet high and is as strong
as a stick. The most prevalent plant of all is a heath
growing to the size of a shrub, and with flowers which
smell like almond blossoms. Besides the general
beauty of hill and dale, there is a great deal of bold
picturesque scenery, occasioned by the craggy character of the high grounds. Colonel Moore's camp is
in a very picturesque situation; his bed consists of
some loose straw covered with meadow hay; and there
he has slept in his clothes ever since our arrival at
San Fiorenzo, generally making a tour of a mile or
two himself in the course of the night; he is in love
with his profession, and as all the services one renders
to a mistress are pleasant, he enjoys all discomforts.
What I have seen of the Army does not reconcile me
to the profession, and I should always feel that Gilbert
was thrown away upon it. It would be a terrible
waste of so many good qualities. On the whole I like
the sea better. The character of the profession is infinitely more manly. They are full of life and action,
while on shore it is all high lounge and still life.

'The country is beautiful. I went the other day to
see the road by which they carried cannon to the top
of a high hill, in order to attack the French battery
on the heights of Fornalli. General Dundas, and
indeed many other people, said it was childish stuff
to talk of getting cannon there—it actually seems im-

possible. But Captain Cook of the Navy, with 200 seamen, carried up four 18-pounders and two mortars, and opened the battery in two days; if this had not been done, we should not have taken San Fiorenzo. The distance about a mile, the ground very steep and rough, considerably steeper than the green face of the craigs[1] leading to the castle from the new strip near the mill, and it is infinitely rougher with rocks and underwood. They fastened great straps round the rocks, and then fastened to the straps the largest and most powerful purchases or pullies and tackle that are used on board a man-of-war. The cannon was placed on a sledge at one end of the tackle, the men walked down hill with the other end of the tackle. The surprise of our friends the Corsicans and our enemies the French was equal on this occasion. The battery played four days on the French redoubt on the heights of Fornalli before it was stormed; during this time Captain Cook and the seamen and several officers and soldiers slept in holes in the rocks.'

The period of ' inaction' was drawing to a close. The new Commander-in-chief, General Stuart, appointed to succeed General Dundas, arrived off San Fiorenzo in the last days of March; and the first impression made by him on those with whom he was sent to co-operate being highly favourable, for once the right man was believed to be in the right place. In council, however, he took the same view as his predecessor of the diffi-

[1] The Minto Crags.

culties attending an attack on Bastia ; and the result of this difference of opinion between the chiefs of the two services was the determination taken by Lord Hood to attack Bastia at all risks with his naval force alone. The command of the seamen employed in the batteries was given to Nelson.'[1]

Sir Gilbert's next letter to Lady Elliot is dated from the ' Victory' off Bastia.

' April 7, 1794.

' How slender is the chance of my seeing you before winter. When I consider how life is fleeting, and what portions are cutting from our loaf that we shall neither eat nor have ; and when I consider the children's childhood, which is, in fact, the parent's share of them, is wearing away without any enjoyment of them, I get very low.

' I am very fond of Corsica ; I mean of its cause and interests ; and I have a real ambition to be the founder of what I consider as likely to prove its future

---

[1] Nelson was profoundly convinced of the importance of Corsica at this period to Great Britain, and not only strongly urged on Lord Hood the course which was finally adopted, but actually concealed from his chief the disparity of the forces which would be opposed to each other. ' When I reflect that I was the cause of re-attacking Bastia after our *wise* generals gave it over from not knowing the force, fancying it over 2,000 men ; that it was I who landing joined the Corsicans, and only with my ship's party of marines drove the French under the walls of Bastia ; that it was I who, knowing the force in Bastia to be upwards of 4,000 men. as I have now only ventured to tell Lord Hood, landed with only 1,200 men, and kept the secret till within this week past ; what I must have felt during the siege may be easily conceived.'—*Lord Nelson to William Suckling, Esq.*, February 7, 1795. *Despatches of Lord Nelson.* See also a curious letter from Lord Hood to General Dundas, given in a note to p. 358 of vol. i. of *Nelson's Despatches*.

happiness. My wish, therefore, would be to settle, as representing Great Britain, our connection with Corsica; to be the first representative of British Government there; to prepare its new Constitution; to see the machine fairly launched and floating with a favourable breeze, and then to resign the helm. This operation cannot be completed in a month or a quarter of a year, but it will not run beyond next winter at furthest, and probably less time will do.

'We sailed from San Fiorenzo on the first of this month, and arrived off Bastia next morning. I went immediately on shore with Col. Villettes, who commands our little army, to reconnoitre. We ascended to the post intended to be occupied by our troops, and looked down on Bastia till our mouths watered. It is a handsome-looking town, aud the country round it is rich and picturesque. In the meanwhile the fleet passed the town and anchored to the southward; when we put off from the shore to rejoin the fleet, we had the honour of receiving the first fire from the enemy, who did not, however, reach us. The next day I returned on shore with Lord Hood, and his barge being distinguished by an awning, was saluted with a dozen of shot which passed all round us, but did not hit. Lord Hood climbed up the hills like a boy, reconnoitred the ground on which our batteries are to be raised, and received a body of 1,400 Corsicans with whom he was delighted. His eagerness for the success of this enterprise is very honourable to him, but is really amusing. The generals, like peaceable gentlefolks, decided that nothing could

be done without our *whole force* against Bastia.[1]   That
being settled after a long and sharp paper war, Lord
Hood, in his way, out of which nothing ever diverts
him, resolved to take Bastia with *half* our force, having
fortunately a right to dispose of it since they are marines
and serve on board ship.   I have been all along scanda-
lized by the inaction of the troops and want of spirit
of the commanders, and desired Lord Hood's leave to
accompany him. Here we are at work, and I trust likely
to prosper.   The troops landed to the number of 1,100
besides seamen, the day after Lord Hood was on shore.
You cannot conceive the spirits of the men and the
ardour and enthusiasm of the officers, high and low, in
this affair ; and the desire to carry our point without
the help of those who are left doing nothing at San
Fiorenzo is so strong that I am sure the sight of our
friends on the top of the hills between the place and
Bastia would alarm our army much more than double
the number of enemies.

' The batteries are nearly ready to open.   They will
play upon the town with bombs and four-and-twenty
pounders the day after to-morrow.   The poor women
and children !   That is a shocking part of these opera-

[1] The disagreements between the two branches of the service gave
great dissatisfaction at home, and ultimately led to the supercession
of Lord Hood; a step much regretted by Sir Gilbert and by the
officers of the fleet, and more especially by Nelson. Intemperance
of language was all the fault *they* recognised in their late chief, and
when he was replaced by Admiral Hotham, Nelson wrote to Sir Gilbert
that the loss of Lord Hood was a calamity to the service. Admiral
Hotham was a good sailor and a thorough gentleman, but his days for
an active post were over.

tions; but I trust they will have influence enough to bring about a surrender, and that the population will be more frightened than hurt.'

While the siege of Bastia was in progress, Sir Gilbert received despatches from England approving in flattering terms of his share in all the transactions which had taken place with regard to Corsica. In reply to the proposal of annexation of Corsica to Great Britain, Mr. Dundas signified the willingness of the King to enter into the terms 'of General Paoli and the other Corsican leaders,' upon certain conditions. One of these was that the supreme executive power, with the command of the military, and with a veto upon all Legislative Acts, should be invested in a governor to be appointed by the King, under any title agreeable to the Corsicans. With regard to the present principles on which the Constitution was to be founded, Mr. Dundas left the most ample powers to Sir Gilbert.[1]

The despatches contained no intimation as to the person likely to be selected to represent the King in Corsica, but desired Sir Gilbert to undertake a new commission to the courts of Italy. ' Nothing,' he wrote, ' can be more flattering than the style and matter of all these despatches, but the Italian Commission throws a great weight of business on my shoulders.' [2]

The idea of entrusting Sir Gilbert with this new Commission, which was one of considerable importance, ' extending to a general superintendence of political

---

[1] Despatch from the Rt. Hon. H. Dundas to Sir G. E., March 31, 1794.
[2] Sir G. E. to Lady E., ' Victory,' off Bastia, April 7, 1794.

affairs in the Mediterranean,'[1] appears to have originated in the very favourable impression produced on the
English Ministers, and especially on Lord Grenville,
by Sir Gilbert's correspondence from Florence. During
his stay there he had made it his business to ascertain,
as far as was possible, the views of the Italian Courts on
the general conduct of the war. A letter, marked
private, to Mr. Dundas had given the result of his observations.

To the Rt. Hon. H. Dundas.

'Leghorn : February 22, 1794.

' I have no opportunity of knowing what steps are
actually taking or taken in the affairs of Italy by those
of the Allies who are most interested in its safety.
But I flatter myself, from many things I hear, that the
importance of this subject is felt, and that adequate
preparation is making.

' I fear only that greatest danger of all human affairs
of being a little too late, especially where the Court of
Vienna is concerned. It used to be said of the old
French Cabinet, that the *clock* of Versailles was always
a *week too slow*.

' Whatever faults the present clock at Paris may
have, slowness is not one of them, and it is the more
necessary to put all others a little forward.

' I have often thought, and I know it is the opinion
of much abler men, that some permanent league of the
Italian States for their mutual defence would be a great

---

[1] ' I understand,' wrote Lady Elliot, ' that you are to be Mentor of the
Foreign Ministers in Italy.'

security, not only to that country itself, but to the peace of Europe. The want of it is particularly perceptible at this time. There is not a government in Italy which is not alarmed, both at the idea of the invasion of its territory, and the disturbance of its internal tranquillity; yet there are hardly any of them prepared, or even disposed, to take a step in their defence. This would not be the case if there had previously existed a systematic, and established provision for this danger, which would have been prepared at once for action, and would have superseded all the littlenesses in the policy and politics of these little courts.

'Tuscany appears to be a strong instance of Italian weakness. The country is extremely rich and very populous. The Government is satisfied that the entry of the French into Italy would both ruin and destroy the country and overthrow the Government, but they seem determined to seek their safety in no other measure than the most abject prostration before the enemy, knowing perfectly that prostration would not protect them while the plunder of their towns and churches affords so many provocations to such an enemy. I think it possible, that if some systematic confederacy in Italy were thought a desirable thing, at least for the present occasion, it might be brought about, and if we are settled in Corsica, I should hope still more from the influence of Great Britain in treating the affair. I throw this idea out merely for your consideration, without presuming to recommend it positively, although I confess it has been lately pretty much on my mind.'

In one of his despatches on the same subject he wrote : 'A number of small states can only be preserved from the aggression of a great Power by federation and faith in the power and honesty of their supports.' To create such a faith in Great Britain, by unfailing demonstration of her ' power to do, and will to dare,' was the object of unceasing efforts on his part during his connection with Corsica and the Italian States.

The announcement of his new powers was made to Sir Gilbert by Lord Grenville, who ' concurred entirely in the views entertained by him on the affairs of Italy,' and in very gratifying terms confided to him the commission ' to promote the great object H. M. has in view of confederating the Italian Powers in a permanent system of general defence.' In virtue of this appointment Sir Gilbert returned to Italy in the course of April, and remained there until the fall of Bastia placed Corsica in the hands of the English.

The irruption of the French into the Genoese territory rendered urgent the necessity for some decisive action on the part of the Italian Governments, and especially on that of the Archduke of Milan, with whom rested the defence of the frontier of Italy and the duty of opposing the progress of the French in Piedmont. Additional powers had been vested in the Archduke Albert by the Emperor, and Milan was thenceforth the ' centre of Italian affairs.' To Milan therefore went Sir Gilbert. Nothing could be more courteous than his reception. The Archduchess gratified his national feelings by carrying His

Majesty's likeness on her fan; the Archduke was cordial in his acceptance on the Emperor's part of a plan for general defence among the Italian States, and for cooperation with Sardinia for her defence; but when the time came for resolving generalities into particulars, there was an evident lack of vigour.

'The Archduke is a clever man, with great application and considerable zeal, but hampered in action by the jealous control of the Austrian Government. If he must send to Brussels or Vienna on every occasion, with an enemy who would be guillotined for waiting for instructions, the match is not equal. There is a want of proper authority and want of proper force. If the Emperor could be persuaded to invest the Archduke with these necessary means of action he might do much,'—but jealousy and distrust at the root of Austrian policy were paralysing all action, and in the days of the Archduke Albert as in those of Maximilian, the Cabinet of Vienna played the game of the enemy. Nor was the recipient of their own delegated authority the only object of jealousy, for Sir Gilbert observed that there was obviously no disinclination on the part of the Archduke to let Sardinia profit by the rude lessons of experience before coming to her aid.

In answer to a distinct question, the Archduke admitted that Piedmont could not defend itself, and the Austrian troops would be obliged to advance when the enemy came before Coni. He admitted the desperate situation of Piedmont and the fatal consequences to the rest of Italy which must follow the loss of that country, ' but seemed contented with exculpating himself and charging the King of Sardinia.' Sir Gilbert left Milan with a strong impression that nothing would be done in that quarter decisive enough to avert the disasters impending over Italy.

From Tuscany he wrote in a private letter, ' the temper of this people is a barometer by which we may learn the progress of the French. The antique virtues are scarce in Cabinets now-a-days. I observe that courage and danger are apt enough to be in inverse ratio, or, like the inhabitants of the Dutch weather-houses, seldom to be at home together. Courage is the lady who comes abroad in fine weather and stays at home when it is foul.'

He did not visit Rome or Naples ; but from the two purely Italian Powers there was even less to be hoped than from the semi-Austrian states. In Southern Italy there was neither commerce, cultivation, nor industry ; and the governments of Rome and Naples confined their internal administration to police regulations which nobody regarded. It was said that the King of Naples lost annually 6,000 subjects by assassination ;[1] and when it was represented to him that nothing short of capital punishment inflicted on convicted assassins would check these wholesale murders, he replied that

[1] Lady Hamilton told Lady Malmesbury at Naples in 1792 that eighteen murderers had lived in Sir W. Hamilton's courtyard one spring, till the King obtained his leave to take them up, and the battle between them and the Sbirris lasted three hours in Lady Hamilton's hearing. Two were killed before they could take the rest.

in that case he should lose 12,000 instead of 6,000.
A fair idea of the impression made on an intelligent
observer by the condition of the Papal States, when
the Pope was not a prisoner in the Vatican, and before
the armies of France had desecrated the patrimony of
St. Peter, may be obtained from the following passage
in a letter written from Rome at a somewhat later
date :—

'The Pope's state seems as near extinction as himself. Nothing but his power and the people's bigotry
could keep off a revolution for four and twenty hours.
The country is remarkably fine and fit for cultivation,
and yet it is a desert from the unjust and absurd restrictions under which the finances labour. There is
nothing to be seen between the rank of princes and
shoemakers, and the houses are palaces or hovels.
There is no trade of any sort, and no money; one pays
18 per cent. for gold and silver, and nobody will take
paper unless in paying large sums. The Pope, however, is going on with great additions to the Vatican:
he has already added two large rooms full of statues.
One of the very striking features of this town is the
total stillness and tranquillity. In fact there is nothing
done, and, what seems more strange, there is nothing
said, which is unusual in Italy.'[1]

The chief difficulty in the way of those who endeavoured to rally the Italian Powers in their own de-

[1] Lady Elliot to Sir Gilbert. Rome: August, 1795.

fence, consisted in the absence of a middle class from
which might have been hoped more energy and activity
than existed among 'princes,' more patriotism and
enlightenment than could be found among 'shoemakers;' nor had the Italians an aristocracy in the
English sense. The difference between the governing
class in England and the selfish and dissolute nobilitv
of Italy was the difference between a head and a wig.
Pleasant manners, a certain culture and refinement—
curls in the wig—they had, but brain-power, force of
character, highest products of active public life, were
wanting.

After six weeks spent in Italy, Sir Gilbert came to
the general conclusion that ' the great difficulty in the
scheme of federation consists in the character of the
men who hold the first rank in Italy. Accustomed to
rule by feeling their way, they shrink from the responsibility of adopting a bold and original policy. Skilful
on small occasions, they are helpless on great ones.
Their experience in administration, and their natural
shrewdness, enable them to write admirable despatches,
but when it comes to action their disposition is to tem-
porise and do nothing.'

He was all the more convinced by these observations
of the importance of Corsica to England, as giving her
a position in the Mediterranean whence she might by
her fleets encourage and protect those in much need of
support, and might by her counsels accustom them
to larger and more masculine views of policy than
they were inclined to adopt. ' The infinite smallness

and tenuity of Italian politics,' he wrote, 'from one end of the boot to the other, is indeed irksome to our gross eyes, and makes them uncomfortable to handle with our coarse fingers.'

Though the Papal Court was not one of those to which he was, or could be, accredited, direct intercourse with it being contrary to law, communications were still carried on with it indirectly through the medium of Mr. Hippesley, with how much reserve on Sir Gilbert's part may be gathered from a sentence in one of his despatches. 'A degree of circumspection is necessary in dealing with that Court that would be superfluous elsewhere. I have had occasion to observe that her policy consists in a diligent collection and skilful application of small materials to great ends.'

One such 'occasion' was doubtless that of the correspondence already referred to, which was only dropped for a time after Sir Gilbert's refusal to enter on an official intercourse with Rome, and was reopened by a long memorandum from Mr. Hippesley. In this it was stated that a free intercourse was already established between the two Governments, and in proof of it, the transactions of victualling agents and other proceedings of a similar nature were cited. The memorandum also laid great stress on the reception given in England to Monsignor Erskine, who had gone there ostensibly on business of his own, but who in fact had been sent by the Pope to sound the sentiments of the English Government and people on the point it was desired to compass. Sir Gilbert was assured that

whatever hesitation might exist as to form, the substance
of the Pope's proposal was already granted, materials
for this part of the argument being found in the ordinary courtesies shown by English statesmen to distinguished members of foreign Courts.

A dinner party at Mr. Pitt's when a foreign minister
happened to be in company, an interview with Lord
Grenville at the office instead of at his private residence, a few gracious words uttered by the King, an
absence of any display of ill-will by the mob—were
circumstances enumerated as indicating the favourable
disposition of England.   To this paper Sir Gilbert
replied with a degree of bluntness that stamped the
communication as informal.

'I really cannot help marvelling to see sensible men,
as you, Erskine, and I may probably add the Pope and
the Cardinal Secretary of State are, amusing yourselves
with all the little, strange, oblique, unmeaning odds
and ends of conversations and occurrences, as grave indications of success in your object.   The others, having
never known any other than Italian ways of negotiating
and judging, have not had time to learn the English
method, and you, my dear Hippesley, must have forgotten it, if you suppose that all these insignificances
signify anything in England.

' . . .   Erskine's conversations would not be much
sought after in London if they were understood to be
so many traps to catch unguarded words, and then put
them to the torture of some purpose that is not expressed.   Of the same kidney are many and many col-

lections of the small ware that you have taken the un-accountable trouble of raking together on this subject. If on a direct proposition for that purpose the Government should be of opinion in England that it is advisable to open a communication with Rome they will do so; but I know enough of the English way of thinking to be quite sure that they will not be drawn a single step forward by all the invisible wires which you are all hooking on to their sleeves.'

In a despatch to the Duke of Portland, after describing at great length the pressure which had been put on himself and on other diplomatic agents of England to obtain the desired result, he sums up the question as follows:

'With regard to the question of opening with Rome an official intercourse, it is impossible to consider it simply, that is to say, as uncombined with many extrinsic considerations. It is undoubtedly an absurd thing in itself, and may perhaps be classed among those barbarisms yet remaining in our law, and which have survived their original cause and motive, that there should be no legal way of communicating on our common affairs with the sovereign of Rome, who, as a temporal Prince, is one of the most respectable Powers in Italy. It is difficult when the question is stated in this way, not to feel one's liberality rise, and not to desire that this antiquated blemish should be effaced from our statutes.

'On the other hand, we state the case imperfectly when we call the Pope a temporal prince, if we do

not at the same time acknowledge that he is a great
spiritual Power, who treats our emancipation from his
authority in that character as an usurpation, retaining
claims and pretensions to the recovery of his lost power
in Protestant countries, and never for an instant losing
sight of that object.   We cannot forget, also, that this
spiritual Power, like all spirit of which we have any
experience, is clothed however in secular flesh ; and
that the spirit and flesh are so intimately blended, and
in such close fellowship, alliance and confederacy, that
they cannot be truly or prudently seen or considered
apart; that the Pope has therefore uniformly, through
all history, down to the present year, employed his
spiritual arms in the conquest of temporal dominion,
authority, or advantage of one sort or other; so that his
Holiness is substantially, in all cases and in every
country, what he is literally in Corsica, both Pope and
Pretender.   Having no temporal force, the Pope is not
a formidable pretender when he is excluded from the
use of other weapons, but when he has an opportunity
of using those arms in which he is most skilful, he is not
a contemptible adversary.   It may therefore be a matter
of reasonable hesitation, whether to place him in a situation, from which we have found him excluded by no act
of ours, but in which, when he is admitted to it, he will
have the opportunity, and he cannot be supposed to
want inclination, to intrigue in many ways that we
do not understand, for many objects which we are not
aware of.   It is the nature of man, how much more of
Popes, to consider a concession or acquisition, no

matter how great, as no more than the step of a ladder, from which to raise the other foot to the next round, and the Pope's ladder, like Jacob's, has its top hidden in the clouds :

> All the rounds, like Jacob's ladder, rise ;
> The lowest hid in earth, the topmost in the skies.'

' On the whole, although the renewal of a free intercourse with Rome must fall in with the general disposition and feeling of every liberal man ; and although, knowing the prodigious structure already designed by the Roman architects, and which they hope to raise on this slender foundation, I am not afraid that this new Babel will ever attain any great elevation ; yet on the whole matter, as we propose to gain nothing and they propose that we should lose much, I am inclined to think, that we may as well avail ourselves of our ancestors' barbarity, and keep well while we are so.'

CHAPTER VII.

THE news of the surrender of Bastia, and of the convocation of the General Assembly of the Island of Corsica at Cortè for June 1, reached Sir Gilbert at Florence towards the end of May, and recalled him to Corsica.[1]

On May 30th we find him writing from Bastia to Lady Elliot: 'The expedition against Calvi will take place in a few days. This garrison was very strong in numbers. There remained at the surrender about 3,500, all regular troops, and much finer men, and better clothed, and more like soldiers than I liked to see them. They were attacked by only 1,100 troops of whom a great proportion were marines, and 200 or 300 seamen, and the success of this business is very favourable to those who were engaged in it. The blockade of the port was undoubtedly the chief means of reducing the place, which was in total want of food when it surrendered. I am glad there were not many

[1] During the second visit to Florence, Sir Gilbert met there his old friends Lord and Lady Palmerston with their children. Among the latter he especially distinguished 'Harry, now nine years old. He speaks French and Italian very well, and has probably secured a knowledge of those languages; but has not yet begun Latin.'

of the inhabitants killed, nor is there much material damage done to the town, except at the end near our batteries.

'I am happy to say that everything seems promising and thriving to our business, and I am also gratified by knowing that it would not have been so in all other hands. It is easy to manage, but also very easy to mar, and the mischief that is to be done in the world by a little nonsense is surprising. I enjoy the entire confidence of this people, and every material point is settled between us. The Consulta is to meet on the 8th, and by the time you receive this I flatter myself I may have set another gem in H. M.'s crown; and that we shall all be fellow-subjects and fellow-citizens here. The change will, I firmly believe, be advantageous to both countries, and I am sure it is so to Corsica. It is impossible to acquire dominion under pleasanter circumstances or by pleasanter means, since it will be brought about in a great measure by the confidence placed in our national character, since it will be not only with the consent, but by the earnest invitation of the people, and since it will, I hope, contribute to their real happiness.'

On June 21, 1794, in a General Assembly held at Cortè, General Paoli in the name of the Corsican people tendered the crown of Corsica to His Majesty the King of Great Britain, represented by Sir Gilbert Elliot as His Minister Plenipotentiary.

This final act, decisive of the union of Corsica with Great Britain, had been before enthusiastically resolved on by the Assembly, in which 'although none but landholders were electors, every man almost without exception voted.' A committee was appointed to prepare the articles of union.

In the Annual Register for 1794 will be found all the state papers which were drawn up at this period by the Plenipotentiaries of the King of Great Britain on the one hand, and by the Corsican authorities on the other: as at the present day they have little· importance, political or biographical, they are not inserted here. Sir Gilbert's impressions of the scenery of the island and of the manners and customs of his new fellow-subjects, freely given in his letters to Lady Elliot, have a more enduring interest.

'Cortè: June 10, 1794.

'A great part of the road here lies through forests of sweet chestnuts, most of them the size of our old ash, and some at least thirty feet in circumference. Chestnuts are the sole food of the people, of their pigs and cattle. We have glens and burns in abundance, and peeps of the Mediterranean at every opening. It is really a fairy land and will delight you as much as me. The journey has been interesting too in other respects; I am come here representing the King to sign and seal our union, and to accept the voluntary tender of their allegiance in return for the protection we give them. There never was an act of the sort better sealed by the hearts of the people. Young and old, man and woman, all sorts and all degrees, are

hearty in this cause. I am not magnificent in my
suite or equipage—myself on a good horse given me by
General Gentili, the rest on mules. We are escorted
as usual by a number of Corsicans with guns on their
shoulders, who are relieved at each village, and by
an escort of the 12th regiment of Light Dragoons,
whose handsome uniforms, seen for the first time in
these hills, make at least as much impression as His
Excellency. We were joined on our way by deputies,
or members of Parliament, coming to this famous
Assembly, in all the simplicity of primitive legislators,
on their little mules, with their musket always slung
over their back and their little portmanteau strapped
behind them. We had hospitality wherever we went
in every form, and where we slept illuminations, bon-
fires, and muskets fired in our faces. The second
night we slept in a monastery, in the village where
Paoli was born, and where the little property he has
is situated. Yesterday when we approached Cortè, I
was met by a handsome prancing horse of Paoli's,
which My Excellency bestrode, and on which I
pranced into Cortè, through deputations of magistrates
and what not, and through male and female crowds
which thickened as we approached. At our arrival
our prancing was prettily heightened by the discharge
of cannon in our ears, and I entered bareheaded, bow-
ing and prancing like Bolingbroke. I met and
embraced *Old Richard* at his door. However, the
likeness does not hold, for although I am a sort of
successor he would have more God bless him's than

I, and could send Bolingbroke into the kennel
without the help of Roan Barbary. As it happened,
however, this very horse had thrown Paoli himself
only the day before; and he had a most narrow
escape, as he is old, very infirm, and pretty heavy.
The Assembly or Consulta meets to-day, but only on
matters of form; to-morrow or next day business
will begin, and the elections having gone *the right
way*, there is nothing to apprehend.'

'Cortè: June 22, 1794.

'I was crowned last Thursday, June 19, and I send
you My Majesty's speech which was spoken in French;
it produced on my new subjects a kingly effect.

'The long and the short, or, as Gilbert would say,
the hexameter and pentameter, of the thing is, that
George III. is king of Corsica. There never was a
pleasanter country than even this part of it, which is
by no means the "crack." It is like Scotland with
a fine climate. The rivers are rapid, craggy, and
crystal. There never was water so perfectly pure and
of such a beautiful white transparency as the Restonica, which flows by Cortè. It falls into another
river almost as beautiful close to this *my capital*.
The brightness and splendour of the Restonica make
it what one may call *precious water*, as one talks of
the *precious stones*. I had heard of the water of a
diamond before, now I see it, for it is really diamonds
in solution. This is no exaggeration, as you will see
when you come. As one walks along the banks the

air is literally perfumed with rich aromatics and sweet
and pungent plants. I purpose to pass the hottest
months still higher up the hills amongst the chestnut
groves. I thought of building a *summer palace* in
some such situation, and my first idea was to build it
of jasper and porphyry, but fearing that as you are
not acquainted with the quarries of this country you
might think me extravagant, I believe I shall go
cheaply to work, and only run it up of common
marble. A deputation of fourteen gentlemen is
appointed to carry the address of the Consulta to their
new sovereign in London. They are all much respected here. M. Colonna[1] is of one of the most
distinguished families in Corsica, like a remarkably
good specimen of a country gentleman in England or
Scotland. Galliazzi is a country gentleman of good
fortune for this country, and is much respected, but
is not so ornamental to the mission as Colonna. Pietri
is a scholar and a remarkably good sort of man. He
has accompanied all my walks, rides, and leisure, ever
since I left Bastia, and has partaken constantly all
those scenes, and many of those hours, in which I was
wishing for you. Notwithstanding that disadvantage
under which he laboured, he has made my time
shorter and pleasanter than it could have been by any
other means within my reach. We have read Dante
together, and talked small philosophy and literature
in a country very favourable to such amusements.

---

[1] M. Colonna was one of the six Corsican Deputies to the Legislative
Assembly of France.

Pray observe, if you see him, whether he is not like Sir
Joshua's Count Ugolino. Notwithstanding this resemblance, and that he approaches fifty, he is a great
lover, and as sentimental as poetical. He repeated to
me Count Ugolino's death out of Dante, and I could
have thought at last it was himself telling his own
story. He was wonderfully fine as well as horrible.
The fourth, Savelli, is also a literary man, and a remarkably sensible, sharp, but modest man. I hope people
will be civil to them in England, but the time of the
year is against them.'

In a letter to Mr. Dundas, written for the purpose
of introducing to him the members of the Corsican
Deputation, we find the first mention of a name to be
hereafter of constant recurrence in Sir Gilbert's correspondence—that of Pozzo di Borgo, with whom he at
this time entered into relations destined to ripen into
lifelong friendship. 'It is a current anecdote, and I
think honourable to the sagacity and long views as
well as to the spirit and courage of the man, that on
June 20, 1792, Pozzo di Borgo, one of the Corsican
Deputies to the Legislative Assembly, said to Pietri,
one of his colleagues, that it was now become impossible to continue any further connection with France,
and that he was sure it must end in the union of
Corsica with England. That very day he bought at
Paris an English grammar and dictionary, and
Pietri, who had been in England and speaks the language, began to give him lessons. On that day two

years precisely he was subject of his Majesty, and has found occasion for his English. They all quitted Paris a few days after the 10th of August, contriving with difficulty to bring their heads safe to Corsica.' [1]

The summer of 1794 was passed by Sir Gilbert at Cortè and Orezza ; where in daily and hourly communications between himself, Paoli, Pozzo di Borgo, and others of the leading Corsicans, the future Constitution of the country was framed.

'Orezza,' he wrote, 'is the name of a district

---

[1] Pozzo di Borgo, Corsican by birth, and born of a noble family, made himself remarked early in life for superior abilities and liberal sympathies. He was a warm admirer of the French Revolution in its early days, and took his place in the Legislative Assembly as a representative of Corsica. According to Lamartine, his personal observation of the virtues and sufferings of Louis XVI. converted him into a supporter of constitutional monarchy. In conjunction with Paoli he sought to deliver his country from the rule of those who were inaugurating a reign of terror in France. In concert with Paoli he offered the crown of Corsica to the king of England, but, unlike Paoli, he continued throughout the English occupation to give the Government his steady support. Lamartine describes Pozzo at a later period of his life as, 'doué de l'extérieur le plus noble, de l'élocution la plus pénétrante et la plus passionnée, des manières les plus simples et les plus élégantes, militaire, diplomate, publiciste, homme de plaisir et d'affaires tout à la fois, Pozzo di Borgo était placé par la seule attraction de sa nature supérieure dans la familiarité et l'estime de l'aristocratie anglaise et continentale.'—*Hist. de la Rév.*, tome v. p. 203.

To the society of London and of Vienna he was introduced by Sir Gilbert Elliot, who from their first acquaintance formed the highest opinion of his abilities, and gave him in all that related to Corsica his most intimate confidence. When the evacuation of the island took place, Pozzo left it for ever, and shared thenceforth the home and life of his friend both in London, at Minto, and at Vienna, until, some years later, he entered the service of the Emperor Alexander. To the day of his death he kept up relations of friendship with those whom he had known in their childhood at Corsica. A considerable number of his letters are preserved at Minto.

where the mineral waters of that name are. The convent at which I am to lodge with Paoli and other grandees and statesmen of this country, is about a couple of miles from the spring. It is in the centre of the sweet chestnut woods, and in a beautiful mountainous country; the elevation is such as to promise a degree of freshness, and there is abundance of shade, of water, and of ferns. The convent, like all others, is built to· be inconvenient, and has nothing but small cells, and a large hall to dine in. I shall have two of the best cells, and we shall all live at one table to be managed by Paoli's servants. There are about eighteen of the monks who will inhabit the convent with us. Here we purpose to keep ourselves as cool and as quiet as we can, and to prepare the future laws of Corsica.'

Representative institutions were familiar to the Corsicans. Every one of the villages clustered like sea-fowl on the sun-baked cliffs; every hamlet hidden in depths of forest, and surrounded by the *macchie* which play the same part in Corsican history as Tarras-moss in that of the Borders; every town perched, citadel-like, on some high crag, had its annual elections, when, besides the Podesta and Municipality, a representative for the National Assembly was chosen by universal suffrage.

From the body of the Assembly [1] were again elected the members of the Supreme Council,[2] and the civil

---

[1] The representatives forming the Assembly were about two hundred in number.

[2] The Supreme Council subsisted through the year and after the separation of the Assembly.

and military chiefs of the Administration, i.e. the President of the Council, and the Lieutenant-General of the Kingdom.

Nothing could be more democratic than the forms, nothing more autocratic than their result. Neither unnaturally, nor unwisely in the existing condition of their country, the Corsicans used their rights to invest with supreme authority the man who had won their affections and their confidence, and except when asked to lay down their arms, or to take up their tools, their submission was complete.

For the authority of this beloved and native leader was now to be substituted that of a foreign Government; and the problem to be worked was how best to adapt the constitutional forms in existence in Corsica with the exigencies of a new political situation. To give a *bonâ fide* weight to the representative body was the first object of the legislators of Orezza.

The Consulta had been far too numerous to be efficient as a Legislative Assembly; it was therefore enacted that the right of sending representatives to Parliament should be taken from the villages, and should be limited to pievès or districts, each one of which contained several villages ;[1] and that the suffrage

---

[1] This limitation of the right of representation to pievès would scarcely have been felt as a deprivation of electoral rights, since it had been customary in many districts for the villages to make over their power to elect a representative in the Annual Consulta to the pievès, in order to avoid the extreme inconvenience to petty proprietors of abandoning their agricultural operations; but the practice had always been considered an abuse.

should be limited to persons above twenty-five years of age ; and that no person should be eligible for a seat in the Consulta, to be henceforth called Parliament, who had not a certain amount of property in land.[1]   With this last enactment was connected another to the effect that henceforth the expenses of members of the new Assembly should be defrayed by themselves and not by the State.   An innovation not likely to have been popular, for the great gathering at Cortè had been an annual holiday, bringing together from *di là e di quà i monti* those whose usual avocations led them to the solitudes of the sea or of the mountains giving them, for one day only, social festivity, political functions, and the cost of their expenses.

In addition to these alterations in the political customs known to the Corsicans, some, to them, wholly novel features were introduced into the Constitution. It was agreed that the Executive should consist of a Governor, to be appointed by the King of Great Britain, who should receive the title of Viceroy and be invested with the powers described in the despatch of Mr. Dundas, already quoted ;[2] that he should be assisted in the civil administration by three Secretaries of State or Ministers, two of whom were to be members of the Supreme Council, the third was to be an Englishman appointed from home.

For British institutions Paoli had always professed unbounded admiration, while Sir Gilbert, like most of

---

[1] In theory all native Corsicans were landholders.
[2] Despatch of Mr. Dundas, March 31, 1794.

his countrymen of that day, was profoundly convinced that the great State which alone had known how to combine personal liberty with legal obedience was the only safe model for all others to follow. To assimilate the Constitutions of Great Britain and of Corsica was therefore the guiding principle of their legislation, and they did not, perhaps, sufficiently recognise the difference of age, of proportions, and of conditions between the nations described by Paoli as *sorelle.* Hence arose some tentative legislation, of which the most striking instance is the institution of Trial by Jury under a special clause of the Constitution, and its subsequent abolition by the Corsican Parliament, after a year's experience had proved it totally unfitted for a country in the condition of Corsica.

'There is not a single instance of the conviction of any prisoner since the crown has been accepted by His Majesty, although there have been many trials in which the offence was proved in a manner to leave no degree of doubt and no possibility of innocence. This evil arises from one of the most remarkable and most rooted peculiarities in the Corsican character—I mean clanship, and the attachments of blood relationship and friendship. A Corsican is deemed infamous who does not revenge the death of his tenth cousin, and he fears the dishonour of convicting his relation, or his friend, or the relation of his friend, much more than that of breaking his oath as a juror. Public spirit has no chance against this stronger principle of private confederacy. The country is so narrow, and they intermarry so exclusively with each other, and are connected in so many ways, that it would be difficult to find twelve men without bias on any cause that could be tried.'

The state of Corsica in 1794 was thus, in some respects, very similar to that of the Scotch Borders in the sixteenth century. Like the Borderers, the Corsicans, while making common cause against a foreign rule, were among themselves divided into a number of clans at war with each other, whose hereditary feuds lasted from generation to generation. Each clan was composed of small landholders and their dependents, to whom it was as inconvenient in harvest time to attend the National Assembly as it had been to Scotts, Kerrs, and Elliots to set forth at a similar season on a foray into England. Among the gentry there were individuals possessed of a relatively high degree of education and of accomplishments, but the people generally were untrained in habits of order and industry.

Like the Borderer the Corsican peasant was content to live on ewe-milk cheese and on a cake, which the Italian made of chestnuts and the Scotchman of oatmeal. Both felt themselves despised unless possessed of a gun and a horse. Both preferred a herdsman's to a labourer's life, partly from a sense of personal dignity, and partly because men care not to sow where they know not who will reap; and both infinitely preferred to all manner of work the excitement of the fray, with the craigs for their strongholds and the desolate places for a safe retreat.[1]

The parallel occurred to Sir Gilbert, for on the publication of Sir Walter Scott's Introduction to the 'Border Minstrelsy' in 1802, he sent a copy to Pozzo di Borgo, remarking that he would recognise therein a state of things familiar to him. Pozzo replied, that while the poetry was unintelligible to him, the history was ' pays de connaissance.'

But two leading traits in Corsican character could not have been matched among the Borderers of Scotland—the universal thirst for place, and the no less universal vanity, which made every man aggrieved who was not promoted.[2]

'July 31, 1794.

' It requires my experience of Corsica to know or conceive the wide field which the character of this people, and the late conditions of the country during an insurrectional revolution, affords to those who would cultivate the discontents of individuals. The pretensions of every man, gentle or simple, are exaggerated

---

[1] Another point of similarity has been discovered by a French author between races so widely different in many respects, for Scotland has not been at all times ignorant of a malady described as well known in Corsica. 'Mal héroïque et populaire dont les vives excitations et l'agitation qu'elles produisent ont été prises souvent pour l'amour de la gloire.'

[2] A recent writer confirms these statements: 'Mattei avait à se plaindre du préfet : " Il trahit la Corse," s'écriait-il avec des éclats de voix sinistres. Pour beaucoup d'habitans celui-là trahit la Corse, qui n'a plus de places à distribuer. Leur rêve est d'être fonctionnaires.'—*Un Hiver en Corse.* 1853.

to a degree that cannot be believed elsewhere, and besides the vanity and egotism of gentlemen as in other countries, you have the whole population of Corsica to deal with, there not being a shepherd who has not acquired a title in one way or other to say he has served *la Patria*, and who does not consider himself entitled to the rank of officer in the Corsican troops, while every gentleman thinks himself neglected if he has not the command of a battalion. Unfortunately there is no industry, nor any notion of acquiring or improving fortune by any other means than by office and employment either civil or military; and it being impossible to salary a whole nation, or even a great proportion of a nation, we have here the unavoidable disadvantage of contending with the private disappointment of the whole body of the people.'

To bring a nation thus constituted into working order, and again into relations of harmony with its new rulers, would have been, under any circumstances, no easy task; in the present case it was rendered doubly ungrateful by the strange negligence of the British Ministers, who for some months after the act of annexation had been carried in Corsica, preserved an unbroken silence towards their Plenipotientiary, and also towards the Legislature, which had voted their supremacy. From June to October they made no sign, Corsica, remaining without any regular administration, while the actual powers of government lay with Paoli. That so exceptional a state of affairs, unduly prolonged, must be pregnant with mischief, was easy to foresee, and subsequent events only too fully justified such apprehensions.

As early as May 12, 1794, Sir Gilbert had written from Milan a letter, marked private, to Mr. Sec. Dundas, and left by him in the Duke of Portland's office, suggesting the desirability of an immediate transmission to Corsica of provisional powers to administer the Executive, as soon as the treaty should be concluded, in order to obviate inconveniences which might arise during an interregnum between the establishment and the execution of a new system.

Of this letter no notice was taken, and on August 7 Sir Gilbert, writing from Orezza, in a despatch to the Duke of Portland, says that the inconveniences foreseen had too surely arisen: ' The civil affairs of the island have necessarily been in a degree suspended since June 19. I am sorry to add that this is not the only inconvenience which has resulted from this awkward interval. The last act of the General Assembly, or Consulta, was to invest provisionally the Executive Government in the persons who before composed the Administration. General Paoli is naturally at their head, but the principal functions of Government have, during this delicate period, been exercised by persons very proper for subordinate offices, but very indifferently qualified to exercise supreme authority at the present moment. There has been by these means an opportunity afforded to conduct business rather in the vexatious and vindictive spirit of an inflamed and triumphant party, than in the conciliatory temper of a new Government, which by its nature supersedes all old rivalships, and has both the power, the interest, and the inclination to soften animosities, and to unite and attach to the new system all descriptions of men in the country. It has been my constant occupation to moderate and assuage, as far as was possible, the vindictive character of the Provisional Government. I have succeeded in many instances, but the British and Corsican authorities have been by this means frequently pulling different ways, and have on many occasions been seen in contradiction with each other. These evils were trifling, however, compared with the uneasiness which the conduct, and I fear the character, of General Paoli have given rise to during this interval. His real qualities have very much unfolded themselves since the heavy pressure of danger and difficulties, which weighed them down some months ago has been removed by our assistance. This *peine forte et dure* (for so it truly was in January last at Murato) being taken off, his ambition has a little room to breathe, and the present interval of power has administered even that sort of wholesome exercise which seems to be restoring health and colour to the convalescent passion.

' . . . It required time and a considerable experience of Paoli to know him well; there are, however, some points of his character which are very manifest, and none more so than a general and habitual distrust of everything and every man around him. Having all his life had to carry on great undertakings with slender means, and to oppose weakness to strength, he is thoroughly exercised in that weapon of the weak called policy by some, and cunning by others. This being his own method, he suspects it in all other men.

‘His habits of distrust have been very much confirmed by living in perpetual apprehension of assassination. Perhaps age and declining strength and health add to this weakness; and the degree of his suspicion, as well as the extraordinary occasions on which it appears, are such as might give to it almost the character of disease.

‘One great object of his late speculation has been the delay that has occurred in the arrival of despatches from England. He has thought that we were treating with every Power in Europe for the surrender of Corsica. On this point he has kept up a correspondence with his countrymen, the tendency of which is to keep them on their guard, and the effect of which is breaking out continually in crosses and quarrels between the Corsicans and us, and in a teazing opposition on the part of Paoli's provisional government, as well as everybody employed by him, to all we were doing.

.   .   .   .   .   .

‘With all this he is pleasant and polite in society. I receive from him every mark of personal kindness and confidence, and I am tempted to think I am one of the few who have any considerable influence over his mind. We are living at the present time under the same roof in a convent in a retired part of the country. He drinks the mineral waters of Orezza.

'What I have said will lead your Grace to conceive that Paoli's total retreat from this country would be a desirable if not almost a necessary thing. It has struck me that something might be done at home to relieve us from this perplexity. I took the liberty of suggesting in my despatch from Cortè,[1] that a letter from His Majesty would be received by Paoli as a flattering and most gracious mark of his royal favour and condescension. If a desire to see him in England could be introduced into His Majesty's letter, it might have a very happy effect. I took the liberty also of recommending a renewal of his former pension.'

'September 6, 1794.[2]

'I have not yet received my commission. The delay is, beyond anything I ever heard of, strange and culpable. It is impossible to describe the mischief it has occasioned and is occasioning. I have been urging it since the month of May, and have been *looking out* at every boat or horseman *since June*, for what I had reason to expect every day. We have neither justice nor revenue nor any other business transacting here, and this has lasted very near three months after it might and ought to have been prevented.'

Again, on September 16, he wrote :—' I cannot sufficiently wonder at the unjustifiable neglect of all our business in the Mediterranean for so many months.

[1] Despatch to the Duke of Portland, June, 1794.
[2] To Lady Elliot.

The Corsicans have borne it wonderfully. In the meanwhile it is impossible they should not feel themselves strangely slighted after the connection they had formed with England. For three months since they gave the crown to the King, there is not one syllable from any member of the King's Government to say " thank you," much less to do the business of the country which we are now bound to attend to as a duty.'

Sir Gilbert's impatience of the delay in the arrival of his powers was aggravated by his separation from his family, which had already endured for a longer period than had been foreseen when he parted from them, and could have no visible term while his own position remained an uncertain one. He repeatedly states in his letters, both to his family and to Ministers, that though it was undoubtedly his desire to carry through the work he had begun, and to establish the relations between Great Britain and Corsica on the footing on which they should be afterwards continued, it was no less his determination not to remain a day longer in Corsica than was necessary for this result. ' When once the Government is fairly started,' he wrote, ' there are many naval or military men who will be found ready and competent to carry it on, and I cannot be expected to settle my family in this climate nor to live here without them.' But though unwilling to ' settle ' in Corsica, Sir Gilbert saw many advantages to the younger members of the family in a temporary residence in Italy, and looked forward himself to visiting, in company with his wife, the treasures of art and the beauties of Nature which

they were both well able to appreciate. It had therefore been determined before he left England that Lady
Elliot, with her six children, should meet him in Italy
in the spring of 1794, but the state of the continent
had hitherto made such a journey impracticable.

'You are mistaken,' he wrote to Lady Elliot, September 14, 1794, 'in supposing that my situation affords more resources against absence than yours. You
have all the children, and the society of those who have
some ideas and feelings in common with yours. There
are many people here that I like from their qualities,
but not one who understands me, or is company for me
by having ideas in common with mine. Yes—one there
is—M. Pozzo di Borgo, who is company for anybody,
and my great resource.' [1]

During the time of interregnum between the Corsican
and British rule in Corsica, the situation already
strained was rendered still more difficult by the in-
trigues of the Pope, who, besides putting in a claim to
the temporal sovereignty of Corsica, affected to believe
his spiritual supremacy endangered by the action in
Corsica of a Protestant Power.

---

[1] During the whole of this time Sir Gilbert was engaged in correspondence of the most multifarious nature, with the Ministers representing His Majesty at the Italian Courts, with the admirals in command of the fleet, with the Grand Master of the Order of the Knights
of Malta concerning supplies, with the States of Barbary concerning
a dispute arising out of the Corsican claim to certain coral fisheries
on the coast of Africa, with the state of Genoa on her claim to Corsica ;
but as none of these correspondences contain matters of interest at the
present day, we pass them over.

The claim to the temporalities rested on communications from Paoli made previously to those addressed to Great Britain.

Both claim and apprehensions were dismissed by Sir Gilbert in the following terms, addressed, as before, to Mr. Hippesley :—

' Depend upon it, we shall admit no claim to Corsica except that of superior force. With respect to religion in Corsica, our rule will be to have *no rule* ; that is to say, to lay no constraint whatever on the inclination of the people themselves in that article ; while we shall not be found unmindful of the grace and honour due to religion.

'. . . . Before I quit the claim to Corsica, I must just say, we all know perfectly that in the struggles of his country against Genoa, and then against France, that in this contest between weakness and force, with nothing but courage on one hand and power on the other, there is no door in Europe, at which, in the distresses of his country, and in its utmost need, Paoli did not knock, at one period or other ; but pray did the Pope send him a fleet and an army to deliver him from France and Genoa ; and now that we have done so, and the Pope says to us, like Scrub, "Take it, *and give it to me*," how can one be grave at such a plagiary from a comic writer ?

' On the subject of religious arrangements in Corsica, I shall only say, for your private satisfaction, that my only rule has been to lay no restraint on the dispositions and views of the people themselves, and all that relates to that subject is entirely their own. You have certainly not read the Constitution of Corsica well at Rome.

' There is no mention of the reduction of bishoprics, parishes, or monasteries in the Constitution: it is only said that these matters shall be concerted between the Parliament of Corsica and the Pope. Such is the letter of the Constitution, which is all that is known at present: what arrangement the Parliament of Corsica will think suitable to the state and resources of the country, it is not for me to say. I am only persuaded that, on the one hand, they will not neglect the temporal interest and welfare of the nation, and, on the other, that they will offend neither the important principles of general piety, nor of the particular religion they profess. . . .

' But I have no extraordinary fellow-feeling towards the *flesh* of this spiritual power, and should have no extraordinary satisfaction in seeing a poor country pay more for its religious establishment than it can afford, not for the purpose of promoting true piety, but to gratify some fleshly appetite of Mother Church. You quote a saying of Madame Coigny, " That it is such and such *princes* that make democrats." I know no better receipt for making atheists than for Popes to be, at this time of day, claiming temporal sovereignties, and laying temporal burdens and inconveniencies on other countries in the name of religion. But fear nothing in this instance: for neither is this Pope an atheist-

maker, nor does Corsica grow *le bois dont on en fait.*
There is, thank God, a great deal of real and sincere
piety in this island, and very little bigotry.'

On the 1st of October, 1794,[1] Sir Gilbert received from
England despatches authorising him to assume the full
powers required for the inauguration of a Viceregal
Government in Corsica. On the following day he
wrote to his kinsman Mr. Elliot a letter which shows
how much he had felt himself aggrieved by the silence
of Government.

'Bastia: October 2, 1794.

'My dear Elliot,—As Burke said on the occasion of a
more difficult reconciliation, my acrimony is dulcified by
the arrival of the despatches which relieve my principal
difficulties, and with the account of Lady Elliot's being
actually on her journey. The provocation has been
really great beyond common powers of endurance, and
on the whole, when I think of it again, I believe I have
not said a word more than was due.[2] On the 12th of
May at Milan I asked for the very thing I received
yesterday, the 1st of October. June, July, August,
September, October—I have been pressing for it ever
since. The evils and the dangers of withholding it
have been extreme and constantly increasing. I might
and ought to have had it on the 20th of June. I have

---

[1] Owing to some delay on the part of the crown lawyers, the actual
Commission was not sent out till November.

[2] In an indignant remonstrance addressed by himself to Mr. E.
shortly before.

been straining my eyes every day, and I may say every
minute of every day, since the 19th of June, for
messengers on the roads or for cutters at sea.　On the
20th of June I told General Paoli that the man we
saw riding at a great distance towards us was probably
the messenger, and that he might depend on his coming
within eight and forty hours, and I would have pawned
my life upon a week—June, July, August, September
—at length the messenger arrived—and he brought me
nothing!　I was told, however, that they waited to receive the account of our proceedings that they might
know how to prepare the Commission, and it would be
sent without a moment's delay.　In the meanwhile I
had only a letter to authorise me to do the needful.
The account of our proceedings was received in London
the 14th or 15th of July.　The letter which I have
just received was despatched on the 15th of September.
Two months—the Commission in hand still.　If it
were only my own concern in the business I am quite
sure I should have endured still ; but when I saw them
spoiling all that had been done, bringing themselves
and all of us to shame, insulting this people, neglecting
such recent as well as interesting duties ; when I saw
the French Republic threatening us with invasion, the
French Princes intriguing, the Pope intriguing, all Italy
looking down upon us, and Corsica kept all this time
in the state that all our enemies could wish ; when I saw
all the ambition, and even all the indigence, of a people
kept gnawing itself for four months, and all looking up
wistfully to me for bread, or cake, which I had not to

give them, I confess I got at last wroth as you have
perceived.   Conceive the number of poor wretches who
expect literally bread from a number of small employ-
ments here, and who have finally lost above a quarter
of a year's subsistence for their families, besides suffering
four months all the agony of suspense and anxiety—for
I did not make a single promise all that time,—and
for want of a letter! Conceive that we have lost for the
public service near 10,000*l.* by the loss of above a
quarter's revenue, for want of a messenger who would
have cost 80*l.*   This is nothing to what might be said
with just truth if I were not dulcified by the arrival
of Forster.'

The utter neglect with which the British Government treated the affairs of Corsica was the more remarkable because at that period, 1794, England had no
footing in the Mediterranean east of Gibraltar, and in
the opinion of the naval commanders the possession of
Corsica was of the highest importance for the protection of British commerce in the Levant, and also for
the maintenance of the influence of England in the
Mediterranean.[1]

---

[1] 'The more I see,' wrote Lord Nelson, February 7, 1795, 'of its
(Corsica's) produce and convenient ports for our fleets, the more I am
satisfied of Lord Hood's great wisdom in getting possession of it . . .
After the evacuation of Toulon, where were we to look for shelter for
our fleet ? . . . All our trade and that of our allies to Italy must all pass
close to Corsica.   The enemy would have had the ports of this island full
of row-galleys, and from the great calm near the land our ships of war
could not have protected the trade . . . . The loss to the French has
been great indeed; all the ships built at Toulon have their sides,

The Mediterranean fleet, 14 sail of the line, was short of men and stores, and Sir Gilbert thought it necessary to make an urgent representation of its condition to Mr. Dundas.

'I am happy to say that, under all the disadvantages of short complements and a very distressing deficiency of stores, no officer of the fleet entertains the slightest doubt of victory, if the enemy should afford them a fair opportunity to try their strength at sea. At the same time it is proper that His Majesty's Ministers should have a just knowledge of our situation, which merits their most serious and most immediate attention ; for although the spirit of our officers and seamen leaves little room for uneasiness in the event of a fair battle, yet, on the general view of the circumstances, I am sorry to say that there is throughout the fleet a strong sense of the discouraging prospect before us, and, in their language, of our going fast to leeward. I speak now of the opinions of those who are most eminent in the fleet for rank and for abilities in their

beams, decks and straight timbers from this island. The pine of this island is of the finest texture I ever saw ; and the tar, pitch, and hemp, although I believe the former not equal to Norway, yet were very much used in the yard at Toulon.' Almost on the same day that Lord Nelson thus wrote from Corsica, Mr. Elliot, writing from London to Sir Gilbert, thus expresses himself, February 9, 1795 :—'The dominion of the Mediterranean is now a matter of the last importance in consequence of the scarcity of corn. The last crop in England, though it had the appearance of abundance, proved to be scanty, and the harvest in America was so bad that corn is now dearer there than in England. Poland is supposed not to have more than is necessary for its own consumption. In Sicily the crops have been very abundant, and that island is therefore the only granary of Europe.'

profession—Admiral Hotham, Sir Hyde Parker, and many others. There is on the whole an unpleasant tone of dejection on the subject. The fleet wants near 2,000 men of its complement. It is so short of stores that an accident or two at sea might become irreparable in the Mediterranean. They are obliged to use both condemned sails and condemned cordage, and are equally deficient in many other articles; so that if they should suffer any considerable damage, either by weather or in action, Admiral Hotham will find himself under the necessity of carrying his whole squadron to Gibraltar, and leaving the enemy in undisturbed possession of these seas. . . .

'The French are much superior both in the number and strength of their frigates. . . .

'I can only repeat my earnest and urgent representations for the necessity of an immediate naval reinforcement. A single ship may be of the utmost consequence, and the arrival of what aid can be afforded two days sooner or later, may very well make the difference of some signal success or calamity.

'The loss of Corsica by the general events and issue of the war, though a great calamity to this island, would not, however, affect our national character. But to lose this country, and to yield the throats and fortunes of all our adherents to a savage enemy so soon after our union, for the want of two or three sail of the line, or of a storeship, or of gunpowder to defend ourselves and them, would certainly leave no favourable impression of us in the Mediterranean. These apprehensions are not, however, entirely visionary in the present circumstances.'

During the whole of his residence in the Mediterranean, Sir Gilbert enjoyed the entire confidence of the naval commanders.   Lord Hood, Sir Hyde Parker, Admiral Hotham, Lord St. Vincent, were constantly in communication with him on political transactions, and were in the habit of appealing to his known zeal for the service when it could be brought to bear on those who had the direction of naval affairs at home. With Nelson he formed still more intimate relations. Of Nelson's genius Sir Gilbert early predicted the results, and Nelson, on his side, repeatedly acknowledged, in later times, the assistance he derived from Sir Gilbert's views on the policy which Great Britain should pursue in the Mediterranean.

The Letters hitherto given treat of this policy mainly with regard to its general scope, the creation of an effective barrier to the encroachments of France in the South of Europe, but Sir Gilbert was no less mindful of the duties and responsibilities assumed by England, when, in accepting the crown of Corsica, she pledged herself to protect the rights and liberties of the Corsicans.

In a despatch addressed to the Duke of Portland, dated Bastia, December 30, 1794, he discussed at length the probabilities of peace, and the concern which Corsica would have in the event, as also the terms on which the island had united herself to Great

Britain.   After considering the engagements that had
been formed between the contracting parties, 'according to the letter and the spirit,' and admitting that
the events of war might possibly render the preservation of the Corsican crown a source of peril or of unreasonable sacrifice to the King of Great Britain,
he proceeded as follows :—' I may be allowed to say,
that before this recent union can be dissolved, and the
promised protection can be withdrawn with dignity or
justice, a very strong case of necessity must be adduced . . . Nothing could be more disastrous for this
country than a conquest made by France in the present
moment.   They will come here in a most savage spirit,
and if we have not a reasonable prospect of defending
Corsica, we ought to seek some other mode of protecting her from this calamity.   It must be remembered
that our present force is so extremely small, that it
may possibly become necessary for the British troops
to evacuate the island altogether.   The consequence of
which would be to deliver up the throats of all our
friends to their butchers and their property to confiscation and plunder. . . .

' I conceive that it would be the bounden duty of
Great Britain, should a disunion become necessary, to
relinquish Corsica with the least evil to that island;
that the possibility of a future evacuation should be
timeously made known to the leaders of the population;
or that, in the event of a peace, Great Britain should
stipulate either for the independence of Corsica, or for
a complete amnesty and oblivion and certain security

to the lives, persons, and property of all concerned in the late Corsican revolution. I consider the condition of amnesty as a *sine quâ non*, and as not less essential to the King's honour than due by every principle of justice and by every tie, human and divine, to the people of Corsica. I can suppose a disadvantageous peace, but I cannot imagine or conceive the possibility of a *dishonourable* one. The same necessity which should oblige us to renounce and surrender our Corsican friends, or a single emigrant, to the vengeance of their enemies, must make us, I think, surrender the Tower of London if summoned to do so.' The despatch ends with the observation ' that unless Great Britain were prepared to make a very great and vigorous exertion in the war, Corsica, as well as Italy, must inevitably succumb to the arms of France.'

As a consequence of the accession of the Whigs to Office, the Duke of Portland had taken possession of the seals of the Secretary of State for Home affairs,[1] and Mr. Dundas became Secretary for War ; but the change brought no fresh vigour into the administration of the War Department.

In a private letter to Mr. Dundas, dated Bastia, February 23, 1795, written after hearing of the loss of Amsterdam and of all Holland, Sir Gilbert wrote as follows :

' War seems more necessary than ever, since to the

---

[1] Mr. Dundas announced to Sir Gilbert that his official correspondence would henceforth be conducted with the Duke of Portland in these words : ' The Government is about to be strengthened by the accession of many respectable characters of whom you think very highly.'

former danger of French anarchy is now added that of
her ambition.   The liberty of Europe was never before
in such danger ; nor has there been, since the Roman
age, so great a prospect of universal empire. . . .   In
the South, everything depends on our maintaining our
maritime superiority, and on the Emperor sending a
great and real force to Italy.   With regard to the first,
I still hope to see it effected ; at the same time the
thing hangs by a thread.   If another ship should be
disabled—and nothing is so possible—I think Admiral
Hotham would quit the Mediterranean.   With regard
to the Emperor I have little faith. . . .   The opinion
of our power is getting low, while that of the enemy is
becoming every week more formidable ; and while this
state of things lasts we must expect our friends to fall
off and all our affairs to decline.   I own I could wish
that it were possible for Great Britain once more to
assert herself ; the want of that reputation which ought
to belong to us has, in fact, lost us the co-operation of
Genoa and Tuscany and neutralised all Italy.   This
circumstance has very probably decided the fate of the
war ; for if we had been able to direct all these Italian
States, the South of France would have been famished
long ago. If you continue the war, I take it for granted
that you expect by exertion to obtain resources equal
to the occasion, for however disastrous peace may be
now, it will be more so after another unsuccessful campaign.   I should therefore hope that you may have
formed a plan and taken measures for a great effort in
the Mediterranean, for that is now a main branch of

the war. A successful campaign here gives you great
chance of disabling, or even bringing over, the southern
provinces of France. Their sufferings are great and
their dispositions unsettled, but while we are thought,
or rather known, to be weak, no good can ever happen
to us. It is a total exclusion of all the favourable
chances on the table.'

In the event of the Government deciding on a vigorous campaign in the South, Sir Gilbert ' was assured
that with a strong fleet in the Mediterranean, a force
of 4,000 or 5,000 British troops to hold the fortresses of
Corsica, would suffice to insure the safety of the island,
and with it, harbours for our ships, and protection for
our trade with the Mediterranean and Levant.'

When established thus in force on their coasts, he
believed that England would have a better chance of
being listened to, ' should the Government then decide
on sending some very able man in the diplomatic line
to Italy, to try whether the different States of Italy
might not be rallied in their own defence.

' If some such measures are not taken, I cannot help
apprehending that we shall soon see a great part of the
Roman empire revived, with the difference only of
having the metropolis on the Seine instead of the
Tiber.'

CHAPTER VIII.

HOWEVER gloomy the aspect of public affairs in the winter of 1794–5, it began under cheerful auspices to Sir Gilbert, for it brought to him those who, to borrow his own expression, were 'the hope, the comfort, the pleasure of his existence.'

The messenger who carried to Corsica the new viceroy's commission was able to announce that Lady Elliot and her six children were following in his foot-steps.

The year of separation had been a time of toil and trouble to both. On Sir Gilbert's departure for Toulon, though warmly pressed by Lord and Lady Malmesbury to spend the winter with them, Lady Elliot had returned to Minto, where, by taking on herself the duties of a landed proprietor and head of a family, she had done all that woman could do to supply the place of man. Her letters testify to the variety of her employ-ments and to her energy in their pursuit. Plans of buildings, drafts of leases, negotiations for the sale and purchase of land, are discussed in them side by side with kindly and playful notices of friends and neigh-bours, and with the fullest accounts of the children; for with the same ardour she displayed in reclaiming waste lands and sowing broadcast the seeds whence have grown our many-tinted woodlands, did she set herself to cultivate the minds and dispositions of her children. If 'bold and honest' they were by hereditary right, she showed them that the noblest form of courage is that which 'hates the cowardice of doing wrong;'[1] and that honesty finds its highest development in reverence for all forms of truth.

When in the spring of 1794, the time came for her elder boys to be given over to the charge of a tutor competent to prepare them for Eton, she wrote to their father with pardonable pride, that he, the tutor, himself a school friend of Mr. Canning and of Lord Holland, highly approved of her educational system. 'He says he would sooner trust Gilbert to conduct himself in any case of difficulty than any boy he ever saw half as old again, and he thoroughly admires his high honourable character. He likes their galloping about alone in all weathers. You know I have always thought hardy and independent habits conducive to health.'

We have been told that this hardihood was sometimes pushed so far as to become alarming to her children's youthful friends, who found themselves expected to laugh at injuries over which honest nature longed to howl; not only, like ancient Borderers, to be 'joyful and thankful' for blows and knocks received in their out-door pastimes, but to fly to their Plutarch for examples how to behave under the discipline of the medicine-chest.

[1] Milton.

'Don't cry, and think of Mucius Scævola,' was the advice she tendered to a weak soul weeping over the torture of a mustard poultice; 'and poor comfort it was,' as the sufferer truly observed some sixty years later, 'for there was no similarity in the cases.' 'I see some people think,' wrote Lady Elliot, 'that Annie's passion for reading is carried too far. I do not; for innocent passions do much to keep out mischievous ones, and simple natural tastes and a love of country life are a great safe guard.'

Early in spring she came up to London in order to be prepared for an immediate start when it should be thought safe for her to join her husband. At this time she grew somewhat impatient of the caution of her advisers.

'April 14.

'I am a little out of patience sometimes with Mr. Elliot for his unwillingness to look at the bright side, always believing implicitly bad reports, but being very cautious in regard to good ones. Burke has filled many people with horror by what he said in the House three nights ago. On Sheridan saying that embodying the emigrants was an act of cruelty, as, if they were taken prisoners they would meet with no mercy, and desiring to know if this was the case and they were all butchered, whether we were to retaliate and give no quarter to any prisoners we took, Burke exclaimed, "Certainly we should revenge ourselves on those in our hands." This seems to me and to most people too horrid to have come from the mouth of a man of humanity and feeling; but as it was from Burke, even Mr. Elliot's mild and gentle character defends it.'

The tales of horror brought to England by the French, who, flying from their countrymen, were crowding the ports and towns of our southern coasts, had familiarised the public mind with deeds of atrocity, and, no doubt, had contributed largely to excite the anti-Gallican sentiments of the nation.

During a short visit to Tunbridge in the spring, Lady Elliot became acquainted with a little colony of emigrants settled there.

'Among them,' she wrote to Sir Gilbert, 'is a most agreeable family, the La Roche's, a father, mother, son, and daughter, people of real fashion and good manners. He told me yesterday, among other horrors, that the *patriots* had murdered two of his nieces; one they had cut into mincemeat with five little children, and the other they had flayed alive. An old uncle, above eighty, they had guillotined. Such accounts make one's blood run cold. I hope I have been able to do a good deal for these poor people, for they interest me above all things. The father is to have a turning machine, and to turn various things to sell; his daughter is to *broder* gowns, for which I have got her the materials, and I think they may by these means make at least 50*l.* or 60*l.* a year, and I have hopes of getting the son into one of the regiments in which they take emigrants. In

general, the *Émigrés* are wonderfully cheerful and contented.'

While learning submission to the decrees of statesmen and warriors, Lady Elliot settled herself and
family at Portslade, on the Sussex coast, preferred
by her to London with all its manifold attractions of
friendship and society; for to the children the great
town was 'a sad hole,' and to her that place was best
in which she could make them her chief companions.
She read her husband's letters to them till her eldest
son knew some of them by heart. While living at
Portslade, near enough to be within reach of friends
at Brighton, and far enough away to be out of the
bustle, the boys assisted at various military spectacles
performed by the troops encamped there in presence of
the Prince of Wales : of these the most original appears
to have been a grand review by moonlight in honour
of Lord Howe's victory of the 1st of June.

'Portslade: June 12.

'There is nothing but rejoicing; it is a most
noble and important victory, and in consequence of
this news we had a grand *feu de joie* last night at
the Camp about nine at night. As soon as it was fairly
dark, the whole seven regiments formed a line of considerable length, consisting of about 6,000 men, and
the crowd attending made at least 2,000 more. We
were all there, and in my life I never saw such a sight.
The cannons fired first separately and then the whole
line followed one another, and after the firing the

bands played " Rule Britannia," and whenever the
music ceased the shouts and huzzas were unanimous :
this was repeated three times, in the finest night possible, with the moon shining full upon the sea.   It is
really quite impossible to imagine a grander sight ; the
children were in raptures. . . The news of the victory
was carried to the playhouses by the Duke of Clarence
and Lord Mulgrave, and the whole audience joined in
singing " Rule Britannia " and " God save the King."
The boys were at Mrs. Pelham's the other morning
when the Prince came in and stayed an hour.   He was
very civil to them, and said he thought he must enlist
one of them.   Gilbert says he was very funny and told
a great many good stories : of course they liked him
extremely.

. . . . . .

' The prisoners taken by the fleet were entirely without money ; the men had nothing and the officers had
only assignats.   A fine trait of English humanity was
shown by the populace when the sailors were bringing
the wounded men on shore.   They had been filling the
air with huzzas ; but on being told that the noise was
bad for the invalids they were instantly perfectly
quiet, and as soon as the sick men got to the hospital
began again their shouts of joy.

. . . . . .

' There is no end of strange metamorphoses in these
times.   Mr. Elliot wrote me word yesterday that he
is become a cavalry officer, and has enlisted himself
in the Surrey Volunteer Company ; and I expect to see

him in a blue jacket and smart boots.   It is I believe
very right, but it is quite impossible not to laugh.   He
has been learning to ride at Astley's.'

The arrival of Lady Elliot with her children in
Corsica opened a new chapter in the family life.   To
the domestic happiness that belonged to them everywhere, were now superadded the vivid interests, the
passionate excitements, bred of their participation in
the great European strife.   A first introduction to
foreign lands is an eventful moment in most lives ; in
those of the youthful Elliots it was probably a turning
point whence might be dated the strong interest in
public matters which became a family characteristic.
Transported at the most susceptible age from their
quiet Scotch home to a scene where their daily existence depended on European complications and the
fortune of war, their minds received an ineffaceable
impression, determining the career of some and the
tastes of all.   In their garden surrounded by the sea,
in the sailing boat they learnt to guide along the rocky
shore, on the decks of the English men-of-war lying off
the Port, and above all, in the society of Nelson and
his gallant comrades, the boys learnt as it were on
England's own element an unswerving faith in her
power and greatness, imbibing at the same time a
passion for naval life which, in the case of George, the
Viceroy's second son, was gratified as soon as his age
permitted by his being entered as midshipman on board
the flag-ship.

His eldest brother Gilbert meanwhile, better fitted by age and tastes to form wider sympathies, learnt not to love England less but Italy too. It was during those years of friendly intercourse with the gifted and gracious natures of the South that a profound sense of their wrongs and a no less ardent desire to see them righted, took root in his mind, whence grew the convictions that ruled his political life and made him in later years one of Italy's fastest friends.[1]

While the still unformed characters of the young people were being subjected to new and varied influences, their elders found endless sources of enjoyment in the beautiful scenery and vegetation of the island, and in their endeavours to make its occupation by Great Britain a source of benefit to the population.

Lady Elliot's letters to her sister, Lady Malmesbury, give a vivid impression of the natural resources and beauty of the country and the unreclaimed condition of its inhabitants.

'Bastia: December 28.

'The weather is now charming; every door and window of the house is open, and the scenery is quite

[1] This is not the place to relate the political transactions between Great Britain and Italy, in which Gilbert Elliot, the late Lord Minto, bore a part. Whenever that chapter of contemporary history is told, it will be seen that he laboured in her cause before it had found favour with English statesmen or been appreciated by the English nation. But as we have shown that his love for Italy grew with his growth we may add that it ended only with his life. Those who watched the tedious and painful illness that in 1859 closed a long and honourable career remember with comfort the ray of gladness shed on a dreary day by news of the victories that ensured the independence of Italy and foreshadowed her unity.

delightful; but there is an anxiety over our situation
which prevents enjoyment. Our ball was really splendid
and gave great satisfaction; the rooms were decorated
with myrtle, orange trees and arbutus. There was one
long passage that was a perfect garden, really very
pretty, and enclosed by a myrtle hedge. If the country
was in a state of cultivation and the people in a state
of civilisation, it would be Elysium; but I am not
reconciled to see every peasant carrying a knife, gun
and pistol. The living here is quite luxurious; I never
saw such quantities of game and fish, and the pork is
the finest in the world—fed on chestnuts. . . . You
would be enchanted with some of the walks here; it is
impossible to see anything more beautiful. Eleanor[1]
and I are the only Englishwomen that have ever
wandered about these hills. There is about a mile
beyond Bastia a convent that is in such a heavenly
spot that if I felt it likely I should spend another
winter here I should certainly make it *my palace*. The
view is quite magnificent over the town, which being
white, has at that distance a charming effect—the sea
and the beautiful islands in front of it; the garden is
immense, full of oranges, lemons, bergamots and vines,
and it lies in a sort of bosom in the hills, rising round it
on three sides covered with cypress, olives, evergreen
oaks, and other evergreens. It is too hot for summer,
but on a winter's day one might sit and bask and feed

---

[1] Eleanor Congleton, daughter of Charles Congleton of Congleton,
and granddaughter of Sir Gilbert Elliot, Lord Justice Clerk, *m.* Col.
Drinkwater.

one's eyes with beauty, and be beyond the nuisance of the dirty town. All that Nature has done for the island is lovely, and all that man has added filthy.'

'Bastia: January 10, 1795.

'There is no doubt but that at all seasons this island is less healthy than the neighbouring continent, so much so, that many invalids who linger on here without improvement find relief by merely going to Leghorn, and return in a short time quite recovered. Intermitting fevers are the chief disease, but everything that proceeds from colds prevails here; yet this is called the healthy season; at the end of summer there is quite a mortality.

'I now feel settled, and have my mornings to myself, and climb the mountains for a couple of hours every day, through groves of myrtle, arbutus, and every sort of charming evergreen. Pozzo di Borgo, the President of the Council, and Sir Gilbert's prime favourite, is an uncommonly sensible and agreeable man. I think he is the only one of the natives that is very distinguished. There are some pretty women, unlike foreigners in general, plain in their manners and very domestic; some two or three are polished and clever. The expense of living is greater here than in London. The inhabitants live so very moderately and require so few luxuries, that people naturally think it a cheap country; but to live handsomely must be expensive, as things of all kinds have to be brought from Leghorn. Your friends the lizards are in great abundance, and do you know that formerly one of the great delicacies at Paris was *Corsican blackbirds?* They are really excellent; but you will be shocked to hear that at least twice a week we have a dish of robins. Nothing escapes the gun, even boys of the age of ours never move without one, as well as a pistol and stiletto.'

A floral calendar might be compiled with extracts from these letters.

December.—' The underwood here is the most beautiful thing in the world; it is chiefly composed of arbutus. now in flower and fruit, looking like a huge strawberry bed, of myrtle and various kinds of heath growing to a prodigious size, and many sorts of lauristine with flowers as large as a hat.'

January.—' There is snow on the hills, but orange flowers, lilacs, and narcissus in my garden.'

February.—' The fruit blossoms in full glory perfume the air.'

March.—' The almond and cherry blossoms have been long over, but the apricots and apples are charming. All the fruit trees are in leaf, excepting figs and vines, and they are peeping. Our garden is a little cape, the sea serving as a fence half round it; it is elevated about forty feet above the sea, and has a beautiful view of the coast; it is full of orange and lemon trees, rose and myrtle hedges.'

' In such a spot,' wrote Lady Elliot, 'my banishment does not sit as heavy on my heart as it did on Seneca's. In this garden the bands of the regiments

play when I have my assemblies, and the company walk
and dance on a terrace above it, washed by the sea ;
last night the scene was quite like a fairy tale, the moon
rising out of the sea exactly opposite the great glass
folding doors which lead from the room to the terrace,
it was one of the most charming things I ever saw.'

As summer drew on, the unhealthiness of the island
increased. 'In summer nights the dews are heavy.'
'The air becomes relaxing and weakening, half the
garrison is ill; but this is as much owing to their own
want of care as to any other cause.' 'There is a considerable quantity of corn raised, but the amount of
waste and undrained land, left so from want of industry,
contributes to make the country unwholesome in hot
weather. Oil and wine are in abundance, but not so
good as they might be with care and attention.' 'If
the island should continue under our protection and
any pains are taken to improve its productions, or
rather the means of cultivating them, it might have as
extensive a trade as any part of Italy in silk, wine, oil,
marbles, iron, and all kinds of minerals, and the finest
wax candles like alabaster. The people are at present
indolent, but when one considers their wretched condition, one can hardly wonder that they should not
choose to sow for others to reap.'

To give their intelligence fair play by education was
one of the favourite dreams of Sir Gilbert's short reign.

Among the chief measures of the first Parliament
held in Corsica after the annexation to Great Britain,

had been an act for the establishment of an university at Cortè and of schools at Bastia and Ajaccio.

It was hoped that another act for the incorporation of levies of Corsican troops for defence of the island would serve in some measure as an elementary educational system, teaching habits of order, of cleanliness, and of self-respect, just as at the present day the half wild natives of certain districts of Sicily are caught and shorn, and washed, and drilled into humanity under the military discipline of the Italian army; and those who have chanced to be their fellow-passengers on the decks of an Italian steamer, when as raw recruits they have been brought northwards, will readily recognise the necessity of some such primary training, as a preparation for school and the university. The intelligence and vivacity of the people never reconciled Lady Elliot to the filth and squalor. They wore to her eye the 'look of conspirators,' and, like Cæsar, she longed for men about her who were fat. Alas! in Corsica nothing was fat but the blackbirds, and they were obese. Nothing could have served better to raise the Corsicans in her estimation than the arrival of some specimens of French Republicans brought into Bastia in the spring of 1795 as prisoners of war.

After a running fight on the 13th and 14th of March, when the English fleet dispersed a French one of equal numbers, capturing the ' Ça Ira' and the ' Censeur;' these ships and their crews were brought into Bastia. ' I am very sorry to say,' wrote Lady Elliot, 'that Admiral Hotham has persuaded Sir Gilbert that the two

French ships could not be cleared out unless the prisoners were allowed to land, and for some weeks, therefore, they will be accommodated in this island. The common men will be packed in large churches, and the officers sent to Cortè, and are to be on their parole; though certainly not one of them has any idea what that means: but if they try to escape the Corsicans will make no scruple of shooting them. The officers came here from St. Fiorenzo in their way the day before yesterday; and only conceive, Sir Gilbert had six of them to dine with us. To describe their appearance is impossible; but my idea of them was a gaol-delivery. We had the two captains of the " Ça Ira ; " the first was a decent-looking man, the second conveyed to me the notion of Blue Beard; their filth was shocking. I was so filled with horror and astonishment that I was perfectly silent for two hours! They were so much surprised at the civility they met with, that they tried to be civil in their turn, saying Monsieur et Madame et Votre Excellence. They seemed very proud of their conduct and really did fight like dragons. They said to the last they looked for assistance from their fleet, and are now so enraged against their Admiral that they said they hoped he was by this time guillotined.'

Lady Elliot went with her children for a few weeks to the Baths of Lucca in the summer of 1795, in order to avoid the season of the great heat in Corsica. During her absence Sir Gilbert made a progress across the island to Ajaccio, and kept a journal for her, whence the following extracts are made.

'First night to La Penta, which was illuminated.

'Second night to Loretta, about an hour's walk from La Penta, considerably higher up the hill.

'Third day to Rostino to breakfast, and to pass the day with General Paoli, who made us welcome. Capt. Duncan has made a good sketch of the convent which he (Paoli) now inhabits, including also the house in which he was born, which might be matched at Minto. It would be difficult for any country to be prettier, wilder, or more picturesque than this. It is all "As You Like It," or "The Fairy Queen." But where is Rosalind? or the Fairy *Vice* Queen's Majesty? There's the rub; and I must play Jaques in my forest, beautiful as it is.

'Fourth day, Ajaccio, June 26.—The journey has been as prosperous and agreeable as possible; never above seven hours on the road; the weather cool; a party of pleasure to all, including the quadrupeds. The officers and men are so much pleased that they have desired to continue the march to Bonifazio instead of being relieved here by a fresh detachment. The detachment consists of 70 British of the 51st, commanded by 2 officers, and 50 Corsicans, commanded by Capt. Colonna and a subaltern. We have 100 mules for our baggage, besides horses for our own riding. Our camps have always been in pretty picturesque situations, close to a chestnut wood, or better, under chestnut trees a quarter of a mile from a village where the horses found stabling and the cook a kitchen. I passed through one considerable forest of pine and quantities of beech-

wood : the pines are immense, but they are far from
the sea and amongst the mountains, and it is difficult,
therefore, but not impossible, to get them to Ajaccio. I
hear there are other forests, which I shall see hereafter,
more conveniently situated for exportation. About
fifteeen or twenty miles of the road from Cortè to
Ajaccio is a mere bridle-path, and in many parts exceedingly bad ; about ten miles next to Cortè and ten
next to Ajaccio, are good enough for a carriage. My companions are, besides the aide-de-camps, Pozzo di Borgo,
a M. Suzzarelli, who is Conservator of the forests, and
a M. Sigaud, a French engineer whom I brought from
Cortè to consult about roads and bridges. Our reception
has been everywhere highly satisfactory, and the sort
of expedition appears to make the proper impression.'

'Ajaccio : June 27, 1795.

'I have had many formalities to perform and to
suffer, and on the whole, though these things are not
amusing to anybody, and to nobody, gentle or simple
so little as to me, my reception here has been what it
ought to be. This ought, one day, to be a considerable
place; it is already an extremely pretty town both
within and as seen from without. The form of the
ground around it, and particularly the shape of the bay,
is beautiful; wood and cultivation are wanting to the
perfection of the coast, but we have the greatest quantity
of the largest myrtles I have yet seen, all in flower and
perfuming the country. I never before knew how well
it is entitled to be the plant of Venus, the symbol of

beauty and of sweetness. The prickly pear, also in flower, grows to the height of a moderate tree. The breeze has never missed a single day and is the freshest and pleasantest thing imaginable.'

The establishment of a naval yard at Ajaccio was one of the objects of the expedition. While Sir Gilbert was there, a French frigate, the 'Minerve,' was brought in from Minorca as a prize by the 'Dido' and the 'Lowestoft,' (Captains Young and Middleton) after a brilliant action in which another French frigate, that afterwards escaped, took part.

'Cauro: June 28.

'A nice rural village ten miles from Ajaccio, and the country residence of M. Peraldi. It is a pretty country and very soon will be as rich as Croesus. The people here are tolerably tidy. I saw yesterday as neat a cottage, with ground and garden round it, as could be found in England, that land of nicety.

'I staid a night longer than I intended at Cauro to see a wood of fine oak about ten miles up the country. It is at a town called Bastelica, which is much the most flourishing and the pleasantest place I have seen ; there is a great quantity of fine oak all round and about it. The ground is divided into small fields, well enclosed and well cultivated in corn and hay. It is perfectly like an English village, with the advantage of a most picturesque highland country. They are about 2,000 souls, and, what I have seen nowhere else, every female, without exception, young and old, hard at work

spinning wool on a distaff. They also spin lint, and
almost every house has a loom and a weaver in it. It
is really a charming place, and so high up the country
that the complaint made of it is snow and cold in
winter but not heat in summer. They gave me a col-
lation at the Convent, and we were served by a Corsican
who had been eight years valet to Lord Heathfield and
was with him at his death.

'This is all I can steal for you to-day, my dear dear
love, and it is rather robbing than stealing, for it is by
main force that I have pushed off my business and the
people waiting to get a word.

'Heaven bless you all.'

'Bonifazio: July 2.

'I am now at my furthest point. This is the most
picturesque place I have seen in Corsica, and I have
gone through much beautiful country and might have
had thorough enjoyment of it with the companion I
ever wish for. My life is really tedious and burthen-
some to me from your absence. Since the summer
of 1783 I have been enduring more or less this worst
of privations. How little of the comfort of family
life I have had; but as there is no remedy at present
we must still *thole* [1] and endure.'

'Bonifazio: July 4, 1795.

'From Ajaccio to this place we have passed through
extremely pretty country, mountainous, but of a gentler
character even on the highest ground, and the lower

---

[1] To *thole*: 'to exercise patience under suffering.'—*Jamieson's Scottish Dictionary.*

parts more cultivated and cheerful. My own party is tolerably large, but besides that we are always attended by a cavalcade of the neighbouring country, who meet me with a set speech, followed by *vivas* and discharges of musketry. These gallop all in a cloud after me, with the noses of the foremost horses touching my horse's tail, a proceeding which he sometimes resents by laying his ears back and stopping dead short amongst them, on which they necessarily huddle all one over the other like falling nine-pins. One cavalcade hands me over at a river or some other boundary to another; but what is most serious is the crowd expecting us at all the halting places, where, instead of repose, I am exhibited to all comers, and circumscribed in a ring of sentinels; and when, forgetting the hardness of my task, I lie down to take a little rest, it is in state, like a deceased nobleman, curious nymphs and fawns surrounding me on every side. At the towns where we lodge we are met by bodies of militia, who fire upon us, take me prisoner and conduct me under various triumphal arches, decorated with myrtle and inscribed with various Latin and Italian compliments to the Preserver of the Municipality; more speeches follow, and I am then led in procession round the town, preceded and followed by great crowds all in their best attire shouting and shooting. The windows and balconies are full of fair ladies, the fashionable part of whom thrust out heads adorned by caps, and other superb and spacious decorations, which can never be seen again in England till the resurrection of our foremothers. I shall get Duncan (an aide-de-camp, equally excellent as a draughtsman and mathematician) to make a survey, plan, and estimate of one of them for you. The females of the humbler class demonstrated their good will, some by firing pistols out of window at me, others by throwing handfuls of wheat over me to make me fruitful as they do to brides. When I arrive at my house it is full of the gentry, and my only refuge is in the custom of the siesta. Then comes a dinner with fifty people in a small room, succeeded by a walk with a hundred people in the party. This is the style everywhere. At Ajaccio it was most splendid, and the inhabitants are considerably more like gentlefolks. This journey appears to have done good, and it has given me much information about a country which it is my business to know, and my real wish to improve.'

' Sartene : July 8, 1795.

' We set off from Bonifazio yesterday, and came to our camp in four hours' ride ; there was not a house nor a man within some miles of us, and I passed a day free from all importunity under the *bield*[1] of crags shaded by evergreen oak and myrtle. In the cool of the evening we moved forward. Travelling in this fashion and in this romantic country takes me to the " Midsummer Night's Dream," " As You Like It," the " Fairy Queen," and Ariosto at every step. The troops, the pitching the tents, the strings of mules, and all the accompaniments of our march make a moving land-

---

[1] *Bield*, Scotch for shelter.

scape while on the road, and a most picturesque scene when we halt, so that I constantly regret your not seeing it, and the absence of Rosalind from these forests takes the edge off all my pleasure.

'We have no sort of inconvenience from heat, not even riding in the sun during the forenoon and evening; this morning it was literally cold. This town is the capital of the Jurisdiction della Rocca, which is the most fertile in grain of any in Corsica, and might be a most flourishing country. It is called the Pays des Nobles—the gentry piquing themselves on their birth, and aiming at more smartness in dress, houses, and manners than in other parts of Corsica. They do not, however, get beyond the pitch of a good yeoman in England, or of the humblest squires of our remote counties. I do what I can to wake the dormant spirit of roads and bridges, fountains and other public improvements, and I hope not utterly without success. I am quite sure that much might be done for Corsica with a real application of Government to its true interests and with a just notion of the means. The French laid out a great deal of public money on public works, some of which do honour to the Government by their magnificence; but in general an immense proportion of the money was pocketed by the engineers and other persons employed, and I cannot find that any means were taken to excite in the people themselves a spirit of improvement. What a Government can execute itself is of little moment, even though a great exertion is made for it.'

'Vico: July 20, 1795.

' We left Ajaccio on the 17th, and came that day to Calcatoggio where we encamped; we passed through Pozzo di Borgo's native district, and over part of his property, and Calcatoggio is the village where the election is held for the Pieve of Cinarca, which he is member for, so that he was amongst his constituents, and I took the opportunity to tell them they had made a good choice. We came the next day to Cargise, the Greek colony, which is as interesting as anything I have seen. I lodged at the house of M. Stephanopolis, the King's advocate, whom you know, and who is chief of the Greeks. He has married, however, a Corsican, Peraldi's sister, which is one of the few, if not the only instance, of their marrying out of their own colony, so that the race is preserved very pure. They continue to dress in the Greek costume, and not a few of them appeared in the identical dresses which their ancestors brought from Greece in the last century and which have been transmitted from father to son. They ' are very splendid, considering the rank of the people, having a great deal of gold and embroidery about them. The colony consists of about 500 souls, who compose 114 families. A pretty extensive territory was given to them, and it is divided into 114 parts, each of which is now the property of a family; when the family increases, so as to become two or more, the family estate is divided among them, as is the case in the rest of Corsica. Their houses were built by the French Government on a regular and uniform plan, which always produces a

handsome-looking town, and this one is the handsomer
for the execution of the work having been given to the
father of M. Stephanopolis, who felt an interest in
doing the thing as well as possible.   These people are
industrious and much more skilful workmen than their
Corsican neighbours; but whether it is owing to the
frequent troubles in Corsica and the insecurity of
property, or some other cause, I think that less has been
done than might have been expected, and their population continues lower than one sees any occasion for.
It is supposed however, to be rather on the increase.
M. de Marbœuf was made their Seigneur with the title
of Marquis de Cargise, and with a grant of the tithe of
all their property.   He built a handsome house, which
being the only thing of the kind in the island, is always
talked of as one of the finest houses and gardens in
the world and as a true Château de Grand Seigneur. . .
It is the sort of house for about 800*l*. or 900*l*. a-year in
England or Scotland.

'This colony came from the country of ancient Sparta.
They are generally well-looking, with a prevalence of
brown skin and black eyes, but there are some fair among
them. A ball was given in the evening in order to show
us Greek ladies in their own costume.   It was in a small
room at the barracks, and the performance was not a
great many degrees removed from a Lochgelly ball, the
rank of the dancers being somewhat similar, there
being but one or two at most who do not labour in the
fields; they dance however much better, and French
country dances instead of reels.   One or two of the

women threw a sort of graceful softness into their
dancing, approaching to the voluptuous, which is described as the character of eastern dancing, but with
not the most remote idea of indelicacy. I got them to
dance a Greek dance : it was accompanied by the singing
of the dancers themselves. The song was a Greek ditty
in the modern Greek dialect, and the dance consisted in
the men and women holding each other by the hands
in a long string and moving, first very slowly, round in
a spiral line so as to have one of the women in the centre.
Then the song quickens and becomes very lively and
loud, and the dancing increases in quickness and
activity too, becoming somewhat violent and rompish,
and then, returning to the adagio movement, which was
again succeeded by the presto, and so on with the two
alternatives to the end.

' I had the song interpreted, and it was a love ditty,
as you may suppose, and from the matter and phrases
not ancient according to our reckoning, though it was
just as imported by the colony, and is, therefore, at
least a century and a half old, perhaps of a much
greater age. The air was extremely pretty and elegant,
and entirely of an Italian character. The headdress of
the women is a small scarlet caul on the back of the
head, enriched with gold lace or embroidery; the hair
in front neatly parted, and clasped close to the head.
From the back part of the caul falls a quantity of
gauze or muslin drapery, which is brought round to the
neck and crosses again to the back, where it is lost, God
knows how ! The dress is a satin or thick silk jacket

with longish skirts, extremely short waists, and a
petticoat of the same material with two or three rows
of gold lace, distant from each other about the breadth
of the lace round the bottom of it : this circumstance is
supposed to be characteristic of the country. Among the
women there are few Helens, though there was one very
pretty girl.   At our departure next morning these
Greek dames sent a plentiful shower of wheat over
me.'

CHAPTER IX.

THESE letters show the dispositions which Sir Gilbert carried with him on the expedition he describes; nevertheless so like tinder was the condition of the population, that a fabled narration of an incident supposed to have occurred at Ajaccio was sufficient to set certain districts of the island aflame.

Sir Gilbert tells the story in a letter to Lady Elliot, but before giving it, it will be useful rapidly to review the sequence of events which had at this date altered the originally cordial relations of the Viceroy with Paoli.

We have seen that when the union of Corsica with the British crown was determined, Paoli, who himself felt that in Corsica he must be *aut Cæsar aut nullus*, announced his intention of abstaining from all further share in the government of the country, and of quitting the island as soon as the British occupation should be fairly established; this step he explained to be imperatively required by the state of his health.

At that period he appears to have been animated by a sincere desire to evolve order out of chaos, and by aid of the strong hand of England to preserve his country from Jacobinical tyranny and secure to

her such popular rights and liberties as she had enjoyed a quarter of a century before under his administration.   It is probable that he was swayed in the same
direction by other and more personal motives, since at
the moment when the English Mission reached Murato
del Nebbio, a price was set on his head by the French
Convention, and his means of continued resistance were
at a low ebb.   It may therefore be assumed that if
matters had been so ordered as to admit of the trans-
ference of the government of Corsica to the British representative on the acceptance of the crown by the
King, Paoli would at that time have been more than
willing to fulfil his engagements and much subsequent
mischief would have been spared.   We have shown,
however, that the English Ministry, though prepared
long before they occurred for the events which laid on
them the responsibility of providing an administration
for Corsica, took no steps whatever towards such an
end for some months after the formal Act of Annexation had been voted by the Assembly of June 21, and
since during this interval no regular or recognised authority existed in Corsica, the real power, as was inevitable,
remained with Paoli.

As if still further to irritate the passions of the man
on whose influence with his countrymen so much depended, the English Ministers treated him with pointed
neglect.   No notice was taken of him by them; nor
until the end of the autumn of 1794 did he receive
any acknowledgment from the King of the part he had
taken in giving Corsica to Great Britain.

'Being informed,' wrote the Duke of Portland to Sir Gilbert, in a private letter dated September 16, 1794, 'of Paoli's disappointment at never having received a line or having been taken notice of by any person in a ministerial situation in this country, I enclose a letter to him.' [1]

A despatch, a few days earlier in date (September 9, 1794), contains the first recognition of Paoli's services as distinct from those rendered by the Corsican leaders in general. In this despatch it is stated that the King has expressed his pleasure to bestow on General Paoli a pension of 1,000l. per annum : and His Majesty's picture in brilliants to be worn by a gold chain round his neck, as a mark of the King's favour.

On October 17, after more than a month's reflection, the Duke of Portland wrote again, that it had occurred to him that it would be an additional satisfaction to General Paoli to be decorated formally by the Viceroy with this picture, that, in short, its presentation should take the form of an investiture, 'the first and only mark of a distinction of this kind.'

Will it be believed that after this pompous announcement the portrait never reached Corsica ? It was lost, how, when, or where we know not, but it never arrived at its destination, and Paoli was led to believe, as he himself stated to Sir Gilbert in the spring of 1795, that the British ministers had inter-

---

[1] The influence that such a letter, with other marks of royal favour, would have in soothing Paoli's feelings, had been pointed out by Sir Gilbert as early as the previous May.

cepted and retained this mark of the King's favour. Extravagant as this notion was, it must be remembered that Paoli was fully endowed with the suspicious disposition[1] characteristic of his race, and that he was profoundly ignorant of the reasons, founded on national character and conduct, which made Sir Gilbert dismiss the imputation as even more insane than childish.

The whole transaction receives a comic tinge when we find that the Corsican agents in England were at the same time insinuating the possible abstraction of the picture set in brilliants by the Viceroy himself, ' on which ' says the Duke, relating the scene in a letter to Sir Gilbert, ' I fairly lost my temper and told them plainly that if Corsican gentlemen were capable of so misunderstanding the character of English gentlemen, the sooner they and this country ceased to have any relations the better.' [2]

It has been shown that, during the interval between

---

[1] This proneness to suspicion is strikingly illustrated in the published correspondence of Paoli. When Mr. North arrived from England to fill the post as Secretary of State, great hopes were formed by Paoli and his friends of finding in him a *point d'appui* for their opposition to the viceroy. Disappointed in this, Paoli wrote to a friend : ' Potrebbe darsi che goda che il vice-rè si perda—aveva egli qualche voce per successore.' — *Lettere del Paoli*, vol. xi. *Archivio storico Italiano*, p. 543.

[2] These gentlemen on their arrival in England had not fulfilled the expectations Sir Gilbert had formed of their conduct. They fell out among themselves in their desire to make each individual's claim to superiority recognised, and, as the Duke of Portland wrote in his peculiar phraseology, ' They soon manifested a disposition to intrigue— (I own I think natural from the observations I have made on the characters of all foreigners in general, and in particular those who are members of second-rate states).'

the meeting of the National Assembly at Cortè in June and the arrival of his appointment to the Viceroyalty, Sir Gilbert's position was a trying one, although he had never ceased to be on an easy and friendly footing with Paoli.   But on Sir Gilbert's assumption of the reins of Government the scene changed, and the disappointment and ill-humour of Paoli were not long in displaying themselves.   Every measure of the Government became the subject of unfriendly criticism ; every disappointed candidate for office received compassionate sympathy ; every successful one was led to believe himself indebted to the good offices of Paoli ; and his residence at Rostino gradually became the centre of an opposition of a very annoying, if not of a formidable character ; the more so, that the many fascinating qualities which gave General Paoli so great an ascendency over those about him, were brought to bear on persons whose position should have prevented them from taking any part in the politics of Corsica.   One or two military officers, more especially allowed themselves to be drawn into the circle of *frondeurs*, oblivious possibly of the evil effects certain to be produced by the sight of divisions among the British authorities, upon a people entirely ignorant of the limit beyond which no Englishman would have carried his opposition to a government sanctioned by his king and country.   'Under these circumstances,' wrote Lady Elliot, 'Sir Gilbert's very uncommon steady composure and most wonderful command of temper were never more necessary, but the life is a laborious one.'

She probably summed up the situation with accuracy in the following words : 'People in general are very hearty in our cause, but Paoli seems adverse to government, for no reason except that Government is stronger than he and that he was not made Viceroy, which was impossible from the beginning; his age (seventy-two), and his feeble health make him quite unfit for habits of business,[1] but he cannot reconcile himself to be a stander-by, though his own friends are the actors.' 'One of his chief complaints,' she wrote again, 'is that all parties are brought into employment, and that it is desired to reconcile all former enmities; this, of course, includes his enemies as well as his friends; people he had banished have been recalled, acts of injustice perpetrated by him have been undone and lands restored to those who had been deprived of them by him for not adopting his policy.' To the same effect Sir Gilbert wrote : 'One of his grand reproaches is

---

[1] Sir Gilbert during his sojourn at Orezza in the summer of 1794 had complained more than once to his wife of the extreme slowness with which Paoli conducted all business ; and he himself, in a published letter to the Cittadino Presidente decano della camera del parlamento, rested his refusal to accept the office of President on his age and bodily infirmities. 'La mia età, le indisposizioni penose alle quali attualmente soggiaccio, non mi permettono in questa stagione intraprendere disastrosi e lunghi viaggi a cavallo ; nè potrei, sotto il loro peso, attendere alla camera giornalmente e constantemente,' &c.—Rostino, 14 febbrajo 1794 (*Archivio storico Italiano*, vol. ii.)

It may be observed that the candidature of Paoli for this office was inconsistent with that clause in the constitution which provided that the President should be elected from the body of the Assembly, and likewise with the assurance given to the English Government that on the annexation of the island Paoli would withdraw from any share in the administration.

against a paragraph in my speech, which recommends
union and charity among all parties. This, he says,
imputes to motives of personal rancour his former
transactions in Corsica.' It must be remembered that
in Corsica, besides the two great divisions of political
opinion which were at that time enrolling Europe into
two hostile camps, there was an infinite variety of
minor antagonisms arising out of private quarrels and
hereditary feuds ; these the British Government was
resolved to ignore, refusing to allow British authority,
money, or soldiers to be used for or against any of the
Corsican factions. 'On this point I have been in-
flexible, and during the whole time of the Provisional Government the Corsican and British Powers
were on this matter pulling different ways. I think it
my duty to prefer the Paolists to others, but not to the
exclusion of others.'[1]   May 23, 1795.

Another grievance of more than a year's standing, as
extracts from Sir Gilbert's despatches already given will
testify, was as lively as ever—the conviction, on Paoli's

---

[1] 'There is no doubt a good deal of party-spirit perceptible here, as
in most other places, and as we have accepted Corsica from those who
are considered as Paoli's friends, and indeed from Paoli himself, I
have always felt that there would be something shabby and inconsistent
in refusing openly to profess our connection with them.

'In the meanwhile, I shall endeavour to prevent anything like a total
exclusion of others, and shall indeed as far as I am able' with propriety
and prudence, encourage the admission of persons of merit and families
of distinction who may not have been precisely orthodox.

'In all attempts to cancel old divisions and to consolidate the interest
of parties in our support, a little time and perhaps a delicate hand are
required.'—Cortè: October 24, 1794. Sir Gilbert to the Duke of
Portland.

part, that the English Government did not mean fairly by Corsica.   He affected to believe that they concealed their policy from Sir Gilbert, but to him he owned in conversation (May 22, 1795), that he believed their design was, by withholding reinforcements, to permit France to recover the island by an appearance of conquest, in order to avoid the disgrace of surrendering it by treaty.   These wild opinions might again, as before, be traced to the difficulty experienced by Paoli in comprehending the neglect of Corsican affairs by the English Ministers.   We have seen the condition of the fleet in February, 1795, which somewhat justified the idea that defence by sea was not intended, and Paoli was probably well aware that for six months after the arrival of the Viceroy's powers he was again left without any official communication from England, while to add to the difficulty of Sir Gilbert's position, Paoli kept up an active correspondence with the Corsican delegates in England, who, for want of better information, furnished him with all the *canards* of the day.

But greater than all these causes of offence to Paoli, was the confidence placed in Pozzo di Borgo by the Viceroy. Sir Gilbert frequently states in his despatches that in Pozzo he found the only coadjutor capable of rising from a consideration of a part to the whole. The subsequent career of Pozzo confirmed Sir Gilbert's early appreciation of his capacity ; but to his fellow Corsicans, and above all to Paoli, there could be no peace while Mordecai sat in the gate.

The most preposterous stories at his expense—Parliament arbitrarily suppressed, troops levied against the people, determined blindness of the Viceroy to their interests—were spread abroad, and Paoli's own published letters display the insane jealousy which had taken possession of his mind.   It is remarkable that these same letters bear testimony, unconscious perhaps, to his conviction that the misgovernment attributed to the Viceroy could only be explained by ignorance of the wants of the people and by the evil machinations of others.

Such being the relations between Sir Gilbert and Paoli, neither cordial nor hostile, for their personal intercourse was ever marked by perfect courtesy, an incident represented to have occurred at Ajaccio was made by Paoli and his friends a pretext for an open rupture.

The charge brought by them was one of wanton insult to Paoli, by the destruction and 'assassination' of his bust, removed under peculiarly offensive circumstances from the ball-room by Pozzo di Borgo and Colonna, the latter one of Sir Gilbert's aide-de-camps.   Of this story Sir Gilbert wrote to Lady Elliot as follows:

'Bastia: August 2, 1795.

'General Paoli is playing the D—— with a vengeance; the pretence is an absurd lie which was invented while I was first at Ajaccio.   The Corsican battalion gave me a ball.   It seems there was a plaster bust of Paoli in the room where we were to dance; it was necessary to remove it in order to make room and to put up some ornaments and devices for the occasion. I never knew of the bust existing, or heard one syllable about it, till ten or twelve days afterwards Pozzo di Borgo received letters from Cortè saying that information had been sent to Paoli that his bust had been insulted, broken to pieces, &c., by Captain Colonna, my aide-de-camp.

'The fact is that Colonna had not been in the house *at all*, and that on my return to Ajaccio I saw the bust with no visible damage, but about the thickness of a wafer rubbed off the tip of the nose, which appeared like an old sore.

'Pozzo di Borgo wrote to Paoli to contradict the story: Paoli's answer treated it as true. Colonna then wrote to deny it on his word of honour. Paoli declared his intention not to answer, and wrote the original story all over the country; he has had Pozzo di Borgo burnt in effigy in several villages, and a petition is being signed asking me to remove him. Of course, all this is mere pretext, nothing in the world shall induce me to move one inch; if this island is incapable of bearing a good government we had better give it up; it is not worth a bad one, even if we were capable of attempting such.'

In the published correspondence of Paoli will be found a letter [1] from him which confirms Sir Gilbert's

'Rostino: 8 agosto.

[1] 'Cari e buoni amici,— . . . Il gesso fu rimosso, e gettato per terra in una camaretta, ora abbandonata ad ogni uso . . . lo che fu il caso la sera del ballo. Due processi verbali, uno del podesta della città,

statement, that in spite of the disclaimers of Pozzo and
Colonna, corroborated by the Viceroy, Paoli did not
cease to write ' this story ' all over the country; instigated, perhaps, thereto by those who sought their own
ends in fomenting the discord between Paoli and the
Government.

To Sir Gilbert the affair was only a ' pretext ' for
getting rid of good government, and he would probably
have taken no exception to the account given by Botta
in his ' History of Italy,' of the mixed motives which
induced certain districts of Corsica to rise in insurrection in the summer of 1795.[1]

Happily the leaders of the insurrection were gifted
largely with that discretion which claims to be the

l' altro del procuratore della medesima, assicurano il fatto, e l' assicurano
le lettere particolari di quelli che hanno veduto il busto mutilato.

[1] " Parva scintilla magnum excitavit incendium." Erano quei signori
arrabiati per una risposta ch'io fece al vice-rè ; e quelle offese che
fecero a quel pezzo di gesso l'avrebbero fatta alla mia persona.
L'altra sera io scrissi a Balestrini e Savelli, e li feci sentire che
questo fatto più si esamina, tanto più puzzara.'—*Lettere di Pasquale
Paoli, Archivio storico Italiano.*

[1] 'The English rule in Corsica was not becoming established partly
because of the natural restlessness of the nation, partly because the
partisans of France were numerous, finally, because the population,
expecting, according to their custom, more from the name of liberty than
she can give, had grown to believe that she would secure them an
immunity from taxation ; and when undeceived had become disaffected,
declaring that they had changed masters but not burdens. Others
there were who, recognising the influence of Paoli's great name and
preferring the independence of Corsica to union with England, turned
their eyes to him as to one who, having prevented the acquisition of
Corsica by France, might still be capable of disputing it with England.

'All these notions, separately or combined,' says the historian, 'led to
disturbances in certain districts, chiefly in the neighbourhood of
Ajaccio.'—Botta's *History of Italy.*

better part of valour, and they at an early period perceived the dangers threatening themselves should
matters be pushed to extremities. 'Treachery,' wrote
Sir Gilbert, ' is the order of the day here, and persons
in the confidence of Paoli have not scrupled to send his
correspondence to members of my Government.'

Under his own hand it now appeared that Paoli was
in communication with the Corsican republican refugees in Genoa and France, and was describing himself
to his partisans in the island as carrying on a constant
correspondence with the King of Great Britain, who
was about to remove the Viceroy and place Paoli at the
head of affairs, with Moore in command of the troops.
With these proofs of Paoli's complicity in the late
troubles in his possession, Sir Gilbert appealed to the
Ministry at home to enforce, though by the most conciliatory means at their disposal, the retirement of
General Paoli from Corsica, and to remove Colonel
Moore, the adjutant-general, whether by promotion or
transfer to another post. In the case of Colonel Moore,
Sir Gilbert explained that the ground he took for the
application was simply the fact of Moore's interference
in the politics of Corsica.   Sir Gilbert ' believed him
to be one of the best regimental officers in the service.'

In the same despatches Sir Gilbert stated pretty
plainly his opinion that the mischief which had arisen
in Corsica owed its existence to the delays and negligence of the English Ministers, who had in the first instance allowed a provisional Government to taste of the
powers of a stable one, and in the second, had given by

carelessness a semblance of truth to the suspicion that
the Viceroy was not in their confidence.   Should there
be any grounds for this notion, which, however, he did
not believe, Sir Gilbert desired to be recalled at once.

'Sir Gilbert,' wrote Lady Elliot,[1] 'is determined to
take no important measures without clear authority
from England; everything is quiet just now, but Paoli
tells his adherents that if it should come to a battle,
the King has promised to supply him with money
against Sir Gilbert and the English military force:
the folly of the whole business is only to be equalled by
its rascality.   Sir G. seems to think it will all end well
when once he gets the absolute powers he expects from
England soon.   In fact he has them now, but he very
wisely does not choose to use them in so important
a case but from absolute authority. . . In the mean*
time there is so much discontent and disaffection that
Sir Gilbert's situation is perilous.   He cannot venture
into the country, and must stay and roast at Bastia and
face all the evils of heat and disease.   He is quite composed, as usual.   He thinks the present discontent will
soon die away, and is determined not to give way to any
of their demands.   He has received petitions from two
districts which are those where Paoli resides, requesting
him to turn out the *Prime Minister*, Pozzo di Borgo,
and I send you his answer.   Nothing will tempt him
to comply with a request made without the smallest
ground but his being a very able man, and weaker ones
wishing for his power.

[1] To Lady Malmesbury.

'Paoli is openly hostile to the Government. I send you enclosed his address to the people, and you will see that he professes loyalty to the King, but chooses to be the head of the State.'

While Sir Gilbert was thus left to roast at Bastia he found no better comfort than to turn his eyes from the 'lift of unclouded blue' above him to that quarter of the sky where heavy masses of cloud hung over the hills of Lucca.

'Bastia : August 17, 1795.'

'I have just received your letters of the 10th and 11th ; the one by Captain Vaumarel, the other by M. de Bosy, and am very glad I received the last letter an hour before the other, as I knew of all your recoveries before I heard of your illnesses. I am thanking God for the change of weather which happened here yesterday. It had been extremely sultry and oppressive for some days though there was wind, but it was not a refreshing one, and I have always been in a fright about some of you. Indeed, though I seem to stand it all better than most people, yet the amount and nature of my present business does not require the aggravation of a debilitating climate. We have now had a quantity of hard rain, and when this happens after the middle of August it is a turn in the year ; and I understood we may reckon the severity of the season over . . . In other respects I repeat my assurances that you need not be uneasy, and I must put you on your guard against believing

[1] To Lady Elliot.

reports; for everything in the world is exaggerated everywhere, even without ill intentions, but in these countries one never hears truth by accident. People went from hence into the country and said that all was over at Bastia, that the whole town was against us, that I never went out in the day, and slept in the citadel every night, and that Pozzo di Borgo never stirred without eight gensd'armes to guard him. The whole is not only false, but without a particle of truth. We have many fast friends, who have behaved handsomely and honourably, and I do not doubt of all being settled much better than ever; but not in a day. I must have my answers from London first. As for myself, I am both tired with work and disgusted with all the baseness I am obliged to witness. While I thought myself employed in founding the happiness of this country and increasing the power and prosperity of England, I was highly gratified and never repined at either labour or risk. I am now more impatient under the sacrifice of all our private happiness and of all my own prospects and views elsewhere, with the risk of health and life, in the service of such monstrous ingratitude, and possibly with the prospect of failing in both objects. When this brush is over I shall have the right to beg that some one else will come and fag in their turn, and I certainly shall do so.'

'September 26, 1795.

'The answers may arrive any day, but I do not depend on them till the end of the month, as the Duke of

Portland will look at his nails and raise his spectacles from his nose to his forehead for a fortnight or so before he answers me. Paoli has certainly made his emissaries here tell some of the countrypeople that he has letters from the King, and that the King would assist them with money and arms against me if I should make war upon them. I should think it rather a shorter method to turn me out.'

Pending the reply to his despatches, the Viceroy adopted a conciliatory policy. He issued a proclamation in which he recalled the various advantages that had accrued to Corsica from her connection with England—-her deliverance from anarchy and from the restoration of an oppressive rule; security to the lives and liberties of her people purchased with English blood; her heaviest expenses, her military establishment, the supplies of the arsenal of Ajaccio, borne at the cost of England; safety on the sea secured to her traders by English fleets; the rights of property rendered sacred and inviolate; the ancient religion of the country respected. This proclamation produced a good effect, and Sir Gilbert was able to assure his wife, who by his desire prolonged her residence at Lucca during the continuance of the disturbances, that she might banish from her mind all apprehensions as to the ultimate result of the troubles, as well as on the score of his personal safety, though he confessed that Pozzo and Colonna were less safe than himself.

In the course of October Sir Gilbert's confidence was

justified by the arrival of despatches from England, approving in high terms of the policy pursued by him since his assumption of the Government of Corsica, dwelling with especial commendation on his forbearance towards Paoli and Colonel Moore, but reminding him that the powers already bestowed on him were more than sufficient to enable him to put down every attempt at opposition and to expel Paoli from the island. This was in fact the case; but as Sir Gilbert had a better knowledge than his chief of the personal position and influence of General Paoli, he preferred to act on an occasion so liable to misconstruction with the greatest circumspection. To this decision of Sir Gilbert it was due that, when the inevitable moment for Paoli's departure arrived, it was made as palatable to him as such a measure could ever be. He was requested to go to England on the invitation of the King, and was promised an addition of 2,000*l.* a-year to his pension while residing there. The offer was accepted with scarcely a hesitation—the only alternative would have been open revolt—and Paoli embarked for Leghorn, attended to his vessel by the Viceroy with every mark of consideration, while the population looked on with indifference and the *Paolists* rejoiced at being out of a scrape.[1]

'Paoli has written to his friends here,' wrote Sir

[1] The Duke of Portland in a private letter informed Sir Gilbert that Paoli's agents in England, speaking through Pietri their mouth-piece, ascribed Paoli's dissatisfaction with the Viceroy to the following causes; 'Your confidence in Pozzo di Borgo, who showed base ingratitude to Paoli, without whose protection and countenance and introduction to you

Gilbert to Lady Elliot, 'that the King's invitation is so gracious that he wishes he had wings at his feet, like Mercury, to be there the sooner.

'I trust we shall now have an interval of tranquillity, and that it will *last my time*. Parliament is to meet at Cortè on November 15th.

'I wish this letter could be carried to you on Mercury's wings before they are buckled on General Paoli's ancles.' [1]

With Paoli's departure from the island he disappears from the correspondence. 'It would take a long summer's day,' wrote Lady Elliot to her sister, 'to draw him;' nevertheless the innumerable allusions to his conduct and capacity leave a general impression on the mind of a character of which the type was essentially Corsican. Nature had endowed him in a conspicuous

that young man would have remained in obscurity ; your retaining your aide-de-camp Colonna, against whom he inveighed in terms as bitter as decency and respect to me would admit, and respecting both, he read a letter from Galiazzi in which they are treated as persons of infamous character, whose conduct at Ajaccio in the destruction and assassination of the bust, had revolted the whole island and brought all the English officers over to their side. His other charges were employment of foreigners instead of Corsicans in subordinate branches of the administration. I told him all these facts were disproved by the enquiry you had insisted on. I told him that in your place I doubted if I should have condescended to make any enquiry into such preposterous charges. On the whole, in spite of all that was said, I am left with the impression they would be glad if Paoli would make an honourable retreat.

[1] It is more than probable that the attitude of the population at this time was resented by Paoli, for in one of his published letters written several years after these events he stated an intention of never returning to Corsica, and added that on two occasions he had been forced to come away at the moment when he had hoped to effect some good by his presence

degree with a lively intelligence, quick perceptions, a fluent and graceful diction : to these not uncommon gifts in his race he added large conceptions, a vivid imagination, and considerable acquirements. 'Les défauts de ses qualités' were also his; the liveliness of his imagination bred a quick suspiciousness, which again, was the cause of much of the insincerity and pusillanimity attributed to his conduct by friends and foes. The very vividness of his conceptions of what should be done for his people seems to have allured him into forgetfulness of the fact that they did very little for themselves. He showed himself truly one of them by never putting himself into collision with their most crying faults—their greed and their spirit of revenge. That he was a man of remarkable powers cannot be doubted, though these had been dimmed by age before Sir Gilbert ever saw him. To Lady Elliot he was 'supremely an actor, and people' she said, 'are amused by Dumouriez's book, in which he makes him a hero.' But the story of his early life justifies the title given him by Dumouriez, while Boswell's account of Paoli tends to confirm Lady Elliot's judgment. He was no doubt fully imbued with the dramatic instincts of the great artistic race whence he sprung, to which they owe the fact of their having produced the ideal types of the grandest rôles ever performed on the world's stage, whether as Cæsars, tribunes, priests, or prima donnas.[1] We incline to think that if, on their

[1] The spirit of the age may have encouraged these natural tendencies, the eighteenth century having been the most histrionic the world has ever

side, the British Government had been less flagrantly deficient in any sense of the dramatic proprieties, they and their Corsican ally might have understood each other better.

For nearly two years before his discontent came to a head Paoli had been prepared to arrange his drapery and fall with dignity as the self-immolating Father of his Country; what was he to think of those who, instead of surrounding his political obsequies with marks of honour, acted as if they thought their inheritance barely worth the succession duty?

In answer to a letter from Sir Gilbert remonstrating on the neglect with which he was treated, Mr. Windham wrote:—

'London: August 28, 1795.

' My dear Sir Gilbert,—Your letter is luckily come on a post-day, for I should have been impatient of every moment that had delayed my sending the answer to it immediately. We are all here so much immersed in the business of our own departments (at least I am in that which I make my department rather than that which is so officially—I mean the concerns of the French within and without), that all that you tell me of recall and successor, opinion of your being out of favour

---

seen. See in England Chatham draping his flannels and wielding his crutch, Burke and his dagger, Wolfe and the flourishing sword which struck dismay into the souls of Pitt and Temple: in France, a whole people masquerading in the *properties* of other nations, ancient and modern; whilst even the great Prussian soldier king insisted on turning his subjects into Frenchmen.

here, and opposition raised in consequence, comes to
me like news from the moon. Your former letter had
in some measure prepared me for this, but not in such
a way as to give me any idea that the effect could be
such as you seem to describe . . . The fault, I am persuaded, is not that anyone has thought or acted wrong,
but that they have not thought at all. It is from
the want of proper attention and culture that all these
weeds have sprung up.

.   .   .   .   .   .

' The trial I have had of official life has not served to
reconcile me to it. It is the period of my existence in
which, I think, I have had the least enjoyment ; but
whether that proceeds from the nature of the situation
or from my having come to a state in which the last
period is likely to be the worst, I will not venture to
pronounce. I go doggedly on, however, resolved that
what good I can do shall not be lost for want of as-
siduity, and enjoying, in fact, the persuasion till lately
that my determination in that respect had not been
without effect. The failure of the expedition to Quiberon, produced by a blind confidence and want of
military capacity on one side, and by the eternal operation of French cabal on the other, joined to the event
of the Spanish peace, has brought things to a state in
which that consolation will probably be denied me. As
long, however, as war goes on—of which I hope the conclusion is still far distant, I mean on any terms short
of the destruction of the present French system—there
will be still something for me to do. Should peace ever

be made with the Republic, I think England will be no
longer a country to live in ; and in that case, as there
will be no country free from the effects of their power
and of their insolence, one may as well choose that
which has in other respects the most recommendations,
and with that view I think I shall be inclined to choose
Italy.   If one is to submit to humiliation it had better
be anywhere else than in one's own country.   What
you mention about the last naval action is wholly new
to me, and I am not sure whether it is not so to everyone in these parts.

    ' Ever most truly and affectionately yours,

            ' W. W.'

             ' September 1.

  P.S.—' The same day on which I had written the sheet
accompanying this I saw the Duke of Portland, who
had been in quest of me, and found him exactly in
the disposition I had supposed.   The question was
only how to get a decision in time, it being a matter
too important to be disposed of without its being submitted to the Cabinet, and there being no Minister
besides himself and me in town.   I am not correct :
upon recollection, Lord Spencer was in town, Mr.
Dundas no further than Wimbledon ;   Lord Grenville,
however, was at Dropmore, and Mr. Pitt at Walmer.
The King, too, is at present at Weymouth.   These
causes of delay will prevent the messenger from being
sent off till the end of the week.'

In order to part as soon as may be from a disagreeable subject—one that strikes us like a false note in
the harmony of Sir Gilbert's life—we shall include in
the chapter of his dissensions with Paoli those with
Colonel Moore, which, indeed, grew out of them. The
despatches which summoned Paoli to England not
only recalled Colonel Moore, but desired him to quit
the island in forty-eight hours. 'This step,' wrote Sir
Gilbert to Lady Elliot, 'I neither asked nor approve.'
It was the Duke of Portland's reply to a confidential
despatch, wherein the Viceroy had simply asked the
transfer of Moore to another post ; the grounds for the
request being the active political sympathies shown by
Moore.

The result of the Duke of Portland's ill-advised
measure was the placing of Sir Gilbert in a painful
and embarrassing situation, wholly unprovoked by any
act of his own ; for as he himself wrote in a private
despatch to the Duke, 'It would be hard indeed on a
public man, were he not able to state confidentially to
his chief his sentiments concerning the judgment,
tact, and temper of those with whom he is acting,
without being supposed to bring public charges against
them.' On Moore's return to England, Mr. Dundas,
probably thinking that he had been ill-used, gave him
his promotion, a step, as we have seen, suggested by
Sir Gilbert himself to the Duke of Portland, as a
proper way of removing him from Corsica.[1]

[1] The Duke of Portland appears never to have communicated Sir
Gilbert's correspondence to the other Ministers.

The news of Moore's promotion following immediately on what might be called an expulsion from Corsica, at the desire of Sir Gilbert, naturally gave rise to many misrepresentations among the partisans of the discomfited party there.

'Colonel Moore,' wrote Sir Gilbert to Mr. Elliot of Wells, 'has written to his friend, Colonel Oakes, not merely that he is appointed to a command in St. Domingo—which I by no means disapprove of, but just the contrary—it was my earnest recommendation and prayer that he might not be prejudiced in his professional views by his misconduct here—but he writes that he has been·received with open arms and caresses by the King and all the Ministers, who tell him he has been *very ill-used*, and offered him any command he chose; that he is much obliged to me for having served him without intending it. This letter is handed about to all who would read it.'

Sir Gilbert, in the meanwhile, sent home a full report of all the circumstances which had led him to ask the removal of Moore, and the next letter he received from Mr. Elliot contained the following passage: 'Your despatch has produced a profound impression on Dundas, who says that had he received it before promoting Moore he should never have done so.' That promotion, however, was never matter of regret to Sir Gilbert, but he did not scruple to acknowledge himself aggrieved by the hasty and injudicious conduct of the Duke of Portland, the effects of which he was destined to feel for some time after the termination of his connection with Corsica.

The two services were on a notoriously bad footing when Sir Gilbert joined the fleet off Corsica, previous to the attack by the naval forces on San Fiorenzo. Sir Gilbert, 'though desirous to give no opinion on military matters, which were beyond his province,' did not conceal his sympathy with the tone and spirit of the naval commanders; hence, as he thought, a little soreness was conceived by the military towards himself, and hence the dissatisfaction which arose when, by his appointment to the Viceroyalty, they found themselves under his command. However this may have been, he had abundant evidence when difficulties arose in his administration of Corsica, that the opponents to his policy found support among the military circles of the society.

With the most eminent members of the sister service Sir Gilbert formed, during his stay in Corsica, relations of close and lasting friendship; and if his footing with the military was less uniformly satisfactory, though among them too he found cordial friends, it must be remembered in how many other parts of the world facts bore witness to the opinion formed by him of the English army officer, as he was at that time. 'Too many of them are equally remarkable for their dread of personal responsibility and their great personal pretensions,' a condition of things out of which military

---

[1] A collision took place very early in Sir Gilbert's vice-reign, between the British military power and the civil authorities of Bastia. Its

quarrels will grow whenever they have to act with foreign allies or with another branch of the service.'[1]

occasion was a very imperious mandate signed by General Stuart desiring the municipality of Bastia to release a native imprisoned by their authority; an interference with their civil rights which they and the population of Bastia naturally resented. The Viceroy thereupon not only condemned the proceeding of the General in the particular case before him, but declared that 'there should be no authority in the island independent of that one of which the powers and limitations had been constitutionally defined.'

[1] Sir Gilbert to Lady Elliot.

CHAPTER X.

The winter of 1795-6 found the family re-assembled in Corsica, and the spring of 1796 was ushered in under unusually agreeable auspices. Two foreign regiments, one of Swiss, another of French *émigrés*, had been sent to Corsica to aid in the defence of the island; and among their officers were several whose society afforded a great resource. ' De Rolle's Swiss regiment,' wrote Lady Elliot, ' is a prodigious fine one. The Lieutenant-Colonel is a most charming man, and was Captain of the Grenadier Guards on duty the famous or rather *infamous* 10th of August. He and three other officers were, I think, all that escaped, and eighty odd soldiers out of the whole regiment. He dined here yesterday, and gave me a full account of that horrid scene and his own miraculous escape, and is to give me a written history of all the various events that preceded that horrid day. Dillon's [2] regiment are a very fine set of men.   There is an old officer and Chevalier de St.

---

[1] These regiments did not arrive in Corsica till 1796.

[2] ' Dillon is still to the taste of vice-queens,' wrote Lady E. to her sister, ' a thoroughly well-bred gentleman, with a certain gentle tedious-ness.' Evidently a charming *raconteur* after the fashion of times when the world had leisure to listen. He was also an accomplished draughtsman, as the sketches he made for Lady Elliot still testify.

Louis in the ranks, and another whose son is his own sergeant. They *must* be men of real character. A shocking thing has happened here: one of the officers who was a supernumerary but thought himself sure of being placed, found on his arrival last Monday (this is Saturday) that he was to be reduced. He was a little unwell at the time, and his disappointment was so great and his feelings so strong, that he almost immediately lost his senses and died yesterday. Whenever he spoke to anybody he said: "Sir, you are not reduced." He has a wife, mother, and daughter in Germany, and has lived nearly *on nothing* on his journey in order to send them his pay. We have dukes and princes as ensigns and lieutenants, who once enjoyed their 10,000*l.* or 15,000*l.* a-year. I protest it makes me unhappy to be amongst them, and I feel as if it were an impertinence to be at my ease.'

They, notwithstanding, bore their penury with cheerful philosophy, or perhaps with that perfection of good breeding which prevents the intrusion of personal cares on the social enjoyments of others. 'They laughed the sense of misery far away.'[1] When to their presence was added that of the officers of the British fleet, Lady Elliot's parties in the wave-washed garden brought together notabilities of the past and heroes of the future; those who had shone in courts and those on whom the existence of courts depended.

Among the rest were three who might almost be

---

[1] Goldsmith's 'Traveller.'

accepted as types of the Past, Present, and Future of monarchical France. Edward Dillon, better known as le Beau Dillon, who had shone conspicuous by his personal advantages at the brilliant court of poor Marie Antoinette.

The Baron de Rolle, who, when that court melted away 'like snow wreaths in autumn,' nobly maintained a soldier's honour, nor sheathed his sword until his sovereigns had been made captives and their last defenders had perished.

Pozzo di Borgo, whose hatred of Bonaparte and influence with the Emperor Alexander had no small share in bringing the Allies to decide on the restoration of the Bourbons, and who was himself among the first to re-enter with the Allied Sovereigns the palace of the Tuileries.

With these at times came another, who did more than any man for years to come to check the Power before which continental Europe was made to crouch; Nelson, with shock head and simple manners and a hero's heart.

The winter having passed over tranquilly, Sir Gilbert was led to hope that a mutual good understanding was growing up between the Government and the population. His views as to the only secure basis on which the English occupation could rest, namely, the cordial co-operation of the people with the Authorities, is set forth in one of his despatches to the Duke of Portland.

'No man could have been more explicit than myself in declaring from the beginning, in everything that I have said or written, that we neither are able, nor should we desire to conquer Corsica, or to hold the Government of this people on any other footing than that of their sincere and cordial support. But I never imagined that any people, much less this one, would remain perpetually in a state of universal tranquillity, and that we should not occasionally have to contend with local and partial disorder; it would be absurd and unwarrantable on one hand to attempt the maintenance of this Government *by force* against the general inclination of the people, and it would be dishonourable, and I cannot help saying absurd, on the other, to abandon a people that are attached to us and faithful to their engagements, because some troubles arise in particular districts and at particular moments.'[1]

The events of the spring—i.e. the disasters of Piedmont, the submission of the king of Sardinia, the retreat of the Austrians to Mantua—produced a very sensible effect ' in heartening the enemies of England and discouraging her friends.' An insurrection instigated by French emissaries and at first confined to a few villages, extended itself in the interior of the island, and with so much secrecy and celerity that Sir Gilbert, who had gone to Cortè to be nearer the scene of operations and had accompanied the troops to some distance from the town on their way to Bocognago, would have been intercepted by the insurgents on his

[1] Despatch of the Viceroy to the Duke of Portland, Bastia, April 8, 1796.

Such ' partial troubles' were, at the moment he wrote, on the point of disturbing the tranquillity of the island.

return, had he not received timely warning of their having assembled in force in the neighbourhood, and of the necessity for an immediate return to Cortè, which he regained in safety.

This escape notwithstanding, his situation was one of great difficulty and delicacy, either of the two courses open to him, of severity or of conciliation, being equally fraught with danger to the future good relations of the government and the people. 'It would have been easy,' he wrote in one of his despatches, ' to drive them from their positions and beat them in the field, but I had reason to believe that a contest between the troops and people assembled on this occasion would be the signal for a civil war.'

Happily the insurgents were equally unwilling to push matters to extremities, and on their showing a disposition to treat, Sir Gilbert consented to hear their grievances.

Persons were appointed to know their terms, and they expressed their desire to send in petitions, with a statement of the causes of their discontent. This they did, after two days had passed in discussion among themselves, during which it was surmised that the leaders and the people were not agreed in their demands. If this were so, the Corsican element must at last have prevailed; for when the petitions arrived, they contained no allusion to what might be termed constitutional questions, they contained no republican, or anti-English sentiments, but they expressed the true Corsican objection to taxation in

general, and the equally national feeling of inveterate
jealousy of their countrymen in office. The petitioners
demanded that the whole Corsican *personnel* of the
Administration should be changed, that the Council of
State and Pozzo di Borgo at its head, should be thrown
into prison, that the Parliament should be dissolved,
and that the new one to be elected should never sit
within reach of cannon. Sir Gilbert, with the advice
of his Ministers, determined to grant the dissolution of
Parliament, to accept the resignation of five members of the Administration, who had placed them in
his hands on becoming aware of the nature of the
petitions, and to take the land and salt taxes into consideration.   Of the other demands no notice was taken.

With this answer the people expressed themselves
satisfied, and returned their thanks to the Viceroy,
offering to form a line for him as he left Cortè, and
to lay down their arms in token of submission.
'Throughout the whole business,' wrote Lady Elliot,
'there has appeared an attachment to the English and
a dislike to the French. They even told one of their
leaders that if he proposed at any time to bring in the
, French he should answer for it with his head.   They
always said it was their own countrymen to whom
they bore enmity; and in their camp they cried,
'Viva il Rè, il Vice-rè e gl' Inglesi.'

These events served to strengthen the growing conviction among the English that unless far more
vigorous measures were adopted than had been hitherto
attempted by the English Ministry, it would be im-

possible to hold Corsica with France threatening Sardinia and Leghorn, and with the population of Corsica not unnaturally impressed by the wonderful triumphs of the French armies under a Corsican leader.

'The first and grand disadvantage,' wrote Sir Gilbert, 'under which we now labour is the progress of the French arms in Italy. Besides the general impression which every fresh triumph of the Republic must make on the rest of Europe, the conquest of Italy, or even her submission to the will of France, will affect us directly in the following manner : the supplies of the fleet and army are all drawn from Leghorn, and general expectation prevails of Tuscany's being compelled to withhold from us any future supplies, and there is reason to apprehend that similar conditions will be imposed on the Roman State and on the kingdom of Naples, as the first article of any peace they may obtain.

'There seems a great probability that the island of Sardinia will be ceded to France, in which event they may send in detail troops and stores to this country.'

.   .   .   .   .   .

'The opinion of a rupture with Spain beginning to circulate, adds another ground of diffidence in the permanence of the present government.'[1]

All these circumstances pointed to a not distant abandonment by Great Britain of Corsica, and justified the restlessness of the islanders.

'To be weak is miserable—doing or suffering,' was

[1] Despatches. vol. ii. p. 147.

the key-note of the Viceroy's correspondence, public or private, at this time.

'You cannot keep Corsica,' he wrote to one of the Ministers, 'against the will of the whole people. You ought not, if you could; but if you can spare a sufficient number of British troops to hold the strong places of the island, with the aid of the fleet, against all external attacks, the knowledge that you can do so will keep this people steady to your cause. If we are weak we shall be set at naught. If we are strong weak powers will cling to us.'

The opinions of Sir John Jervis and of Commodore Nelson coincided with those of Sir Gilbert. 'With harbours of refuge for our fleets and a position for our troops and stores such as Corsica afforded, they had no doubt of being able to command the Mediterranean, and to protect or threaten the coasts of Italy, according as they should be held by friend or foe, without the dismal necessity of bolstering up our incompetent allies.'

The contemplated cession of the island of Sardinia to France produced several despatches from Sir Gilbert, urgently pressing on the attention of Government the disastrous results of such an event to Great Britain, and suggesting that proposals should be made to the Court of Turin for a British occupation of the island during the war. The relations of the islanders with the court had been as bad as possible for some time past, and it was thought that both parties might find their advantage in the course indicated.

In reference to some late insurrectionary movements

in Sardinia, Sir Gilbert wrote : ' It would be desirable
to know what is the sincere sentiment of the major
part of Sardinia on the late occurrences, for insurrec-
tions, though apparently general, are often the act of
the smaller number. Those who concur or acquiesce
in them letting themselves from weakness follow the
stream of events, till they arrive at objects from which
they would have shrunk with horror if they had been
originally presented to them.' If any such transfer of
Government were intended as had been suggested by
Sir Gilbert, he considered that the entire and sincere
consent of the Sardinians themselves must be obtained,
as an indispensable condition of the project: ' it is
on that datum alone it can receive a moment's consideration.'

To these letters, such was the slackness of his correspondents at home, Sir Gilbert rarely received replies.
' Their silence is inexplicable, and inconceivable in the
harm it produces, yet I know them to be good friends
to the cause and to me.'

' You ask whether Corsica is to be given up, a question that can only be answered at home,' wrote Lady
Elliot to Lady Malmesbury, ' from whence we have
heard nothing official for eight months.'[1]

---

[1] June 8, 1796. When at last a messenger from England arrived, he
brought with other despatches a private letter from the Duke of Portland,
in which the following paragraph occurs, needing no commentary. ' You
must remember that the possession of Corsica is not more gratifying to the
public than that of Gibraltar; and that the expenses belonging to it are
not likely to make it popular. Recollect that our worthy countrymen are
not foreign politicians; they cast up an account well enough; but as for
power or even protection beyond the Channel, the bulk of the people of

One weak power after another was drawn into the vortex of French ascendency.

On May 15, 1796, a treaty of peace [1] was signed at Paris between France and Sardinia.   On the 16th Nelson wrote to Sir Gilbert, 'I very much believe that England, who commenced the war with all Europe for her allies, will finish it by having nearly all Europe against her.'

As an immediate result of the Peace of Paris, the Pope shut his ports against the English, and it was only due to the strenuous efforts of Sir W. Hamilton, backed by the support of the Viceroy, that Naples did not do the same.   'In that distracted country, divided by internal feuds, there is a general detestation and horror of the French and great promises to act against them, but at the same time they are more than ready for peace, and are believed to be in treaty for it.'   A

this country are incapable of feeling the necessity as of estimating the value of it.'   At this very time, Admiral Jervis was blockading Toulon, of which post he never lost sight for a single hour during six months, a measure rendered practicable only by daily communications with Corsica.

[1] On April 23, the King of Sardinia had requested a suspension of arms, and sent plenipotentiaries to Genoa to treat.   The French demanded a cession of two out of the three fortresses of Coni, Alessandria and Tortona as a condition of the suspension of arms; but when the conferences were opened, Bonaparte insisted upon the possession of all three, and of the conquered country between the Genoese territory and the Po.   This armistice was signed on the 28th.

The Duke of Parma was the next Italian sovereign who followed the example and fortunes of the King of Sardinia, and he was the first to be plundered of his works of art.

On entering Verona, Bonaparte announced that had Louis XVIII. not previously left the refuge of its walls, he should have given the city to the flames.

course one can hardly condemn if their means of resistance were limited to such troops as had formed the Neapolitan contingent at Toulon.

Lady Elliot to Lady Malmesbury.

'Bastia: May 24, 1796.

'The advances of the French into Italy will have reached you, and if you are like me you will not be surprised at the success of all their attempts. We received yesterday the accounts of their being in Milan, and of Beaulieu having retreated to Mantua. He has left, it is said, a strong garrison in the citadel of Milan with orders to resist to the last; but what can be done against the force of the French and the inclination of the greater number of the inhabitants wherever they go? The poor in all states are more numerous than the rich, and are all favourable to the new system of plunder and the chances before them.'[1]

A month after the Peace of Paris the French were in possession of Leghorn, and in defiance of the neutrality of the Grand Duke, the cannon of the forts were directed against the English shipping in the roads.

How suddenly these events came about are related

---

[1] In a proclamation dated May 19th, and addressed to the people of Lombardy, after discoursing on the fraternity of nations, Bonaparte demanded a contribution of 20,000,000 francs to be levied from the rich, the easy classes, and the ecclesiastical corporations, the indigent class to be alone spared.

'Cette contribution devait être frappée sur les riches, sur les gens véritablement aisés, sur les corps ecclésiastiques, et épargner la classe indigente.'—Lanfrey's *Napolcon.*

in a letter from Lady Elliot to her sister, written in the early days of June. To escape from the heat of Corsica in its most unhealthy season, she had ventured to remove with her children to the mainland, encouraged thereto by the assurances she received from His Majesty's Minister to the Court of Tuscany,[1] that the French intended to respect the neutrality of Tuscany. She was in the neighbourhood of Pisa when she heard of the arrival of the French at Bologna, a fact that produced in her mind the instantaneous conviction that the preliminary of a justifiable pretext would be dispensed with and that Tuscany would be entered next.[2]

'In spite,' wrote Lady Elliot on the 26th of the month to her sister, after her arrival at Bastia, 'in spite of all the assurances I received from Mr. Wyndham, of there being no danger in Tuscany, I took the liberty to make use of my own reason and understanding, and from the moment I heard of 22,000 men having arrived unexpectedly at Bologna, I saw what was to follow; their declaration was that they were there as *friends* at the invitation of the people, and they only gave the Pope's Legate *one hour* to remove himself and all that belonged to him. They took the garrison prisoners and sent them to Milan. On the morning of my leaving Pisa, I had an express from Modena and another from Lucca informing me of the French being at Bologna, and of the

---

[1] Mr. Wyndham.

[2] The orders of the Directory authorising Bonaparte to make *main basse* on Leghorn, were dated May 7.

possibility of their intending to make a *coup de main* at Leghorn; that there was reason to think a small detachment was to be sent by a short route through the mountains from Modena to Lucca Baths, and that from the particular circumstances of my situation I should be exposed to great risk and be considered as an object if they could take me and my family prisoners. I instantly resolved to return to Corsica; but the wind was extremely high and contrary; even boats could not get to the ships. The next day the wind remained the same, and in the evening came an express from Mr. Wyndham, saying that the French had demanded that day a passage for not less than 7,000 nor more than 10,000 troops to pass through Tuscany, and that they might send a garrison to Leghorn. The wind was something abated, but still contrary; however Captain Freemantle undertook to get the children on board the "Dolphin" (about eight in the evening), which lay about half-a-mile from the shore. He thought this material in case of any fresh accounts which might produce confusion in the town, which is half filled with French Republicans. The next morning, at eight o'clock, I received a message from the Governor of Leghorn, desiring me not to lose a moment in getting away, as he had just received an express from Pistoïa that the advanced guard of the French army had arrived there, and that 7,000 men were advancing and were at that time within only two posts of Pistoïa— 3,000 of which were cavalry, and all mounted on horses they had just put in requisition at Bologna. We did

not stop one moment.   Captain Freemantle had had
the precaution of having his boat ready, and went to
it with us through all the bye-streets, and Eleanor and
I went on board the "Dolphin" in a state of perfect
horror.   The wind had happily changed to a most
favourable quarter about two hours before.   As, however, the captain of the "Dolphin" was on shore,
we remained within cannon-shot from the town for
about two hours, when Captain Freemantle sent off his
boat to order the ship instantly under weigh—that he
had seen the captain of the "Dolphin," who would
follow us out in a smaller sailing boat, but for God's
sake not to wait for him.   So many of the ship's company were on shore, that we had not men enough to
heave the anchors, till we got them from the "Incon-
stant," which lay pretty near us, and we set sail about
two o'clock, having been on board since between nine
and ten in the most anxious state of mind possible to
imagine.   Had the town risen we never could have
embarked, had not the wind changed we should have
been under fire from the forts.   We had a very good
passage, and arrived here at four o'clock yesterday.   I
could not but be struck with the change; the day before I had run away without anything more than the
clothes I had on, and I was received here with every
kind of honour—guns firing, shouting, and the streets
full of people, quite *en reine*.'

The conquest of Leghorn by the French was the signal for the immediate seizure of the forts and town of
Porto Ferraio in the Island of Elba, by Lord Nelson,

acting under the orders of Sir Gilbert, who, at this conjuncture showed a spirit of prompt and energetic decision, such as in later years distinguished the most memorable part of his career, his government of India. Sir Gilbert and the naval and military commanders in the Mediterranean were equally well aware that the independence of Corsica could not be maintained in the face of a hostile occupation of Sardinia; for this reason he had for months before the cession of Sardinia to the French, urged on the Home Government the importance of a temporary occupation of that island; in default, however, of the necessary means to accomplish such an object, the time at which it might have been effected was allowed to go by, and Sardinia became incorporated with the French dominions. The importance of obtaining a more defensible position than could then be found in Corsica, was thus rendered urgent, and it was with a view to secure a receptacle, whenever the evacuation of the island should take place, for the troops, stores, and all loyal subjects of the King of Great Britain, whether Corsican or English, that Sir Gilbert determined on the seizure of Porto Ferraio in Elba. ' An invaluable port and harbour,' wrote Lord Nelson, ' which I have now taken in execution of your plan.' [1]

So prompt was this measure in its conception and execution that the Admiral, Sir John Jervis, was not aware of it until it had become a *fait accompli*, and the excellent understanding which existed between the Viceroy and the Admiral could not be more clearly

[1] Despatches, vol. ii. p. 210.

shown than by the letters that passed between them on the subject.

The foresight which had prompted the occupation of Porto Ferraio [1] was speedily justified; for before the month was at an end, the declaration of a defensive alliance between France and Spain, determined the English Government to order the immediate evacuation of Corsica, and the consequences would have been disastrous to the English had they not been in possession of Porto Ferraio. [2]

Another less important conquest closely following on that of Porto Ferraio is described by Lady Elliot.

'Bastia: September 18, 1796.

'There has been a little fracas between Commodore Nelson and the Genoese. He had lost a boat in the night, and sent one out in the morning to look into the little harbour to see whether it could be found; and he told the crew if the French battery, by which they must pass, fired upon them they might take a small vessel that lay close to the battery, which was unloading stores for the French, but not to touch it unless they fired. Nelson's boat was no sooner under the guns of the battery than they fired, and the crew took the

[1] Sir Gilbert's letter to the Governor of Porto Ferraio, justifying his seizure of the town and fort, and solemnly engaging that the troops should retire and the place be restored to the grand Duke of Tuscany at the peace, is published in *Nelson's Despatches*, vol. ii. p. 208.

[2] See Sir Gilbert's Instructions to Lord Nelson respecting the capture of Capraja, which contains a full explanation of his motives for adopting that strong measure.' *Nelson's Despatches*, vol. ii. note to p. 274.

vessel and brought it off. The Genoese then began to fire on our ships, and continued to do so from seven in the morning till one o'clock, without one shot hitting. Commodore Nelson returned three shot only to the battery and none to the Genoese, whereas he could have half destroyed the town; and at one o'clock he sent a flag of truce to know what had occasioned this conduct towards His Majesty's ships, and desired it might be noticed that from humanity he had not fired a shot in return upon the town. The answer he received was that the port was shut to the English, and an answer should be sent to him in a few days. He immediately came here, and after remaining twenty-four hours and consulting with Sir Gilbert, it was determined to send an expedition against Capraja, which belongs to the Genoese, and has been a nuisance ever since we have had Corsica. Being half way between Corsica and Leghorn it facilitates small boats passing to and fro, as they can take refuge there from weather. The embarkation took place the night before last, but the weather has been so calm that the ships have only just reached the island, and I have been spying at them this morning till my eyes ache. The place is thirty miles from hence, but with the naked eye we can see the ships close to it, and the town we suppose them going to attack.'

'September 19th.

'Capraja is taken without bloodshed, and the troops, excepting a small garrison, return to-day. The Pope, though he has refused the terms the French offered him—too ridiculous for even priests and cardinals to listen to—will not have assistance from Naples. There is no guessing what he means, but he is so much afraid of his people, that he dared not go to the last great day at St. Peter's.[1] The Corsican prisoners were brought into Bastia to-day, and the militia who attended them halloed all the way " Long live the King and the English." The prisoners said this was very different from what they had heard at Leghorn.

' The island is as still as the sea ; we ride every evening till nine o'clock by moonlight, and have no more palpitation when we meet a man with a gun than in England a peasant with a stick.'

On September 29th Sir Gilbert acknowledged the receipt on the previous night of a despatch from the Duke of Portland, dated August 31st, desiring the immediate abandonment of Corsica, or, as he paraphrased it, announcing the intention of the Government ' to

---

[1] To the honour of the Roman people, it should be remembered that they were the first to resent the plunder of their galleries and churches by the French. ' At Rome there has been an insurrection. The people will not allow the Pope to give either money, statues or pictures. (July 19.) The Pope seems to be in a great fright, and has again sent orders, if the French come to treat them civilly. The people assert that the statues and pictures are not the property of the Pope, and that they will not part with them.'—*Lady Elliot to her Sister.*

How the French were instructed to act we know ;—' Si Rome fait des avances, la première chose à exiger est que le pape ordonne immédiatement des prières publiques pour la prospérité des armes françaises. Quelques-uns de ses beaux monuments, ses statues, ses tableaux, ses médailles, ses bibliothèques, ses madones d'argent, et même ses cloches nous dédommageront des frais que nous coûtera la visite que vous lui aurez faite.'—*Instructions of Directory to Bonaparte.*

withdraw the blessings of the British Constitution from
the people of Corsica.'   They, apparently, having ' entertained the blessing unawares.'   This was the first
intimation received by the Viceroy of the measure
thus summarily decided on; one in the necessity or
propriety of which he by no means concurred, while
taking it in connection with similar instructions respecting Elba and Capraja he accepted it as the abandonment of the whole Mediterranean policy he had
so anxiously sought to inaugurate.   To secure a strong
and independent position in the Mediterranean as a
basis for naval and military operations seemed to
him the first element of success in a policy aiming at
the encouragement and support of a common action
among the Italian Governments, by which alone
they could hope to defend themselves against the
advance of France.

The abruptness of the decision by which Corsica was
given up to her fate—in other words, to France—
was painful to him on other grounds.   Reference to
a despatch already given, of November 1794, containing his sentiments on the consideration due by Great
Britain to those Corsicans who had committed their
families, properties, and lives for the common cause,
will suffice to show how acutely he could not but feel
the course adopted towards them; no ' timeous' information concerning it had been given them; no terms
were made for them or for Corsica.   Great Britain was
simply to save herself with all possible expedition from
the advancing French.   The evacuation of Elba and

of Capraja was to be simultaneous with that of Corsica, and the fleet was ordered to ' leave the Mediterranean,' that is, to retire to Gibraltar.   For the first fortnight after the receipt of the despatches from London, the secret of their contents was closely kept in order to give time for the arrival and distribution of transports before the public should be made aware of the impending retreat of the British.   According to the Viceroy the news when known was received with consternation in Corsica ; and he ascribed in large measure the success of the subsequent arrangements required to execute the orders from England to the good and friendly spirit of the people.[1]

But the conduct of the people of Bastia may perhaps be as fairly attributed to the Viceroy's personal influence

---

[1] Admiral Sir J. Jervis in a despatch to Lord Spencer, described a revolutionary outbreak as having occurred at Bastia as soon as the news of the evacuation was made known, in consequence of which the government had been wrested from the Viceroy by the municipality of Bastia, and delegates had been sent by them to the French authorities at Leghorn.

Sir Gilbert, on the other hand, in a despatch to the Duke of Portland says, that Sir J. Jervis having been good enough to read him his despatch to Lord Spencer, he thinks it his duty to state that Sir J. Jervis has misapprehended several points relative to the affairs of Bastia concerning which many false and exaggerated reports had been circulated, based on the fact of there having existed some movements of uneasiness when the populace had sought to profit by a moment of anarchy, to make disturbances for the sake of plunder, ' as under similar circumstances would probably have been the case in any other part of the world.'   While the committee and people of Bastia had acted with prudence and discretion to the very last moment, they had undoubtedly sought to make terms for themselves with the French Republicans of Leghorn when abandoned by us, and for this ' I could not blame them.'

over many of his late subjects, who were well convinced
that their rights and interests lay near his heart and
who viewed his departure with unfeigned regret. ' It is
impossible,' wrote Lord Nelson to H.R.H. the Duke of
Clarence, ' I can do justice to the good arrangement of
the Government or the good management of the
Viceroy with the Corsicans, not a man of whom but
cried on parting with him : even those who had opposed
his administration could not but love and respect so
amiable a character.' [1]

The total evacuation of the island was not completed
until the garrisons of San Fiorenzo and of Calvi had
been withdrawn. On October 26th Sir Gilbert wrote to
the Duke of Portland that the last British detachment
had reached Porto Ferraio in safety, and that he himself was about to proceed there on board Commodore
Nelson's ship the ' Minerve.'

To Lady Elliot, who, with her children, had sailed for
Gibraltar on the 23rd in a man-of-war, of which the
captain had orders if pursued ' to run and not fight,' he
wrote :—

'S. Fiorenzo Bay: October 24, 1796.

' I stayed at Porto Ferraio till the 22nd, when I embarked on board the "Captain" with Commodore Nelson
for this place, wishing to confer with the Admiral, and
being anxious about the Ajaccio people.

' We arrived here this morning and found that the
Spanish fleet had been two days off Cape Corse, but is

---

[1] *Letters of Lord Nelson*, vol. ii. p. 301.

now on the coast of Provence.   I was very uneasy lest
they should prevent the convoys from Ajaccio and Calvi
joining us here, but the Admiral makes light of it and
assures me the Spaniards will never do anything
themselves, or prevent us from doing what we like.
We are looking out earnestly for Admiral Man's
squadron, on which a good deal turns.   San Fiorenzo
was evacuated last night, leaving nothing behind of the
smallest value.

'I have had a full and satisfactory conference with
the Admiral, who is as firm as a rock under difficulties
that might shake tougher stuff than Hotham.   He has
at present fourteen sail of the line against thirty-six,
or perhaps forty.   If Man joins him, they will certainly
attack, and they are all confident of victory.

'Porto Ferraio is a blessing ; for if he can do no better
he may find shelter there till he is reinforced.   Government has never said a word to me about Porto Ferraio.[1]
They have gazetted Nelson's letter to the Admiral, but
not mine, so that I seem to have nothing to do with it.
George continues perfectly well, and is a great favourite
with everybody.'

'S. Fiorenzo Bay: October 26, 1796.

'Yesterday, to my great joy, the garrison came in
from Calvi without an accident, and we received accounts from Ajaccio that the evacuation took place there
on the 22nd.   They sailed on the 23rd by the passage of

---

[1] In regard to its occupation by British troops, a measure taken on
the Viceroy's responsibility, and of which the idea originated with him.

Bonifazio for Elba, where I trust they are now safe.
The whole of this business is therefore happily and
satisfactorily terminated, with the enemy on shore, and
a very superior fleet against us at sea.

'I return to-day to Porto Ferraio . . . and go from
thence to Naples on my Italian plan ; Naples, however,
is most material, the continuance of the fleet in these
seas depending altogether on the exertions of that
court and country to supply them. The Admiral is
strongly against my relinquishing any of my present
powers, particularly my direction of military affairs, and
he seems to consider my continuing to exercise them as
absolutely indispensable to the co-operation of the Navy
and Army in a service so much mixed with politics.
God bless you, my dearest love. If I could hear of your
safe arrival at Gibraltar, though I can see no further
into your destiny I should at least be without any
immediate burthen on my mind. For myself, and on
all other points, the evacuation of Corsica being so
fortunately accomplished and completed, I am exone-
rated and free from care—I mean personal care. I
retain a great interest in the Mediterranean branch of
the war which is more important than it appears ever
to have been thought in London.'[1]

[1] 1796. 'We are all,' wrote Nelson, 'preparing to leave the Mediterranean, a measure which I cannot approve. They at home do not know
what this fleet is capable of performing ; anything and everything.
Much as I shall rejoice to see England, I lament our present orders in
sackcloth and ashes, as dishonourable to the dignity of England, whose
fleets are equal to meet the world in arms, and of all the fleets I ever saw
I never beheld one in point of officers and men equal to Sir John
Jervis's, who is a commander-in-chief able to lead them to glory.'

The exigencies of the military situation absolutely required that Porto Ferraio should be retained until further measures could be taken for the security of persons and property endangered by the French occupation of Corsica. Sir Gilbert, therefore, took on himself the responsibility of delaying the execution of the orders to abandon Elba. Unless this had been done, 'our Smyrna convoy and transports would have been lost,' wrote Nelson; and, in conjunction with the naval chiefs, he determined also on the detention of the fleet. It must have been with a strange revulsion of feeling that a few hours after Sir Gilbert had gone on board the 'Minerve' he received despatches from England annulling the orders so lately executed in regard to Corsica, and containing counter-orders respecting the movements of the fleet.[1]

That the change of policy regarding Corsica was not known until the island had fallen into the possession of France, was considered by Sir John Jervis a matter of thankfulness. The moment for defending it was past, when the vacillation of English policy had weakened the confidence of the Corsicans, and the successes of France in Sardinia and on the coast had laid the island open to the invaders; but Sir Gilbert probably read with more of pain than resignation the words in

[1] 'A great point was gained,' wrote Sir W. Hamilton to Commodore Nelson, October 31, 1796, 'by your (his, Nelson's, and Sir Gilbert's) joint endeavours to prevent the king's fleet from abandoning the Mediterranean, and by which I verily believe these kingdoms and all Italy are saved from the absolute ruin with which they were immediately threatened.'—*Despatches*, vol. ii. p. 289.

which Mr. Windham told him of the 'new instructions which will continue you in the situation you have filled so ably, and preserve us from a policy as false in my opinion in both senses of the word as that which I may now say we were about to pursue. I tremble lest this change in our determination should come too late, and that the process should be too far advanced to be stopped before considerable mischief will have been done, or even to be stopped at all.'[1]

Admiral Sir John Jervis to the Viceroy.

'"Victory," Island of Minorca: November 11, 1796.

'By the "Cygnet" cutter which arrived last night I have orders to support you in the sovereignty of Corsica, and in case of the evacuation having taken place, to establish ourselves at Porto Ferraio. Thus far we sail before the wind, but alas! poor Admiral Man has for the present frustrated my plan of operations by a resolution taken in concert with the captains under his orders to cruise off Cape St. Vincent until the latter end of October, and then to proceed to Spithead with his whole force, in direct disobedience to the orders which he acknowledges to have received from me. His reasons are those of a man who has lost his powers, and I conclude the queries he put to the captains were so framed as to point their answers, which happened upon a former occasion. Thus circumstanced, it is my intention to proceed to Gibraltar

[1] The Right Hon. W. Windham to Sir Gilbert Elliot, October 20, 1796.

with the convoy, in hopes of receiving a reinforcement : should none appear within a reasonable time, I will make the best of my way to Porto Ferraio, where I hope to arrive before your return from the Continent.

'Although I have nothing to offer against your re-tiring from a scene where you cannot act with the dignity and authority necessary to justify to the public and to your own character a longer continuance with us, I look forward with very great anxiety indeed to the situation I may be placed in by the loss of your able counsel and honest support. I entertain the highest opinion of the honour and integrity of General de Burgh, but inexperienced as he is in business of such a complicated nature, diffident and doubtful where prompt decision is necessary, I dread the mo-ment of your final departure. I will, however, hope the best, and in truth form great expectations from the plan of operations you have in contemplation to lodge with the General.

' I have the honour to be, with the truest esteem and regard, dear Sir, yours most faithfully,

'J. JERVIS.'

The altered tone of his instructions probably en-couraged Sir Gilbert to a measure which was required to complete the security of the new station at Porto Ferraio, namely, the capture of Piombino, on the coast of Italy, whence alone supplies could be furnished to Porto Ferraio.

'We take Piombino this evening,' he wrote from

Porto Ferraio on November 6, 1796. 'This will be the last act of my reign, and in truth the measure of Porto Ferraio was not complete without it. I shall then feel very comfortable about our supplies. This is my first continental conquest. I believe it would not be difficult to take Rome ; but it must be done by some Admiral, for military men seem to me much too good generals to make conquests. We are eagerly looking out for Admiral Man's squadron, on which much will depend.'

The reception given to Sir Gilbert by the Court of Naples was of the most cordial description.

'The civilities, or rather the real kindness of the King and Queen, and especially of the latter, surpass everything I could have imagined. They are so far honourable to themselves that they are clearly founded in a principle that is creditable even to kings and queens. I mean in gratitude and in a desire to express their sense of the good I wished to do them. By far the most agreeable evenings I have passed since we parted have been with the Queen in very quiet parties. She often talks of you and the children in a way which she certainly knows is not unpleasant.'[1] After de-

---

[1] While Corsica had continued in a state bordering on insurrection, Sir Gilbert had forbidden the return there of his wife and children, and they, after the heats of summer, made a journey to Rome and Naples which had delighted Lady Elliot's artistic nature. Sir Gilbert ever counted among the minor trials of his life the disappointment caused him by the necessary relinquishment of an old and early dream, that they should visit those scenes together, and that such should be the crowning enjoyment of their foreign life. Lady Elliot's visit to Naples had shown her the Queen in her best light. Unfeignedly fond of children,

scribing a royal hunting party at Carditello, where they killed fifteen wild boars, four foxes, two fawns, and a hare, in the course of the forenoon, which the King did not, however, consider good sport, Sir Gilbert says: 'The evening ended with a dinner, at which the King toasted the English nation, and turning to me said, "and especially your health, who have done so much for me and to whom I and all my people are under such obligations."'

Lady Hamilton was one of the marvels of Naples that could not be passed over in silence. 'She is the most extraordinary compound I ever beheld. Her person is nothing short of monstrous for its enormity, and is growing every day. She tries hard to think size advantageous to her beauty, but is not easy about it. Her face is beautiful; she is all Nature, and yet all Art; that is to say, her manners are perfectly un-polished, of course very easy, though not with the ease of good breeding, but of a barmaid; excessively good-humoured and wishing to please and be admired by all ages and sorts of persons that come in her way; but besides considerable natural understanding, she has ac-quired, since her marriage, some knowledge of history and of the arts, and one wonders at the application and pains she has taken to make herself what she is. With men her language and conversation are exaggera-tions of anything I ever heard anywhere; and I was

and with many natural simple tastes, she arranged several meetings at various country palaces with Lady Elliot and her young party, and there the royal children and the Queen 'romped' with their young guests, 'William pulling the Queen's hair down all about her ears.'

wonderfully struck with these inveterate remains of her origin, though the impression was very much weakened by seeing the other ladies of Naples.

' I go to Caserta to-morrow, and the day after the King has appointed to show me the manufacture at Belvidere. I have been as prudent as I can about buying pictures and drawings, but cannot entirely refrain.

' *December* 24.—The King did the honours of Belvidere excellently, and appeared in a better light than in killing wild boars and ducks. He showed me the whole process of silk, explaining everything very distinctly and intelligently from beginning to end, and taking me into most of the manufacturers' houses, where he seemed like a father in the midst of his family; this is certainly an amiable and laudable amusement. We passed the night at Caserta. The Queen showed me her four eldest children, and the next evening, being the last I was at Naples, she had the great theatre of San Carlo lighted up on purpose to show it to me. It has been shut for some time and been altered and newly decorated for the arrival of the Princess who is expected from Vienna. The Queen conducted me round the theatre herself, arm in arm with your spouse, and was as gracious as any queen could be.

' We had the *attitudes* a night or two ago by candlelight; they come up to my expectations fully, which is saying everything. They set Lady Hamilton in a very different light from any I had seen her in before; nothing about her, neither her conversation, her manners, nor figure announce the very refined taste which she discovers in this performance, besides the extraordinary talent that is necessary for the execution ; and besides all this, says Sir *Willum*,[1] " she makes my apple-pies." '

Sir Gilbert went to Rome the day after this letter was written, and remained there long enough to be satisfied that the Papal Court was by no means disposed to a tame submission to the French, but was anxiously looking for the advance of the Austrian army. Early in January he returned to Naples.

' Naples : January 13, 1797.

' The Court have come to Naples to celebrate the King's birthday. The King and Queen dined in public, and underwent a general *Bacio mano*, or hand-kissing. I could not but help recollecting that the last public royal dinner I was at was at Versailles, where the Queen of France, then Dauphiness, was in all the glory and lustre of Burke's morning star, and there was then much less probability of her dreadful reverse, than there can be now of any catastrophe to a sister crowned head. The Queen whom I really admire and like was far from cheerful.

' The Queen has a strong powerful mind, and is full of courage, vigour, and firmness. I have *written* demonstration both of her understanding and character. Acton is exactly made to suit her, and if they could

---

[1] Lady Hamilton's manner of pronouncing her husband's christian name.

decide on their own views, I should not be at all uneasy ; but the rest of this country may probably see, in
the common way, only the present danger and the inconvenience that is next that, without perceiving the
greater evil or the certain ruin that is behind.

'I like Lord Malmesbury's answer to the Directory
extremely well.   It is dignified, and leaves his adversaries completely in the wrong.'

The letter, a long one, ends with an aspiration not
destined to be fulfilled :—

'God bless you, my dearest love.   We have often
said this shall be the last absence.   I hope in God that
once met we part no more in this world.   I am
thoroughly determined to let my happiness depend
hereafter on nothing out of myself, excepting yourself
and the children, and by this means I am as secure as
a mortal can be.   My love to Gilbert; I hope Eton
will not soil his pure character.   But it is a pickle
education.   Young C—— is here a midshipman ; a
very clever boy, but such a pickle, and such a *deep* one
as I would not have Gilbert for twenty worlds.'

While Sir Gilbert was at Naples he heard from Lady
Elliot of her safe arrival in England.   Her description
of the incidents of her voyage gives a lively picture of
the perils of her passage.

'December 12, 1796.

'We had the worst possible passage from Gibraltar
to Weymouth, every danger that war and tempests can
present, white squalls and black squalls and contrary

winds. I never quitted the coach, and lay on two boards just a month. Two days we spent under the storm-stay sails; every sail was torn to pieces at different times and our masts in continual danger. Even Dixon's face grew pale; nevertheless, pray tell Nelson that I never was out of my coach night or day, and got into a state of resignation to anything that would end the scene. The night we left Gibraltar we were hailed in the night three times by three Spanish frigates within pistol-shot; no answer was given, and luckily we were going at a great rate, and passed them, I believe, before they made up their minds what to do, but had they hailed us with a broadside I and my coach might have taken a swim.

'We arrived without one morsel of meat for the crew, and only two chickens and two ducks for ourselves, no fuel for three or four days, and scarce of water, which was the colour of mahogany.

'Only forty effective men. O'Hara gave us forty invalids; he said to assist, but all they could do was to eat our provisions; seven died in the passage, and they were half of them in such a condition from sores that if the weather had been hot the ship would have been filled with infection. The provisions you had given for the ship's company were all we had to serve us home, we could get nothing at Gibraltar but thirty fowls, and we were sixteen people to feed, so you may guess we were at short allowance. Had the wind not changed just as it did Dixon said he must return to Lisbon. This idea was too shocking, for besides doubling the voyage, we were told at Gibraltar Portugal was making her terms with France. Dixon said it was the worst voyage he had ever made in any seas. I am more confirmed in my hatred to that element than ever. We arrived at Weymouth at eight at night; Dixon was to go with despatches from O'Hara to London, and I and Eleanor went on shore with him, in a little boat that came out to us and would only hold eight people and rowed five miles. At Gibraltar they had taken from us the launch, and we had no boat but that you gave Dixon which was in very bad order.

'The children were to come next morning. Dixon left us at supper, and soon after came in a horrid custom officer and said we had broken through the laws of quarantine and must return on board. I told him he might lock me up in the room, but no power on earth should make me ever return to a ship. I sent for his master, who held the same language, but I was firm; he said that neither my children nor baggage could be allowed to land; I told him I would submit as to the baggage till I got permission, which I should instantly send for to London; but for the children I would have them by some means or other. He left me about one in the morning, and I instantly sent for the boatmen who had brought us on shore, and sent them by means of bribery to fetch the children. They were very drunk, and I was very miserable; but the night was calm and moonlight, and they were all brought safe to land by three in the morning. I could not have been easy to have left them at anchor on such a dangerous coast, and indeed they had not the common necessaries of life. Our chimney had been blown away so that we could never have any fire, and the cold was intense, for we had passed from the latitude of Corsica to England in six days, and it was a bitter frost. After I had got permission for my things to be landed the wind was too high for boats to go out, and I was detained in all ten days at Weymouth.'

During Sir Gilbert's visit to Naples and Rome, Nelson wrote to him repeatedly in such strains as the following:

'"Minerve": December 24, 1796.

'I have reserved a place for you on board the "Minerve"; I long to see you, for your advice is a treasure which I shall ever most highly prize. Only tell me where to send a ship and she shall attend you.' And to Lady Nelson he wrote from Porto Ferraio,—'I expect Sir Gilbert Elliot here every hour. He goes down to Gibraltar with me. He is a good man and I love him.'

The point on which Sir Gilbert's advice was at the moment most earnestly desired by Nelson, related to the evacuation of Porto Ferraio; the Admiral having despatched to the Commodore stringent orders to co-operate with General de Burgh, commanding the British troops in Elba, in its evacuation.

The Admiral's orders were precise and clear, but the General had had no instructions to the same effect from

England, and he demurred to co-operate with the Commodore in their execution. Sir Gilbert Elliot was urgently desired by both to return and lend his counsel in a question of so much difficulty.

Immediately on his arrival in Elba, a consultation was held between himself, Lieutenant-General de Burgh, and Commodore Nelson respecting the late orders from Government at home, which Nelson had been specially deputed by the Admiral to carry into effect. The subject was one of great difficulty, involving many interests, and it received the most deliberate consideration. The result was, that under existing circumstances it was deemed of paramount importance to retain possession of Elba, until His Majesty's Ministers could be fully apprised of the many cogent reasons for continuing the British occupation notwithstanding the orders from home.[1]

The motives which guided this decision are explained in the following despatch.

His Grace the Duke of Portland.

'Porto Ferraio: January 24, 1797.

' My Lord Duke,—I sailed from Naples on the 15th inst., and arrived here on the 22nd. I embark tomorrow on board the " Minerve," Captain Cockburn, in which frigate Commodore Nelson has hoisted his

---

[1] Elba was not evacuated by the British troops till the following spring, when General de Burgh, in command there, received His Majesty's instructions to withdraw his forces. These were the first instructions which were sent him.

broad pendant. The "Minerve" will join the fleet, and I hope to find a speedy opportunity from thence to England. Commodore Nelson proposes to look into Toulon, Mahon and Carthagena, so that our passage may be somewhat protracted. I found General de Burgh under great embarrassment for want of pre- cise instructions. He had prepared a letter for me, which he delivered to me on my arrival, and of which he has no doubt sent a copy to Your Grace, as well as a copy of my answer. On that answer he had deter- mined to regulate his conduct on this occasion. He required of me in substance to authorise in writing the departure of the troops from hence, to annul the orders under which they came hither, and to declare that I considered this the wish of Government. If I did not comply with this request, he declared his de- termination to remain here until he should receive further orders from home. I answered of course, that since the 15th of last November I have had no autho- rity to confirm or annul any order whatever; that I could not declare it to be the wish of Government that the troops should be withdrawn from Porto Ferraio, and that I entertained on the contrary a real doubt whether such were the intentions of Government or not.

'On receipt of this answer the General determined to stay; and I confess his conduct in that respect appears to me prudent and proper. The General I know writes in strong terms on the inexpediency of retaining the post. I ought perhaps to be silent, my

opinion not being called for by any official duty; but
zeal is an importunate, perhaps impertinent thing,
and cannot always be restrained from meddling. I
have indeed the better excuse for mentioning my
opinion on this subject, as it has now been referred to
under the word *politics* in General de Burgh's late
despatches both to Your Grace and to H.R.H. the
Duke of York.

' Your Grace has, I believe, already had occasion to
know by the whole tenor of my correspondence from
the year 1793 down to my latest letters of July
1797, what my notions are concerning Italy. I have
always thought that it is a great and important object
in the contest between the French Republic and the
rest of Europe, that Italy in whole or in part should
neither be annexed to France as dominion, nor affili-
ated in the shape of dependent republics; and I have
considered a superior British fleet in the Mediterranean as, amongst others, an essential means for securing
Italy and Europe from such a misfortune.

'These are my politics, and I have every reason to
be satisfied that Your Grace and all His Majesty's
Ministers have uniformly entertained and indeed
avowed the same sentiments. They have, indeed, been
a ruling principle of your measures during the three
years that I have been honoured with the confidence of
Government. To the general principle I must now
add a particular one founded on perhaps temporary
circumstances, that the possession of Porto Ferraio is
highly desirable if a British fleet is to remain in the

Mediterranean, and to be employed, amongst other objects, in protecting Italy. If other services more important and more urgent make it impossible to maintain any longer a Mediterranean fleet, I then agree with General de Burgh entirely in the inutility of retaining this harbour. What I differ with him in, is only in considering that point as less decided than he does.

'I have, &c.,

'G. E.'

To Lady Elliot.

'Porto Ferraio: January 24, 1797.

'We sailed from Naples on the 15th, and arrived here the 22nd, having had fine weather and a pleasant passage, though a very slow one. I sail to-morrow with Nelson on board the "Minerve," Captain Cockburn's ship, to join the fleet whenever we may find it. Nelson proposes to look into Toulon, Mahon and Carthagena, which may make some delay. When I get hold of Sir J. Jervis he has promised to forward me to England. I hope, hope, hope for a speedy passage and to meet with you once more, my dearest love, and with the children, perhaps in a month, but perhaps it may be two. . . . The troops remain here till further orders from home, and if it is not already too late, I have still a hope that things may yet fall into the old course—I mean that a superior fleet may be kept in the Mediterranean, and that Italy may be preserved. I fight a hard battle for that boot, though it has been every day more and more a losing one.' . . .

Sir Gilbert arrived at Gibraltar on February 9th; on the 11th he left it again with Nelson in the ' Minerve,' in order to join the Admiral, Sir John Jervis, to whom he was desirous to report his observations on the state of Italy before proceeding home. The passage was destined to enrich his store of naval experience in a very remarkable degree. The ' Minerve ' had scarcely reached the Straits when she found herself hotly pursued by two Spanish line-of-battle ships, and the frigate being cleared for action, Sir Gilbert was requested to have certain parts of his papers ready to be sunk if necessary. At the hottest moment of the chase, the danger was averted by an incident which is related in the spirited narrative of the Battle of St. Vincent by Colonel Drinkwater. The sudden cry of ' a man overboard ' having led to the lowering of the jolly boat with a party of sailors and the gallant young Hardy[1] in command,· the current of the Straits rapidly carried the boat far astern of the frigate, a circumstance which combined with the fast sailing of the headmost ship of the chase, rendered the situation of the crew extremely perilous. At this crisis, Nelson, casting an anxious look at the hazardous situation of Hardy and his companions, exclaimed: ' By G——, I'll not lose Hardy! Back the mizen top sail.' No sooner said than done: the ' Minerve's ' progress was retarded, the boat's crew recovered, and the Spaniard, confounded by this man-

---

[1] Afterwards Admiral Sir Thomas Hardy.

œuvre and shrinking from the challenge he believed to be offered to him, shortened sail and was soon lost to sight.

In the course of the ensuing night, described as 'very foggy,' the 'Minerve' found herself surrounded by strange sails ; 'something like a scrape' it was allowed to be by Nelson himself, but one from which, with address, he doubted not they might be extricated. If the ships did not belong to the Spanish fleet, he thought they must be a convoy, proceeding to the West Indies, in which case it would become his duty to give the earliest intimation of their approach to the British Commander on the West Indies station. Sir Gilbert, who had quietly slept through Nelson's first visit to his cabin when the discovery was made of their being entangled in a strange fleet, was roused by his return to discuss a possible trip to the West Indies, an announcement which he received with his usual equanimity, observing to his A. D. C. Colonel Drinkwater, who narrates the scene and had evidently been on the alert all night, that as they were only passengers they must submit to circumstances. When morning broke, no ships were to be seen, and Nelson became assured that he had passed through the main fleet of the enemy, and on the 13th he joined that of Sir John Jervis 'to the gratification of all parties.' Sir Gilbert then left the 'Minerve,' and repaired on board the 'Lively' frigate, under orders to proceed with him immediately to England, but he could not bear the idea of leaving the

British fleet at this critical juncture, and having been refused his request to remain with the Admiral as a volunteer on board the 'Victory,' he obtained the Admiral's assent to his second proposal, that the 'Lively' should be retained to carry home the despatches concerning the expected naval engagement.

Thus it was that Sir Gilbert Elliot was an eye-witness of the Battle of St. Vincent, and that his descendants now possess a sword taken from the captain of the 'S. Josef' by Nelson himself, and by him presented to Sir Gilbert.

'"Lively," off St. Ives: March 1, 1797.

'You will think it strange, that I do not land with Captain Calder, who is going ashore with his despatches, but he is very anxious to have the start of everybody with his good news. . . . Captain Calder carries the accounts of the most famous sea fight that ever was fought at which I had the superlative good fortune to be present. Sir J. Jervis with fifteen sail of the line, engaged the Spanish fleet off Cape St. Vincent on the 14th February with twenty-seven sail of the line. He has taken four sail of the line, of which two are three deckers of 112 guns each, one of 84 and one 74 guns. There is next to a certainty of another Spaniard of four decks and 140 guns having been destroyed by our frigates the day we came away, as she was floating about alone without a single mast, and the frigates were gone on that service. . . . Sir J.

Jervis is immortalised and Commodore Nelson a hero beyond Homer's. It is impossible to give you a notion of his exploits.

'We are at this moment come to anchor where ends an eventful period of my life. There are few months into which one could crowd more interesting events, adventures, and chances than since we left Port Ferraio, not to speak of the three years and a half that are passed.'[1]

Colonel Drinkwater, in his account of the battle of St. Vincent, relates, that when Sir Gilbert and his party landed at Plymouth on Sunday the 5th of March, they were met by all classes with long faces and desponding looks, instead of being hailed, according to their expectations, as the bearers of tidings of triumph. The news of the shutting up of the National Bank of England, and the *general suspension of cash payments*, had arrived at Plymouth that morning; not a word of the great naval victory had been dropped by Captain Calder; and the good people of Plymouth were firmly persuaded that the French and Spanish fleets had effected a union, and that ruin and invasion stared them in the face.

When told of the glorious battle which had 'confounded their enemies,' they would hardly believe the statements they heard; and 'such was the panic pre-

[1] March 4, 1797.

vailing' that only fifteen guineas in gold could be collected at Plymouth from the Admiral, the General, and other friends towards enabling the Viceroy and his party of six individuals and their servants to pay their travelling expenses to London.

CHAPTER XI.

1794–1797.

The three years of Sir Gilbert's absence from England had produced events entirely subversive of the expectations which he carried with him to Toulon.

The French Republic, become a great military Power, had not only freed the soil of France from hostile forces, but had humbled Austria, liberated Northern Italy, made allies of Holland and of Spain, and forced Great Britain to betake herself to the seas where she had reigned supreme.

But the advantage was not all on the side of the Revolution.

The rapacious and insincere policy of the French rulers was doing much to create in their antagonists a principle of cohesion that had previously been wanting to them. The sentiment of national independence was awakening, and every forward step of the French armies was destined to increase its strength. In 1796 the French began their famous march ' to carry the torch of Liberty round the world.' In 1797 they had carried home by its light a considerable portion of their neighbours' goods, and there were some who doubted whether the game was not worth more than the candle.

It was perhaps as yet only those who had had a near view of French lust of conquest, as it had been displayed in Italy since the beginning of Bonaparte's great campaign, who were capable of thoroughly realising the nature of the gigantic despotism which in the name of Liberty was being fastened on the neck of Europe. But thoughtful men who in 1790 had been alienated from Burke by his passionate distortion of the facts of history, began to ask themselves if there was not more than they had seen in his prophetic forecasts.[1]

[1] The following lines from 'France,' an ode written by Coleridge in Feb. 1797, show the effect wrought on those who had watched the proceedings of the past year, and who under all circumstances 'still adored The spirit of divinest Liberty':—

> 'When France in wrath her giant-limbs upreared,
>   And with that oath which smote, air, earth, and sea,
>   Stamped her strong foot and said she would be free,
> Bear witness for me, how I hoped and feared!

.   .   .   .

> '"And what," I said, "tho' Blasphemy's loud scream
>   With that sweet music of deliverance strove!
>   Tho' all the fierce and drunken passions wove
> A dance more wild than e'er was maniac's dream!

> '"Ye storms, that round the dawning east assembled,
>   The sun was rising, tho' ye hid his light!"

.   .   .   .

> 'Forgive me, Freedom! O forgive those dreams!
>   I hear thy voice, I hear thy loud lament,
>   From bleak Helvetia's icy cavern sent;
> I hear thy groans upon her blood-stained streams.'

There are two lines in the ode which are little more than a paraphrase of a sentence of Burke's, applied to the same nation:—

> 'The sensual and the dark rebel in vain,
>   Slaves by their own compulsion.'—*Coleridge.*

> 'Intemperate minds forge their own fetters.'—*Burke.*

Nowhere were there more elements of mischief at work than in Great Britain. Ireland was on the eve of open rebellion, and the 'extinguisher' if not 'on fire' was smoking.[1] The army had notoriously been tampered with. The Channel Fleet was in a state of mutiny. Burke, the great champion of the established order of things, was dying broken-hearted; and accusations of feebleness and incapacity were directed against the Government, alike by their old opponents and their new allies.

It has been seen that the negotiations which had been for some months in progress between the Portland Whigs, as they were called, and Mr. Pitt, were not finally closed by the accession of the former to the Ministry until the summer of 1794. The ground on which the Coalition took place was the impossibility of co-operation in the direction of the war, or of co-responsibility in its results, without a common knowledge of measures and means, such as could only be properly shared by the members of one Administration.

In the spring of the year, in January 1794, the Duke of Portland notified to Mr. Pitt his final resolve to separate himself from Fox, still, however, retaining his favourite notion of acting as chief of an independent party in Parliament who should support the war in the most unqualified manner. Months before Sir Gilbert Elliot had pointed out the utter impossi-

---

[1] Mr. Luttrell on being told (at a much later period) that the army in Ireland was disaffected, remarked that ' it was a serious thing when the *extinguisher caught fire.*'

bility of working such a scheme with any good result;
an impossibility founded on the Duke's personal character, and on those general instincts of party nature
which would prevent any Minister from counting on
the candour and forbearance, still less on the consistent
support, of a party occupying the position of a 'detached
auxiliary force, to act on one occasion, to retire on
another, and to be a perpetual object of anxiety to
those whom they mean to serve, of hope to the enemy,
and of speculation to the rest of the world.'[1]

Accordingly, a month later, when the question arose
of a subsidy to Prussia, the Government desired to
know if they might rely on the support in Parliament
of the Duke and his friends; to which the Duke's
party returned for answer that their confidence in
Ministers would induce them to concur in the measure,
but in their ignorance of the causes which rendered it
necessary, they could give no opinion as to its expediency.[2]

[1] Sir Gilbert to the Duke of Portland, on his taking office under Mr.
Pitt in 1794.

[2] 'Pitt about ten days ago communicated to the Duke of Portland,
through the medium of the Chancellor, that the King of Prussia had
demanded from the Combined Powers a subsidy of upwards of 2,000,000*l.*
sterling, as the only terms on which he would adhere to the alliance.
Pitt at the same time intimated that it would be necessary that this
country should contribute 1,200,000*l.*, and wished to know whether the
Duke and his friends would support the measure in Parliament. The
Duke, after having consulted Lord Fitzwilliam, Lord Mansfield, Burke,
Windham and a few others, returned for answer, that their confidence
in the Ministers would induce them to concur in the measure, but that
they could not give any opinion respecting its expediency, as they were
unacquainted with the plan of the campaign and other circumstances
on which the necessity of it might be founded. The Chancellor, I

A clearer proof of the utterly false position in which they were placed could hardly be found. In July the Coalition was publicly ratified by the accession of five new Cabinet Ministers from the ranks of Opposition to the Treasury Bench; and yet so little were the contracting parties in each other's confidence, that the whole arrangement nearly fell through on the very day before it took place.

The point at issue was the conduct of the war, which Mr. Pitt intended should remain with Mr. Dundas, while the Duke of Portland considered that it should be connected, as heretofore, with the duties of the Secretary of State for the Home Department, in which office he was to succeed Mr. Dundas.[1]

The new ministers, or at least those among them most under the influence of Burke, were far more uncompromising in their war policy than the older members of the Cabinet. The war had been originally forced on Mr. Pitt's Government by the action of France, and it followed the course of all other wars, extending its area as measures of self-defence or of retalia-

---

understand, afterwards told the Duke of Portland that the plan of the campaign was a cabinet secret among the Allied Powers, and could therefore not be disclosed. He also added, that the contribution of 1,200,000l. was essential to secure the King of Prussia's assistance, without which it would be difficult to Austria to carry on the campaign. The Duke upon this repeated the assurance of support, &c. March 15, 1794.' —*Mr. Elliot to Sir Gilbert.*

[1] Pitt created a third secretaryship of state, dividing the powers and duties hitherto combined. Thus to Dundas were given the Colonies and the East India Department, and he was also charged with the conduct of the war. The Duke of Portland was to have Great Britain and Ireland.

tion required, and paying material losses by material conquests. But the Whigs of Mr. Burke's school, of whom Mr. Windham was one of the most distinguished, had consistently protested against Mr. Pitt's war policy as half-hearted and unintelligible.[1] While his attention was chiefly directed to the preservation of the Balance of Power in Europe, they cared less for what France achieved beyond her borders than for the establishment within them of a government founded on principles subversive in their eyes of social order and of political freedom. Their policy was to struggle with Jacobinism till they or it should go down ; with this view they desired to embrace openly the Royalist cause, and considered those military expeditions of paramount importance which had for their object co-operation with the Royalists within France. According to Mr. Windham, to seek popularity for the war by running after material

---

[1] 'London : January 27, 1795.

'Affairs here have an aspect as little pleasant as those in your part of the world. The worst symptom of all, however, is the cry of Peace which is beginning to be heard from all parts, the result partly of the base interested spirit which seems to have got possession of this country through the medium of its trade and its wealth, and partly of the wicked Jacobin spirit which we have drawn from the common reservoir of France. At the head of this cry is the wicked little fanatical imp W——, who from motives which he must be answerable for, but which I am far from thinking unsuspicious, is acting against Pitt, under the forms indeed of friendship, but with all the alacrity of determined opposition. We shall weather this storm for the instant, but the prospect before us hardly affords a hope that it may not prove fatal in the end. I must not however go on in these reflections; I am already I fear too late.

'With unalterable regard and affection, yours ever, my dear Sir G.,
'W. W.'

advantages was ' to pander to the avarice of the country.
What are possessions in the West Indies to us if Jacobinism is triumphant in France?' and in the same
uncompromising spirit, when Wilberforce spoke of
peace they accused him of ' cant;' when Pitt was supposed to desire it they deplored his ' weakness;' when
the liverymen of London petitioned for it they complained of ' clamour' and ' sedition.' These differences
of sentiment in the Ministry rendered the choice of the
individual with whom should rest the conduct of the
war a point of some significance. Pitt was firmly resolved that it should remain with the Minister who
had most of his confidence, while the leading Whigs,
who would have gladly seen Mr. Windham assume the
direction of the war, had less sympathy with the pretensions of the Duke of Portland, and acquiesced in the
arrangement by which he assumed the reins of the
Home Office, a post for which however all agreed in
thinking him eminently unfit.

The difficulty on this occasion was amicably arranged,
yet the differences of opinion which had nearly brought
about a rupture continued in full force.

A few months later, in November of the same year,
1794, the Ministry was again on the verge of dissolution, the subject of contention being Ireland. It was
well known that the Duke of Portland had always
earnestly desired to remodel the Irish administration
and to emancipate it from the faction of jobbers which
had so long governed it. On the first opportunity that
occurred he asserted his views, by the appointment to

certain important offices of persons either connected
with or trusted by the Catholic party in Ireland.[1] These

<hr />

[1]   'November 1, 1794.
'It is the Duke's desire to widen the basis of the Irish Administration
by the admission of Grattan's friends, who last year relinquished their
opposition to the measures of Government on account of the critical
situation of the times, and have conducted themselves with such prudence and moderation, as prove that they are actuated by motives of
real patriotism and an ardent zeal for the real benefit of society in
general.   This measure, however, cannot be carried into effect without
the removal of the Irish Chancellor, Lord Fitzgibbon, who is said to be
a proud, arrogant, violent man, and who by his animosity against the
Catholics has rendered himself very obnoxious to them.   The Duke of
Portland, therefore, proposes to compensate Lord Fitzgibbon, in the case
of his resignation, by high promotion in the peerage and even by a
pension ; but he is unwilling to relinquish his office, and Pitt seems
resolved to support him, under the idea of not seeming to desert his old
friends.   The Provostship of the University of Dublin is also vacant
by the death of Mr. Hutchinson.   This office is reckoned a most
important one, but has been generally *jobbed* away, like most of the
Irish offices.   The Duke, at present, wishes to confer it on the Vice-
provost, who is a very learned man, and a person to whom the
university is under the most essential obligations.   The Ministry in
Ireland are nevertheless determined to dispose of it otherwise.

'There is also another job to which the Duke refuses his consent, and
that is in the person of our friend Douglas, who has obtained the promise of the office of Secretary of State for Ireland, which is a sinecure
office for life, and which clearly ought not to be given to a person who
is not a native of the country.   This is not all.   If Lord Fitzwilliam
goes to Ireland, the office of President of the Council will be vacant, and
the Duke of Portland is very naturally desirous that Lord Mansfield
shall succeed to it.   Pitt, however, says, that on Lord Westmoreland's
departure to Ireland, he promised him that he should, on his return to
England, have as good a situation as .that which he left, he being then
Postmaster-General; and he therefore insists on Lord Westmoreland's
promotion to the Presidency of the Council.   To this the Duke will not
consent, and I think most persons will agree that Lord Mansfield's
qualifications give him great pretensions to an office of consequence in
the state.   Thus matters stand, and are to remain till Lord Spencer's
return, which will probably be in a couple of days.   The Duke, I must
own, appears to be on good ground in the dispute.   If he goes out
Windham will, *I know*, follow him.

c c 2

intended arrangements were, however, resisted by Mr. Pitt, who alleged that the Duke had not sufficiently explained his views concerning Ireland before the Coalition, and who visibly shrank from endangering his interest with those who had long given him their political support.

Again the resolution of Pitt overcame the opposition of his new colleagues. But in the following year, 1795, a serious schism took place in the ranks of the Liberals acting with Mr. Pitt, once more on the subject of Ireland. The appointment of Lord Fitzwilliam to the Viceroyalty had been immediately followed by a series of changes in the *personnel* of the Irish Government which gave dire offence to the dominant Irish party; the result was the recall of Lord Fitzwilliam, a measure approved by the Duke of Portland and palliated by Windham, while Burke embraced Lord Fitzwilliam's cause with his usual warmth, and Mr. Elliot of Wells wrote to his cousin, Sir Gilbert, that the course taken by the Duke of Portland ' would frustrate all the hopes which the people of Ireland had derived from the Coalition in England, and would throw Grattan and some of the most valuable political interests in Ireland into

'Pitt alleges that this intended arrangement for Ireland was not sufficiently explained to him before the Coalition; but it is almost impossible that *he* should not have been acquainted with the Duke's views upon the subject, as they were well known to the *public*. The truth is that he is jealous of the ascendency which he conceives the Duke may gain by his Irish patronage, and thus, instead of associating to himself the stable and permanent interests of the country, he seems resolved to trust himself entirely to the support of persons who exist only by the sunshine of his favour.'—*Mr. Elliot of Wells to Sir Gilbert.*

opposition.   I have endeavoured to form as candid and impartial a judgment as I can, and think that Lord Fitzwilliam was induced by the Ponsonbys to proceed rather hastily and rashly in his new arrangements, but I cannot bring myself to consider his recall as founded in wisdom or justice.' [1]

Shortly after the nomination of Lord Camden and of the Hon. Thomas Pelham as Lord Lieutenant and Secretary for Ireland, they pressed strongly upon Mr. Elliot of Wells the appointment of Under Secretary, temporarily re-assumed by Mr. Sackville Hamilton; this was the more honourable to Mr. Elliot because he was known to have condemned the recall of Lord Fitzwilliam, a step judged ' prudent and even necessary ' by Mr. Pelham, and was equally well-known to be favourable to the Catholic cause, a question on which the policy of the Ministry was still dark, for, to use his own words, ' he could never be persuaded that any government is good which is founded on a principle of monopoly ; ' while greater than his dread of immediate insurrection was that with which he contemplated the probability of ' an inveterate disgust to the English Government being imbibed by the Irish nation unless a new system towards them were speedily adopted.'   In spite, or in consequence, of these opinions, Mr. Elliot had no taste for an active part in Irish politics, and he declined the offer, accompanied though it was with a suggestion that he might look to succeeding his friend Mr. Pelham in the

[1] Mr. Elliot to Sir Gilbert, June 19, 1795.

Chief Secretaryship, from which it was probable he would shortly retire. In the course of the summer, however, the pressure put on Mr. Elliot by Burke, Windham, Pelham, and others, and the difficulty experienced by the Irish Government in finding to fill the vacant place a politician equally conversant with the state of Irish parties while totally disconnected from them, decided him to accept the post of Under Secretary; hence the chief part of his letters subsequent to February 1796, bear the date of Dublin Castle, where he was residing at the time of Sir Gilbert's return to England in 1797.

Beside these notorious differences of opinion among the members of the Government, there had been others on the policy to be pursued in the Mediterranean; and the relations of the Ministers were less confidential and candid than in the interest of the public they ought to have been. Lady Elliot, writing from Bath in December 1796, after she had been in daily communication with leading members of the Government, says: ' It appears that they never agree on any point. The jealousy is so great between the old and the new party that they have no communication. Harriet says that Pitt knows nothing of what passes in the Duke's office, and that he (Pitt) was totally ignorant of every circumstance about Corsica, and would scarcely believe the total silence that the Duke had so long persevered in towards you.'

From all this it appears that England is justified in not loving coalitions; the parties to them finding it so hard to love each other.

On Sir Gilbert's return from abroad he learnt that unfavourable representations of his relations with the army in Corsica had been given to the King and to the Duke of York; and that no steps to counteract these had been taken by the Minister with whom his official correspondence had been carried on.[1]   Under these circumstances, he obtained the Duke of York's permission to lay before His Royal Highness the whole of his correspondence with the staff of the army in Corsica, as also his despatch to the Duke of Portland concerning Colonel Moore.   The result of the Duke's perusal of these documents will be seen in a letter which will be found in its place in the correspondence.

Lady Elliot went down to Scotland in May 1797, when the following series of letters begins :—

Sir Gilbert to Lady Elliot.

' May 12, 1797.

' I saw Mr. Dundas this morning at his office, and was entering on business when Pitt came in, which prevented our proceeding.   I talked, however, of the Duke of York's affair with both of them.   Both assured me of his uncommon candour and justice, and it ended in Dundas's undertaking to speak fully and seriously to the Duke of York, and to deliver to him his own opinion and that of Mr. Pitt; after which

---

[1] The late Lord Minto used to relate, on his father's authority, that Sir Gilbert, in his first interview with the Duke of Portland after his return to England in 1797, found some of his own despatches lying with the seals unbroken on the Duke's table.

Mr. Dundas promised to tell me what was best to be done, and to assist me in getting right in this quarter, in which they both seemed to think there would be no difficulty. This, however, is not to be till some day next week.

'The news from Portsmouth continues good. Lord Howe went to St. Helens' yesterday and was on board all the ships. On his return to Portsmouth in the evening he wrote to the Admiralty that the reception had been everything he could wish; that the mutiny is entirely over, and that the seamen are anxious for nothing but the Pardon under the King's hand. That has since gone to them.

' There has been an attempt to seduce the guards at the Tower, by exciting them to a demand for higher pay. Some few of the men had, it seems, listened to these suggestions, but the soldiers had generally behaved extremely well on the occasion, and the experiment seems to have increased the confidence reposed in the guards, rather than diminished it. Nothing can be worse than Ireland. In the North it is said that the people very generally have taken an oath to support the French. The religious question seems to be laid aside, and the object of the malcontents now is to break off altogether the connection with England and to put themselves under the protection of France. This is very bad. A speedy peace seems to have become extremely necessary; but the necessity for it may probably make it less attainable; for the enemy may be naturally expected to insist on worse terms, and indeed on conditions that may be thought impossible. It is reported that the French will demand a restitution of all our conquests to France, Holland, and Spain, and a cession of Gibraltar to Spain. I wish you a thousand joys of being at pleasant Minto.'

'May 13.

'It now appears that two ships, the "Duke" and "Mars," still hold out at Portsmouth. They are said to be manned principally by Irishmen. One does not like to have the thing kept alive at all, but I should imagine those two ships will be soon reduced to order. There is a fresh mutiny at Sheerness on board the ship which has the pressed men to man the ships which come down the river. I understand that their grievances relate to pressing, and to the length of their detention before they are put on board their ships, and the severity of their treatment at Sheerness.' [1]

---

[1] 1797.—The mutiny on board the Fleet broke out in April 1, the second, and most serious, at the Nore on May 17. 'Many of the officers were sent on shore, the red flag was hoisted, and all authority was usurped by the revolters, who chose as their organ a committee of delegates, the principal of whom was Richard Parker, a man of some intelligence and education.

'Encouraged by the arrival of the North Sea squadron to take a share in the revolt, they at length had the audacity to blockade the mouth of the Thames. They were soon after reinforced by part of Admiral Duncan's fleet, which increased the number to twenty-four, or twenty-five sail, more than half of which were of the line.

'Troops were poured into all the towns as though an immediate invasion was expected. At Sheerness, where a bombardment from the fleet was expected, numbers of the inhabitants fled.

'One sign of the universal depression was the fall of the stocks, till at the beginning of June they sank to 47½ per cent.'—Hughes' *History of England.*

'May 16.

'It seems ascertained that the mutiny is now finally settled at last; but Lord Bridport's fleet had not sailed by the latest accounts. Ferguson of Pitfour told me just now that he had seen a letter from Ireland, in which it was said that the Committee of the House of Commons at Dublin, which was charged to enquire into the plots in the North of Ireland, had reported that a conspiracy had been formed to proscribe—that is to say, to murder —30,000 persons, including all the members of both Houses, without any exception. I do not answer for this.'

'May 17.

'I have received to-day from Elliot the two reports of the secret committees of the Houses of Commons and Peers, on the conspiracies in Ireland. It is really true that the proscription of 30,000 persons was part of their plan. I shall send you the reports, but I suppose they will be in the papers.'

'Tuesday, May 23, 1797.

'The last news from Ireland is that Grattan and the rest of their Opposition, after losing their motion for Parliamentary Reform have seceded from the House, declaring their further attendance there useless. This conduct naturally countenances every sort of violent proceeding out of doors, as it acquaints the people that they cannot obtain redress in Parliament in a regular or constitutional way. If the seceding members are in earnest, they will probably themselves take a part in the revolutionary measures which they are countenancing, and what with their weight as members of Parliament, what with their talents, may furnish dangerous leaders to the insurrection. It is said to-day that the intention of our Opposition is to follow the example, or rather to act in concert with that of Ireland, by seceding from the House of Commons after their motion for Parliamentary Reform which stands for Friday. I should apprehend less, however, from this course in the English Opposition than in that of Ireland, as they do not stand in high repute here, and this country is not generally so disposed to disorder as is the case in Ireland. Such a measure would either bring them into contempt or would rouse the friends of order and of the Constitution. We may weather all these ugly points and brush through our difficulties, but there certainly are many symptoms of approaching disorder, and none of us can be surprised if it should come on upon us any day of the week. The mutiny at Plymouth is not yet quelled. Several of the best officers are dismissed by their crews. They have sent delegates to Spithead, to learn with certainty that everything was settled there, not giving credit to the assurances of the officers.

'At Sheerness things were still more serious. Two regiments having arrived there, the seamen took offence or alarm on the supposition of the troops being sent to coerce them. They seized the gunboats, and took other measures which left it doubtful whether it was not their intention to attack the garrison when the recruits came away.

'I dined with Windham at Fulham on Monday; Windham violent in censure of his colleagues, particularly Pitt and Dundas. He appears to have been for firm measures throughout, and particularly on the mutinies, but to be constantly over-ruled. He seems to consider Dundas as a feeble and pusillanimous character, notwithstanding his sturdy manner. All this is very confidential. Windham seemed leaning to what I should call desperate courses the other way, such as for joining Sheridan, or anybody that can prevent our becoming a province of France. Sheridan of late has affected moderation compared with his associates, but I would not advise Windham to *ride the water* with him. This is *very* confidential.'

'May 24.

'The mutinies are still alive at Weymouth and Sheerness, though hopes are entertained of a settlement; but there is no longer anything like real subordination or obedience in the Navy. They will obey and serve just as their opinions or humours go, but no further. Every squadron that comes in regularly takes the command from their officers and elects captains from among themselves, who supersede the real captains, leaving them only a little exterior show of respect but no authority whatever. When or how this dreadful state of things will be changed is uncertain, and it is equally uncertain what England can do with a Navy of this sort.

'The affairs of Ireland are in a most precarious state

A plot has been discovered to assassinate Lord Car-hampton, Commander-in-Chief, in which two of his own servants were concerned.'

' May 25.

' The most interesting news is that Charles Fox went yesterday to the levee, and asked an audience after the levee, which was granted of course.   I do not know on any certain authority what passed ; but Harriet told me last night what she had heard ; that Fox had spoken in very moderate and becoming terms, had said he could give the King better information on some points than he could receive from his Ministers.   He described the great dangers and evils that were impending, and thought it his duty to apprise the King of the true state of things.   That it was perhaps still possible to retrieve our affairs, but that there must be a total change of measures and of his Ministers.   That he gave this advice with the less scruple as he was himself determined not to accept office, and thought on the present occasion it would be improper for him to do so. The King received what he said graciously and in good part, and thanked him for the good intentions he had shown on the occasion ; but of course it is not known whether he made him any answer to the advice he had given.   It is indeed unlikely he should have com-mitted himself.   There are many speculations on this event.   The mutiny at Sheerness is as bad as ever. The artificers and several of the yards have also begun combinations for increase of wages and other advan-tages.'

'Friday, May 26, 1797.

'There was last night an ugly business at Woolwich, which has terminated, however, in a most satisfactory way. Some men of the Horse Artillery, whose turn it was to clear out some litter in the stables, being called yesterday in the evening to that duty, called out suddenly, *No fatigue*, in a mutinous way and refused to work ; on which the officers seized some of them and confined them. The remainder ran to the barracks and as soon as they were there gave a cheer ; this was immediately answered by all the rest of the Artillery soldiers in the barracks, and also by some other soldiers of the Infantry in a neighbouring barrack. The officers, being alarmed at these appearances, placed a guard on the barracks with a sentry at each room door, and with orders to fire at the first man who should attempt to come out during the night. It was remarkable that this guard, which was the usual guard that happened to be on duty, behaved perfectly well, assuring the officers they might depend on them ; although every man was on duty the whole night and there could be but one man at each door. In the meanwhile, accounts of the mutiny having been sent to London, orders were given for cavalry to march, and it happened to be Lord Pembroke's regiment and himself to command it.

'Very early in the morning the commanding officer of the Artillery called out the men from the barracks to the parade, and spoke to them. He asked them if they had any grievances, and told them that they knew

very well that their officers would always be ready to
receive any complaints made in a soldier-like and
proper manner.   They declared they had no grievance
or wish whatever and that they were perfectly satisfied
with everything.   Being asked what then was the reason for their present behaviour and what they meant,
they said they could give no account of it themselves;
that they had no ill intention whatever; that hearing
the shout they had answered it without well considering
what they were about, and that perhaps they had fallen
into this fault the more readily for having been so
often bantered and abused in the town for not preferring complaints and making demands; that they
respected, liked, and would obey their officers, and
were determined to serve their king and country faithfully.   Some of them came forward with tears and
begged the commanding officer to be their friend, and
to prevent the affair from becoming a stain on the
Artillery.   The officer informed them that he would
stop the march of a regiment which had been ordered
to march upon them, for which they expressed their
thanks.   The officers then proceeded to take away their
arms, to which the men submitted without any opposition, saying they were sensible it was the duty of the
officers to take away their arms, though it was not
necessary, as they might be depended on not to use
them in any way that their officers would disapprove
of.   In short, this affair ends better than well, and
proves that although there is a general relaxation and
wantonness in the times, yet no progress has been

made in really detaching the army from its duty. Lord
Pembroke told me all this himself to day, just as he
came from the Duke of York, where he had carried the
account. He also told me of several regiments of
cavalry and infantry who had entered into voluntary
subscriptions—I mean the common soldiers, corporals,
and serjeants—for the prosecution of all persons who
should attempt to seduce soldiers from their duty.'

'May 27.

'The mutiny of the Artillery, of which I told you yesterday as settled proves somewhat more serious than
Lord Pembroke imagined. It seems the men did prefer
some complaints and demands, which were thought
to have been satisfied by Lord Cornwallis, who you
know is at the head of the Artillery, and is along
with them; but some appearances in the night were unpleasant, and Lord Cornwallis has asked for more forces
at Woolwich, which looks uncomfortable; yet on the
whole it still appears likely that this business will soon
be settled; but when the general disposition to
mutiny and licentiousness, which is showing itself in
so many quarters, will be suppressed, it is not so easy
to tell. There is another ship in a state of mutiny, or
rather of rebellion, at Purfleet. The crew has threatened to land and attack the town.

'I was with Dundas this morning; he had been up
half the night, and seemed not only busy but fatigued.
One distressing and alarming event succeeds another
so fast that they have not a moment's rest.'

'Monday, May 29, 1797.

'I received this morning your two letters of Wednesday, the last of which brought me the account of Mr. Elliot's death.[1] I do most sincerely pity the Admiral; no man ever sustained a more serious loss, nor one that must be felt by him as more irretrievable. I confess that painful as such scenes are, I am sorry I was away at this season of affliction; as I believe there are few now alive in whose sympathy and affection the Admiral would feel more comfort. I have written to him by this post, and begged him to make Minto henceforward his home, if he finds it any relief or pleasure to him.

'All business is at a stand-still here. Things are indeed very threatening and gloomy. Some unsuspected turn of fortune may come to cheer us, but the dejection and dismay of Government are not calculated to produce such a change.

'Lord Spencer has gone to Sheerness with the Board to try to compose the rebellion of the seamen there, but it is not yet known with what success. At Portsmouth some ships of Lord Hugh Seymour's squadron are in a state of the most violent mutiny, the men dismissing their officers and taking the command of the ships. The frigate intended to carry the Prince and Princess of Würtemberg[2] to Hamburg is at the Nore, but the mutinous, or rather the rebellious, ships at Sheerness will not permit the frigate to depart.

---

[1] Andrew Elliot, uncle of Sir Gilbert, and Ex-Governor of New York.
[2] The Princess Royal of Great Britain and Ireland, just married to the Prince of Würtemberg.

They are therefore to sail from Yarmouth in another.
The mutiny of the Artillery is said to be settled. It
seems pretty certain that we have taken Porto Rico in
the West Indies. The news from Paris is considered
good, by the influence of the moderate party in the
Council, in consequence of the new election of a third.
They are supposed to be strongly inclined to peace.'

'May 30.

' Lord Spencer and the other Lords of the Admiralty
having gone down to Sheerness in compliance with
the requisition of the mutinous ships, who insisted on
the same attention being shown to them as had been
done at Portsmouth, have just returned, without having
settled the affair. It is reported that the Admiralty,
after hearing their demands and treating with them,
had declared their demands to be so extravagant and
absurd they were inadmissible. They have therefore
come away, and orders are left to permit no boat to
land from those ships. It is said that two frigates
which were there have returned to their duty ; but the
guardship and another line-of-battle ship are in a state
of open rebellion, blocking up the mouth of the river and
even threatening the shore. It is also reported that three
of Admiral Duncan's ships are in a state of mutiny, his
fleet having been hitherto sufficiently steady.

' If discipline should not be quickly restored in the
Navy, and we are left at war. with France, Spain, and
Holland, without a fleet, the situation is more serious
than was ever known before in England.'

'June 1, 1797.

'I am going to-day to a most melancholy duty. I accompany Mrs. Crewe to Beconsfield, where Burke is now come from Bath. This visit is most doubly painful and uneasy to me by other circumstances besides his illness. There has been no intercourse between us since I went abroad, and he has openly professed dissatisfaction with me ever since my arrival at Toulon, on two grounds. First, because I did not take Cazalès with me, and secondly, because he supposed I was not sufficiently royalist. On the first point I should plead guilty, for I confess I had a most violent repugnance to put myself, my character, and the affairs entrusted to me into any other hands than my own, especially into those of a Frenchman—and nobody can be more a Frenchman than Cazalès, though on many accounts I have the highest regard for him. On the second point he is completely wrong in the fact—for from the time of my arrival at Toulon nothing was heard there but the purest royalism, and I strongly solicited Government to let me send for the Princes and put them at the head of the counter-revolution at Toulon and in the South. However, Burke is now too much reduced in strength to bear a discussion on these subjects or any other; and I must submit to any impression he has received. I have no doubt he will receive me kindly and be pleased with my visit; yet I have never heard this directly from him; and on asking Windham, Walker King, and some other of his friends, I have rather their opinion than their knowledge that I shall

be welcome. You see that in this world all it is possible
for anyone to do is to do right; but no one can depend
on avoiding censure, or can trust to the opinions or even
justice of the best friends. The experience one has acquired of the very general defects of the world ought
to give one contempt enough for its opinion to prevent
one's happiness depending on it; yet one can no more
help feeling the injustice of mankind, especially of
friends, than one can help feeling the comforts of
domestic affection; which to me have always been and
will always be a true consolation and an effectual
refuge under the worst evils.'

'June 3, 1797.

' I returned from Beconsfield yesterday, and found
there the kindest and most affectionate welcome it is
possible to imagine. It is strange that Windham should
never be able to form an opinion on any question. I
saw him only the day before I went to Beconsfield,
and asked him as a serious point—whether, from all
he knew, he thought on the whole my visit to Burke
would give him pleasure or otherwise? He hesitated
and could not tell what to say;—" Yes—I don't know!"
in short, would have deterred me from going if I had
not asked Walker King the day before. Instead of all
this, no father could receive a son who had been long
absent with more tenderness or treat him with more
friendship or solicitude about his welfare. I have not
time to-day for the particulars of this visit. I had
been prepared for the extreme alteration in his looks

and told to expect his skeleton rather than himself;
yet what with my doubts concerning his sentiments
towards me and the effect of his kindness in these circumstances, what with the shocking change in him, I
was overcome in a way in which I never was, or at
least but seldom in my life.   I felt I might be doing
harm by the chance of agitating him.   However, this
proved otherwise, and he was affected, but pleased with
these marks of feeling for him.   He is emaciated to the
greatest degree, has entirely lost his powers of digestion.   He considers his own case as quite desperate,
and is rather irritated than flattered by the supposition
of his recovery being possible.   He entered most warmly
into all my affairs, public and private.' [1]

'June 8, 1797.

' The sailors at the Nore have sent a memorial to the
King, which is said to be very impudent as well as
unreasonable.   The buoys are taken up below the Nore,
which it is supposed will prevent the fleet from getting out of the river, and carrying the ships either to
the enemy or Ireland; it will also expose them to want
of provisions and water.   It is believed the Dutch fleet
is out, and it seems difficult to find a squadron of ships
in sufficient discipline to send after them.   However,
I understand a squadron is provided for that purpose,
though less numerous than the enemy.'

[1] Burke died on July 9, 'without pain or struggle, having preserved
his mind entire to the last moment.'   In a letter to one of his relatives,
written not long before his death and sent after that event to Minto,
these words occur: 'Sir Gilbert is one of the best men I have ever
known, and one of the ablest.'

‘Saturday, June 10, 1797.

‘Three ships came in last night from the Nore Mutiny —the "Leopard," the " Repulse," and the " Ardent "—to Sheerness; their crews were not all agreed, and there was a battle in the " Leopard " between the mutinous part of the crew and the loyal, in which seven or eight men were wounded, and I believe a midshipman killed. The " Repulse " got aground in endeavouring to escape, and received the fire of another ship before the tide rose so as to float her; she got safe off however at last, with some damage, but little loss in men; a lieutenant lost his leg, but I think there were no men killed. There are fourteen of the ringleaders of these ships' crews sent ashore in irons.   In addition to this news, accounts are this moment received by the telegraph that all the red flags are struck and the proper colours flying on *all* the ships at the Nore. Captain Knight of the " Mountagu" is coming to town it is supposed with offers of capitulation; but Lord Spencer has declared that he will accept nothing short of unconditional submission.   This is authentic.

‘I pass to-morrow at Richmond with the boys, and some Corsicans, viz. Pozzo di Borgo, Balestrino, and his daughter.’

‘June 15, 1797.

‘You will see by the papers that the mutiny at the Nore is finally subdued.   Parker and most of the delegates are in custody, and will no doubt be made examples of.   This is an event of great and real importance, as

it seems to remove the great obstacle to the continuance
of the war, the *possibility* of which seems to me to
furnish the only chance for such a peace as we can accept, or as would not be much worse than war. I
cannot help fearing that peace will be found more
difficult than seems expected. It is true, on the one
hand, that France is supposed to be very generally desirous of peace; but, on the other hand, the Government
in France may not wish it very sincerely, and they seem
strongly possessed with the desire to take this opportunity of humbling the power of their only rival.'[1]

---

[1] Something of the mutinous spirit which assumed such formidable
proportions in the Channel fleet had shown itself in the Mediterranean
fleet on more than one occasion; and once at least it had received in
some degree the sanction of officers high in command, who by their own
conduct set an example of want of discipline.

In a letter dated Bastia, July 28, 1795, addressed to Lady Elliot, Sir
Gilbert mentions that great dissatisfaction had been caused in the fleet
under Admiral Hotham's command, by an order to cease pursuit, when,
after some days' chase, they were on the point of coming up with the
enemy, some of the British ships being actually in action. 'Admiral
Goodall was one of the pursuing ships, and he is described as kicking
his hat about the deck in a frenzy of rage when he was called off. It
was his ship's company who came on deck after their return from San
Fiorenzo and declared they would not sail again under such an admiral.'
The anecdote shows enough of the spirit animating both men and
officers to explain the extraordinary rapidity with which they forgot
the antagonism of 1797, when fairly entered on the career of glory
just opening to them under the leadership of Nelson. The affair in
which Admiral Hotham was concerned, though considered very disastrous
at the time, is related in Hughes' *History of England* (see note to page
235, vol. iv.), with circumstances which are not borne out in Sir Gilbert's
account of it, given to him by Sir Hyde Parker who was second in command. Admiral Hotham is therein described as a most brave and gallant
sailor, but of too advanced an age for active service; and to his fear of
losing his ships on a rocky shore, and of the responsibility he would con-
sequently incur, was ascribed the order which gave so much offence to
the fleet under his command.

' I went to Eden Farm yesterday to dinner, and stayed all night. We passed the evening quietly in the library, surrounded by the girls: they all draw very tolerably in a style that I think good, because it is quick, easy, and produces a great effect. On my way to town I called on Mrs. Hoare, and found her full four years older, living with her brother Prince in the old solitary cynical way, but preserving her friendship for me. She told me what people had said of me in my absence, and particularly of my great severity and sanguinary cruel violences against the people of Corsica, whom I had hanged up without trial, etc. Though she had not believed this, she seemed surprised to hear that there had not been a single instance of any capital punishment inflicted on a Corsican during the whole of our connection with that country.

' The Cabinet is much divided on all this affair of the Peace, and it seems highly probable that they will split upon it. Pitt differs with Lord Grenville, and Dundas with both; in short, all is in great confusion. Meanwhile the mutiny is fairly got under, and the delinquents are in the hands of the law, which I hope will deserve the reproaches cast on it better than I did in Corsica. Tom Erskine, I am told, goes about saying it will be murder if they touch a hair of Parker's head. I don't exactly know why. I saw Lady Plymouth on Saturday at the Opera, and she told me a few of the stories she had heard about us in Italy and since she came home. One was, that besides sitting under

canopies, etc. as you have already heard, we never went
to bed at home without having two candles carried
before us in state by a government officer of the house-
hold, the title of whose office she did not recollect. The
Bonaparte story you have heard.' [1]

'June 26, 1797.

'Lord Malmesbury talks of going to Lille on Friday.
George Ellis attends him. The Cabinet has objected
to Lord Pembroke's going with him, but Lord Granville
Leveson and Lord Morpeth are to go as secretaries. The
opinion concerning the probability of peace is more
favourable since the return of the last messenger than
I ever remember it. The answer of the Directory
consents to the negotiation's including the allies of
both nations. They also consent to Lord Malmesbury's
appointment, but say it is *de mauvaise augure* for the
expeditious termination of the peace; alluding, no
doubt, to the frequent messengers that he sent for in-

[1] The Bonaparte story had been written by Lady Elliot herself to her
husband, soon after her arrival at Bath from Corsica.

'To show how the greatest nonsense gains credit, Lord Galloway
asked me yesterday what sort of a man Bonaparte was. I told him I had
been fortunate enough never to see him, though at the evacuation of
Leghorn I was very near it. He seemed quite astonished, and said,
"What! did you not know him in Corsica?" I told him he had not been
there for many years, and gave his history. He exclaimed, "Good
God! Why, everybody believes that he applied to Sir Gilbert for promotion in a Corsican regiment, and on being refused went to Paris,
where he was immediately appointed to his present command, and by
that refusal of Sir Gilbert's has become our bitter enemy, when he
might have been secured as a friend." He added, that I ought to put the
truth in the newspapers, for that it had been much talked of, and that
such lies were very prejudicial.'

structions.   Lord Malmesbury wrote to Lord Grenville
on hearing the objections made to him, desiring that
no personal considerations respecting him might induce
Government to employ him if it was thought subject
to the slightest inconvenience, and suggesting the possibility of some disadvantage arising from his nomination after these objections had been made to him.
Lord Grenville answered that it was thought advisable to employ him, notwithstanding the objections
alluded to, and I think they are right not to let the
enemy have any hand in the appointment of our Minister.   There seems a strong cry for peace in France,
aided by the appearance of a rupture with America, and
by the extreme distress of their finances.'

                                        'June 27, 1797.

   ' I understand that Dundas's resignation depends on
the giving up of the Cape of Good Hope and Ceylon.[1]
I hope neither may be parted with ; they are material
conquests and some little compensation for the war.'

                                        'June 29, 1797.
   ' I had my audience of the Duke of York yesterday,
and it terminated as pleasantly and satisfactorily as
all the former discussions on the same subject.   We
sat together from three till six o' clock, and the Duke
entered into every part of the case with perfect atten-

---

   [1] In an earlier letter he had mentioned rumours of a break-up of the
Administration. The Duke of Portland and Windham denied the truth of
them, declaring it was *impossible* to hand over Government to Opposition.
Dundas, however, hinted to Sir G. the probability of his going out.

tion and patience, reading most of the despatches and letters himself. He assented distinctly to my assertion that Colonel Moore had taken part in a faction against me, saying frequently that nothing could be more clear, and using other expressions of assent and conviction. I showed him General de Burgh's testimony concerning the harmony that had prevailed between us, and showed him the list of officers I could refer to as friends. Our sitting concluded by his assenting to the conclusion I drew from the enquiry that the imputation of disagreement with the army, provoked by me, was totally false, and that there really existed the faction which I have accused ; that Moore was the head of it, and while such a faction was acting against me I could not be responsible for the appearance of differences with the few individuals who composed it. He has promised to set me right with the King.'

Sir Gilbert felt that the misrepresentations which had made such explanations on his part necessary, should have been arrested on their first circulation by the Ministers who were in possession of the facts of the case ; but they were thinking of other matters, and to this supineness on their part he was indebted for the extensive circulation of much mischievous falsehood. That they did not themselves entertain any unfavourable impressions of Sir Gilbert's conduct may be seen in the following passage from a letter to Lady Elliot, July 22, 1797 :—

'The Duke of Portland is delighted with a conversation he had yesterday with Pitt about me. Pitt had spoken in the highest terms of commendation of me, and expressed again how ill-used I had been, and that I was the most injured person in the world; that my conduct had been admirable and exactly the contrary of what had been imputed to me, and that he was all anxiety to find an opportunity to show the world the esteem in which the Government held me. All this the Duke related with the most friendly joy and satisfaction as if he had not been the cause of all the mischief.'

'July 13, 1797.

'My departure this week is out of the question, for I go on Saturday to Mr. Burke's funeral at Beconsfield, which will be attended by some of his most particular friends, but in other respects will be private. Francis seems to have more feeling and a more proper feeling on this occasion than might have been expected. Talking of his difference with Burke and the rest of us the other day, he let out, inadvertently perhaps, his *real* sentiments, and, I believe, those of many others of that party. He was saying that he had yielded more to Burke's mind and opinions than to any other man's in the world, but that the questions on which they differed were too important to admit of concession to any authority whatever; that he had a right to his own opinions on all subjects, and on this particular one it was his duty to follow it. Then breaking out, he called out, " I am a republican; my mind is inclined to that mode of Government. This old limited monarchy

is worn out and will do no longer; I am sorry for the
calamities that are coming on, but it cannot be avoided
much longer." You see this is very strong, and our
Opposition are to be considered as real revolutionists.[1]
Don't mention this story.

'I took Pozzo di Borgo the other day to see an English
trial. We were invited by the Lord Mayor to dinner
with the Judges. Lord Macdonald, the Chief Baron,
was one of them, and cracked old jokes and told old
stories in the old way. Jekyll has given him the nick-
name of the Arabian Knight, for having a thousand and
one tales.'

'Great Russell Street: Monday, July 17, 1797.

'I have come here in a hurry on hearing of a most
shocking accident which happened last night. Lord
St. Helens' house was burnt down to the ground; providentially no life was lost, but he has literally saved
nothing, and the house contained everything he possessed in the world. He has lost every scrap of paper
he ever had. Conceive how inconsolable that loss must
be to one who has lived his life. All his books, many fine
pictures, prints and drawings in great abundance, are
all gone. I never saw anybody so perfectly composed and
resigned as he is about it. His behaviour seems to me

[1] In the diary of Thomas Moore, edited by Lord John Russell, the
following curious passage occurs, vol. iv. p. 219 :—' Mr. Fox was never
a member of the " Friends of the People; " never a Reformer in the sense
of those who think the people have a right to change the representation.
When he was for reform in 1797, " *meant really revolution*," because he
thought that a revolution of another kind was coming on, and preferred
of the two a popular one.' The words quoted were spoken by Lord
Holland in 1824.

quite edifying, and much beyond any degree of philosophy I could command on such an occasion, though I
know you would expect a good deal more from me. He
was in his night-gown just going to bed, and alone in
his room, his servants being already gone to bed, when
in an instant his window-curtains were in a blaze, and
in less than a minute and a half his room was in flames.
I went on Saturday with Francis to Beconsfield and
assisted at Mr. Burke's funeral. It was an affecting
scene, and I was deeply and most sincerely moved
about it. It was attended by persons of great distinction, although, according to his directions, the funeral
was plain and without expense.' [1]

'July 29.

' I am writing to you to-day at Windham's. I hope to
be off with the boys on Tuesday, giving up Birmingham,
where I wished to show the manufactories to Pozzo di
Borgo and to myself, never having seen them ; but the
boys will consider every day on the road a slice cut out
of their holidays. I refrain even yet as much as I can
from letting my thoughts of Minto loose, or laying the
reins on the neck of my impatience, for there is nothing
more lengthening to a journey than for the man to ride
faster than his horse. Yet when I do venture to let my
mind take a side glance of Minto, it seems so delightful
and so much like heaven that I hardly dare look for it
on earth.' I go back to Sheen after dinner. You

---

[1] A few days later Sir Gilbert returned to Beconsfield to see Mrs.
Burke. On this occasion he visited the Emigrant School, instituted by
Burke. 'This is an institution that really does us credit, and great

cannot conceive the comfort of the green garden and
chestnut trees when I awake, for I sleep on the ground
floor, in the great green velvet canopy bed—or rather
you can conceive it. I must go, Windham having come
in, and saying something very fine, and I am sure
sincere, to you. I hope not to write much oftener to
you in my life. God bless you ! '

A few days later Sir Gilbert was again at home; but
he found there more of earth than heaven, as the next
letter will show :—

'Minto: August 28, 1797.

' My dear Lady Palmerston,—We all continue well,
and in whole skins, which is more than we can quite
reckon on at present in this country.   It is rather
hard upon us to find ourselves once more in Corsica
when we thought ourselves at home. We were hugging
ourselves in the comfort of this quiet country, when it
went mad all at once on the Militia Bill for Scotland,[1]
and that part of Great Britain is now in a flame from
one end to the other. It began in Berwickshire, where
a mob, composed in great part of women, attacked the

honour to him.   There are sixty French boys, principally the orphans
of Quiberon and children of other emigrants who have done or suffered
something in the cause.'

[1] A Bill passed in the session of 1797 for the establishment of a
militia consisting of 6,000 men in Scotland, was highly obnoxious to
the Scotch peasantry, among whom the most false and absurd reports
were spread with respect to its tendency. In many places when the
time for carrying it into effect approached, large mobs collected together
and violent riots were the consequence. This was especially the case at
Jedburgh, Eccles, Selkirk, Tranent, and Dumbarton.

gentlemen employed in carrying the Act into execution, nearly murdered one of them, and forced the rest, by threats of instant death, to subscribe a paper promising to have no further concern in the Militia. They burnt the stackyards of two gentlemen who were obnoxious to them, and committed every sort of outrage. The flame soon spread to this county, and there is hardly a gentleman who has not been threatened with death or the burning of his house by the country people in the neighbourhood, if the Militia is persisted in. We—I mean this family—are rather in favour at present, but that is a distinction we cannot wish to preserve, as it can only be done by deserting the common duty. Indeed, as it is, we have had an alert, and were informed two nights ago that we were to have a visit. It was, I believe, not at all intended, but having made no preparation for defence, I really never saw Lady Elliot in so great a terror before. Major Rutherford, one of our neighbours, was knocked from his horse a few days ago at Jedburgh, five miles from hence, at the head of a party of our yeomanry, and has very narrowly escaped with his life. His foot hung in the stirrup after he had been knocked down with stones and bludgeons, and he received in that situation several cuts on the head with his own sabre, before he was rescued. In short, we are in considerable confusion. The worst, however, seems to be over in this part of the country. We have got a few dragoons, and have taken pretty firm measures, which appear to have subdued the first spirit of the revolt, and if the rest of Scotland were no worse than we are here, the business would probably be carried through with very little further opposition. The Bill is in reality quite unobjection-able; but it has been misrepresented, and is generally misunderstood by the common people, who are alone concerned in these tumults; for it is fortunate that the farmers are not only well-disposed, but are almost as forward and zealous in yeomanry and all sorts of volunteering as the gentlemen. We are endeavouring to explain and to conciliate, I think with some success, not neglecting, at the same time, the more effective methods of troops and prosecutions. On the whole, I consider this part of the country as in a tolerably pro-mising way, and none of this house have anything to apprehend in person or estate, though I take as strong a part as I can in carrying this business through.'

The business was ' carried through ' with no worse results than the agitation described. The remainder of the summer was passed by the family, now including Pozzo di Borgo, in Scotland, and was no doubt enjoyed by Sir Gilbert in pursuance of his ideal of summer delights, ' bruising the daisies, with a book in his hand,' and by Lady Elliot with the thorough satisfaction of a true Northerner who greatly preferred the summer which calls men out of doors and fills the fields with life and movement, to that which drives them to spend the hours of sunshine in darkness and repose.

APPENDIX.

Despatch from Sir Gilbert Elliot to the Duke of Portland on the Relations of England and Rome.

Bastia : September 24, 1794.

MY LORD DUKE,—I learned on my first arrival at Toulon in November 1793, that the Pope had conceived the design, and was taking measures with great earnestness, for establishing an avowed communication between the Courts of London and Rome. From that time to the present, every occurrence in the Mediterranean has been used to the utmost in promoting the success of that object, and every person employed by His Majesty, amongst whom I have not been forgotten, has been either importuned to enlist, or has been tried to be kidnapped, into that service. Two methods have been pursued. First, to prevail on His Majesty's servants and officers to make direct and official applications and to enter into direct correspondence with Rome. Secondly, on that being refused or avoided, to allege that it had actually been done, and to cite all the transactions of the victualling agents and other proceedings of a similar description, to prove that a free intercourse was already established.

Both these means have been employed with equal diligence in London. Monseigneur Erskine was sent to England with a commission from the Pope to carry this point. He took the pretence of his family connections for the journey, and he obtained with ease, from the liberality and hospitality of England, that welcome which his rank and situation, and the ostensible motives of his visit, not only justified but entitled him to. In the meanwhile the true motives of his journey being really known, it' became easy for Monseigneur Erskine to convert his travels into a mission, his visits and conversations into conferences, and himself into a Nuntio. He is so considered at Rome, and, as I before observed, this Minister pursues the two methods above mentioned in promoting the objects of his mission. He negotiates *directly* by solicitation, argument, and intrigue. And not having yet succeeded in obtaining by that mode an avowed assent to his proposal, he endeavours in the meanwhile to prove that you have done in substance what you have refused in form. For this purpose he goes about London, partly extorting from the facility and good humour of those with whom he converses, partly obtaining by surprise, without even the knowledge of those who furnish them, materials for this part of his argument. If Mr. Pitt invites him to dinner, and there happens to be a foreigner or foreign minister of the company, it is sent to Rome as an indication that Mr. Pitt acknowledges his public character. If Lord Grenville receives his visits at the Office instead of his own house, this circumstance is relied on in his next despatches. If his name appears in a newspaper as having been at the King's levee, and there is no motion in Parliament or no mob the next day, it is insisted on as an acquiescence of the public in his mission, and as a proof that the times are favourable to this change. The King himself has been already cited as having authorised, and indeed actually opened, the communication with the Pope, for having expressed some gracious sentiments to Lord Amherst, when His Lordship acquainted His Majesty with the compliment paid by the Pope to the 12th Regiment of Light Dragoons.

In the meanwhile the counterpart of this proceeding is acted at Rome by Mr. Hippesley, who, with the most sincere zeal for the public service and the purest intentions (but approving of the Pope's views on principle), is co-operating with them by every means he can employ, and, amongst others, by repeating with great precision at Rome the motions of Monseigneur Erskine in London. He is ostensibly an English traveller in Italy for his health, but is in fact performing all the functions of British Envoy at Rome ; is treated as such by the Pope and his Ministers ; and is accumulating materials to make out a mission *de facto*, until His Majesty is pleased to grant one *de jure*.

I take it for granted that Government has deliberated on the question ; and if, on the whole, the determination is contrary to the Pope's wishes, I should humbly conceive that it would be advisable to take some means of declaring that intention so explicitly as to afford no opportunity to claim your constructive assent, in opposition to your formal refusal, or of extorting from you acts, which, though ineffectual for the present purpose, would, I assure Your Grace, be all treasured up in the interim as precedents, as admissions, and as the basis or instruments of future claims to be urged on more opportune occasions.

His ambition has no visible limits, and its ascending quality has been perfectly illustrated in this very instance. Having been made to believe that he should probably carry the first point of having an acknowledged Minister from Great Britain accredited to Rome, he saw that he should obtain as a natural consequence the reception of a Nuntio in London. Feeling already his foot firm in this step, the other seems to have mounted quite naturally of itself to the next. We therefore heard immediately of legalising his spiritual authority over the English Catholics. His rescripts were to be registered, or, in other words, acknowledged as binding, and the civil power was to concur in

giving validity, by affording the sanction of a public
Register, to this exercise of foreign authority within the
realm. The Pope makes this new concession result, either
as a corollary from the other (by an argument of which I
am not master), or derives it from some general notions of
unlimited toleration which he supposes us to possess; for
he says the Catholics of England are disturbed in the exercise or enjoyment of an essential part of their religion if
they are cut off from the privilege of receiving his commands, and they are persecuted if the law does not
protect them in this article by legalising those acts of the
Pope's authority in England which their religious opinions
teach them to consider as binding on themselves. I do
not propose to examine the validity of the argument, or
to what extent this principle, if conceded in the precise
form demanded now, would be sure to stretch itself by
abuse, and probably to retain, if not daily increase, its extension by perpetual encroachment, on one hand, and sufferance on the other: but I content myself with observing
that the step is *one higher* than the other, and that if you
agree to receive a Nuntio in England it will be expected
the day after that you should admit the Pope's bulls to run,
like any other legal process, freely through the kingdom
without debating the merits of the question. I should
imagine that, however liberal the public spirit may be in
England on the article of Toleration, this innovation would
nevertheless be of difficult digestion, and that it is not likely
to be offered by Government to the people.

The mere exchange of an Envoy for a Nuntio would be
a barren acquisition, if the residence of a Nuntio were to
produce no fruit. There are therefore many points, yet
undreamt of in London, which have long since been seen
rising on the horizon of Rome as that horizon has been seen
to extend itself.

The various repeals and modifications of the penal

statutes that have taken place of late years in Great Britain and Ireland, and the late concessions to the Irish Catholics, have been enumerated as trophies of the policy and able administration of Pius VI. The hospitable reception of the fugitive French priests in London, and the preference given to that class of emigrants in the charitable contributions of the public, have been adduced, not merely as proofs of the generous and christianlike character of the English people, or of the good conduct of the priests, but as an indication that the prejudice against the Catholic religion has abated, and has even given way to some show of partiality and predilection in its favour. As a further proof of this partiality, they quote the grounds on which Mr. Dundas is stated to have opposed Mr. Sheridan's proposition for admitting the English Catholics into the army and navy on the same footing with the Irish ; namely, that the bill professed in its preamble to confer this benefit on the Catholics, but that the provisions of the bill extended the same benefit to Protestant Dissenters. Catholics are therefore represented as enjoying a greater degree of favour in England than the Dissenters, and this remarkable change in the temper and feelings of England is made the subject of present exultation and of future expectation at Rome. In the panegyrics bestowed on the great Pontiff and Prince whose work these wonders are, it is said with some triumph, that since so many unexpected exploits have been achieved, it is impossible to say to what extent the glory and prosperity of Holy Church may be restored under the same auspices, after so many ages of affliction and humiliation. I am pretty nearly translating a paper printed by authority at Rome. I am not so much an *alarmist* as that my apprehensions should keep pace with the sanguine hopes of Rome; and I should not fear a revolution, either in Church or State, from the residence of a Nuntio in London.

But I am quite sure that the Court of Rome would propose and the Nuntio would exhaust all the resources of Italian policy to accomplish *both*; and that from the moment of that establishment it would be the work of one Secretary of State to transact the affairs of the Roman department alone. I cannot help enclosing a very curious paper which was sent to me by a friend, who probably did not think it curious in the same way that I do. It is an account of some interviews between His Royal Highness Prince Augustus and the Cardinal of York. Your Grace will see the frank and manly virtues of our soil and of *our true* blood royal, singularly and happily contrasted with the cold-blooded craft of Italy, and with the qualities, such as they are, of the Pope's.

END OF THE SECOND VOLUME.

LONDON: PRINTED BY
SPOTTISWOODE AND CO., NEW-STREET SQUARE
AND PARLIAMENT STREET

7